THE REGAL FAMILY

A Kingdom of Andover Novel

Restless Children Media, LLC

Published 2010

First Edition

Published by Restless Children Media, LLC, 93 S. Jackson St. #96908, Seattle, WA 98104-2818

www.restlesschildremedia.com

First published in the United States of America

ISBN: 978-0-615-35093-6

A Guide to the Kingdom of Andover

Characters

His Majestic Regal Highness The King Michael of Andover (53) The reigning monarch of the Kingdom of Andover; he lives and works at Andover Palace

Her Regal Highness The Dowager Queen Cassandra of Andover (83) The former monarch of the Kingdom of Andover, mother of the King; she lives at Andover Palace.

His Regal Highness The Prince of Kemp, Prince Alexander of Andover (29) The heir to the throne of the Kingdom of Andover & son of the King; he lives and works at Kemp Castle.

Her Regal Highness The Princess Helena of Andover (25) The only daughter of the King; she lives at Andover Palace.

His Regal Highness The Prince Joseph of Andover (23) The youngest child of the King; he lives at Andover Palace.

Her Regal Highness The Princess Sophia of Andover (47) The daughter of the Dowager Queen and sister of the King; she lives in at state apartment at Andover Palace.

Her Regal Highness Lady Margaret of Andover (50) The cousin of the King, niece of the Dowager Queen and sister of Lord Walter; she lives in a state apartment at Andover Palace.

His Regal Highness Lord Walter of Andover (47) The cousin of the King, nephew of the Dowager Queen and brother of Lady Margaret; he lives at Blake Manor.

His Regal Highness Samuel of Andover (10) The son of Lady Margaret and His Highness Edward; he lives in a state apartment at Andover Palace.

Her Regal Highness The Princess of Kemp (29) The wife of Prince Alexander; she lives at Kemp Castle.

His Highness Prince Robert of Andover (51) The husband of Princess Sophia; he lives in a state apartment at Andover Palace.

His Highness Edward of Andover (42) The husband of Lady Margaret; he lives in a state apartment at Andover Palace.

Kingdom Counties

Old Andover, Kemp Forest, Blake Hill, Port Agnes, Lord's Pass, and West Andover

Regal Residences

Andover Palace: The official residence of the King and members of the regal family. It's located in Old Andover.

Kemp Castle: The official home of the heir to the throne, the Prince of Kemp. It's located in Kemp Forest.

Blake Manor: The home and work base of Lord Walter. It's located in Blake Hill.

Port Agnes House: The official summer residence of the regal family. It's located in the county of Port Agnes.

Styles:

His/Her Majestic Regal Highness is only used by the ruling monarch.

His/Her Regal Highness is only used by direct descendants of King Christoph, Andover's first monarch, the spouse of the monarch, and the spouse of the heir to the throne.

His/Her Highness is used by spouses of the regal family.

His/Her Reverence is used by the grandchildren (and their descendants) of His/Her Regal Highnesses.

Titles:

King/Queen of Andover*:* the current ruling monarch

Dowager King/Queen: the former ruling monarch

Duke/Duchess of Andover: the spouse of the ruling monarch

Prince/Princess of Kemp: the heir to the monarch and their spouse

Prince/Princess of Andover: the children of a current or former monarch

Lord/Lady of Andover: the children of a prince or princess; the spouses of a prince or princess

His/Her Regal Highness of Andover: the children of a lord or lady; spouse of a lord or lady

Marquis/Marchioness/Baron/Baroness: hereditary aristocratic titles given to grandchildren of His/Her Regal Highnesses

Count/Earl/Countess: inherited aristocratic titles, which can be awarded by the current monarch

Dane/Danisi: life titles awarded by the monarch, which cannot be inherited and rank above 1st and 2nd Peers

1st Peer/2nd Peer: life titles awarded by the monarch, which cannot be inherited and are the lowest form of titles

1

His Majestic Regal Highness The King Michael of Andover stood before the arched window in his private suite with peace of mind. This morning, like every other morning, would begin with tradition, purpose, pomp, and a bit of irony for good taste. Yet in this moment of personal solitude and reflection, the current monarch felt better than he had in years. Could it have been the ease with which the past few weeks seemed to drift by, or the realization that all was not lost, despite thoughts to the contrary? The King let out a small sigh before turning his attention to the small silver alarm clock near his bed that was due to go off at any moment. No one in the kingdom knew that their monarch rose at five-thirty every morning in order to reflect upon what his life meant to him without the opinions of the many denizens who wanted nothing more than to bend his ear towards their own personal agenda. In the next two hours, his personal valet would come to ensure the King was ready for the day. After breakfast, he would go through his daily schedule with his private secretary, which would sustain him until he retired for the evening.

Today was going to be a day where life would finally come together for King Michael. No longer was he going to hide behind the edifice of duty, but he would allow his heart to love after so many years of being alone. As the King walked from his bedroom through his dressing room, into his closet, and into his vast private bathroom, he recalled the times love seemed to evade him. Michael stepped into the warm shower as thoughts of his dearly departed wife, Her Regal Highness The Princess of Kemp, Princess Katherine, entered his mind for the first time in months. How he missed her free spirit, no nonsense attitude, and compassionate view on life. Her passing nine years ago had been a blow, not only to him, but to the entire regal family and the Kingdom of Andover. Their children dealt with their mother's death in their own way, but there was no way to console them when they could barely process the brevity of the situation. One year later, after what seemed a lifetime without Princess Katherine, Michael's mother abdicated, making him the ruling monarch of Andover. However unprepared Michael felt for the role this was his chance to shine…his chance to make a difference in the kingdom and in the lives of his people.

The King began to lather his lean body just as the clock struck six; he had ninety more minutes of quiet reflection before his day officially began. His memories of Katherine were always pleasant, but they carried the scepter of deceit; not hers, but the one's perpetrated and carried forth by those who influenced the man all those years ago. Now, after all of those years, he was finally prepared to pursue an event which he'd anticipated for years. Today, Michael thought, was the beginning of his life. Yes, it would certainly change Michael's life forever, but in ways he couldn't even imagine.

Life had already begun in the private state apartments which constituted the protruding east wing of the Gothic inspired Andover Palace. These private state apartments were designed for the exclusive use of Andover's regal family who were married with their own families, or felt living in a private suite within the palace was an invasion of privacy. Luckily for these members of the regal family, their private state apartments were kept to the same high standard as the palace, which was easily accessible through an adjoining corridor.

Her Regal Highness The Princess Sophia of Andover awoke with a jolt just before seven o'clock in the morning. Her heart raced at a speed which frightened her, so she reached for the crystal tumbler she always kept by her bedside. As she sipped the water, her husband stirred and pulled the bed sheets around his broad shoulders. His Highness Prince Robert let out a soft snore, which made her smile. How she loved him. Even after twenty-one years of marriage, Princess Sophia loved her husband as much as she did the first time they'd met. His kind brown eyes and gentle soul were the trademarks of his personality, and he was the best lover she'd ever had. The princess placed the tumbler onto the mahogany table with great care and slid her feet into a pair of cashmere slippers as she pulled on a silk azure morning robe.

Princess Sophia walked to the vast window in front of her bed with a view of the expansive grounds of Andover Palace. She always marveled at the fact that the palace was only three miles from the center of Old Andover, but within the palace walls it was a world away. Despite the fact this palace had been Sophia's home since the death of her grandfather, His Majestic Regal Highness The King Henrik of Andover, Princess Sophia felt restless. No matter how hard she tried to ignore these feelings stirring in the pit of her stomach, the restlessness within her soul refused to recede.

"You're up early." Sophia snapped out of her reverie as she turned to her husband. Prince Robert gave his wife a mischievous smile. "Are you all right?"

Sophia nodded. "I couldn't sleep…again."

Robert slid out of bed. Sophia noticed his waning morning erection through his soft pajama bottoms. His brown chest heaved as he exhaled and stretched towards the heavens. He wrapped his arms around Sophia's waist, kissing her on the nape of her neck. "Maybe you should see Dr. Hyatt…"

"No. The last thing I need is press speculation concerning a visit to my doctor. I'll be fine."

Robert watched as his wife broke his grasp. Although he'd always loved her, he knew that there were issues he would never understand about her. For instance, she always worried about what the press would write about her. However, he knew this was due to the fact that her brother, mother, grandfather, and great-grandfather had been the monarchs of the Kingdom of Andover and she had a sense of duty on her slender shoulders. Despite Robert's best efforts over the years to assuage her fears, they always fell on deaf ears. "Shall we have breakfast with the family," he called after his wife.

"I suppose." Sophia pulled open the door to her bathroom. "Robert?"

"Yes?"

"Do you love me," she asked.

He smiled. "Of course."

With that, Sophia disappeared into the bathroom as Robert pulled on his bathrobe. There were many moments when he wondered if he ever truly belonged to this rarefied world, or if his presence was simply a matter of design. Growing up in the kingdom as the son of an aristocratic family, Robert had met the regal family on many occasions, but he never felt as if he knew them. Hell, after twenty-one years of marriage to Princess Sophia he still doubted whether or not he was a member of this family or just Sophia's husband. Whatever the true answer, he couldn't worry himself with it this morning or any morning for that matter. Duty first, self second, Sophia always reminded her husband. And, he sighed to himself, she was always right.

"Mommy! Mommy!"

Her Regal Highness Lady Margaret of Andover stirred in the comfort of her down feather bed as her ten-year-old son's voice sailed down her ear canal. Margaret let out an exasperated grunt as she shuffled across her bedroom, slipped into her mauve dressing gown, and stepped into the corridor. Standing in his black pajamas with his hands folded across his chest, His Regal Highness Samuel of Andover, stared daggers at his tired mother. She yawned. "What is it Sammy?"

"Look." He opened his little hand to reveal a surprise – his dead pet hamster. "He won't wake up."

Margaret took a closer look, but jumped when her son tried to put the dead rodent into her soft hand. "Honey, he's dead."

"What?" His eyes grew wide and quickly began to fill with tears. "But Mom, he's only two. Why'd he die?"

"I don't know, Sam. Put him back in his cage and I'll have Ellie tend to it."

Samuel closed his hand with defiance. "I want Daddy."

Here we go again, Margaret thought tersely. Whenever she didn't do what her son demanded, he always requested his father, His Highness Edward. Thankfully, he was due to return today from a three month dig in the Sahara Desert. "Samuel, he'll be home today."

"Good." Samuel spun around and ran down the corridor to his bedroom.

Lady Margaret walked down the corridor of her state apartment with a sense of purpose. She may not have been a princess like her cousin, Sophia, but she was still a member of the regal family, a fact she never let anyone forget. Her mother, Her Regal Highness The Princess Fiona, was the younger sister of the Dowager Queen Cassandra. Growing up, Margaret felt as if she were made to feel less than by the staff and some members of the family – especially her grandmother, Her Regal Highness The Duchess Victoria – but she never let it bother her. Margaret felt as if she'd spent her entire life proving she was just as good as her cousins and it shaped the course of her life. When her mother, Princess Fiona, died eight years ago, Margaret's brother, His Regal Highness Lord Walter of Andover, moved into Fiona's regal residence, Blake Manor. Whether it was out of defiance or refusal to be carted off to Blake Manor, Margaret retained her state apartment at Andover Palace, to the unspoken consternation of Princess Sophia. The feud between the princess and the lady was well documented in the press, but they never commented on it in the public sphere. But that didn't matter, Margaret reminded herself as she sat on the chaise lounge in her private sitting room. With Edward's return in a matter of hours, Margaret had too much to attend to and lending her thoughts to her feud with Princess Sophia was quite counterproductive.

"The morning air always refreshes me." Her Regal Highness The Dowager Queen Cassandra, the former monarch of Andover, took in the misty April morning with great abandon. Her three West Highland Terrier-Cairn Terrier crossbred dogs sniffed the grounds of the palace with the same curiosity they dedicated to this task every morning. "Don't you agree, Joseph?"

"Yes, Grandmother."

"Now, you know what I always say: If one can't enjoy the small details of life, how will they ever enjoy the gifts they seem to strive for?"

His Regal Highness The Prince Joseph of Andover couldn't help but laugh at her philosophies of life. As the youngest child of King Michael and the deceased Princess Katherine, Prince Joseph was always close to his grandmother. Their morning walks were a tradition that went back to Joseph's fourteenth birthday and continued until this very day. Whenever Joseph went way, he called her each and every day to discuss the recent events affecting the kingdom, as well as the family. When his mother died nine years ago, it was his grandmother, then Queen Cassandra, who dedicated her time and attention to ensuring that he got through the tragedy. Joseph always remembered his grandmother's undying kindness, despite what the press wrote about her from time to time.

"Darling," continued Cassandra, "what's on your agenda for today?"

"I'm reading to a nursery school at ten and having lunch with Alexander at Kemp Castle to discuss Mother's charity, but my afternoon is wide open. Why?"

"Maisie, don't touch those mums," Cassandra whispered. Maisie, the oldest of Cassandra's dogs, quickly ran to her mistress's side. "Well, you do know that Edward is returning to Andover today. Don't you?"

"I heard Margaret discussing it with my dad."

"Really? What did they say?" Although she always denied it, Cassandra was a lifelong gossip, a quality she always had to suppress during her twenty-eight year reign as Queen of Andover.

Joseph leaned into Cassandra. "Apparently, Edward's dig is over and he's coming home."

Cassandra huffed to herself. "Well," she began, "it's about time. He has a wife and child! Not just any wife! He's married to a regal highness! I never understood how Edward could run off to the Sahara Desert to dig for bones when he has *responsibilities*. If Fiona were alive, that never would have happened. My sister would have seen to that."

"From what I've heard, Edward and Margaret have never had a conventional marriage."

"You don't know the half of it!"

"Grandmother!"

"Joseph, we all have a past. Margaret has hers; Edward has his. That's all I'll say on that matter. Now, tell me, what are we having for breakfast?"

As the regal family began to file into their breakfast room, the Blue Parlor, to enjoy the fresh eggs, warm pancakes, French toast, rare tea and coffee, and the other delicacies dreamed up by the palace's chef, one member of the family was conspicuously absent. It wasn't His Regal Highness The Prince of Kemp, Prince Alexander, who resided at the heir's residence, Kemp Castle; His Regal Highness Lord Walter, who resided at Blake Manor; or His Highness Edward who was boarding the regal jet to Andover. No, it was King Michael's middle child and only daughter, Her Regal Highness The Princess Helena of Andover, who was sulking in her bedroom.

Most mornings, Helena's absence from the regal breakfast was overlooked. This morning however, her father demanded her attendance. When word reached Helena fifteen minutes ago, she wanted nothing more than to scream to the heavens, but she knew she had no choice. God, she thought, not today. The princess walked by her floor length mirror once again to catch a glimpse of her slightly rotund body. She knew she was a bit plump, but the newspapers were being especially cruel today. This morning's edition of *The Pass Observer* sat on a silver tray next to her silver coffee pot. "Princess Porky Goes to Town!" shouted the headline in black ink. Had she known a photographer with a photo lens was stalking her from two hundred feet away, she wouldn't have eaten that burrito so quickly, but she had an engagement in twenty minutes.

Stop it, she told herself once more. Stop making excuses for them, she sighed. Life had been like this for the past two years and, until she lost the weight, she feared that she may never have a quiet moment again. The longer she remained a walking target for Andover's press, the longer they would watch her every move. But there was only so much one could do. Last month, she even asked her father to take away *The Pass Observer*'s operating license, but he declined because it could violate their right to free speech. But what about my right to live a private life, she wanted to scream. But a private life was something she'd never had. As the daughter of the current monarch, Helena lived in a veritable fish bowl and she hated it. There were times she even considered giving up her regal entitlements, taking her trust fund, and disappearing into a vast city like London or New York. But, for the time being, her presence was requested in the Blue Parlor

Helena slipped into her black Manolo Blahnik Mary Jane's, took a deep breath, and ventured down the vast labyrinth of corridors to the Blue Parlor where her family waited.

"How nice of you to join us, Helena," smiled Lady Margaret.

"Guess what, Helena? My hamster died," Samuel said sharply.

Helena waited as the butler pulled out her chair between Cassandra and Samuel. "I'm sorry to hear that."

"See!" Samuel reached into his blazer pocket and dropped the rodent on her plate.

Princess Helena let out a scream. Margaret quickly scolded her son. Within an instant, a maid had removed the plate and replaced it with a clean one. "I told you to put that the hamster in its *cage*," Margaret snapped.

"I did. Then I took him out again," Samuel countered.

"Samuel, I'm sorry to hear your pet has died. We should get him a real pet. Like a dog. You do know that Maisie is about to burst," Cassandra stated blithely.

"Can I have a dog, Mom?"

Margaret gave Cassandra a steely gaze, which Cassandra conveniently ignored. "I'll discuss it with Aunt Cassandra. Later."

Michael rose from his seat at the head of the table. "May I have everyone's attention? Sam, I'm sorry to hear that your pet has died, but such is life, is it not? I have news. Count Matthew Hall will fly into Andover tonight and he will stay - as my guest - in a suite within the palace."

Silence filled the room. They all knew who Count Matthew Hall was – the whole kingdom knew – but he usually stayed at The Nightingale Inn, Andover's most exclusive hotel. If Count Matthew Hall stayed at the palace during this trip to the kingdom, who knew what the press would make of the situation or how the people would react. This notion, to a certain degree, weighed on all of the minds present in the Blue Parlor.

"Dad, what's going to happen with you two?" Joseph knew that Michael wouldn't have arranged for Count Matthew to stay at the palace without good reason.

Michael sat in his chair as he prepared to break the news to his family. "The Count and I have been together for three years. I thought it was time he stayed here…in a suite. Logistically, it's easier."

Cassandra stirred her coffee absentmindedly. "Michael, he could easily stay at Blake Manor…"

"Mother, this isn't open to discussion. I simply wanted to inform everyone that the Count will be here tonight, so please let's make him feel welcomed." Michael turned to Margaret. "Will Edward be with us tonight?"

She nodded.

"Then I want us to have dinner in the dining room. I'll have my secretary organize your schedules accordingly." Michael stood again and left the room as everyone else stood out of respect.

A look of confusion, concern, and outright curiosity filled the room, but no one quite knew what to say to break the spell cast by their monarch. "Well," Cassandra said dryly, "it looks like this is going to be an interesting day after all."

2

In his private suite in Kemp Castle, His Regal Highness The Prince of Kemp, Prince Alexander of Andover listened as his secretary shared the news of Count Matthew Hall's stay at Andover Palace. To Alexander, this is the sort of news that always made him doubt whether or not his father had been completely honest with him throughout his life. There were a plethora of things Alexander didn't know about Michael's life before he met his mother, the late Princess Katherine, but answers were the only thing that could assuage the endless speculation that occurred in the young prince's mind. Alexander had always tried to be understanding of his father's situation, but the simple fact that his father could begin to see someone – a man, no less– six years after his mother's death was too much to bear.

However, Alexander's anxieties as heir to the throne were only heightened due to the fact that his residence was Kemp Castle. The castle was isolated on two thousand acres in the northeastern part of the kingdom, which was over four hours way from Andover Palace. To add a bit of insult to injury, the castle itself was built in the middle of a lake with its own drawbridge. While Alexander was raised in this castle, there were times he yearned to be in Andover Palace with the rest of his family. He often grew bitter because unlike his siblings, Princess Helena and Prince Joseph, he'd never lived at the palace. He was simply a visitor. Now the news that his father's boyfriend of three years was staying at the palace made the prince even more jealous than he was on a normal morning.

Alexander promptly dismissed his private secretary. Gathering his coat from a nearby chair, he left the inner sanctum of his bedroom, passed through the anteroom, and into the brick halls that made up the interior of this intricate castle. Several servants stepped out of Prince Alexander's way and bowed as he strode down the halls with purpose and confidence. He made his way outside into the fresh afternoon air, climbed into an electric golf craft, and whizzed towards the stables.

She sat on her brand new stallion with a broad smile. As her husband came towards her in the electric golf cart, Her Regal Highness The Princess of Kemp, Olivia, dismounted the stallion, ran towards the prince, and threw her arms around his neck. "Thank you for the stallion. He's wonderful," she cooed.

Alexander gave her a soft peck on the mouth. "I'm glad you like him."

"I do. I'll have to invite your sister and aunt over for a ride this week."

"You can ask them tonight. We're going to the palace for dinner."

Olivia gave Alexander a perplexed look. More often than not, her plans for the evening changed due to his father's sudden whims of fancy. But there was no way to defy the King in a place like Andover, Olivia constantly reminded herself.

"Is it a problem," asked Alexander.

"Well…Wendy and I were supposed to have dinner here tonight. I told you about it days ago."

Sensing the disappointment in her voice, Alexander caressed her soft hand. "I'm sure your sister will understand. You're a member of the regal family. You'll be the Duchess of Andover when I'm the King. These are the sacrifices we must make."

Olivia forced a weak smile. "I know…Do you want to go for a ride?"

"I can't. I have to meet with the estate manager of Kemp Castle before my lunch with Joseph." Alexander climbed into the electric golf cart. "Do you want a ride back to the house?"

"Not right now. Midnight Thunder and I are going for another ride." Olivia watched her husband drive towards the castle. These were the moments when she wondered whether or not she'd done the right thing by marring the heir to Andover's throne. Yes, she loved Alexander, but she always thought that her reality would be like the dream she had before becoming his wife. Her life was excellent, which was why she never complained. However, her life wasn't her own. Her new life was filled with regal obligations, last minute changes, and forced smiles in order to keep the peace. But this is what she wanted, she reminded herself for the third time this morning. One day soon I'll be the Duchess of Andover, she smiled to herself, and then it will all be worth it. Olivia mounted Midnight Thunder, gave him a gentle nudge, and began to ride into the distance. It'll all be worth it, she told herself, but in this moment, she began to reconsider everything she thought she knew.

"What do you want me to do with her, Your Regal Highness?"

"Let her in…but to the front room. Have Marigold give her water or tea and then you'll go in to tell her that I'm busy with regal affairs. Be sure she leaves and do not let her in again, do you hear me?"

"Yes, Sir." Jasper gave a low bow, took three steps backwards, and exited the private office of His Regal Highness Lord Walter of Andover.

How do I always end up in these situations, he thought to himself. Walter rubbed his weary eyes for the third time in three minutes because he'd forgotten to take out his contact lenses last night. After an evening of debauchery with a woman he'd met at a charity function, it was time for his staff to give her the regal blow off. Walter never wanted to be the one to cast out a poor woman into the streets, so he made sure his staff was adept enough to handle this task.

Just then, there was another knock at the door.

"Yes?" In walked Jasper. He bowed again, handed Walter a soft cream envelope on a silver tray, bowed, took three steps backward, and exited the room. Walter opened the envelope and pulled out the heavy card. The top was embossed with King Michael's crest and the words: *From the Office of His Majesty The King*. In short, the note instructed Walter to attend a dinner at the palace at seven o'clock in the evening to welcome Count Matthew Hall during his stay at Andover Palace. Walter inputted the necessary information into his Google Calendar which was perfectly synced to his iPhone and his private secretary's web calendar.

Evenings at Andover Palace with Michael and the rest of the regal family were events Walter rarely enjoyed. Yes, they were his family, but the years he'd spent in Luxembourg before the death of his mother, Princess Fiona, had made him the black sheep of the group. Walter marveled at the ease with which Margaret resided at the palace, but even staying there for two days made Walter uneasy. That was why after Princess Fiona died, Cassandra implored Walter to stay in the kingdom instead of flying back to Luxembourg. However, he chose to reside in the regal residence where he'd grown up, Blake Manor. It was one hour north of Andover Palace in the middle of rolling countryside. The five hundred acre, thirty bedroom manor was fit for regal living, which was made even more appealing by the fact that it had its own hunting grounds. The peace and isolation of Blake Manor allowed Walter to perform his regal duties while indulging himself with the pleasures of women who weren't of his class, but too naïve to fully understand his social status.

Walter's iPhone vibrated careless. *She's gone*, the message read. He breathed a sigh of relief, but his moment of accomplishment was interrupted when his sister, Lady Margaret, barged into his office. "What are you doing here," he asked pointedly.

"Walter, I need a favor."

"What?" He motioned for her to sit as he went to the wet bar and made her a Bloody Mary. "Is everything all right?"

Margaret rolled her eyes. "Edward's coming back today."

"Edward and Count Matthew in the same day? We must be blessed." Walter handed his sister her drink. "What's the problem?"

"I told the driver to drop Samuel off here after school. Edward and I need time alone." Margaret took a long sip of the cocktail. "Whatever happens, I don't want Samuel to see…or hear…whatever goes on."

Walter gave his sister a confused look. "I thought you wanted Edward to come back from his dig. That's all you've talked about for weeks."

“Edward left because we had…issues. Now he’s coming back and we still have the same issues.” Margaret emptied the glass. “I’m so tired.”

“Look, I’ll watch Samuel and bring him to the palace tonight. Did you bring a change of clothes?”

“I gave them to someone…I’m sure they’ll find their way to his bedroom. Thank you, Walter.” She smoothed her Eli Saab dress as she rose from the damask chair. “You’re so lucky that you’ve never been married or had children. It’s all too much. I don’t know how Mother and Father did it.”

“They didn’t. Aunt Cassandra and Uncle James raised us, along with a full time staff. Mother and Father were too busy being seen in Monaco to give two shits about us.”

“You always know how to make history interesting,” she stated snidely. “They tried.”

Not wanting to get into a war of semantics with Margaret, Walter let it go. He escorted his sister to the foyer of the manor, kissed her goodbye, and took in the lonely setting that was his life. Blake Manor had become his world, but it was all too incomplete for his tastes. While the some members of the regal family did come to Blake Manor on the weekend, Walter never felt as if they were coming to see him. Hell, they rarely came to see him when he lived in Luxembourg or New York, so why should it be any different now? Walter walked by the mirror in the foyer when he caught sight of himself. He backed up and came face to face with the man he’d been so desperate to hide. There he was: A mass of quiet desperation. He longed for a wife and children, but for some reason, they seemed to evade him. The lines around Walter’s eyes made him look ten years older than his forty-seven years, but life wasn’t slowing down even if his libido had. In time, Walter told himself, he would have the fairy tale ending he deserved. After all, he was His Regal Highness Lord Walter of Andover! No one could take that away from him. But if he could only let himself love without putting up the walls that always resulted in one night stands, he might stand a fighting chance of happiness. Walter shook his head with discontent. I need to rest, he told himself. On his way up the flight of stairs to his private suite, he instructed Jasper to take any messages and to wake him in exactly eighty-three minutes. With that, Walter pulled the heavy silk curtains shut, crawled into bed, and let the world pass him by.

"I am so humbled to present to you the newly renovated Andover Horticultural Society's Green Gardens." With that, Princess Sophia cut the blue ribbon. The lawn filled with applause and flashbulbs as the princess shook hands with the society's chairman, Countess Gwendolyn Moore. After twenty minutes of photographs, the princess was whisked into her waiting car, and driven to Andover Palace where she was scheduled to have afternoon tea with her mother, the Dowager Queen Cassandra.

During the twenty minute ride back to the palace, Sophia sank into the soft leather of the black executive Lancia Thesis. Before she could clear her mind her iPhone rang. It was Robert. "Yes?"

"Sophia, it's me. Can we talk?"

"Robert, I'm on my way to the palace. Can this wait?"

"I suppose. Goodbye."

Sophia was a bit taken aback by Robert's abrupt salutation. In fact, her husband had been acting quite strangely for a while now, but she'd chosen to ignore the signs. She likened his behavior to that of a man who cheats on his wife: The wife, no matter what her IQ, knows within her soul that her husband is being unfaithful even if she doesn't have the proof to confront him. That, Sophia deduced, was pure animal instinct; the hunter in us all. But in this moment, she couldn't decide what Robert wanted because he was so aloof that it was hard for her to see her husband for who he really was.

Within minutes of returning to the palace, Sophia sat in her mother's private tea room on the first floor of the palace facing south. Cassandra loved this room, and while it was always used by the monarch from the days of her grandfather King Christoph, Michael allowed his mother to use this room for her world famous afternoon tea parties. Today, however, Sophia was the only guest. Twice a month, mother and daughter got together to discuss the rest of the family in great length.

"Matthew is staying in the Wesleyan Suite," Cassandra murmured. "President Carter stayed in that suite. I remember his visit well…"

Sophia gently sipped her cup of Darjeeling tea. "Michael loves him, Mother. Don't tell me you're surprised."

"Aren't you," countered Cassandra.

"No. Michael may be the monarch, but he's a man. Men do what they do."

Cassandra shuddered. "I wish you wouldn't use those phrases! I've heard people utter that on afternoon talk shows. One might think that you did not have a proper upbringing." Cassandra leaned in closer to her daughter. "Do you think Michael will marry Matthew?"

Sophia chewed on the question as Voltaire, the youngest of her mother's dogs, sniffed her Christian Louboutin high heels. "I do. Katherine died nine years ago. Michael's grieved. I think it's time for my brother to move on with his life."

"Well! I suppose one shouldn't stop Michael from living his life; however one must consider the responsibility that comes with being the King of Andover."

Sophia walked over to the tea service and poured herself another cup of tea. "Mom, may I ask you a question?"

"What is it, dear?"

She shifted uneasily as she tried to find the right words. "I'm perfectly secure in the fact that Robert loves me, however…"

"However? There shouldn't be a however. You're a regal highness…A princess!"

Sophia continued. "There's something inside of me that says all isn't as it appears..."

"Tell Michael," Cassandra stated. "He's the King and your big brother. He'll fix your problem."

"Mother, this isn't a matter of national security. I don't need to involve Michael."

Cassandra fed Voltaire half of her strawberry cookie before turning her attention to Sophia. "Then what's the matter?"

"I..."

"Sophia," Cassandra said sternly. "Stop this! You do this all the time. You imagine the worst possible scenarios just to amuse yourself. Robert loves you. The whole world knows that. Don't you remember that *Vanity Fair* proclaimed you to be the most glamorous couple in the world? You have always been adored my dear and so it will always be." Sophia began to protest. "Just be happy," interjected Cassandra. "I'm eighty-three and I haven't been this happy in years. You have a wonderful life and a dashing husband. Don't let your mind tell you otherwise." Cassandra collected Voltaire and left the tea room.

Feeling smaller than she'd ever felt before, Sophia reassured herself that her mother was right. After all, Robert did adore her and she did have a penchant for creating drama in her head. Sophia quickly finished her drink before leaving the tea room with a newfound sense of self.

Lady Margaret lowered herself into the warm bubble bath. She closed her eyes as a smile crossed her face. In this moment, she had everything she ever wanted: A wonderful son and the best lover she'd ever had the good fortune to run across. As she thought back to the last twenty minutes, she couldn't help but recall the energy with which he'd entered her and the way he kissed her breasts. He was gentle and passionate, yet he was also full of the energy reserved for men in their twenties. Margaret opened her eyes as he stepped into the quaint bathroom, his semi-erect penis still visible through his boxer shorts. Despite the fact that they hadn't made love in so long, she still marveled at his fit body. "Going so soon? You just got here," she cooed.

"I know." He sat on the edge of the bath, kissing her forehead.

"Don't leave," she whispered into his ear.

Prince Robert gave her a wistful smile. "I have to. If I don't go now, Sophia will get suspicious."

Margaret felt her skin crawl at the mention of her cousin's name. Sophia had everything including the man she loved. Where was the justice, Margaret often asked herself. "She's never going to find out," Margaret reassured her lover.

Despite the fact that he and Margaret had been sleeping together for a little over a year, Robert was beginning to think that Sophia knew more than she let on. While his wife was the perfect princess in public, he knew that she was far from inane; Sophia was probably the smartest person he knew. "Anyway, you should get to the airport because if the press shows up and you're not there to greet Edward, it will certainly raise…concerns…to say the least."

Margaret was all too aware that Robert made perfect sense, but a small part of her wished life were different and that they had been married all those years ago. But by the time they'd met, he was already desperately in love and engaged to Sophia, the Queen's daughter. "Then I'll see you at Michael's dinner for Matthew," she sighed. "Goodbye, darling."

Robert gave her a quick kiss before returning to the bedroom of The Hunting Lodge, dressed, climbed into his BMW X3, and drove onto a tiny country lane.

As Robert drove from his personal home, The Hunting Lodge, to the palace, he couldn't forget the suppleness of Margaret's skin or the taste of her intimate surprises. While he never intended to sleep with his wife's cousin, there was something about Margaret that he couldn't resist. Could it have been her feistiness or her willingness to do many things that Sophia deemed too inappropriate even within the privacy of their bedroom? Robert truly loved his wife, but he also loved the times he and Margaret spent at The Hunting Lodge. It was the only place they could be alone. And due to the fact that he'd purchased The Hunting Lodge years before he'd met Sophia, it wasn't deemed a regal residence and was off limits to the rest of the regal family. When the going got tough, the lodge was his refuge from the politics that so often engulfed his wife's family.

He turned onto Route 3 just as his iPhone chirped next to him. Pressing the hands free button near his radio, Robert said, "Hello?"

"Robert, it's Sophia. Where are you?"

"Honey, I had to run to The Hunting Lodge to retrieve a few files for my father. I should be home in forty-five minutes."

He could hear her typing away on her MacBook Air. "Fine. Goodbye."

"I love you." With that, he hung up.

That was a little too close for comfort, he told himself. Yes, he had been able to keep his year long affair a secret, but something within him started to nag at his soul. For the past few weeks he'd had irritating pains in his stomach, which his doctor diagnosed as stress, but Robert knew better. The fear of his wife discovering his covert affair was enough to keep him up at night. Hell, the maelstrom that could erupt with Michael if the press found out made him think of expulsion from the kingdom or worse. To clear his mind, Robert turned on the CD player. The next instant, Chet Baker came to life and Robert began to relax. In less than half an hour he would be with his wife and all would be fine. However, one nagging question still bothered him: Now that Edward was returning to Andover, what would happen to his relationship with Margaret? Not wanting to know the answer to that question, Robert quickly forced it out of his mind with little success.

Princes Alexander and Joseph sat in the study at Kemp Castle with a bottle of cognac between them. Lunch consisted of pheasant from the Kemp Castle grounds, vegetables from the organic garden, and sides of cheese from the sheep and cattle kept at the castle's barn. The brothers had never been close growing up, and after the death of their mother nine years ago, they'd managed to grow further apart. When their father ascended the throne and Alexander was invested as the Prince of Kemp, they met sporadically to have lunch and discuss everything from politics to women to their family. Today, the conversation was skewed towards Count Matthew's impending visit.

"Dad seems happy," Joseph reasoned. Unlike some members of his family, Joseph was always supportive of his father's decisions. "Who knows? Maybe Dad will ask Matthew to marry him."

"I hope it doesn't come to that," Alexander replied with a raised eyebrow. "I don't think the kingdom needs *that*."

Joseph chewed on his pheasant. "Alex, don't be provincial. It's time Dad moved on with his life."

"Yes, but there are some things the King of Andover shouldn't do. Dad knows that." Alexander took a long sip of cognac. He could never understand why Joseph was so protective of his father. From where Alexander stood, his father had more power than he needed and at times like this, it seemed like he was flaunting his position. "Can you imagine? The King of Andover marries a man. The press would crucify us."

"You don't give Dad enough credit. Andover has the Marriage Equality Act. Two people of the same sex can get married without incident. That includes Dad."

Alexander cleared his throat. "And how are you, Joey?"

"I can't complain. Life's a party and I'm the DJ."

"I wish you would find a girl and settle down. You need to stop your carefree ways."

Joseph groaned at Alexander's flimsy attempt to show brotherly concern.

While he appreciated Alex's pithy observations, Joseph didn't feel like being lectured by anyone about the state of his love life. When he found the right girl, the world would know. Unlike Walter, he didn't have a fear of commitment, just the fear of finding someone who would love him for him. "Alex, let me live my own life. I mean, you don't hear me asking you when you'll produce an heir."

"It's not for lack of trying," sighed Alexander. "Olivia and I are doing everything to get pregnant."

"Maybe one of you is barren," Joseph replied. His brother shot him an icy glare. "I was kidding."

"Joey, my wife and I are trying to get pregnant. It hasn't happened yet. It will."

Joseph eyed his older brother carefully. "And if it doesn't?"

For a moment, Alexander was stunned by his brother's forthrightness. This was the question no one had the gall to ask him in the sixteen months since his wedding to Olivia. They were both twenty-nine and they had years to have a child. However, as Olivia reminded him, the longer she didn't have a child, the harder it could be to conceive in the future. Alexander refused to face this fact, just as he refused to have a fertility test. "It will," he finally responded. "My wife and I will have a baby, Joey."

Joseph quietly nodded, but his brother's confident demeanor didn't sway him in the least.

"Your Majesty, you have a call."

Michael placed his reading glasses on his oak desk. Glenn, his private secretary, patched the call through to Michael's private line. The line rang once. "Yes," Michael said.

"Your Majesty, it's me."

In an instant, Michael felt as if he'd been given the gift of life. Hearing

Matthew's voice only made him love this man even more than he already did. "Matthew. Where are you?"

Matthew closed the latch on his Louis Vuitton suitcase. "I'm still in Amsterdam. The car is on its way to take me to the airport."

"I'm sorry that the regal jet can't bring you to Andover. Edward is returning today and I thought it would be best if a member of the family was on the jet." Michael quickly stopped himself when he heard how the words had fallen out of his mouth. "I didn't mean it in that way, Matthew…"

"It's fine," Matthew replied as he sat on his bed. "I understand. I've always understood."

"Well, I'll treat you like the prince you are when you get to the palace. I have so many activities planned for your visit."

"What about your official business?"

Michael laughed. "I sign bills…it's not that time consuming, despite what people tend to think."

Matthew heard his housekeeper tell him that the car had arrived. He began to walk down the stairs of his four million dollar canal house as he said, "Is it going to be a problem for me to stay at the palace?"

"Absolutely not," Michael snapped. "You are my boyfriend…lover… whatever. You are mine and you will be treated as any member of my family while you're in Andover and that will include staying at the palace."

"Okay."

Michael sat up because he felt there was a bit of hesitation on Matthew's end. "Is everything all right, Matthew?"

"Yes. I'm just a little nervous," confessed Matthew. "But I'm ready. Listen, I have to go. I love you, Michael and I'll see you in a few hours."

With that, Michael hung up the phone. He sat back in his chair, put on his glasses, and tried to finish reading the novel his sister had given him by Anthony Trollope. Finding it difficult to continue with the novel with thoughts of Matthew on his brain, Michael turned his attention to the confidential files that sat on his desk and demanded his attention.

As Michael made his way through the state papers concerning the armed services, regal charters for a new green energy corporation, and issues regarding the Andover Equities and Securities Exchange, his minded drifted to the first time he'd met Matthew. While it all seemed to happen a thousand lifetimes ago, the images, sounds, and smells were still familiar to the King. Despite the powers that seemed to keep them apart so many years ago, Michael and Matthew were in a different place. Times and people had changed for the better and the future seemed to be more enthralling than before. The King quickly signed the papers in front of him, stepped into the anteroom of his official office, and instructed Glenn to return the papers to their necessary officials.

Michael stepped onto the lawn of Andover Palace when his mother and her dogs, Maisie, Voltaire, and Bramble came towards him. He took his mother by the arm as they walked in quiet surrender by the palace lake. The lake was a natural part of the estate, but over the years, Cassandra made small changes to suit her own tastes.

"My secretary told me that Edward has landed," cooed Cassandra. "It's so good of him to leave those bones in the ground and attend to his wife and son."

Michael shook his head. "Mother, you don't even know why Edward went to Africa."

The Dowager Queen sniffed. "Well," she began, "in my day a man stayed with his family. I told Fiona - may God rest her soul - Edward didn't respect Margaret and she told me the same thing. If he actually respected her, he wouldn't have disappeared for three months."

Michael bit his lip. As Andover's monarch, he knew about everything that went on in the kingdom, and that included the inner workings of his family. While he sometimes wished he didn't know the intimate details of their lives, he needed to know what they were doing in order to protect them. Such was the cross he had to bear. The truth behind Edward's self-imposed exile to the deserts of Africa wasn't his secret to tell and he refused to tell anyone, especially his mother.

"Son," Cassandra continued, "do you think this is right?"

"It's not for me to say."

"Come! I taught you all about monarchical diplomacy, but you can tell me!" Cassandra felt Bramble jump on her leg. She pulled a small piece of chicken out of her Hermes handbag and fed it to the dog. "Michael…"

"Mother, no. What happens between a man and his wife should remain between them." Michael gave his mother a sly look. "You should know that."

"Yes... Quite right." And that was all the Dowager Queen had to say on the matter.

3

His Highness Edward of Andover stepped onto the tarmac of Andover International Airport. To his surprise, photographers snapped his picture in rapid succession as a news crew from the Independent Broadcasting Channel documented his return. He'd only been gone for three months, but it did feel like a lifetime. Edward had spent the majority of last night preparing for this spectacle. Three months in the Sahara Desert did things to the skin his wife wouldn't appreciate. My wife, he chuckled to himself.

Edward waved to the crowd with great fervor. This was the part he enjoyed most about being a member of Andover's Regal Family – the attention. A reporter from IBC did a quick interview with him, during which a black town car idled a few feet away. The chauffeur opened the back door and out stepped Lady Margaret of Andover. She was wearing a cream colored Chanel suit with a string of pearls wrapped around her neck. A black hat completed her ensemble. They approached each other with the familiarity of old friends and a couple who had less in common that they ever thought possible. Margaret and Edward smiled for the cameras before getting into the town car.

An hour later, Edward and Margaret walked into the restrained elegance of their lush state apartment. It had changed little since Edward left for Africa three months ago; the only new addition was a portrait of Margaret's mother, Princess Fiona, on her wedding day. Edward had always admired Princess Fiona and he took her death quite hard. A maid came into the front room with tea, cakes, and sandwiches. The sight of the rich food made Edward slightly nauseous, due to the fact that his diet in the Sahara consisted of nothing more than true grit and human determination. He and his wife sat next to each other on the pale green sofa. She leaned in and kissed Edward on the mouth. He returned her affection, albeit tentatively.

"What's the matter," she asked softly. It had been too long since they'd been together. Margaret desperately missed the smell of her husband, the taste of his mouth, and the power of his rugged lovemaking. “I’ve missed you.”

“I’ve missed you, too.” Edward rang a nearby bell. The maid reappeared with a low bow. “A glass of water and lime, please.”

“Yes, Your Highness.” With that, the maid left the room and within a minute she returned with the glass of water.

As she left, Edward said, “You look well, Maggie.”

“I am.”

“Where’s Sam?” Edward picked up an egg sandwich and ate it with great intensity.

Margaret poured herself a cup of tea. “He’s at Blake Manor with Walter. Oh, I don’t know if you’ve been told, but Michael is hosting a dinner for Count Matthew Hall tonight. Everyone’s attendance is mandatory.”

“I need to sleep. I’ve been up for hours.”

“It's one dinner, Ed. It won’t kill you,” she replied tersely.

Edward rolled his eyes. “I didn’t say it would. When you’ve been in the midst of the Sahara for three months then we can see how interesting a regal dinner sounds to you.”

“You don’t have to be such an ass,” Margaret snapped. “It's just one tonight...”

“Fine.” Edward stood up and walked towards the bedrooms. “I’m going to take a nap. What time is this dinner?”

“It's in four hours.”

Edward nodded before leaving the front room. He sighed to himself as he turned down the corridor towards the private bedroom suites. There were four bedroom suites in this state apartment, but his and Margaret’s was at the end of the corridor. Once in the mauve bedroom, Edward peeled off his clothes and climbed into the soft four poster bed. The soft sheets felt like heaven against his weather-beaten skin. The perks of being a regal family member, he told himself. Edward set the alarm on his iPhone for an hour before dinner. He began to doze off when Margaret came into the bedroom.

"Can we talk," she asked. Edward sat up at full length. Margaret couldn't stop staring at his cut, nude body. "You…should put something on…one of the help might see you and there'll be a scandal…"

Edward moaned. "That's the least of our problems, Maggie."

She shifted uncomfortably. "Can we please talk?"

"Do you really want to do this now?"

"Ed…"

"I'm tired. I'm jet lagged. I have to attend a family dinner. Maggie, I need my rest. Please. We haven't talked in three months. I don't think three hours of not talking will further damage our marriage. Do you?"

Knowing that her husband was right, Margaret left their bedroom. She wandered into her study, called in her secretary, and ran through her schedule for the next week. Despite her attempts to keep busy, all Margaret could think about was the fact that her husband was finally home, but she'd never felt more alone.

"Daddy! You're home!" Samuel ran across the Crimson Room and jumped into Edward's arms.

Edward held his son for dear life. No matter how much he loved being a part time archaeologist, Edward's love for his son was paramount. He inhaled the scent of his son's bubble bath and looked into Samuel's big brown eyes. "Sammy. I missed you, buddy."

"Me too. Bugger died this morning."

"The hamster?" Samuel nodded. Edward said, "We'll have to get you another one."

Samuel grabbed his father around the neck, not wanting to let go. "I'm glad you're home."

"So am I."

As Edward talked to his son about the last three months, Lady Margaret and her brother, Lord Walter made their way into the Crimson Room. It was customary for the regal family to have drinks in this room before moving to their private dining room for the main meal. As usual, Margaret turned up early. Walter, who was still feeling rundown from this morning, signaled to the barkeep for his favorite drink: a double Martini Bianco. Walter gently sipped the refreshing liquor when Margaret whispered in his ear, "You look like hell."

Walter gave his older sister a deft look. "Not now, Margaret."

"Walter! Margaret! Isn't it a lovely night? The whole family together again… My, it's just like the old days." Cassandra smiled as she gilded into the Crimson Room. She loved family dinners, which had been a staple at Andover Palace since the time of her grandfather, King Christoph. A waiting maid handed Cassandra her personal drink: two-thirds gin, one-third orange juice, a splash of vermouth, and one ice cube. "Edward," she called across the room, "it's so nice to have you back."

Edward gave Cassandra a light kiss on her cheek. She couldn't help but blush. "You look radiant, Your Regal Highness."

"Oh, Edward!"

Walter rolled his eyes. "I need another drink."

Moments later, Prince Alexander and his wife, Olivia, entered the room; Princess Helena and Prince Joseph quickly followed. As the family fell into their familiar patterns of tradition and conversation, Princess Sophia and Prince Robert made their grand entrance. Their glamor enveloped them and, as some people noted, it couldn't be turned on or off; it just was. In the moments before Michael entered with Matthew, Olivia took Edward by the arm for a quiet chat.

Edward gave Olivia a familiar hug. Even though they were related by marriage, they were also first cousins who happened to marry into the regal family. Many in the public eye considered this to be a happy coincidence, but as His Regal Highness Duke James, Cassandra's late husband noted, "Having two people from the same family marry into ours greatly reduces the need for due diligence on our part." In a way, he was right. Despite this, Edward and Olivia relied on each other when it seemed they were true outsiders within this truly unconventional regal family.

"How was the dig," asked Olivia.

Edward let out a slight chuckle. "Take a guess."

"Are you glad to be back?"

"Of course. I've missed my son."

"And…"

Edward took a long sip from his glass of lager. "There is no 'and'."

"Edward," sighed Olivia. "Does this mean…"

"Olivia," interrupted Alexander. "Grandmother wants to tell you something."

"I'll be right there." She turned her attention back to her forlorn cousin. "Why don't you come to Kemp Castle for a few days? We can talk." With that, Olivia joined the Dowager Queen and the Prince of Kemp.

Matthew stood outside of the lively room with trepidation in his heart. Dressed in a bespoke Tom Ford dinner suit, he couldn't help but feel slightly out of place amongst the old world extravagance of the regal family. In spite of the fact that he'd grown up in Andover and had known Katherine and Michael since they were teenagers, Matthew knew that intermingling with the family was much different than simply being in their presence. A feeling of dread rushed through his stomach. He was about to enter the Crimson Room, when Michael approached him with his secretary, Glenn, in tow.

"Once dinner is over, I will call Minister of Government Patricia Ali. Not before." With that, Glenn bowed and left the two lovers alone. "You look dashing," Michael gave Matthew a light kiss on the mouth.

Matthew couldn't help but squirm. "Should we do that…here?"

"It's fine. I'm the King of Andover. I can do whatever I want."

Matthew looked at Michael quizzically because he couldn't tell if he was serious or simply joking. Michael nodded to a waiting valet, who pulled open the door to the Crimson Room. "Your Regal Highnesses, His Majestic Regal Highness The King of Andover," announced the valet.

Everyone turned towards Michael with a bow or curtsy. Matthew followed behind him because he wasn't sure how he should behave in such a foreign situation. Despite the fact Matthew and Michael had dated for three years, this was the first time that he had been exposed to the personal pageantry displayed behind the closed doors of Andover Palace.

The first regal to approach him was Prince Joseph. Joseph, Matthew thought, was the nicest person in the regal family. In Matthew's opinion, Joseph was the only one without an agenda or very obvious personal demons. "It's good to see you again, Count Matthew," Joseph said, as he extended his hand.

Matthew shook with it great aplomb. "Likewise, Your Regal Highness."

"I hope the staff is treating you well."

"They are," replied Matthew. A waiter came by with a glass of amontillado sherry, which Matthew drank quickly.

"Listen, later this week my brother and I are going to Blake Manor to go shooting. You do shoot, don't you?"

"I do." Matthew could tell that Joseph was sizing him up, but in this moment, he was glad to have someone to talk to. Michael was across the room in an intense conversation with Prince Robert and Princess Sophia. "What will we be hunting?"

"Quail or duck. I'm not sure. Anyway, it'll be an event. Oh, just so you know, my brother is a lousy huntsman, so try not to laugh."

Princess Helena watched with envious disgust as the delicate hors d'oeuvres floated around her. Sitting on a plush settee, Helena quickly grabbed two salmon encrusted scallops and popped them into her mouth. She savored the taste. How she missed food. Since this morning, she'd been on a self imposed hunger strike in personal retaliation over her new nickname, "Princess Porky". It was bad enough that she was being dubbed as such in the press, but even a reporter for one of the evening news channels made the same remark an hour ago. Helena vowed that she would have the last laugh, but for now, the salmon encrusted scallops were enough to soothe the deeper pain.

As Helena reached for a platter of minced duck and veal, King Michael sat next to his daughter. "Are you enjoying yourself?" The King asked as he took a sip of his favorite drink, a single amaretto.

"I suppose." Helena let out a defeated sigh. "Dad, I'm a little tired. Do you mind if I retire for the evening?"

Michael checked his watch. "It isn't even eight o'clock." He eyed his daughter carefully. Out of all his children, Helena was the most difficult to understand because she kept everything internalized. With Alexander and Joseph, they would eventually reveal what was bothering them, but Helena would keep it inside until it ate her alive. "I saw the newspaper this morning."

Helena felt her cheeks turn to fire. "Daddy, I can explain…"

"It's not your fault, but I thought we discussed this."

"Discussed what?"

Michael took a sip of his drink. "Helena, you shouldn't put yourself in a position to be ridiculed. I know how much it hurts you, but if you must eat on the go, do it in the privacy of your car."

She stopped for a moment. Was her father taking the side of the press?

She was his daughter! "How was I supposed to know that damn paparazzi had a zoom lens?" Helena's voiced quivered with anger.

"I'm sorry you're upset. But if we work *together* they will leave you alone." He patted her on the back. "Don't you agree?"

"I suppose." Michael quickly turned his attention to Matthew and Alexander. Helena couldn't believe what she'd heard. No matter how hard she tried to fight back the tears, she couldn't help but wish that her mother was here to sort this out. God, she thought, I need you now than ever, Mom.

As the palace staff cleared away the dishes from the second course, Michael took in the lovely sight. Three generations of Andover's regal family sat side by side without a care in the world. Michael had fond memories of Sunday dinner being held in this room with his grandfather, King Henrik. It was a tradition that his mother, the former monarch, kept alive. To his right was Matthew, who was seated next to Prince Alexander. Next to Alexander sat Lady Margaret, His Regal Highness Samuel, and the Princess of Kemp; Prince Robert sat to Michael's left, followed by Prince Joseph, Princess Sophia, Princess Helena, and His Highness Edward; the Dowager Queen Cassandra sat at the other end of the table. The conversation drifted from politics to the arts to the plight of Andover's people.

Once the third course was laid, King Michael turned to Robert. "Robert, I heard that you were at The Hunting Lodge this morning."

Robert cut his steak with immaculate precision. "I was. I had to get some papers for my father."

Michael nodded. "How is Hider?"

"Quite well, thank you." Robert chewed the tender meat. He always hated when Michael played these mind games with him. Ever since he'd married Sophia, Michael had kept his brother-in-law at arms length. Robert didn't know why Michael insisted on treating him as if he'd done something wrong, but it always made him uncomfortable.

Michael bit into his steak with a smile. He knew all too well that Robert was hiding something, but he chose not to know. Michael was very protective of his little sister and this husband of hers was too cool to be taken lightly. Behind Robert's eyes, Michael always felt that something wasn't right. He couldn't place his finger on it, but he was very certain that one day it would all come out. "My security team has brought it to my attention that the security around The Hunting Lodge is very lax. We could rectify that…at the palace's expense, of course."

Robert nodded gently. "That's very kind of you, Your Majesty." Although Robert had been told time and again to call the King by his birth name in the privacy of Andover Palace, he never felt comfortable breaking tradition. "But I like The Hunting Lodge as it is. It's quiet and private."

"That it is," Michael said in a low voice. "However," he continued, "if Lady Margaret continues to visit you there, we will need to protect her. After all, she is fifth in the line of succession."

With those words, Robert thought the floor would open up and swallow him. Yes, he knew that as the monarch, Michael knew everything, but how much did he know? This cageyness Michael displayed put Robert on edge. But if he let it show, he would literally ruin his life in an instant. "Sire, many members of the family come to The Hunting Lodge. The issue of security has never come up before."

Michael sighed as he took a sip of water. "That is true. My concern is when Lady Margaret spends more time at The Hunting Lodge than your wife. We must do whatever is necessary in order to preserve the integrity of the crown, the monarchy, and those directly – and indirectly – involved. Don't you agree?"

All Robert could do was nod. For the rest of the meal, Michael droned on about the stock market, but Robert knew he had to let Margaret know that Michael was on to them. If Michael was beginning to question their relationship, reasoned Robert, it was only a matter of time before Sophia started asking the same questions.

***

After dinner, the regal family retreated to their own corners of the kingdom. Alexander and Olivia said their goodbyes as their chauffeur drove them back to Kemp Castle; Walter's driver took him back to Blake Manor; and Prince Joseph went out on the town for a drink with Edward. As the palace began to wind down for the night, Matthew retreated to the Wesleyan Suite. An hour later, he was joined by Michael. They sat on the large bed without a care in the world. "Did you enjoy the dinner," asked the King.

"It was lovely. But I don't think the Prince of Kemp likes me."

Michael let out an uncharacteristic laugh. "Alexander doesn't like anyone. Sometimes I wonder if he likes himself."

Matthew kicked off his shoes. He moved in closer to Michael, planting a soft kiss on his lips. "God, I've missed you. Oh, I forgot to tell you. Prince Joseph invited me to a shoot at Blake Manor."

"Good..."

"What's wrong?"

"Nothing."

"You and Prince Robert had a very intense conversation."

"That?" Michael simply shook his head. "That was nothing. My brother-in-law and I have an interesting relationship."

"So I see. You know, it's very intriguing to see the way you interact with your family."

"How so?"

"Well," began Matthew, "you seem so authoritative, but normal at the same time. I don't know. I mean, I've been around them before, but not like this."

"Matt, you saw us as we really are."

Matthew could sense the irony in his words.

Michael started for the door. “I have a few matters to take care of tonight. For tonight, I’ll stay in my own private suite, as a matter of decorum and protocol. Do you understand?”

“Of course I do. I’m just happy to be here.”

“Matthew, I want you to know how much I love you, and how ready I am for you to become a permanent part of my life.” With that, Michael said his final goodbyes, leaving Matthew alone. Matthew prepared for bed, but Michael’s words still sounded in his head. A permanent part of his life? Would Michael propose? Is this what this visit was about? The excitement of it all proved too much, and within minutes, Matthew was fast asleep.

4

The King of Andover sat at his desk within the wood paneled walls of his official office. This office, the one in which he received official visitors, members of his government, and distinguished guests from abroad, was three times bigger than his private office and much less intimate. The adjoining anteroom was always a hive of activity, while the official reception room was always filled with the sound of anxious footsteps of those waiting to have an audience with the King. On this day, King Michael was to receive the head of his government, Patricia Ali. She was a smart woman who had won the hearts and minds of the kingdom through her platform of change meeting tradition. For the people of Andover, it was very important to maintain their high quality of life, while allowing enterprise to stay one step ahead of the rest of the world. The agenda for today consisted of a new environmental strategy and the current political climate.

This was Minister of Government Patricia Ali's fourth year of a five year term as the head of the kingdom's government. Needless to say, the King dreaded their weekly meetings. She was a woman who seemed to fight an invisible battle simply because she thought it would help her popularity in the opinion polls. By the King's estimation, she tried too hard. Had he been allowed to vote in the election (no member of the regal family was granted the right to vote), he most certainly would have voted for her opponent. The clock on monarch's desk struck ten o'clock in the morning, and as if by magic, Glenn entered with Patricia Ali. The King rose as she performed a low curtsy and the odd couple got down to business.

"There are members of the government," she stated, "who feel that the regal fleet of vehicles should be replaced with fuel efficient cars."

Internally, the King rolled his eyes. He was tired of having this discussion. His mother had signed the energy efficiency bill into law which proclaimed that within ten years, every car owned by the people of Andover would be replaced by an environmentally friendly model. In order to sway the people to adopt such a drastic strategy, the government and the regal family paid for sixty percent of the list price of any car that met certain criteria under thirty thousand Andover dollars. So far, the initiative had worked. The only downside was that the regal family felt that they weren't the people; they were regal.

"Your Majesty," Patricia called, snapping Michael out of his reverie.

"I heard you," he replied tersely. "Ms. Ali, we've been through this before. Replacing the regal fleet will be placed on the taxpayer's shoulders. As stated in Article 7, Subsection 9A of The Kingdom of Andover's Civic Law, the maintenance of the regal fleet, when so used by the regal family for personal and professional duties, will be paid from public funds. Do you really think the people of Andover would appreciate having to replace perfectly fine vehicles?"

Patricia shifted ever so slightly in her chair. Everyone knew the King was smart, a fact she always forgot. "I think the regal family should consider replacing the fleet at their own expense, Your Majesty."

"I'll consider it." That was that. "What's next?"

"Well, it's been two weeks since Count Matthew Hall came to Andover to stay at the palace. Many people are wondering what this means for the regal family."

Michael bit his bottom lip. He knew this would eventually rear its ugly head. "May we keep this between us? I do require the strictest confidence."

Patricia nodded. "Yes, Sire."

"The Count and I are examining the longevity of our relationship. The palace will release an announcement in due time. That's all I have to say on the matter." Michael glanced at his clock. It was 10:30. He rose. "Have a lovely day, Ms. Ali."

She shook his hand with a curtsy. "Thank you, Sire." With that, Glenn escorted the Minister of Government out of the palace.

Michael began to rethink the past two weeks with great intensity. He loved Count Matthew Hall more than the world, which is why he intended to propose to him next Wednesday. Michael had a ring commissioned for his beau. The only reason this had been kept a secret from the regal family, as well as the public, was due to the fact that the jeweler, Rebecca Lane, 1st Peer, was Michael's childhood riding partner. She was the epitome of discretion and if he, as the most powerful man in the kingdom, could trust anyone with this life altering news, it was her.

Michael walked towards the large window that overlooked the palace lake, when Glenn came into the room. "Your Majesty, Her Regal Highness Lady Margaret and His Highness Edward are here for their appointment."

"Yes. Show them in." The King stayed by the window as Glenn ushered Lady Margaret and His Highness Edward from the reception room into the grand office. He didn't turn around, for the reason behind this visit was known to them.

Lady Margaret handed her cousin a small manila envelope. "It's been in my safe for two months. I don't know the results, Michael."

Michael cradled the envelope in his hands. This was the aspect of his position that he hated more than anything else. Knowing the secrets of his entire family was like knowing the exact date the world would end, but not being able to tell a living soul. The blissful ignorance they all displayed thinking that they'd pulled one over on him made Michael cringe. Michael motioned for everyone to be seated. He sat on the sill of the large window, while Edward and Margaret sat across from each other in two high backed chairs.

"Mike, if I may…"

"Yes, Ed?"

Edward cleared this throat. He caught sight of Lady Margaret, but the look on her face was too blank to decipher. "I want to apologize to you, and my wife, for going to Africa for three months without reason…"

"You had a reason," surmised Michael. "I think we can all agree that the situation was not…ideal…but we must reap the fruits of our actions. Besides, the three of us agreed that it would be best if you went on that dig in the Sahara. I hope you were able to clear your mind."

"I was."

"Margaret? Do you have anything to say before I read this?"

Lady Margaret said nothing. She already felt like she'd committed a sin and she loathed the fact that Michael treated her like Hester Prynne. However, she knew she should be on her best behavior because Robert had informed her that Michael alluded to their affair. "I think life will be easier once we know the results," Margaret finally stated.

Michael ran his index finger along with sealed flap. He pulled out a medical document which was folded into thirds and read it quickly. The King's face was a mask as he handed it to the couple. For better or for worse, their fates were sealed.

"Now Matthew, I know Michael is very fond of you, which is why I thought it was important for us to get to know each other. I'm famished," the Dowager Queen exclaimed.

They were seated in the private dining room of her favorite restaurant, Le Amore. The Dowager Queen Cassandra scanned the menu as Count Matthew Hall sat on tenterhooks. According to Cassandra, Princess Sophia and Princess Helena were supposed to stop by for coffee, but until then, they would manage. From Matthew's vantage point, he could see the main dining room which was filled with executives and aristocrats making deals and trying to steal a glance of the Dowager Queen in public. On their way to Le Amore, Cassandra informed Matthew that she always dined out twice a week because, "It makes the people of Andover feel as if you're real and not a remote figurehead."

The waiter returned, took their orders and left their drinks on the table. "Tell me, Matthew, how are you finding your stay at the palace?"

He marveled at the fact that he was sitting across from the Dowager Queen, who was the most powerful woman in the kingdom. "It's lovely, Your Regal Highness."

"Isn't it? I was telling my daughter this morning that it is so nice to have you with us. It's refreshing to see a new face around the palace. Yes, we use to have all sorts of dignitaries and royals in our midst. Mind you, they still come quite frequently, but there hasn't been a definite change of guard for so long that we've all stayed at each other's palaces. Oh, that reminds me! The King of England is scheduled to come for a visit in September. That'll be a lovely occasion. He may not be very bright, but his wit outshines his ineptitude." Just then, Cassandra's iPhone chirped in her vintage Hermes Matte Crocodile Birkin Bag. She handed the phone to Matthew. "My dear, who is it?"

"The Princess of Kemp."

Cassandra answered the phone. "Olivia, I can't talk now…Yes, I'm with Count Matthew…Goodbye." Cassandra dropped the phone into her green handbag. "Prince Alexander bought that phone for me. I still can't figure it out. I'm from the time of rotary dialing…Matthew, there's something I want to discuss with you."

He could feel body temperature rise seventy degrees. "Yes?"

She lowered her voice. "As you know, my son loves you."

"And I him."

"Yes. Quite right," she replied. "I say this with the utmost ambiguity as I do not know what my son's plans are these days. That being said, if I had to estimate a guess, I would assume that he wants to make your relationship… known…in every sense of the word, if you follow me." The Dowager Queen continued, "After the death of Princess Katherine, my son fell into a depression that I thought would never end. Luckily for us, once he became the kingdom's monarch, he seemed to be lifted from the rigors of mourning for Katherine. Matthew," she said, moving in closer to him. "I think my son may ask you to marry him."

Matthew couldn't speak. For weeks he'd guessed that Michael may ask him to be his husband, but he wasn't given any indication as to his true intentions. This visit, Matthew hoped, might be the reassurance he needed to take his own life to the next step, whatever that may be. This unofficial confirmation from the monarch's own mother made him feel as if everything was actually falling into place. "That would be wonderful. I wouldn't want to share my life with anyone else."

"That's good to hear," Cassandra replied tactfully. "You must remember that the people of Andover, while they are accepting of the King's sexuality, still hold the late Princess of Kemp in their hearts. Time will only tell if you can match her level of popularity. Now, I'm not saying this to upset you – no – I'm only saying this to make you aware of the many…particulars…that come when marrying into the regal family. Ask Prince Robert or the Princess of Kemp. It's not easy, Matthew."

The head wait staff reappeared with their first course of seasonal soup and smoked trout. When they left, Matthew was still trying to find the hidden meaning behind Cassandra's words. He finally asked, "Do you want me to refuse his proposal?"

Cassandra looked up wistfully. "Did I say that?"

"No…"

"What I meant to say," Cassandra interjected, "was for you to think about how your life will change. Because, my dear, we must think of the greater good. In all honesty, how do you think the kingdom would react to the news that their monarch wants to marry a man?" With that, Cassandra said no more as she paid dutiful attention to her decadent lunch.

Matthew, on the other hand, suddenly wished he was anywhere else in the world.

***

Edward and Margaret sat in silence in their state apartment for three hours. They did not want the staff to get wind of the newfound revelation shared between them, so they'd given the staff the rest of the day off. While Lady Margaret knew she was the least self sufficient person in the world, she had the palace's main kitchen on speed dial just in case she needed nourishment. Prince Joseph had taken Samuel to the opening of The Lawson Museum of Contemporary Art's new instillation wing, which was supposed to provide the couple with time to hash out the realities of their situation. Anxious, Margaret moved back and forth between the piano in the Morning Room and her study, while Edward stared transfixed out of the window in the library.

It was Edward who finally broke the untenable silence. "This is what you wanted, isn't it?"

Margaret paused as she passed the library door. "Yes," she nodded.

"At least we know..."

"Edward…"

"Margaret, I'm thrilled to death Samuel is my son. When you told me that there was a chance that he wasn't… I didn't know what to do." Edward ran his hands through his thick strawberry blonde hair. He let out a guttural cry. "How could you put me through that hell, Margaret?"

"I didn't intend…"

"Like hell," he snapped with mounting fury. "You wouldn't have cheated on me a year into our marriage if you didn't intend to hurt me. The only thing I keep asking myself is what I did to deserve this level of unbridled hostility."

Margaret glared at her husband. He always made himself out to be the victim. God, she thought, he was worse than the women she knew. The reason she slept with her courtier had nothing to do with Edward. She did it because she wanted to do it; nothing more, nothing less. It was fun and the courtier did not disappoint her in the bedroom. Margaret constantly cursed the heavens when she wound up pregnant at the same time she called off her affair with the courtier. She managed to keep her affair a secret for all these years, but when the courtier resurfaced months ago with a blackmail suit that could have ruined the regal family, Michael ordered a paternity test. Edward, unable to stomach the betrayal of his wife, went back to his first love: archeology. The dig in the Sahara was the best option for them because no one within the regal family or in the public eye would ever consider that Edward was reeling from his wife's deception. Although the results came back two months ago, Margaret decided not to read them until her husband came home. "Edward, I do not want to discuss this! Samuel's your son. The proof is there. Let's just put it behind us."

"Can you promise me that you won't do something like this again," he asked.

"Yes," she answered abruptly. Although she knew this promise was an outright lie, Margaret decided that being with Edward in this moment was more important than the truth.

She touched his soft face, kissing his mouth with the fury of a starved lover. Margaret thrust her breasts against her husband's chest, while he undid his belt with lightening speed. Having almost forgotten the sensations that arise from making love, Edward picked up Margaret, placed her on the old leather chair, pushed up her skirt and began to perform cunnilingus. She did everything she could to stop from screaming with pure ecstasy, for his beard provided a thrill she'd almost forgotten. His throbbing penis teased her rock hard, aching clitoris, to the delight of both parties. Margaret dug her nails into his back as he climaxed on her thigh. He collapsed next to her on the soft sofa, and they fell asleep well into the night.

His Regal Highness Lord Walter sat in the middle of a long conference table covered with orchids. To his left sat members of the University of Andover Board Of Governors, while the Board of Administrators sat to his right. He tried to suppress another yawn, but it was futile. Six o'clock. Great, he thought. How he hated being the regal patron for the University of Andover. This wasn't a position he wanted – it was unwillingly thrust upon him. When his father, His Highness Lord Nicholas died, his mother, Her Regal Highness The Princess Fiona assumed his position. Upon her death so many years ago, Margaret refused to assume the position, which prompted Michael to name his cousin its new regal patron. Sitting through these bi-monthly meetings was a chore. The only consolation lay in the fact that he was supposed to meet King Michael, Princess Sophia, Prince Robert, and the Dowager Queen for dinner at the stock exchange to mark its one hundredth birthday.

As Dane Mark Patton, Head of the Board of Governors, droned on about the current state of the university and its pledge to increase funding for incoming students, something caught Walter's eye. He sat up with great delight. In all of his years in Andover, he'd never seen anyone so beautiful. She sat in the third row eagerly listening to Patton's speech. In her hands lay a small black leather notebook with a black fountain pen. Walter didn't know who she was, but he was intent to discover the identity of this creature. Lord Walter scribbled a quick note, folded it, and handed it to Jasper, who stood dutifully on the sidelines. Walter watched as his secretary read the note. Jasper nodded before leaving the stage. Time seemed to move at a glacial pace, but at least Walter now had someone to hold his interest for the next thirty minutes.

"Your Regal Highness," Jasper said at the conclusion of the event, "her name is Miss Daisy Herman."

"I must meet her. Have you told her that someone would like to speak with her?"

Jasper shifted. "Sir, I must advise against this. She…isn't of the right sort."

Not this again, Walter thought to himself. He'd heard that load of drivel his entire life. Princess Fiona would always educate her son about the type of girl that was suitable for him because, there was a very small chance, that he may actually ascend the throne. At the time of his birth, Lord Walter had been fifth in line for the throne and now he was seventh; that day, he assumed, would never come. “Jasper, I don’t pay you to organize my personal affairs. Would you please tell Miss Herman that His Regal Highness would like to have a word with her?” Sensing Jasper was about to protest, Walter raised his hand. “Thank you, Jasper.”

Minutes later, Jasper returned with Daisy Herman. By Walter’s estimation, she was more beautiful than he thought. She was no taller than five foot five, but what she lacked in height she made up for in pure personality. Daisy curtseyed dutifully. “How do you do, Your Regal Highness?”

“Very well. Thank you.” Walter gave Jasper a dismissive smile. With that, Jasper fell into the crowd, keeping an eye on the errant lord. “Did you enjoy Dane Patton’s speech?”

“I did. I graduated from the university four years ago, but I come back from time to time to hear what’s going on.” Daisy gave Walter a small smile.

“What was your concentration?”

“Art History,” she replied. “But as of now, I teach art to high school students.”

Walter was smitten. Even though her accent could use a bit of work, she had a fire within her. So many of the women he met from proper aristocratic circles were only concerned with meeting Michael or being invited to one of Cassandra’s tea parties. Daisy struck him as a genuine person. “I do hope it fulfills you.”

Daisy shrugged. “From time to time.”

Jasper signaled for Walter that it was time to leave.

Walter extended his hand. “It was a pleasure meeting you, Miss Herman. I do look forward to speaking with you again.”

Daisy accepted his hand as she curtsied. “Thank you, Your Regal Highness. Goodbye.”

Walter stared out of the window of the black executive Lancia Thesis. Jasper sat in the passenger’s seat next to Walter’s driver. As Walter performed a

Google search on Daisy through his iPhone, he said, "Jasper…"

"Yes, Your Regal Highness?"

"I'd like a full dossier on the young woman I spoke with this evening," replied Walter with finality.

"Yes, Sir," sighed Jasper.

Walter sat back in the seat as the party drove towards the stock exchange. No matter what, he was going to find out more about this woman. A small smile crossed Walter's face as they came to the entrance of the stock exchange because he finally felt like he could actually fall in love.

King Christoph opened the Andover Equities and Securities Exchange one hundred years ago in order to open the Kingdom of Andover to the free markets of the world. However, once the kingdom saw the effects of The Great Crash on their counterparts in the rest of the world, the government set stricter rules to keep the markets from wild swings that could prove deadly. On this occasion, the floor of the exchange was littered with Andover's aristocracy, and, for ceremony's sake, the regal family of Andover. Their presence was always an anticipated addition to any event. If one could get the regal family to support their cause it was bound to succeed. The regal family was very aware of this, but they performed their duties with grace and no hint of irony. To the rest of the world, this is what they longed to do. However, the regal family owned a substantial stake in the Andover Equities and Securities Exchange, which is why they took a very strong interest into the daily mechanics of the operation. The King was the Regal Chairman of the Exchange, while Prince Robert was the Regal Patron of Note. Everyone knew that Prince Robert did the majority of the work, while the King simply signed the papers. So it was, and so it would always be.

Princess Sophia posed for a photographer from the *Andover Business Journal*. Her feet were killing her. She knew these shoes were far from sensible, but the kingdom expected the sister of the monarch to be fashionable at all times.

The princess took another glass of champagne from a passing waiter. Sophia watched as Robert interacted with the people of Andover in a manner she never could. Although Robert was an aristocrat of the right class, he had a way of making everyone in his presence feel as if they were his trusted confident. Princess Sophia didn't know how he did it, but it was one of the many things she envied about her husband. There were other aspects of his personality that she couldn't stomach, much to her dismay.

"Are you enjoying yourself," a voiced called from behind her.

Sophia turned to see her brother, King Michael, coming towards her. He was flanked by two nondescript men from Andover's Secret Police. Ever since he'd become king, Michael was surrounded by security in public. Despite his nonchalance towards their presence, he hated feeling as if he were a prisoner in his own skin. Every monarch since King Christoph was assigned a security detail and Michael was no different.

"Your Majesty," she cooed with a slight bow. While it wasn't required for Sophia to bow to her brother in public, she did it anyway.

"I'm ready to go," confessed Michael. He twisted the vintage Rolex his father had given him twenty-five years ago.

"Just enjoy it."

Michael eyed her carefully. "I could tell you the same thing."

"Excuse me," she said playfully. "I'm having the time of my life."

"If you say so. Those shoes are anything but practical."

"If you only knew. I heard around the palace that Matthew is leaving tomorrow. Do you have anything planned?" Sophia had always been supportive of her brother's love for Matthew, despite the resistance from certain members of the regal family. The fact of the matter was that Sophia knew the truth…a truth that only Michael, their late father His Regal Highness Duke James and Cassandra knew. If that hadn't happened, Sophia wondered from time to time, where would they be today?

"Well, I'm taking him to Port Agnes House."

"That's on the other side of the kingdom! How will he get to the airport for his flight?" Sophia sat at the regal table to give her feet a much needed rest.

Michael joined her. "I'll have my helicopter take him. I need to be alone with him." Michael lowered his baritone voice. "I just hope that…let's just say…"

Sophia nodded knowingly. "I figured. I'm very happy for you, Mikey."

He felt his cheeks turn red. "Thank you. But," he continued, "I haven't told the rest of the family and until I have answer, I don't want to make this public knowledge."

"You have my word. Do you think he'll accept?"

Michael drummed his fingers on the maple table. "I hope so. After everything we've done through, we're still here."

"What is he doing tonight? Was he furious with you for deserting him," laughed the princess.

"No," Michael retorted. "He and Helena are having dinner at Cabo. Then they're going to watch a film in the palace viewing room."

"Still, if I were him, I would have loved to have spent the evening with my boyfriend."

Michael glanced across the room. There, Prince Robert was chatting away with Lord Walter and Countess Mara Flynn, the heiress to a respectable textile fortune. "Your husband is right there."

She let out an annoyed sigh. "I'm aware of that, big brother. But he's in his element. He lives for these nights."

"This hasn't been his entire life," reasoned the King. "You and I have lived through it – literally."

The truth behind Michael's words stung Sophia. While she performed each regal duty in support of crown and country, she could never shake the feeling that she was a pawn on the chess board of life. Growing up, her mother and father reminded her of the duty she must perform, while her grandmother, Duchess Victoria, stressed the importance of giving herself to her role in life. "It's strange," Sophia began.

"What?"

"Everyone in the kingdom wonders what it's like to be us, but we spend just as much time wondering how to be less like them."

"Don't let the press hear you say that," whispered Michael. "It could be the end of us." Michael took a long sip of water. "How are things with Robert?"

"Fine." Princess Sophia rubbed her hands together. "Everything's fine."

The sound of a ringing iPhone startled the siblings. Sophia leaned across the table to find it was Robert's. He had the worst habit for leaving his personal affects in public places. Sophia constantly instructed him to act with caution, yet he continually ignored her. As the call went to voicemail, Sophia picked up the phone to see who it was. She assumed it was his father, Hider, or his sister, Nicola. To her surprise the number was all too familiar…it was her cousin, Lady Margaret. Sophia's face turned to stone.

"Who was it," Michael asked gently.

"No one." With that, Sophia stood up and marched across the room. She whispered something into the ear of her secretary, Kelly Washam, 2nd Peer before leaving the exchange.

Princess Sophia wasn't seen for the rest of the night, but Michael assumed that his sister knew much more about the relationship between Lady Margaret and Prince Robert. And if she didn't know something before, she knew now.

Her Regal Highness The Princess of Kemp pulled on her nightgown with the help of her night maid. For Olivia, one of the perks of being married to the heir to the throne was that she never had to bother dressing herself. The night maid zipped up her nightgown before leaving the princess' bedroom for the night. Olivia sat at the small writing desk near the window. She took her brown leather journal from the drawer and proceeded to record the events of the last few weeks.

Edward's return to Andover had been a welcome surprise. Olivia always loved spending time with him, even though he seemed to be terribly preoccupied these days. No matter how deftly she handled the situation, Edward refused to discuss the matter. He would only say that it had been taken care of. Olivia was aware of how volatile Edward's marriage to Margaret could be, so she tried to stay out of his marriage. Yes, she was slightly frightened of Lady Margaret, but most women in Andover were terrified of her.

Olivia's mind began to drift towards the small details of everyday life, when Alexander knocked at the door. "May I come in," he asked.

Placing her journal in her desk, she said, "Yes."

Alexander stood in the doorway dressed in nothing but a pair of old hunting pants. She could smell his scent from across the room. "Were you hunting this late?"

"The damn buck kept us on the run. Doland finally got the damn thing an hour ago." Alexander flopped onto the soft bed. His brown skin was littered with sweat. "You should've come."

Olivia sprayed her scent onto her wrists. "I'm no fan of hunting. I find it barbaric. You knew that when you married me," she said wistfully.

"One of the few things," Alexander responded tactfully. He propped himself up on the bed. The sight of Olivia in that nightgown made him want her in ways he couldn't express. However, their marriage as of late had been very difficult.

Olivia took a deep breath. "That was uncalled for, Alex."

"So, what? This is my fault now?"

"It's your sin too, Alex!" Olivia faced Alexander with fire in her eyes. "I'm not in this alone."

Alexander was too tired to have another fruitless fight with Olivia. He made his way to the door as his heavy hunting boots scuffed the wood floor. "If you want out, just tell me. You'll be well compensated."

"I don't care about the money. I love you…"

"And my title," he groaned.

"Have you been drinking again?" Olivia didn't want to get too close to him. She could never be too careful in these situations. "You're not supposed to have more than two drinks in a night…"

"I know! Damn it… I don't need you telling me… I'm going to my bedroom. Good night."

Alexander opened the door to his vast bedroom suite and collapsed on the bed. His hunting boots made a thud on the floor as he kicked them off. Rubbing his eyes, Alexander began to reevaluate the state of his life. He was the heir to the throne of the Kingdom of Andover. Sooner or later everyone would expect for him to produce an heir. Hell, even his father had managed to have three children with his wife. But for Alexander, the task at hand was much harder than it should have been. He'd loved Olivia for years, but on the advice of many within the regal fold, he'd decided not to sleep with her before the wedding. Their wedding night was magical. However, some time between their honeymoon and a return to regal protocol, Alexander had lost the power to maintain a lasting erection. Olivia tried to help by telling him that she saw the same thing happen to someone named Trey on one of her television programs, but he wouldn't hear of it. To think that the Prince of Kemp was impotent could be a blow to the long term stability of the monarchy. The worst thing about his condition resided in the fact that he couldn't maintain an erection while watching adult films or taking mood enhancing supplements. Alexander toyed with the idea of telling his father, but he feared an apocalyptic fall out.

Two months ago, Alexander suggested that he and Olivia maintain different bedrooms until this matter were resolved. She agreed. He was too nervous to broach the subject to his wife, but he was aware that she was growing restless. He didn't blame her. They were in the prime of their lives. Yet the longer they waited to have children, the more complicated the matter became. Different options ran through Alexander's head. A few minor members of Andover's regal family who were descended from King Henrik's younger brothers, Prince Christian and Prince Erich, resided in Europe and America. There, Alexander knew he'd have the privacy to see a specialist. The thought entered his head from time to time, but he'd done nothing about it.

Frustrated with himself, Alexander pulled his nude body under the familiar sheets. He managed to fall asleep, but the thoughts of his physical condition continued to plague him throughout his dreams.

The crystal blue water crashed on the rocks below. In the distance, the morning sun still hung low in the sky. On the jagged cliff, Count Matthew Hall sat in quiet surrender. Of all the places in Andover, this was one he'd never seen. It was beautiful. Matthew's feet dangled from the cliff with boundless optimism. His trip to Andover had been the best time he'd ever spent in the kingdom. In all of the years he'd spent living in Amsterdam, he seemed to forget the many treasures to be held in his own home land. Matthew decided there and then that no matter what the outcome, he was going to purchase a home in Andover because the kingdom was in his blood.

Michael approached Matthew with fear in his stomach. The King of Andover was many things, but a coward was not one of them. Yet in this moment of intimate seclusion, he was petrified. During their three year relationship, Michael had imagined this moment in its splendor. As Michael glanced ahead of him, he caught Matthew lost in his own thoughts. Suddenly, Michael felt as if he could accomplish anything. For a moment he paused to take in his surrounding.

Unlike the other three regal residences, their summer home, Port Agnes House, was closed to the world. The regal family relished the summers spent at their summer home. Even though Port Agnes House was officially opened from June until September, the regal family used it whenever it struck their fancy. Today, no one was allowed at the old seaside castle.

"Michael," Matthew called. "A pod of dolphins just broke the surface. I can see why your family keeps this part of Andover to themselves."

"Matt," interjected Michael, "I have something I want to discuss with you."

"Yes?" Matthew turned to Michael. He realized in this moment that he loved him more than he could ever express. "What is it, Your Majesty?"

Michael cleared his throat. "You and I have been through a lot. Don't you agree?"

"Yes…"

"Matthew, I…I loved Katherine. You know that. When she died nine years ago, I didn't think I would ever recover. But I did. Then you walked into my life. You showed me that life could be as wonderful as it had been years ago. During the past three years, you've shown me how to laugh again. You've taught me how to be a better person… I can't thank you enough, Matt…"

Tears came to Matthew's eyes. He ran his hand down Michael's face. Out of impulse, Matthew planted a kiss on the King's mouth. "You know how much I love you."

Trembling, Michael pulled a small black box from his trouser pocket. Opening it, Matthew's eyes filled with tears at the sight of the platinum band. "Count Matthew Hall, will you marry me?"

As Matthew wiped the tears from his face, a flood of emotions invaded his body. In that moment, he gave His Majestic Regal Highness The King of Andover an answer.

5

In the two weeks since the King of Andover proposed to Count Matthew Hall, the Summer Season had arrived in Andover. The season was strategically placed on June seventh before the official start of the summer. Needless to say, the start of the season was the most important event in the regal calendar. With the start of the season came polo tournaments, symphonies in the park, fireworks at Kemp Castle, the opening of the regal residences to the public, and the official opening of Port Agnes House. The household staff at Andover Palace worked overtime to facilitate the logistical nightmare that occurred when the family moved from the palace to the castle: the staff needed to be housed on the other side of the kingdom; favorite desks, chairs, and the like had to appear without delay for the regal family.

Her Regal Highness The Dowager Queen dabbed her bespoke perfume behind her ears before answering the ringing telephone. Normally, she would never perform such a menial task, but since this was her personal line, she made an exception. "Yes?"

"Mother, may I have a moment?" The King asked hurriedly.

"Why, yes." Placing the phone down, Cassandra began to replay the events of the past two weeks. Ever since Michael took Count Matthew to Port Agnes House before he was due to leave for the Netherlands, he hadn't been himself. The Michael she knew could be dry and witty with the staff; the man who was king was now delightfully happy. Cassandra had her suspicions. Had Michael actually proposed to the count without consulting her? Did he consult the Minister of Government Patricia Ali?

"Mother," Michael said as he came into her sitting room. "You look lovely."

Today was the first day of Andover's Summer Season, which always started with a ceremonial polo tournament. Dressed in her regal regalia, Cassandra was a vision in diamonds. Her crown lay on a satin pillow at the foot of her bed. "As do you, son. I was telling one of the maids this morning…you know how I sometimes speak with them to gauge the mood of the people…and she told me that there are rumors spreading about your relationship with Count Matthew."

"Is that so?" Michael folded his arms in defiance. He knew how crafty his mother could be when she wanted privileged information. "And what did she say?"

"Well," she replied blithely, "she thought that there could be a regal wedding in the works."

Michael studied his cuticles. "And what did you tell her?"

"Me? I told her that *I* hadn't been made aware of any such plans! Can you imagine a regal wedding without my knowledge?!" She laughed heartily. "How absurd!"

"Oh, Mother, you can stop the theatrics," Michael said bluntly. "You know very well how I feel about Matthew."

Cassandra straightened her posture. "Be that as it may, if you are planning to propose, it would be nice to know before I hear it through the kingdom's gossip mill."

"I did propose to Matthew," Michael admitted. He suddenly felt as if his biggest secret from the last fortnight had been whisked away.

"What did he say," she asked.

Michael grinned. "Yes."

Cassandra gave her son a pert smile. Betrayal and deceit were the two words that instantly came to mind. How could Michael do this to me, she thought angrily. "Son, it would have been polite for you to tell me of your intentions before performing such a callous action!"

"Callous? I love him. And furthermore, I don't need to run every decision past you. I'm the monarch of this kingdom. You are not." The bluntness of this statement stunned Michael. He'd never spoken to his mother in that manner, but after so many years of kowtowing to her whims and demands, it felt good.

Cassandra, on the other hand, refused to be silenced. "After everything I've done for you, this is how you repay me? Michael, this is bigger than you! This will affect the entire kingdom! Not just domestically, but internationally as well! The ramifications…we may never survive this. Think about the headlines! 'Andover's King Marries a Man!' Can you imagine?!"

"Actually I can," he retorted wistfully.

"I'm serious, Michael. You know full well that all engagements must be run past the monarch…" Cassandra stopped herself. She caught her breath. This wasn't thirty years ago, she had to tell herself. She was no longer Andover's monarch. These days she was just Her Regal Highness The Dowager Queen, mother of His Majesty The King. That was all. Cassandra knew that Michael was within his right to propose to Matthew as he did. That fact alone made her realize that she longer possessed any true power. "I'm sorry," she said after moments of quiet reflection. "You'll have to excuse me. I feel… Dear, could you get me a glass of water?"

Michael quickly returned with the water. "Are you angry?"

The Dowager Queen shook her head. The cool water helped clear her mind. "I'm surprised. Granted, I had a feeling that this could happen. Why didn't you tell me?"

"You can't keep a secret."

Cassandra was surprised by his candor. "When you get to be my age, a bit of gossip keeps you young. Of course," she added, "when I was the Queen of Andover, I couldn't gossip. I didn't miss it. But when I abdicated, I found it to be a wonderful way to connect with the people. They all seem to get a thrill out of it. Have you told Patricia Ali?"

"Not yet. I'll tell her this afternoon at the polo tournament."

"Yes…that's a good plan… Less of a chance she'll make a scene." Cassandra sighed as she moved towards her bed. "When is the wedding?"

Michael bit his bottom lip. "Within the year; it will give the palace enough time to plan the perfect wedding."

"And Matthew? Is he moving back to Andover or will he stay in the Netherlands?"

"Once the official announcement is made," Michael began, "Matthew will return to Andover. He will stay with his parents, Count and Countess Hall, at their estate in Kemp Forest. After the wedding, he will move into the palace."

Cassandra absorbed this rush of information. "You seem to have it all planned, Michael. Just remember that there are people who still hold Princess Katherine in high regard. We must consider that. Have you?"

"I will inform Katherine's sister, Mary."

"Good. And the rest of the family?" Cassandra placed a large canary yellow diamond onto her small finger. "What shall we do about them?"

"Mother, I can handle everything. Do I have your confidence?"

"Yes," Cassandra smiled. "After all, if you can't trust your mother, who can you trust?"

Oblivious to the frenzy around the corridor from her, Princess Helena prepared for the polo tournament. Of all the events on the regal calendar, this was by far her favorite. Horses had never been her favorite animal, but the athletically inclined polo boys made her heart flutter. Over the past few weeks, the princess had successfully lost sixteen pounds through a diet of water, lettuce, and sheer willpower. Her father's comments about her weight combined with her new moniker, "Princess Porky", had finally pushed Helena to her breaking point.

The young princess admired her new body in the privacy of her dressing room. Beyond the doors, her personal secretary, Bertie, chatted with Helena's dressmaker, Mrs. John Langdon. Mrs. Langdon was Princess Katherine's dressmaker, but when she died, Helena assumed her role as Mrs. Langdon's regal patron. Needless to say, their relationship was stormy at best. This was the reason Bertie sat in on Helena's fittings; Helena hated Mrs. Langdon. While she never said anything to the contrary, Helena always suspected that Mrs. Langdon resented the fact that Helena was not built like her mother. But now, after nine years of Mrs. Langdon's disapproving stares, Helena was going to show that uptight social climbing wannabe. Princess Helena took a triumphant breath as she stepped into her dusty pink bedroom suite. Bertie clasped her hands together in delight, while Mrs. Langdon came over to inspect the dress. "You look beautiful, Your Regal Highness," cooed Bertie.

"Yes…Your Regal Highness, if I may say so, this dress fits you perfectly." Mrs. Langdon took a step back to admire her work. "I'm speechless, Ma'am."

Helena simply smiled at her nemesis. Her weeks of starving had finally paid off. There she stood in her pale canary yellow dress without a care in the world. After all of these years, she'd finally won. A knock at the door pulled Helena back to earth. It was a junior valet from the Precious Stones regiment of the palace with her tiara. She sat in her high back chair as the junior valet gently placed the diamond tiara on her coiffed head. Perfect, she thought to herself.

"Your Regal Highness," Bertie said as she glanced at her watch, "your car is here."

Princess Helena caught one last look at her new self. She hadn't felt this calm or self assured in years. Although the methods of her weight loss could be deemed risky by some, she didn't care. Helena lifted her chin, took a deep breath and prepared to introduce her new self to Andover society.

Princess Sophia stared out of the window of the limousine. Over the past two weeks, she tried to devise a plan, but alas, nothing she thought of seemed appropriate for the situation. In her mind, she knew that Robert wasn't sleeping with Margaret. However, her heart begged to tell a different story. Torn between the conflict raging within her, Sophia had retreated to Port Agnes House one week ago. The rest of the family would decamp to the ancient castle today, much to her chagrin. Princess Sophia glanced at her watch once more. In ten minutes, they would be at The Hunting Lodge. Sophia would have preferred to stay in bed, but she had to attend the first day of the Summer Season out of duty.

By the time the driver turned from Route 3 onto the isolated country lane where The Hunting Lodge stood, she noticed something odd. A regal car sped away with deft precision. The princess had a hunch as to who it could be, because there was only one person in the world who hated her that much. Margaret was three years older than Sophia, but their relationship had always been difficult. As teenagers, they fought over boys, which later turned into men. Margaret managed to sleep with the first man Sophia ever loved. For two years after that betrayal, Sophia never spoke to Margaret in private. Their rivalry lasted all of these years because Sophia suspected that Margaret was simply jealous of her for no apparent reason. Yes, Sophia was a Princess of Andover, the sister of His Majesty The King and the daughter of the Dowager Queen. By Sophia's estimation, Margaret was nothing more than a cousin of the regal family. Margaret was simply a Lady of Andover, as well as an additional expense on the Regal Expenditure. The world could do without Lady Margaret, Sophia surmised, but she was a necessary cog in the regal machine.

Sophia's bodyguard opened the door of The Hunting Lodge. Looking around, Sophia heard Robert rustling through the kitchen cupboards. She stepped through the rustic living space into the tiny kitchen. This was Sophia's least favorite place in the kingdom, but her husband loved it, which is why she merely tolerated the time she spent there. "Robert," she called.

Prince Robert came from the utility room with freshly chopped firewood. "Sophia. Hi," he said. Placing the firewood in a nearby basket, he kissed his wife. "What are you doing here?"

“We’re expected at the Prince Christian Polo Club in two hours.” She studied Robert for a moment. “Go shower.”

Robert shook his head as he began preparing a pot of tea. “I’m not up for the season this year. Please send my regards…”

“I will not,” sounded Sophia. She could feel her temper beginning to escape her. “Go get dressed. If you need a morning suit, I have a spare one in the car. We can stop at Blake Manor so you can change.”

“Blake Manor,” Robert queried. “Why would we go there?”

“It’s on the way,” snapped Sophia. “Besides, you cannot change in public. What will people say?”

“I don’t know, but I’m sure you’ll tell me.” Robert brushed past his wife on his way to the living room. He began to strip out of his dirty clothes.

Sophia couldn’t believe the way her husband was behaving. Over the past twenty-one years, she’d done everything for him. She was the reason he was given the title of a prince instead that of a lord, as was regal tradition for the spouses of a princes and princesses. There were times he acted like a petulant child, which never sat well with the princess. Watching her husband change, Sophia said, “There is no reason to take that tone with me. I’m only keeping with regal tradition and protocol. You are my husband. You are expected to attend regal events. If I turn up alone to the most important event of the season, what will I say?”

“You’ll think of something,” Robert muttered.

Sophia ignored him. “What will the King say? Can you imagine the questions from my mother? Andover society will assume things are rocky between us.” She walked to her husband, gently touching his muscular shoulder. “I love you.”

His eyes met hers. No matter how many times he slept with Lady Margaret, the allure of Sophia always remained in the forefront of his mind. “I love you, too."

"Why don't you shower? You can dress here…"

Robert nodded as he stepped into the small bathroom. His mind was racing. It was a very fortunate thing that he and Lady Margaret had not slept together today. But they had slept together yesterday and twice last week. Even though Edward was back in the kingdom, Margaret seemed to need her lover more than ever. It wasn't that Robert minded, but with Sophia off at Port Agnes House, he knew something was amiss. When they were first married, Sophia suffered two miscarriages in rapid succession. Each time she was ordered to recover by her doctor, she went to Port Agnes House. She once told him that it was the one place in the world where she could think without the responsibility of her regal duties. Prince Robert had always admired her strength, but whenever she went to Port Agnes House for more than a night, he knew it could not bode well for him.

As Robert cleaned his body, he began to think that maybe Michael had tipped off his sister about his suspicions regarding Margaret. Robert quickly banished the thought from his mind. Michael may have always been weary of Robert, but Robert knew Michael would never upset his sister. Could it be that Margaret said something in passing? The feud between the princess and the lady was legendary. But Robert deduced that Lady Margaret wouldn't risk losing everything just to spite Sophia.

He wrapped a towel around his waist as he stepped into the living room. His morning suit was hung on the back of the front door. Sophia was in the kitchen pacing. Robert dressed quickly. "Honey, could you tie this for me?"

Sophia came towards her husband with a small smile. Placing the tie around his neck, she proceeded to tie it. "Who was that I saw leaving?"

Robert shrugged. "It was Margaret."

"Oh? What did that shrew want?"

"She and Edward are going through some stuff. She just wanted to talk."

Sophia examined the finished tie. "She should talk to her brother. If people were to see you with her in such a secluded location, they might get the wrong idea." Stepping back to take one final look at her husband she added, "Don't you agree?"

"Yes."

"I think I'll have a word with her," Sophia murmured.

Robert grabbed his jacket and followed her outside. "Sophia, I don't think that's necessary."

"I know you don't. But I do." With that, Sophia climbed into the back of the car.

Robert sat beside her and took her hand. Sophia gently squeezed his hand. In that moment, Robert realized that his wife knew much more than she let on.

Since its founding ninety years ago, the Prince Christian Polo Club was the heart of Andover's social world. It was named after the second son of His Majestic Regal Highness King Christoph, Prince Christian, who held Andover's first polo game on the site where the present club stood. From that day forward, the game of polo had been a fixture in the kingdom. The next year, King Henrik (the new monarch and King Christoph's eldest son), proclaimed that a polo tournament at the club with the attendance of the regal family would commence Andover's Summer Season. Today, there were five polo clubs throughout the kingdom, but this was the only club that mattered.

The crowds always started to form at half past six in the morning for the start of the season. Everyone from Andover's aristocracy to the politicians to the invited guests and the few lucky members of the wider public, dressed in their best morning suits and dresses for this event. Many hoped to catch a glimpse of the regal family in their private enclosure, while a select few would venture into the rarefied box.

The first to arrive was the Dowager Queen Cassandra with her granddaughter, Princess Helena and her nephew, Lord Walter. They greeted the press, waved to the crowd, and ventured into the regal enclosure, which was safely guarded by Andover's Secret Police. Next to arrive was Lady Margaret, His Highness Edward and their son, His Regal Highness Samuel. Princess Sophia and Prince Robert arrived at the same time as the Prince and Princess of Kemp. The King of Andover arrived alone, to the elation of those gathered by the entrance of the polo grounds. Watching the people from behind the bullet proof glass of his double wide limousine, Michael felt a sense of happiness because in just two days he would announce the news of his engagement to the entire world.

The polo players began to lead their horses to the field. Leading the way was His Regal Highness The Prince Joseph. From the age of ten, Joseph had been the most avid polo player in the regal family. When he decided to form his own team at the age of eighteen, his father donated the horses and the staff. Joseph's team was known as The Kings. Joseph knew that being the most visible member of the regal family in the eyes of the public would always benefit him in the long run. Joseph and his team mounted their horses, and with the shot of a gun, the game commenced.

Halfway through the first game, Lady Margaret retired to the cool anteroom of the regal enclosure. While she admired Joseph's athletic ability, she wanted nothing more than to leave at once. Yet regal tradition stated that each member of the family had to stay for the entire tournament. And with Joseph's team playing, Margaret knew that this would be a long day. "Would you like some company," Cassandra asked as she sat on a chair near the door, with a fan in her hand. An attentive valet fetched her personal drink: two-thirds gin, one-third orange juice, a splash of vermouth, and one ice cube. "What a day. I just love the start of the season! Your mother - my sister - always said that the start of the season was just like the beginning of life: New, but with the promise of a thousand better tomorrows." The Dowager Queen gently sipped her drink as she eyed Margaret. "My dear, are you all right?"

"I'm a bit tired, Aunt Cassandra. The new puppy kept me up most of the night." With the birth of Maisie's three puppies a few weeks ago, Cassandra gave one to Samuel. Luckily for Margaret, the puppy, Austin, was nothing but a nuisance.

"Dogs do that, Maggie. Have the night maid look after it. Would you like a drink?"

Margaret continually marveled at how Cassandra could drink all day long. The most shocking thing was, Cassandra never got drunk. Maybe she was immune to the effects of alcohol, Margaret thought, wistfully. "Sure."

Cassandra silently motioned for the valet to fetch another drink. "Well then, it must be nice to have your family together again."

"It is. We're thinking about taking a trip to New York in the fall…"

"Oh," interrupted Cassandra, "you could do a regal tour of the United States! A goodwill tour! You haven't done one of those in years. Don't you remember when Michael and Katherine and Sophia and Robert did theirs? Oh, Margaret, let's run it by the King. I'm sure he'll take to the idea."

"Aunt Cassandra," Margaret said firmly. "That's a nice idea; however, I thought it would be nice for Samuel to meet Mark and Vincent."

Cassandra paused for a moment. In her years as the Queen of Andover, she thought about her extended family and even attended their weddings and funerals. If she couldn't, she would dispatch Michael, Fiona, or Sophia to make a regal appearance. These days, her mind rarely thought of her uncles, Prince Christian and Prince Erich, or their families. Her own family was enough to keep her busy for two lifetimes! But as Cassandra began to recall the rich family tree from which she was descended, she thought of His Regal Highness Vincent, the grandson of her cousin, Her Regal Highness Lady Sharon of Andover, daughter of Prince Christian. Vincent was a second year student at Yale University and his father, Sharon's widow, Mark, His Highness of Andover, resided in New York City. Cassandra couldn't recall why Vincent had never been to the kingdom, but he did receive a small annuity of one hundred thousand Andover dollars from the Regal Expenditure. After all, he was eighth in line for the throne.

"Well, you may see them sooner than you think," Cassandra finally murmured as she finished her drink.

"What do you mean?"

"Well, Michael and…" Cassandra stopped herself. If she told Margaret about Michael's impending announcement, he would most certainly banish her to Port Agnes House for the rest of her life. "Excuse me," she cooed to a waiting butler. "Tell me, what is the score?"

"The Kings are leading six to three at the end of this chukka, Your Regal Highness," replied the butler.

"Very well." Cassandra turned to Margaret. "I'm off."

Indeed you are, Margaret laughed to herself.

"Edward," Sophia called as she approached him. "May I have a moment of your time?"

"Sure." Edward took Sophia by the arm as they walked to a secluded part of the regal enclosure. They had been friends since they were teenagers. The bond between them was unbreakable. Even when Michael disapproved of Edward's marriage to Margaret and Sophia saw that Edward was too good for that woman, their friendship endured. "What's on your mind, princess?"

"Why did you go to Africa?"

"It was a personal matter, Your Regal Highness. I needed to get away. You know I'm an archaeologist at heart."

"You're a regular Howard Carter," she replied wryly. "Could you please give me an honest answer?"

Edward looked around to ensure no one was listening to their conversation. "It's a personal matter concerning myself and Margaret. However, it's been resolved."

Sophia studied Edward's eyes. "Is it?"

"Yes."

"Are you lying to me?"

"No," he stated. "Why would I?"

She bit the inside of her cheek while she debated whether or not to tell him what she'd suspected for weeks. "Does your wife's relationship with my husband concern you?"

"What?" Edward couldn't believe how preposterous this statement sounded. "That's ridiculous, Sophia. Prince Robert is crazy about you."

"I know *that*. Listen, the night of the Andover Securities and Equities Exchange centenary party…"

"Margaret and I were having dinner at Cabo," interjected Edward.

"I was speaking with Michael," Sophia continued, "when Robert's phone rang. It was your wife."

Edward simply chuckled. "So? Sophia's we've known each other for most of our lives. I know how you feel about my wife. What's all of this? I thought Robert was the love of your life."

"He is," she snapped. "But why was she calling him?"

"I don't know. Maybe she wanted something…"

"Obviously," Sophia retorted. "Do you think I'm being paranoid?"

"A bit." Edward shook his head. "Don't let this drive you crazy."

Sophia walked to the edge of the enclosure as a polo player rode by. She gave him a regal wave before saying, "But I saw her leaving The Hunting Lodge this morning."

Edward couldn't believe what he was hearing. He knew he couldn't take

Sophia's word because she never liked Margaret. Everyone in the regal family knew that. But this was a different story… With Margaret's past, it was all too likely that she was straying right under his nose. "What does that prove," he asked.

"Edward, where did she say she was going this morning?"

Edward shifted uncomfortably.

"Edward?"

"To pick up something she'd left at Blake Manor." Edward stuffed his hands in his pocket, kicking the dirt beneath his feet.

Sophia shook her head in fury. "How convenient! The woman has the entire regal household at her disposal and you fall for that?!"

"You don't have any proof, Sophia. This is pure conjecture and you know it."

"No. What I know is that Margaret has had it in for me for as long as I can remember. Don't you remember what happened with Victor Kerby? He was my boyfriend and she threw herself at him! The only reason she stayed away from Robert was because we had a very public courtship…"

"Stop," Edward said.

"And," Sophia continued, "two weeks before her engagement to Count Thomas Hale was to be announced by Princess Fiona, she met you and dumped him!"

"That's enough," he growled. "Are you done sullying my wife's name?"

"She did that herself," sniffed Sophia. "Edward, I don't want to upset you, but this is what Margaret does. She wants what she can't have. If she and Robert are sleeping together we have a problem."

"What do you want me to do, Sophia?"

Princess Sophia took a deep breath. "Keep your wife away from my husband and I'll do the same."

Edward nodded slowly because he knew all too well that Sophia's suspicions were well founded.

When the whistle sounded for the twenty minute half time, Joseph and his team joined the regal family in their enclosure. Prince Joseph took the time to introduce his team members to his family, but one family in particular took a special interest in number four. Princess Helena first noticed him on his horse, and he looked like a white knight. During the first half of the game, she couldn't keep her eyes off him. She'd already received compliments on her new shape, which gave her the confidence to ask her brother for a regal favor. "Joseph, may I have a moment?" she asked.

"What is it?"

"Who's number four?"

"Derek Sharpe."

"Introduce me…"

Prince Joseph groaned. He could vaguely recall when his sister fell for a polo player a few years ago who ended up running off with a much thinner woman. It was then, Joseph guessed, that Helena really put on weight. Would history repeat itself, he wondered.

"Please," she begged.

Joseph signaled for Derek to join them. To Helena, he was even more handsome up close. He was six foot five with a slightly stocky build, gray eyes, and a head of short black hair. Perfection, she thought. "Derek Sharpe, this is my sister, Her Regal Highness The Princess Helena of Andover."

Derek bowed. "It's a pleasure, Your Regal Highness."

"Yes…it is. You play well," she smiled.

"Thank you," he replied.

Just then, Bertie interrupted the group. "Your Regal Highnesses," she said with a curtsy

Helena rolled her eyes. “What is it, Bertie? We’re in the middle of something.”

“The press need Prince Joseph and Mr. Sharpe.” Bertie quickly left, followed by Joseph and Derek.

As Helena watched them go, she decided then and there to learn everything she could about that dashing young man.

“Glenn!” The King called.

“Yes, Your Majesty?”

King Michael sat behind his large maple desk in his office at Port Agnes House. The sun seeped into the large airy room as the sound of Samuel’s laughter drifted through the open window. Michael always felt more relaxed at Port Agnes House, although his monarchical duties never ended. As the sole unifying and guiding force of the kingdom, it was his responsibility to ensure that life continued as normal, regardless of the political, fiscal, or international issues that could turn the world on its head at a moments notice. “What time is the art dealer arriving?”

Glenn consulted his oversized notebook. “After lunch, Sire.”

“Good. Have you coordinated the details of the Prince of Kemp’s birthday with Kemp Castle? Do they have the itinerary I wrote this morning?”

“Yes, Sire.”

Michael nodded. With Alexander’s birthday five days away, Michael had to ensure that his son was kept busy and happy. Michael was due to make his big speech from the Throne Room at Port Agnes House. Tonight, the whole world would know that Michael intended to wed Count Matthew Hall. “Very good. When will the news crews arrive?”

“Seven o’clock for a live broadcast on every channel in the kingdom at half past seven."

"Grandmother," Princess Helena called as she walked down the beach. She was dressed in a flowing Diane von Fürstenberg wrap dress with a pair of strappy sandals in her left hand. In her right hand, she carried a large book with a slightly worn red cloth cover.

"Yes, dear… What is it?' Cassandra was still recovering from yesterday's opening of the Summer Season. Like always, it was a smash hit. The regal family received favorable press in every newspaper. To top it off, Joseph's team won the tournament for the second year in a row. Nothing could stop the regal family now, Cassandra thought blissfully.

Helena sat on a wooden beach chair next to her grandmother. In the distance, Samuel played with Edward and the new puppy; Margaret lay on the sand, her face covered by an oversized straw hat. In the sea, Robert kayaked with Joseph. Taking in the sight, Helena said, "Isn't life wonderful?"

"That's my credo! My, you've been in an unusually cheerful mood since yesterday, Helena." Cassandra's eyes lit up. "Why! You've fallen in love, haven't you?"

She couldn't stop herself from blushing. After the polo tournament, Helena managed to have her picture taken with Derek and Joseph. The picture appeared in *The Pass Observer* with a complimentary blurb. Helena was truly on top of the world. "I wouldn't call it love, but I am infatuated."

"Oh, I remember that feeling. Now, when I met your grandfather – may he rest in peace – my mother and father arranged the union. Mind you, I'd known James for some time, but in those days, it was considered proper for a young woman's parents to chose and approve of her future husband. I've always said that the vetting process is quite important. My father thought the same thing, as did your grandfather, and my sister," rattled Cassandra. "It's a pity they're all dead," she concluded with marked irony.

"I've never felt like this before," admitted Helena. "Well, once. But… well…"

"He left you," finished Cassandra.

Helena gave her grandmother a tight smile. "I need your help."

"Oh, I do hope it's not a scheme. If you need someone to scheme with you, recruit Margaret. She's excellent at those things. I always told Fiona that if Margaret had been born into a common family, she would have made a great politician." Cassandra gently sipped her special drink. The gin certainly hit the spot.

"It's not a scheme. Since I am a princess, I realize that I simply can't fall for anyone and marry them. I'm very aware of my responsibilities."

Cassandra nodded in agreement. "You are second in line for the throne."

"Which is why," Helena began, hoisting the book onto her lap, "I need your help. The gentleman I met yesterday is Derek Sharpe."

Cassandra frowned. She picked through the newspapers at her side. After a moment she came to the picture of Prince Joseph and Princess Helena with Derek Sharpe. He was cute, Cassandra thought, but he looked quite common. Cassandra knew she had to keep her opinions to herself – for now – because Helena was very sensitive when it came to the opposite sex. "Oh, yes. I remember him…vaguely."

Helena handed the large book to her grandmother. "Can you find him in this thing? I always get lost within the boring details."

"Helena! This book contains the most prominent families in Andover! The entire history of Andover's regal family and proper society can be traced in *The Andover Peer Review.* It's far from boring; to the contrary! It's truly essential," the former queen exclaimed.

With purpose, the Dowager Queen began to turn the pages of the one hundred and eighth edition of *The Andover Peer Review.* Everyone who was anyone was included in this book. Each regal line was traced, including the families who married into the regal family. Whether she was at Andover Palace, Port Agnes House, or Blake Manor, Cassandra instructed the staff that a copy of this important book was to be in her private suite. As she thumbed through the S's, Cassandra's face fell. There in glorious black and white was Derek's name with a very strong caveat: While his maternal grandfather was Count Daniel Roland, 1st Peer and his maternal grandmother was Danisi Anne Roland. Anne's title was a mid-ranking life title, but it was better than nothing. However, things got interesting when their daughter, Derek's mother, Blythe, refused to accept an aristocratic title. Blythe, Cassandra seemed to recall, was what some would call a feminist. While Cassandra didn't truly understand feminism, she refused to judge women who followed the movement. However, when it came to Blythe's marriage, as stated in *The Andover Peer Review*, she married a local carpenter named Jay Sharpe. Although Derek didn't have an aristocratic title, this didn't mean he couldn't assume one with the death of Blythe's father.

"Well," Helena asked impatiently.

Cassandra closed the book. "Darling, you've only just met him. Take it slow."

"What did it say? Grandmother, don't tease me…"

"His maternal grandfather is a count, but his father is a carpenter. How Joseph met him is beyond me…but he could inherit his grandfather's title upon his death. Helena, let's not worry ourselves with this, all right?"

Helena knew her grandmother very well. Maybe this wasn't a good idea after all, she surmised. "Whatever you say," answered Helena. With that, Helena decided that she would focus on having fun this summer, but thoughts of Derek Sharpe were not far away.

His Regal Highness Lord Walter sat in the back of the West Andover Country Club with his gaze fixed towards the entrance. In the weeks since he'd met Daisy Herman, he'd become smitten with her. Walter reasoned that since she wasn't caught up in the world of the aristocratic climb into the regal family, Daisy was what some would call common. While they couldn't date as of yet, they had spent a lot of time together at official occasions. Daisy managed to "appear" at more than a dozen functions where Walter represented the regal family. At these functions, everything remained official, but it was clear to Walter that their relationship was developing into something much more meaningful. It had been years since Walter had felt this way about a woman. It was, he reasoned wistfully, about time.

The country club manager led Daisy to his table in the private section of the dining room. Alone, they could talk in a manner that no one would approve of within the regal household. While the regal family wiled away the summer at Port Agnes House, Walter decided to stay on at Blake Manor. The fewer run-ins he had with his family, the better. Daisy was dressed in a chic Vivienne Westwood ensemble with a pair of black Jimmy Choo's to match. Although she was far from wealthy, Daisy knew how to make the most of her limited resources.

Walter rose when Daisy reached the table. She curtseyed as she said, "Your Regal Highness."

"Daisy," he replied, sitting in his chair. "How do you do?"

"Very well. Thank you. The flowers you sent to my apartment were beautiful," she smiled. "You're too kind."

Walter gave her a shy smile. "It's a small token of my affection."

"I can tell." Daisy pushed her hair behind her ears. "I read in the newspaper that the regal family is at Port Agnes House for the summer. Are you staying there, too?"

"Not exactly. I'll spend the majority of the summer at Blake Manor, but a few days at Port Agnes." Walter lightly touched her hand. "But I don't want to talk about that. Tell me about yourself."

Daisy shrugged. "What's there to tell? My life isn't nearly as interesting as yours."

"Come on," plied Walter, "tell me. I want to know."

She sighed. "I don't know… My parents were originally from America. They came to Andover because my father got a job for Locke, Nicholas & Co. Three years later, I was born. I grew up in Lord's Pass, but in a three bedroom apartment… I graduated from the University of Andover and here I am. Very unremarkable," Daisy replied.

This is why Walter enjoyed spending so much time with Daisy. She was refreshing. The women of his world were too uptight to enjoy life. With Daisy, she was unaware of the nonsense that surrounded her to care about what people thought about her. Just then, a foreign thought came into his head.

"Daisy…"

"Yes, Sir?"

"Have you ever been to Blake Manor," he asked.

"Once when it was open in the summer my mother and I walked around the gardens. It was lovely."

"Well, I live there. Would you like to come over for dinner in a few days?" His eyes twinkled. "We can talk without the rest of the kingdom gawking at us. How does that sound?"

All Daisy could do was smile.

Two hours before Michael gave his press conference, he called his entire family to Port Agnes House for a very important meeting. The Prince and Princess of Kemp came from the north of the kingdom, while Lord Walter came directly from the country club. Gathered in Michael's private sitting room, the regal family talked amongst themselves before he joined them. The mood within the room was that of the calm before a life altering storm. No one knew what Michael wanted to tell them, although Margaret suspected that an engagement announcement was inevitable.

Ten minutes later, Andover's monarch made his way into the airy sitting room. Without delay, he sat behind his desk and said, "As you all know, I am giving a press conference from Port Agnes House tonight. The reason for this press conference concerns the future of the monarchy…"

"Are you abdicating," interjected Prince Alexander.

Everyone threw a look of disbelief Alexander's way.

"Why do you always go there," asked Prince Joseph.

"I'm not the only one who thought that! Don't you all remember what happened before Grandmother abdicated? She called us into her office at the palace to break the news," retorted Alexander. "Is that what this is about?"

King Michael shook his head. Alexander's response was far from surprising to the King because he knew that his son coveted his position. "I will never abdicate," Michael said firmly. "The reason I've called this meeting… Two weeks ago, I proposed to Count Matthew Hall. He's accepted my proposal of marriage."

Sophia gave her brother a tight hug. "I'm so happy for you. I truly am."

"That's great, Mike. Congratulations," added Walter.

"You're what?" Alexander couldn't believe what he was hearing. The kingdom accepted the fact that Michael was dating Matthew. But how would they react to the news of that the King of Andover wanted to marry a man? How could he, thought Alexander. "Dad, have you thought about this? I mean, really thought about it."

Olivia grabbed her husband by the arm. "Let it go," she whispered in his ear.

"Alexander, if you have something to say to me, we can discuss it later. Now isn't the time," Michael stated.

"When's the wedding," asked Prince Robert.

"Those details will be worked out by the palace," Cassandra stated officially. "We never concern ourselves with such triviality!"

Margaret gave Michael a light hug. "I'm sure it'll be the wedding of the year. Edward, your parents are arriving soon."

"They wanted to see Samuel and this was the only time in their schedule for the next two months. If you'll excuse us," Edward smiled.

Margaret and Edward left, as Sophia watched her husband look forlornly after her cousin. Disgusted, Sophia turned to Michael. "If you need any of my help, I'd be more than happy to contribute. As is Robert," she added.

Robert blinked. "Of course."

"Dad, can we please talk," begged Alexander.

Michael excused the rest of the family, leaving him alone with his eldest child. The relationship between the monarch and his heir had been particularly strained in the years since Michael ascended the throne. While Michael knew that Alexander wanted to be Andover's monarch more than anything else, he still wanted a relationship with his son. However, in Michael's eyes, it seemed as if that was the last thing Alexander wanted from his father. Now, the news of Michael's impending marriage to Count Matthew Hall seemed likely to ruin the final remnants of their fragile relationship.

"Your outburst was uncalled for," Michael stated calmly. "I'm ashamed of you, Alexander."

"Me? You're the one who's about to make a fool of himself! The King of Andover cannot marry a man. The scandal alone will ruin the kingdom!"

Michael clenched his hands. "I am the monarch. I have earned the respect of everyone in this kingdom. Whether or not you agree with my personal choices is irrelevant. I have given my life to country and crown, and I intend on finally giving myself the same right to happiness as everyone else."

"That's crap, Dad." Alexander paced the spacious office with fury in his heart. For all of his life, he'd looked up to his father, but lately, he felt more distant from him than ever before. To Alexander, the problem was Count Matthew. If that man had simply stayed away from his father, none of this would have happened. He and Michael would still be as close as they once were. "Have you considered the repercussions? I mean, have you?"

"I'm the monarch, son. I don't need permission to marry the man I love."

Alexander threw his head back in frustration. "But when I wanted to marry Olivia, I had to get your permission, Grandmother's blessing and Patricia Ali's approval. And she had to be vetted by the regal household to ensure she was of the right sort. Let's not forget the dossier! Do you know how humiliating that was?"

"It's protocol. Matthew's of the right sort. Your grandmother and Patricia Ali are aware of my decision; I have their support. Alex," Michael said in a calm voice, "why is this suddenly an issue? You knew this would happen sooner or later…"

"Is that why you signed the Marriage Equality Act," snapped Alexander. He had his suspicions about Michael signing that act, because it was the first bill Michael signed into law as Andover's monarch.

Michael couldn't believe what his son was insinuating. "No," he answered. His voice grew steely as he said, "And if you ever mention that to anyone, you will regret it."

"Why do you have to marry this man? You barely know him!"

"I've known Matthew my entire life. There are a lot of things you know nothing about, Alex," sighed Michael. "It's best you leave this issue alone. It's not up for discussion."

Alexander started for the door with anger in his soul. "Did you ever love my mother," asked Alexander, hotly.

"I always did; I always will."

"Then how can you marry this man? Dad, I'm not being flip, I'm being serious."

The King of Andover stared at his son for a long second. His children had no idea how or why he married Princess Katherine all those years ago. While he grew to love Katherine, they were both aware of the truth behind their union: Michael needed to produce heirs to the throne. However, in spite of the circumstances behind their marriage, they did love each other. Michael and Katherine never cheated on each other. When Katherine died unexpectedly nine years ago, Michael was torn to pieces. It wasn't until three years ago when Matthew re-entered his life that Michael allowed himself to think that he could fall in love again. As Michael quickly recalled the last thirty years in thirty seconds, he caught Alexander staring at him. "Son, I love Matthew. I loved your mother. She knew that."

"Still, this is by far the stupidest thing you've done as monarch. You should know that."

Michael had heard enough. "Now you listen to me, you petulant boy! I am your father and the King of Andover. You will show me respect. If you don't I will strip you of your title as heir to the throne and give it to Helena."

Prince Alexander couldn't believe his ears. "You wouldn't do that," he said, calling his father's bluff.

"Try me," Michael countered. His eyes were as dark as coal; his words as cold as night. "You may go, Alexander."

"Yes, Your Majesty," Alexander muttered as he left the room.

Emotionally drained, Michael sank into the plush chair behind his desk. No matter what anyone said, this was going to be worth it, Michael told himself.

In that moment, not even the King of Andover could have predicated what was to transpire next.

***

"Good evening. I come to you tonight from my official office at Port Agnes House. In the eight years I have been your king, the Kingdom of Andover has grown from strength to strength. Even in times of despair, we have pulled through as a united people. After the death of my late wife, Princess Katherine, I did not think I would ever love someone in the same manner. However, I was wrong. As many of you may know, Count Matthew Hall and I have been together for the last three years.

"The Count is a source of joy in my life. Although he has resided in Amsterdam for the last three years, he has recently stayed in Andover Palace as my personal guest. Upon the consolation of the Minister of Government Patricia Ali and Her Regal Highness The Dowager Queen, I have proposed to Count Matthew Hall. Thankfully, he has accepted my proposal.

"I ask you to join me, the regal family, and Count Matthew Hall's family in the celebration of our impending union. More details will be released through Andover Palace as the wedding date draws near.

"Thank you for joining me this evening. I wish you a happy evening from my home to yours."

With that, the stage manager gave Michael the signal they were no longer live. The King took a deep breath as his handlers spirited him into his private state apartment. The news was out. In a few short months Michael's life would finally change forever. Yes…indeed it would.

6

The Prince of Kemp was in a state of shock. Today was his thirtieth birthday. The well wishes were pouring in from all corners of the kingdom, the royal houses of Europe and Asia, and even the Office of the President of the United States of America. Yet all of the birthday greetings in the world couldn't cure the prince of this feeling of ultimate betrayal. The events from several days ago still resonated through his head. Needless to say, after his private talk with the King before the press conference, his own family had given him a regal reaming for his behavior in the presence of His Majesty. The Dowager Queen deplored her grandson's behavior so much so that she only sent him a birthday card signed by her office; not her. His brother and sister had kept their distance, while Princess Sophia remained his only link to his family on his birthday.

From the window of his private bedroom suite at Kemp Castle, Alexander could see the castle staff running about, preparing for his birthday party. The entire regal family would be here tonight, but thankfully, Count Matthew Hall would be absent from tonight's event. Why couldn't the King have waited to make this announcement, Alexander continually asked himself. But that's how his father operated, Alexander sighed. He could do whatever he wanted.

The defiant prince remembered how different life had been when his mother, Princess Katherine, was alive. His father exhibited a reserved exterior and restraint was his middle name. These days, King Michael did as he pleased. Alexander even wondered whether or not his father remembered that today was his birthday. So far, he hadn't heard a word from his father or his father's office.

This is the worst birthday I've ever had, Alexander whimpered. He walked into his private office to clear his mind. My life is falling apart, he told himself.

A knock at the door startled Alexander. "Your Regal Highness," a valet said with a bow.

“Who is it?”

“Her Regal Highness The Princess Sophia.”

Alexander straightened his tie. “See her in.”

Princess Sophia sauntered into the room. She performed a small curtsy as the valet left them in silence. Sophia sat in a large leather chair across from her nephew’s desk and handed him a small box. “I wanted to give it to you before the party.”

He untied the ribbon, opened the lilac box, and pulled out a small diamond lapel pin.

“It belonged to King Henrik. He gave it to my grandmother, who gave it to my mother, and now it’s yours.”

Alexander placed the box on his desk. “Thank you, Aunt Sophia. It’s beautiful. Is…my father coming tonight?”

Sophia gave her nephew a sympathetic glance. “Yes. I don’t know what happened in his office, but whatever it was… You need to rectify this situation, Alex.”

“Me? It’s just as much his fault…”

“He’s the King of Andover,” Sophia snapped. “He’s due respect, Alex. When you’re the monarch, you’ll expect nothing less.”

Alexander crossed his arms with pure defiance. “My father seems to think he’s immune to other’s opinions.”

“Alex, you have no idea what you’re talking about.” Sophia removed her gloves with great care. Placing her hands in her lap, she closed her eyes for a moment. “There’s something you need to know about your father.”

“Yes?” Intrigued, Alexander sat in the chair near his aunt. He knew she was no gossip, unlike his grandmother, so whatever she had to say must be important. “What is it?”

"Years ago, long before you were born, your father was a lively, active young man. Our mother had been the Queen of Andover for about four years. Michael had settled into his role as the Prince of Kemp, while I reveled in my new life as a princess. But I digress. Around this time, Michael fell in love for the first time."

"With my mother," Alexander interjected.

Sophia shook her head. "No. With Matthew."

Alexander couldn't believe what he was hearing. Yes, his aunt was one of the most honest people he'd ever met, but this didn't make any sense. "What do you mean? They've only known each other for a few years."

"Your father grew up with Matthew…as well as your mother. Michael, Katherine, and Matthew were friends when they were teenagers. They were best friends," she recalled with loving nostalgia. "When your father was twenty-one, he told our mother that he wanted to marry Matthew. Now Matthew came from the right sort of aristocratic family, so it would have been the perfect union within regal circles. However, our parents, Aunt Fiona, and our grandmother, the Dowager Duchess Victoria, wouldn't hear of it. At those times, two men falling in love was only talked about in the corners of artistic cafes, not in the halls of Andover Palace.

"Needless to say, our mother vetoed Michael's plans. I don't know what really happened behind the closed doors of our mother's office, but I do know that Michael was heartbroken. For two weeks afterwards, he shut himself away in Kemp Castle. He only went to official regal events. I knew things were bad when he wouldn't receive me at the castle. When I broached the subject to our mother, she merely said that Michael was acting out. That was all. But I could see how much he was hurting.

"As time went on, he seemed to heal, but Matthew had already left the kingdom. That's why he moved to Amsterdam. For almost thirty years, he and your father stayed away from each other. The Queen, Princess Fiona, Duke James, and the Dowager Duchess decided that Katherine Pierce would be the best bride for the Prince of Kemp…"

"My mother was a sacrifice," Alexander asked.

"No," Sophia asserted. "They knew how Michael felt about Matthew. They also knew that Michael and Katherine were great friends and she was the best person to wed the Prince of Kemp. Michael agreed to their plan. My brother and Katherine were in love, Alex. I have no doubt about that. She loved your father and he loved her. Her death almost killed your father. Do you know when happens to a man when he loses the two great loves of his life? Count yourself lucky that you have Olivia."

Alexander tried to process what his aunt had just told him. Maybe his reaction was out of place. Maybe his father actually knew what he was doing. "Why are you telling me this, Aunt Sophia?"

"Your father has made a lifetime of sacrifices for this country, the crown, and this family. When Matthew re-entered Michael's life three years ago, it was a second chance at love. If you can't see that, I don't know what else to tell you," Princess Sophia sighed.

"Then what? You want me to shut up and endure this…spectacle?"

"Yes. That's part of the duty of being a member of the regal family. You should know that by now," muttered Sophia. "Your personal life always takes a back seat to what is best for the kingdom."

"But I don't agree with what my dad is doing and I also don't agree with this marriage."

Sophia stood. Her pink Prada heels resonated through the drafty office. "You don't have to like it or support it in the privacy of your private suite, but when you're in public, give them all of the support in the world."

"Do you support this marriage," Alexander asked before his aunt left the room.

Sophia put on her gloves. With a small laugh she replied, "I'll see you tonight, Alex. Have a lovely birthday."

The princess left the moody prince alone in his private office. Now more than ever, the Prince of Kemp knew that something had to be done. But what?

Before arriving for his brother's thirtieth birthday party at Kemp Castle, Prince Joseph ordered his driver to make a detour. As the car sped along Route 14, Joseph took in the sights of the kingdom at dusk. Although he rarely spent much time in the kingdom, he still loved his home country. A sense of pride always rushed through his body at the sight of the kingdom's mountains, sea side, and the irresistible Andover women. While the prince had been on his best behavior during this trip, he knew that his next jaunt abroad would be a chance for him to unleash his pent up sexual energy.

The black executive Lancia Thesis came to a stop in front of an imposing country style brick mansion. As Joseph climbed out of the car, he took a moment to take in the sight of his mother's childhood home. Situated in the Kemp Forest county of Andover, this was the refuge of the kingdom's oldest families. Although a few of the families had downgraded their homes during the last recession, few people with newer money ventured into this exclusive enclave. The prince waited by the car as his driver, knocked on the door, talked to the housekeeper, and ushered him into their music room.

Joseph sat at the baby grand piano with childlike purpose, as Beethoven's "Moonlight Sonata" sprang from his fingertips with great ease. "Your Regal Highness," a woman's voice called from behind him. "I forgot you were a maestro."

"Aunt Mary," Joseph said warmly. He gave her a long hug. "It's good to see you."

"You too. Will you have a seat?"

She guided him to the rose colored sofa. "I'm surprised to see you tonight. I thought you'd be at your brother's birthday celebration."

"I'm on my way. The Prince of Kemp won't even miss me. Why aren't you and Uncle Ted coming?"

Mary Walsh, who was a second peer due to her contributions to the improvement of Andover's artistic education, was a woman unto herself. While her sister, Katherine, became the Princess of Kemp, Mary devoted her life to the arts and her horses. Throughout Katherine's marriage to Michael, Mary kept a respectful distance from the regal family because she simply didn't understand them. Katherine seemed to fit in well, but Mary never quite knew what to make of those people. She twisted a long, salt and pepper dreadlock before saying, "You know me and Ted. Despite our upbringing, we're not those sort of people."

Joseph shrugged. "You should come. It's what my mom would have wanted."

"Joey," Mary said softly, "if my sister were still alive, I would still have reservations. It's not my world. I've sent Prince Alexander a birthday gift and a card. I don't need to stand in the ballroom of Kemp Castle to show him how much I care. Besides, it's not as if he or Princess Helena ever contact me."

Joseph could hear the disappointment in her voice. It's true that Mary wasn't the press favorite that Katherine was, but Joseph found her fascinating. When he was little, he always tagged along to this house whenever his mother visited her parents and sister. Maybe that was the reason why he could never deduce why Alexander and Helena simply ignored their aunt. "Well, those two have their own problems. I do know that my dad would love to see you," reasoned Joseph.

"The King called me yesterday. He wanted to explain his announcement to me." Mary's housekeeper delivered a coffee service to the music room. "Your father and I have never been close, but we've always respected each other."

"My dad's a good guy."

"He is," smiled Mary.

Joseph poured his aunt a cup coffee. "Will you come to the wedding?"

"I remember when my sister married your father. I'd never seen anything like it," she reminisced. "Ted and I may come."

Joseph stirred his coffee twice. After tasting it, he said, "Are you okay with my dad's decision? I mean, it does concern you…in a way."

Mary was touched by her nephew's devotion. "If this were nine years ago, I wouldn't have been very understanding. However, time has gone by. My sister isn't coming back. The King deserves to get on with his life, in spite of what some people may think."

"You're right," Joseph said. "Where's Uncle Ted?"

"He went to Lindman Square to get a cake. We're having a few friends over tonight for dinner and music. You're more than welcome to stay. Our cook is making her famous roast duck."

Prince Joseph couldn't help but smile at the offer. He always loved Rhonda's cooking. At one point, he even ordered the palace chef to acquire her recipes, which did not go down very well with the household staff. "I'd love to, but I do have to get to Kemp Castle before they notice my absence." Joseph made his way to the front door with Mary by his side. "Did you get an invitation to the Dowager Queen's garden tea party at Andover Palace?"

"I did. Unfortunately, I'll be in Rio. Ted's giving a lecture on social entrepreneurship."

"You two are the best people I know," the prince said truthfully.

Mary walked her nephew to his waiting car. The driver stood with the door open, as two bodyguards lingered behind the car. "Good night, Your Regal Highness. I love you."

He gave his aunt a tight hug. "I love you too, Aunt Mary. Give my love to Uncle Ted. Good night." With that, Prince Joseph climbed into the car and was whisked away to Kemp Castle.

***

The State Ballroom at Kemp Castle was festooned with the finest decorations from the regal household. Waiters glided around the ballroom with trays of special concoctions, while the musicians played the Prince of Kemp's favorite music. And, true to form, the regal family mingled with a select few of the Prince of Kemp's three hundred closest friends.

The Prince of Kemp chatted to one of his best friends from childhood, when his secretary instructed him that his father wished to speak with him. While the prospect of leaving his party to attend to the whims of his father did not appeal to Alexander, he decided to err on the side of caution, especially after the events of the past few days. Alexander found his father in the Smoking Room, just above the State Ballroom.

Although they hadn't spoken in nearly a week, the coolness between the King and his heir seemed to evaporate in this moment. The King walked over to his son and gave him a tight hug. Alexander found this show of affection out of character for his father. Michael could feel his son tensing up, so he loosened his grip and patted his son on the back. "Happy birthday, Alexander."

"Thank you. Are you enjoying yourself?"

"Yes. May we talk?"

"Sure…but I do have to get back to my guests."

Michael nodded. "I understand. Did you know you were two weeks late? Your mother refused to have the doctor induce labor, so she was bed ridden for two weeks. Even then, you didn't do anything until you were damn ready. When Helena was born, you wouldn't acknowledge her presence for a whole week. I didn't know what to make of that. But when Joseph came along, you didn't hold him for three months. You've always done things on your own time. That's the one thing I know about you..."

Alexander failed to see the meaning behind his father's words. "What does this have to do with anything, Dad?"

"I know you're not ecstatic over my engagement to Count Matthew. Granted, I should have run it by you and your siblings before the family meeting. Just know that I love you, Alexander. Whatever has happened in the last few days is behind us. I want us to move forward from here. Can we do that?"

"I suppose," muttered the prince. Alexander did his best to hide his emotions, but his father could see the tears beginning to form in his eyes.

Michael placed his arm around Alexander's shoulder as they started for the door. "Happy birthday, Alexander."

7

The newspapers wrote of the elaborate bash at Kemp Castle for the next two days. Life, as it was, returned to normal for the regal family. The Prince and Princess of Kemp joined the family at Port Agnes House, while His Regal Highness Lord Walter stayed at Blake Manor for the majority of the week.

Six days after the party, His Regal Highness Prince Joseph of Andover embarked upon a European regal tour of duty with His Regal Highness Samuel of Andover. After their two week tour, they were scheduled to be hosted on the yacht of an Asian royal who was old friends with the Dowager Queen Cassandra. Joseph's supervision of Samuel on this tour was entirely His Highness Edward's idea.

Over the past few days, Edward had begun to re-evaluate the state of his marriage. In the ten years that he'd been a member of the regal family, he had endured his fair share of scandal at the hands of his wife, Lady Margaret. Granted, Michael kept these indiscretions out of the press, but there was only so much he could do. For Edward, monogamy in a marriage was the most important thing. Without it, he reasoned, we might as well become wild animals. But his wife failed to share his views on marriage. She continued to lie to him, even when she promised that her lies would stop. If Margaret didn't respect him, he wished that she would be honest with him. Being made a fool of was the worst thing in the world.

In the privacy of his own thoughts Edward wondered if he could get custody of his son. If they managed to move to another country without the regal family lording over them, maybe they could have a normal life. However, that would never happen. The regal family would never let an heir to the throne leave the confines of their safe world. Yes, the descendants of Prince Christian and Prince Erich lived in Europe and America, but King Henrik's heirs still lived in Andover. It was, Edward had been told, their duty to country and crown. Under these conditions, Edward knew they wouldn't let him take his son away from his inherited duty.

Divorce seemed to be the only feasible option. There had never been a regal divorce in the history of the kingdom. The scandal would be more than he could bear. Edward had the security of his own family who still lived in the kingdom, but his life would be under more scrutiny than it was at the moment if he filed for a divorce. No matter what Edward thought of his wife or her family, they were masters at keeping their lives as private as possible. If Edward were to become a member of the general public, but as the ex-husband of Her Regal Highness Lady Margaret, he would be under constant pressure to reveal everything he knew about the regal family.

As Edward sat on the beach of Port Agnes House, he wondered what would happen next. Ever since he'd spoken to Sophia at the opening of the season, Edward began to pay much more attention to Margaret's comings and goings. In the past he'd simply turned a blind eye to her behavior. Lately, he noticed that her three hour lunches could be suspect, especially when His Highness Prince Robert disappeared to go for a walk around the sixty acres of forest surrounding Port Agnes House.

Sleep was no longer Edward's friend. He sat up late at night watching the ocean waves, while his wife slept soundly. There were times that he hated her. He wanted her to die. Death would be the best way for him to get on with his life; it would be the only way. Banishing the thoughts from his mind, Edward kicked the sand at his feet. He closed his eyes, and began to dream of things yet to come. But more importantly, he had to devise a way to protect his son, expose Margaret's deceit, and find a way to restore normalcy to his life.

"It's the event of this season!" Cassandra flipped through a thick black folder with purpose. She balanced her special drink on her knee. Bramble, Voltaire, Maisie and her two puppies, Yonkers and Edison, tussled in the corner of the spacious Sun Room.

Princess Sophia finished a tall glass of water. The cool air in the room refreshed her although she longed to be on the beach. "Mother, your tea party is always an event to remember."

"Of course it is, Sophia! All of the young ladies looking to enter proper society are vetted by me at this event, before Michael's final list at his autumn ceremony." Cassandra stared at her daughter. "Sophia, before the others get here, there's something we need to discuss."

"What is it? You're not sick, are you?"

"Me? Heavens no! I'm built like a Vuitton Steamer Trunk; I'll never go out of style," laughed the former monarch. "No… When Michael marries Matthew…and once I'm gone…there will be no one to carry on these tea parties for society. Yes, Matthew and Alexander will co-host the one for the young men in the kingdom, but a woman needs to oversee my tea parties. You do know that my grandmother started them. When she died, my mother took over, followed by myself and Princess Fiona. Now, when I die…"

"Mother, don't say 'die'. Say pass…" Princess Sophia always shuddered at the word "death".

Cassandra shook her head. "Death is the only certainty in life. One can evade taxes, but one knows that death always reserves the final dance." The Dowager Queen finished her drink. "Now," she continued, "once I'm dead, I want you to carry on this tradition with Princess Helena."

"What about Olivia? Surely you'd want the Princess of Kemp involved…"

"Once you and Helena are dead, then we can talk about that. You and Helena are my direct heirs. You're also princesses of the regal blood. That's what matters," Cassandra stated in an imperious tone.

"And Margaret," asked Sophia. "Is she exempt?"

Cassandra rolled her eyes. "I love Margaret, but she's never shown much of an interest in planning these tea parties. Her mother and I tried to get her involved, but she always slipped away to chase some man."

Princess Sophia laughed at the irony. If her mother only knew, thought the princess. "Mother, I'm honored. I'll be glad to carry on this legacy."

The valet opened the large door with a bow. "Their Regal Highnesses Princess Helena, the Princess of Kemp, and Lady Margaret."

Cassandra rose. The other women curtseyed to the Dowager Queen and Princess Sophia. While Princess Sophia was currently ranked below Olivia since she was married to the heir to the throne, Olivia still curtseyed to Sophia in the presence of the regal family. After all, Cassandra often reasoned, Sophia's of the regal blood and the King's sister.

The valet and butler quickly laid out the drinks and luncheon before leaving the regal women alone.

In the privacy of each other, a strange thing happened. The Dowager Queen became the most important woman in the room, while Princess Helena and the Princess of Kemp jockeyed for Princess Sophia's approval. Meanwhile, Lady Margaret did whatever she could to steal the limelight. Princess Sophia saw this as sad, but she simply shook her well coiffed head.

As they consumed their first drinks, Cassandra got down to business. "Ladies, this year I want the tea party to be the event of the season. I know that every event cannot be the event of the season, but one must try!" With that, Cassandra handed them large folders with her regal crest embossed on the cover. "As you'll see, I've put each of you at one table. In this manner, you'll be able to mix with the guests. It's very important that we show them everything they expect of the regal family. Is that clear?"

"Quite," Margaret stated. Lady Margaret was not in the mood to be in this meeting with the rest of the regal women. She wanted nothing more than to go horseback riding on the beach. Also, the coolness she felt radiating from Sophia annoyed her to no end. That's why I'm sleeping with your husband, Margaret smiled to herself.

"Does anyone have something to add," asked Cassandra.

Olivia fed Yonkers a piece of her chicken. "I have something," she said, tentatively.

"Yes," Cassandra smiled.

With all eyes on her, Olivia took a deep breath. No matter how long she was married to Alexander or how much they told her they accepted her, Olivia was still paralyzed by fear in the presence of these women. "May I be frank?"

"What is it dear," Cassandra asked kindly.

"I feel like my marriage is a sham!" Olivia felt as if her greatest sin had been cured. In that moment, the past few months of internal strife vanished. She hadn't felt this good in ages.

However, the regal women looked quite uncomfortable. Even though they all had issues of their own, they were never brought up in situations like this. Olivia would be excused, as usual, because she was still new to regal protocol.

Princess Sophia rose first. "Ladies, why don't we leave the Princess of Kemp and the Dowager Queen to discuss this matter?"

Princess Helena wanted nothing more than to stay. Lately, she'd been craving good gossip. Talk about a windfall! However, Sophia took her niece by the hand as they left the Sun Room.

"I'm sorry," Olivia cried. "I…it's just – I don't have anyone to talk to at Kemp Castle. The rest of the family is four hours away at Andover Palace. I'm sorry, Your Regal Highness. I didn't mean to ruin your meeting." Olivia did her best to contain her emotions. Crying in front of Cassandra would have been a catastrophic misstep. Olivia reached into her Hermes Kelly bag for a handkerchief. "I'm sorry…"

Cassandra looked at the young woman with kind eyes. Cassandra's entire life had been in service to the Kingdom of Andover. From the moment of her birth eighty-three years ago, she was destined to be the Queen of Andover. For twenty-eight years, she was. After the death of her husband and sister in the same year, she decided to abdicate the throne in favor of her son and heir, Prince Michael. In the eight years since her abdication, Cassandra began to learn more about the needs of people on a human level than she had in her entire life. Growing up in a cosseted world with maids, secretaries, drivers, attendants, dressers, and the like distanced her from the true cost of human strife.

"My dear," Cassandra said. "What's the issue?"

Olivia proceeded to tell her husband's grandmother about the events surrounding the non-sexual aspect of their relationship. As Olivia recounted the fact that she and her husband hadn't had sex in months, Cassandra gasped in shock. It never occurred to Cassandra that her handsome grandson and his breathtaking wife could have a sexless marriage. "That's an important issue," Cassandra finally replied.

The Princess of Kemp dabbed her soft brown eyes. "I'm sorry… I didn't mean for it to come out this way. But after so long… I couldn't keep it to myself anymore."

"My dear, if you don't produce an heir, the throne will pass onto Princess Helena. I have no doubt that, if forced, she could become a great monarch. But the Andover throne has passed down the line of the first born since my father inherited the throne from my grandfather. To interrupt that would be detrimental to the monarchy. Do you understand?"

"Yes," the princess replied weakly. "What do I have to do?"

Cassandra walked to the large window. The waves crashed on the beach below. Cassandra watched as Edward swam in the sea; Michael was on a phone call; and Margaret sat on her horse as she talked with Prince Robert. "You have to have a child."

"I know…"

"But it must be the Prince of Kemp's *natural* and legitimate heir. A *blood* heir," stressed Cassandra. "If there is doubt, a test will be done at the birth."

Olivia couldn't believe what Cassandra said. Yet, her words were the honest advice she needed. "But what are we to do if we can't…perform…"

Cassandra held her breath. "Through whatever means necessary you must produce an heir for the Prince of Kemp. It's that simple, my dear."

The Princess of Kemp tried to process what the Dowager Queen meant. "What are you saying?"

"If it involves a fertility treatment, so be it. I'm sure we can twist the press so it works to our benefit. You could become the patron of a fertility charity." Cassandra's eyes lit up. "This is what you'll do: We'll find a proper fertility charity that needs a regal patron. After a year or two, you'll undergo the necessary tests. If they prove that you need treatment, you'll have the sympathy of the press and the kingdom. The most important thing is that you produce an heir," stressed Cassandra.

This sounded great in theory, but Olivia remained skeptical. "But what if I can't…or what if it doesn't work…"

Cassandra filled her crystal tumbler with water. "There's never been a regal divorce, but if you can't produce an heir…well… We'll find the Prince of Kemp a wife who can," Cassandra stated bluntly.

Olivia watched the elderly woman walk out of the room with her dogs in tow. Horrified by what she'd just heard, Olivia tried to come to grips with the reality of her situation. She was expendable in the eyes of the monarchy. If she didn't have Alexander's child, her days as his wife would be over in an instant. She'd come too far to not become Andover's duchess one day. In that moment, Olivia resolved that she would have the next heir to the throne, no matter what.

The white horse galloped through the thick overgrowth in the forest surrounding Port Agnes House. Lady Margaret kicked the horse in the sides, demanding it go faster. After she left Olivia alone with Cassandra, Margaret ran into Robert on the beach. What he said disturbed her then; it still bothered her now. He essentially told her that they were over.

How could he, she thought for the millionth time in the last fifteen minutes. How could he?

She'd given herself to him during the last year, but now he was ending their sweet love affair. He claimed that Sophia was getting too close to the truth.

By Lady Margaret's estimation, Prince Robert wanted to be the good guy who didn't hurt anyone. Well, she thought ruefully, you broke my heart! Tears streamed down her face. As the cool wind hit her in the face, she almost forgot about Robert's betrayal. They were supposed to have a future together. With Edward's return, all hope of a better life was dashed. Damn them all, she seethed.

As the horse jumped over three fallen trees, Lady Margaret pulled the reins, prompting the horse to come to a dead stop. She tried to catch her breath, but it was useless. Turning the beast around, Margaret rode with lighting speed towards Port Agnes House.

As she approached the castle, she could see her aunt walking about fifty yards away with her dogs. Margaret grew closer, but then something happened.

Two of Cassandra's dogs saw the horse running towards them at full speed. They barked like mad as they ran towards the purebred horse. Before Margaret could think, the horse whinnied, rose into the air, and threw her onto the hard, dry ground. The horse ran into the forest as two handlers ran after it.

Margaret lay on the ground, broken. She could feel nothing, but everything hurt. The next few minutes were a blur. Someone called for a doctor, as the regal family rushed to her side. Then everything went black.

8

For two nights, the regal family kept the outside world away from Port Agnes House. The family doctor brought in the minimal amount of staff to tend to Her Regal Highness Lady Margaret. The injuries she sustained from her accident were still unknown, but the doctor was close to his final diagnosis. The palace did issue a statement saying that Lady Margaret was involved in a minor accident; more information would be released as it became available.

His Majestic Regal Highness The King instructed his mother to keep her dogs under lock and key for the moment. He even accosted his mother for being blatantly irresponsible when it came to her pets. The Dowager Queen didn't fight her son; the sense of guilt she felt already consumed her. Princess Fiona, the Dowager Queen's sister, lost her youngest child, Lady Constance, when she was fourteen years old. It took Fiona years to recover from her daughter's death. Before Fiona died, Cassandra promised to look out for Margaret and Walter. If Margaret died as a result of her dogs, Cassandra didn't know how she would ever live with her niece's blood on her hands.

Princess Sophia was a constant presence at Margaret's bedside. No matter how she felt about her cousin, this was the worst thing to happen. Luckily, reasoned Sophia, Samuel was out of the kingdom with Joseph. If things took a turn for the worse, they would be informed, but not now. Sophia sat by Margaret's bed and pitied her. Although Margaret's image was that of a woman who owned it all, she wasn't powerful. No, thought Sophia, she was just a woman.

When the doctor had the results of his many tests, he was sent to see the King in his official office. All matters concerning the health and welfare of the regal family were always run by the monarch first. Whether or not anyone agreed with it, it didn't matter. In order to protect the regal family and the kingdom, King Michael had to know what was really going on beneath the surface. His Highness Edward joined the King and the doctor for the results of the exams.

The doctor bowed in the sight of the men. "Your Majesty; Your Highness. I have Her Regal Highness' results."

"Will she walk again," asked Edward. Over the past two days, he worried that his wife would be a shell of her former self. The sheer thought of Margaret slipping from his life scared him into action. He was now committed to his marriage, in spite of their issues.

"Yes," the doctor responded. "However, as a result of the fall, she lost the baby."

The King gave Edward a curious look, a look which Edward returned. He and Margaret weren't planning on having another child; this was news to him. Sensing that something was amiss, the King replied, "How terrible. How far along was she?"

The doctor consulted his notes. "By my estimation, she was approximately three to three and a half months pregnant."

"Thank you, doctor," the monarch said.

With that, the doctor bowed, leaving Michael and Edward.

"Did you know about this," asked Michael.

Edward shook his head. "No. I… Your Majesty… The dates…"

"What about them? It was your child…"

"I was in the midst of the Sahara Desert."

Michael stopped. It was happening again. Michael never knew why his cousin seemed so intent to ruin her own life. If Edward was right, that meant Lady Margaret was up to her old tricks. After everything he had done for her, he was livid. He felt even worse for Edward because the test results from a few weeks ago proved that Edward was Samuel's father, not the courtier. Now this, Michael though angrily. If he didn't know any better, he would have sworn that she was intent on bringing down the monarchy.

"Why did she do this," Michael asked Edward.

"I don't know... She promised me that she was done with this bull." Edward felt angrier than he had in a long time. Leaving the kingdom – and his wife – seemed like the best thing in this moment. "That wasn't my child, Michael."

"Edward, this cannot get out. You must keep this between us. If the press were to get wind of it...well... it would be a nightmare."

Edward nodded. He knew how the regal family worked; Michael reigned supreme. What he said was non-negotiable. "Yes, Your Majesty. I understand. What are you going to do," he inquired.

"I don't know, Edward..." Michael left the office with Edward. At this moment, his most pressing matter was discovering the father of this unborn child. However, he already had his suspicions about who it was. And, he deduced, so did Edward.

His Regal Highness Lord Walter stepped out of his sister's sick room. During the last hour, she'd finally come to. She didn't remember much about the accident, but she swore she would never ride again. Margaret told her younger brother that her body ached like hell. However, she was glad to know she would be better in a few days.

Walter walked up the north wing staircase to the second floor of Port Agnes House towards his private suite. He'd had the same suite since he was a child, while Prince Alexander and Princess Sophia had their suites in this wing of the house. Before he reached his suite, his private secretary, Jasper, rushed towards him.

"Your Regal Highness," his secretary said breathlessly.

"What is it," asked Walter. He wasn't in the mood for whatever Jasper wanted to tell him.

“There’s a young woman here to see you, Sir. She’s demanding to see you…at the gates…”

“Who is it?”

“The woman from the university lecture.”

Daisy, Walter thought. A friendly face could be the trick to cure his foul mood. Walter knew that he couldn’t invite her upstairs. He instructed Jasper to have her ushered into the Silver Library. There, they could talk in private.

Once in the library, Walter was delighted to see that nubile creature. Daisy wore a flowing vintage wrap dress with simple sandals. To Walter, she looked like a Bohemian dream. “Daisy,” he sighed.

“Wally,” she cooed.

Ever since Walter invited her to dinner, they had been on very intimate terms. The regal family still didn’t know about her, which only made her visit to Port Agnes House much more risky. “What are you doing here,” he asked.

“I heard about your sister. I had to see you.” Daisy took in the sight of the room. “This place is amazing. I mean, I’ve seen a picture before, but it’s huge!”

Walter felt queasy. “Daisy, I will pass your good wishes onto my sister, but you do have to go.”

“But I just got here!”

He could hear the disappointment in her voice. “I know, but… The whole family is here. Her Regal Highness isn’t well. We need privacy.”

“I thought you loved me.”

“I do,” he replied. “I just need you to respect our privacy.” He could see the hurt in her eyes. “These aren’t my wishes. They’re His Majesty’s wishes.”

Daisy realized this was a useless battle. She grabbed her purse and kissed Walter on the cheek as they prepared to leave the Silver Library.

Just then the door swung open.

There stood Princess Sophia with a first edition of *Walden* in her hands. She quickly surveyed the situation. The woman standing in front of her looked like a bag lady for a lack of trying. Her cousin, on the other hand, looked as if his world was about to implode.

"Your Regal Highness," Daisy said. She performed a quick curtsy.

Princess Sophia remained stoic. "How do you do?"

"Very well, thank you."

"Jasper," Walter called into the hall.

"Yes, Your Regal Highness," he replied.

"Could you please show my guest to her vehicle?"

Jasper led Daisy away. Sophia brushed past Walter and returned the book to its proper place. As she turned to leave the library, she said, "You shouldn't have done that."

"I don't need a lecture, Sophia."

Sophia jammed her hands into the pockets of her pant suit. "Who was the woman? If you lie to me, I'll find out."

Walter shifted his weight. He hated these situations. Although he was barely three months older than Sophia, she still exerted a massive amount of control over his life. To be frank, he was tired of her. "She's someone I'm seeing. That's all you need to know."

Sophia couldn't believe what her cousin was telling her. His sister barely escaped death, yet he was already bringing common women into Port Agnes House. "After everything that's happened in the past few days, do you think that's wise?"

"This doesn't concern you, Sophia. Let it go."

"I would, but she shouldn't have been here to begin with. Those aren't my orders, they're the King's. No outsiders while Lady Margaret recovers." Sophia shook her head. "Heaven forbid you think with your big head," she snapped.

"I've heard enough," Walter bellowed. He started for the door, furious with his cousin's constant intrusions into his personal life. "Just because I don't have someone like Robert or Olivia doesn't mean I don't deserve the chance to find someone. Daisy was only here for two minutes before you came bursting in. I didn't know she was coming. I'm sorry she came. She's gone. It's a non-issue. Can you please stop minding my business?"

Sophia rolled her eyes with annoyance. "I'll stop minding your business when you start behaving like a member of the regal family."

And with that, Sophia stormed out of the library.

Something within Princess Sophia erupted late one evening. Whether it was before dinner or just after she climbed into bed, she couldn't recall. However, in that solitary moment, everything she felt she knew was suddenly erased. As Robert slept soundly, the princess pulled on her robe and walked to the south wing of Port Agnes House towards Cassandra's bedroom. From the hall, she could hear the low murmur of Beethoven. Princess Sophia nodded to the attending guard before entering her mother's private suite.

"What is it, dear," Cassandra asked. She lowered the volume on her iPod with grave concern. "What can I do?"

"I want the truth." Sophia couldn't believe the ease with which the words fell from her mouth. "Mother, I need you to be honest with me."

Cassandra was baffled. "I'll do whatever I can," she replied, cautiously.

Princess Sophia sat on the soft down bed. "There's something I need to tell you. I've had my suspicions for a very long time, and I need an answer."

"Regarding?"

"My husband and Margaret. Do you think they're having an affair?"

Sophia's candor startled her mother. In Cassandra's day, no one ever said such a thing! Yes, many people alluded to them, but they never expressed the truth. "Sophia! Someone might hear you!"

"I don't care," she moaned. "He's my husband and she has a past. We all know about her…tricks..."

"Sophia, stop. She's your cousin; my sister's daughter!"

"I don't care," snapped Sophia. "She's always wanted everything I have. You know that. When you became Queen and I was invested as a princess, she loathed me for it. It's not my fault! She went after Victor Kerby without a second thought!"

"Stop it. I've heard enough. Margaret has made quite a few catastrophic mistakes, but that doesn't mean that she's having an affair with Prince Robert," Cassandra stated in a low voice. "Now I want you to drop this nonsense now. What if one of the staff heard you? Or the King?"

"Mother, I'm not crazy. I know exactly what I'm talking about. I can't even believe how you can sit here and defend Margaret. I'm your daughter. You should be on my side."

"I don't take sides," sniffed Cassandra. "I take note of both sides, but I never take sides. It seems to me that you're having problems within your own marriage. You see Margaret as a threat, which is why you are assuming that she's up to her old tricks. She has a husband and child… I think Lady Margaret is simply too old to exert herself with the deception needed to carry out an affair." Cassandra shook her head with great finality. "Now, if you don't mind, I need my sleep."

As Princess Sophia walked to her suite, there was something she couldn't shake. Her mother's flip attitude bothered her, but there was something more. That night, Sophia couldn't sleep because she knew all too well that her life was about to fall apart at the seams.

***

His Majestic Regal Highness The King finished his call with Count Matthew Hall before his first appointment of the morning. In the week since Lady Margaret's accident, Michael watched her recover without incident. The news of her untimely miscarriage was a shock to her, but she refused to comment on the situation. Maybe that was best, the King thought to himself. However, there were certain things he needed to clear up. After seeing how angry Edward was at the news that his wife was carrying a child that they both knew wasn't his, Michael suspected that his sister's husband was the child's father. No one had told the princess or the prince, but Michael feared that Edward would explode in a moment of fury, thereby ruining everything the regal family allegedly stood for.

Scandal within the regal household was nothing new, but this almost incestuous relationship between Lady Margaret and Prince Robert bothered Michael. Had they actually been careful, this might have ended differently. But the careless actions of two adults could ruin the monarchy if this wasn't handled in the most delicate fashion.

That's why the King ordered Prince Robert to see him this morning. As far as he knew, the prince wasn't aware of Margaret's pregnancy or the fact that her riding accident caused her to lose the child. In order to protect his sister, Michael felt he needed to confront Robert directly.

"Your Majesty," the attending valet said with a bow. "His Highness Prince Robert."

Robert walked into Michael's official office with a low bow. The valet closed the door, as Robert said, "Your Majesty. It's nice to see you."

The King sat behind his desk. "Did you know Lady Margaret was pregnant?"

Robert sat up in shock. His mouth went dry; his face went slack. He and Margaret had done everything right. Sophia suspected that something was amiss, but Robert had done his best to keep his indiscretion discreet. "Good for her," he choked.

"I'd say. But she lost the child during the riding accident."

"She… How is she coping with the news," asked Robert. He could feel his palms grow moist.

"As well as can be expected. His Highness Edward and I were informed by the doctor. Edward was shocked, to say the least."

"Losing a child is hard," reasoned Robert.

Michael nodded. "However, this is the third child you've lost," acknowledged Michael.

Robert looked confused. "Excuse me?"

"The two children that Princess Sophia miscarried and Lady Margaret's child," surmised the King. "One could assume that having your child is simply bad luck."

Robert bristled at the King's hostile tone. In all of Robert's years as a member of the regal family, Michael had never spoken to him like this. Robert suddenly realized in that moment that Michael knew everything. It's all over, Robert realized. He turned his attention to the sight of his wife on the beach below. She wore a two piece McQueen bathing suit that truly complimented her slender figure. The only thing the prince wanted to do in that moment was scoop her in his arms and make passionate love to her. But depending on the outcome of this meeting with Michael, Robert was unsure about the state of his marriage.

"That's not true," Robert stammered. "Margaret's child isn't mine…"

"She was three months pregnant. Edward was in the Sahara Desert. Unless Lady Margaret impregnated herself with his frozen sperm, it's doubtful that the child was his. I've been aware of your affair for four months, Robert. While I should've stopped it, your marriage is your responsibility."

Robert shifted uncomfortably in his chair. "I'm… I'm sorry."

Michael was unmoved. "It's too late for apologies. You and Margaret thought only of yourselves. Edward loves his family. No matter what anyone says about him, he's always been committed to Samuel and his wife. My sister has given you her heart; no questions asked. Yet you've managed to hurt her with her own cousin."

The room started to spin as Robert's life flashed before his eyes. "What now?"

The King walked towards Robert with a firm look on his face. "Count yourself lucky that Margaret lost that child. The ramifications would have torn apart this family, as well as the kingdom. You must tell your wife everything before Edward does. He and the princess have been friends for years… I would be surprised if he let it this news slip."

Robert nodded. As he started for the door, Michael called after him.

"Robert, if you hurt my sister or scandalize this family one more time, I will ensure that your life is a living hell. We both know I have the power to do it." And with that, King Michael answered his ringing iPhone.

In the anteroom outside of the monarch's official office, Michael's words reverberated through Robert's mind. He knew that Michael could exert his limitless power and essential crush him. Robert made his way towards the beach because he had to make this right. But, Robert reasoned, it would be harder than it seemed.

Lady Margaret sat in her bedroom at Port Agnes House. The guilt, dread, and shame she felt in this moment weighed upon her. After her riding accident, Lady Margaret was resigned to bed for a week, but now she was up and around. However, the news that she had lost a child she didn't even know she was carrying shocked her more than anything. She assumed the reason her menstrual cycle stopped was due to menopause. Since she was nearing that age, Lady Margaret told herself that she was getting it early.

In hindsight, her refusal to admit the true nature of her condition was a way to shield herself from the unwelcome barrage of questions from the regal family. Since the accident, the King had only paid her a short visit. Margaret knew this was unlike Michael, but it didn't take her long to put the pieces together. Due to the fact that she was three months along, it was easy to deduce that the child was not Edward's. Before the accident, Margaret suspected that Michael was getting close to the truth, but she told herself that she and Robert were being too careful. However, they weren't careful enough.

How she missed her parents and her son, however, Samuel would return from his trip with Prince Joseph just before the start of the school year. However, Margaret did her best to console herself with the memories of her parents, Princess Fiona and Lord Nicholas. They always supported her, even when she was clearly in the wrong. But being shunned by the King was the worst feeling in the world.

The only other thing that hurt more than her cousin's refusal to talk to her, was Edward's refusal to address the subject. After everything they'd been through in the past few months, she knew she'd crossed the line this time. With Samuel's paternity, Margaret was sure that her husband was the child's father. They looked alike and Samuel bore more than a passing resemblance to the men in Edward's family. In spite of their time apart and the paternity results, Margaret knew that Edward had forgiven her. But this would prove to be bigger than them. This was Robert and Margaret's sin. No amount of passion fueled sex or expensive watches could cure the evil pall Margaret and Robert had cast across two marriages.

As she sat in the window of her bedroom, Margaret thought of a simpler time. She laughed at herself when she realized that those times never existed. Margaret couldn't fathom what the future held for her. Would Edward stay with her? Or would Robert stay with Sophia? Would Sophia try to have Michael exile her to a far region of the world? Or would the entire regal family act as if everything was normal?

The only thing Lady Margaret knew for sure was this: Once Princess Sophia learned of her husband and her cousin's betrayal, all hell would break lose. But the one thing Margaret never realized was that Pandora's Box was already open, and her life would never be the same again.

***

His Regal Highness The Prince of Kemp examined the rose garden at Port Agnes House with great interest. While his mother was alive, this rose garden was her summer passion. At Kemp Castle, she commissioned the award winning horticulture expert, Rosalind Diaz, to turn the once depressed spaces into an appealing piece of artistry. Today, the gardens at Port Agnes House and Kemp Castle were world renowned. With his mother's passing, Prince Alexander ensured that her beautiful gardens were not neglected by the regal household.

The Prince of Kemp walked through the vast garden, when he saw his wife coming towards him. In the past week, their love life had exploded in ways he'd never imagined. Olivia actually seemed interest in sex. Meanwhile, the prince was able to make love to his wife for the first time in months. And it was amazing. Alexander joked that it was the sea air; he even suggested they make Port Agnes House their full time regal residence.

"Hello, darling," Olivia smiled. She wore a form fitting pink sundress with matching sandals, black sunglasses, and an oversized light blue hat. "Your father said you were out here."

"I was just inspecting the gardens. Where have you been," asked Alexander. He kissed her passionately. "I've been waiting."

Olivia giggled. "I met with your aunt to see what we should get the King and Count for their wedding."

Alexander grumbled. "Let's not talk about that."

"I thought you and your father were making progress after your birthday party."

"We are… But I still have my reservations."

"If that's the way you feel, I won't mention it. By the way, last night was sensational."

A wide smile appeared on Alexander's face. "What can I say? Whatever was blocking me before is gone. Life is great."

"Alex," she began, "something's not right here."

"What do you mean?"

The regal couple sat under a large tree as the sun rose to its prime position in the sky.

"People have been acting quite odd since Lady Margaret's accident. It's as if everyone knows a secret, but no one's willing to admit it."

Alexander shook his head. Having grown up in the confines of regal life, he knew that this was the way in which his family operated. They rarely spoke of the issues that affected them until they were out of control. Alexander always likened it to Frankenstein and his monster. "Listen, just ignore it. After thirty years of being around my family, I've learned that it's best to keep yourself to yourself. That way, you're never a target."

With that statement, Olivia felt a pang of guilt run through her body. Her confession to the Dowager Queen made her feel better, but now she realized it violated her husband's personal code of discretion. In that moment, she decided to leave it in the past. "That's good to know," she said weakly.

"You haven't said anything to anyone, have you?" Alexander gave his wife a cautious look. He knew she could say the wrong thing from time to time, which was of great concern to him.

"No," she replied quickly. Olivia rose. "I think lunch should be ready now. Shall we?"

Alexander took his wife by the arm, as they walked to the castle's terrace for lunch. Olivia decided to forget her talk with Cassandra because it was void. But she still felt uneasy because she had to remain on the Dowager Queen's good side or else her past troubles with her husband could be exposed.

9

His Regal Highness Lord Walter of Andover waited anxiously for Daisy. It had been weeks since they'd seen each other because she was attending to family business in the United States. Walter grew restless with each passing day because he assumed that this is what love felt like. It was now late August and Walter relished the idea of making Daisy a permanent fixture in his life. No matter what her breeding dictated, Walter was intent on having Daisy as his wife. However, he couldn't ignore the shadows cast over their relationship.

After Daisy's run-in with Princess Sophia at Port Agnes House, Walter kept his distance from his cousin. He wasn't afraid of her, but he was terrified by the storm of controversy that could erupt if Sophia felt the need to share Daisy's visit with Michael or Cassandra. But shockingly, Sophia remained silent. Walter knew that this was unlike her, yet he welcomed the chance to get to know Daisy without regal protocol rearing its ugly head. Maybe Sophia wasn't so bad, he told himself.

In the privacy of Blake Manor's library, Walter and Daisy shared a passionate kiss.

"You look great, Wally," she smiled.

"As do you," he replied. He guided her to the sofa. "How was America?"

She shrugged. "It was okay. I had to see my grandmother in Baltimore. Thankfully, she's fine."

"That's wonderful to hear." Walter kissed the nape of her neck. "I'm so happy to see you."

"I can't stay long. I have to prepare for the new school year."

"I've been thinking about that," he said. "How would you like to work at the Lawson Museum of Contemporary Art? The King's the regal patron and Prince Robert's father funded the entire renovation of the museum. I could get you a position as a curator."

Daisy's eyes lit up. "That would be wonderful! Oh, Wally," she exclaimed. "But will it be okay with the King and all?"

Walter nodded. "The King has more pressing things to consider, like his wedding."

"Everyone says that it'll be the event of the decade! When's the wedding again?"

"The eighth of April."

"If we're still together then…"

"What makes you think otherwise?"

"You never know what can happen," she said wistfully. "But if we are lucky enough to be with each other, could I go with you?"

Walter was lost for words. It was one thing for him to have an illicit relationship behind the closed doors of Blake Manor, but to make their relationship public before the regal family was aware of it could be suicide. He did love Daisy, but his sense of duty and tradition played a bigger role in his psyche at that moment. "We'll see," he stated.

Daisy winced. "It was a dumb idea. Like I always say, 'Nothing's certain.' Do you want to have lunch or something else," she cooed.

"How about both," Walter whispered.

As the summer came to a close, Her Regal Highness Princess Sophia did everything she could to keep herself sane. However, the truth about the accident was something she never wanted to know. There were plenty of times over the past few weeks when Prince Robert tried to tell his wife, but she simply walked away. The King even sat her down for a talk, and she walked out of the room. No, Sophia continually told herself, I don't need to know.

Today was the day of the Dowager Queen's Annual Tea Party in the State Reception Room at Andover Palace. Every year, twenty young women of note from within the kingdom were invited to take part; of those women only the few personally vetted by the former monarch would go before the King to receive a first or second peerage. As Sophia thought of the many tea parties she'd been to since the age of eighteen, she shuddered. Yet, this was her regal duty and she always put her regal life before her personal life. But now, she began to wonder if that had been a colossal mistake.

Princess Sophia placed her tiara on her head, when her personal secretary informed her that her presence was requested in the State Reception Room. As she walked down the familiar corridors, she caught sight of Lady Margaret descending the stairs. How she hated her. In that moment, Sophia wanted to slap her ungrateful cousin, but that would accomplish nothing. No, Sophia reasoned. The only way to make Margaret pay would be to hurt her in the one arena that even Michael couldn't control beyond the palace walls – the press. A wicked smile crossed her face. Yes, that's how she would exact her revenge upon that woman who seemed intent on ruining every aspect of her life. Sophia made her way into the State Reception Room where Princess Helena, the Princess of Kemp, and Lady Margaret were talking amongst themselves. The princess forced a warm smile onto her face, but the thought of sweet revenge was the only thing on her mind.

Upon Cassandra's entrance into the room, the first guests made their appearances. The regal family took their places at the five perfectly decorated tables. Lady Margaret chatted to the woman next to her about issues concerning international policy, while Princess Helena shared a witty remark with the ladies at her table. The Princess of Kemp was a bit thrown to find the woman next to her was a member of a fertility charity called, The Andover Center of Hope. The Princess of Kemp couldn't help but feel as if Cassandra was doing everything she could to ambush her.

Olivia regretted ever telling Cassandra about her problems with Alexander. Although Cassandra hadn't mentioned the subject since, Olivia continually worried that the Dowager Queen would let everything slip in front of Alexander. That, Olivia knew, would be a true disaster. In the past few weeks, she and Alexander made great strides in the bedroom. She wasn't pregnant, but she knew it would only be a matter of time. As long as they tried, no one could replace her as Alexander's wife. Losing her status as the Princess of Kemp, the wife to the heir of the throne and the future Duchess of Andover, Consort of The King, meant more to her than anything else. After all she'd gone through a lot to arrive at this point; Olivia knew that she had to play the game, but having her husband's child was of extreme importance. As she sipped her tea with great care, Olivia simply smiled and nodded as the woman from the fertility center went on about their good work.

The Dowager Queen held court at her own table to great success. In her old age, these were the events she always enjoyed. Tables filled with her personal blend of teas, homemade pastries, and the right women from the right families looking to enter the aristocratic fold; and, if they were extremely lucky, the regal family. Many years ago, this was where Cassandra had the idea to pair Katherine with Michael, an idea that was met with support by Cassandra's husband, mother, and sister. Today, there was no one that jumped out at Cassandra as being truly worthy of Prince Joseph's hand, but she did see one or two lovely women who could replace Olivia. Yes, it could be seen as extreme because the Princess of Kemp was generally liked, but producing an heir was more important that being popular. Cassandra still couldn't believe that her grandson and his wife had yet to have a child, but with the sorry state of their love life, she feared it may never happen. But, Cassandra remembered, in the past few weeks, she noticed a change with the young couple. Maybe it was the thinly veiled threat to Olivia that she was replaceable that made the difference. Whatever it was, things seemed better. And to Cassandra, as long as everything seemed perfect in the eyes of the public, that was all that mattered.

"Your Regal Highnesses; Invited Guests! Please join us in the garden for the musical portion of our afternoon," the butler announced.

As the twenty women and five regal women moved through the glass door into the garden, Lady Margaret found herself alongside Princess Sophia. They hadn't exchanged two words in a matter of weeks, but Lady Margaret decided that this was the time to break the stalemate with her cousin. "It's a lovely day, isn't it," Margaret said calmly.

Princess Sophia gave her an icy glare. "Yes. It was."

With that, the princess made her way across the garden as Margaret watched her with disdain. These were the moments when Margaret felt no remorse for what she'd done. Even though Michael still shunned her, Edward was distant, and Robert did his best to ignore her, Margaret still justified what she'd done. Princess Sophia had everything, and now it was her turn to get what she wanted. This would pass, reasoned Margaret, and when it did, she'd have Robert for herself. In the past few days, Margaret had begun to think that losing the baby she didn't know she was carrying was a blessing. This way, she wouldn't be scandalized, but she and Robert could make a clean break from Andover in a few years. While it seemed like a far off dream, Lady Margaret decided to focus on the future…a future where Princess Sophia was without the love of her life.

"Princess," Cassandra called to Olivia. "Miss Nancy Houghton told me that she's from a fertility center. Isn't she remarkable?"

"Yes," nodded Olivia. She took a sip of tea before adding, "Their work helps so many people."

Cassandra smiled. "I do agree. Now, tell me, should my office inquire as to whether or not they would like you to be their regal patron?"

"That won't be necessary," beamed Olivia. "The Prince of Kemp and I are doing quite well."

"Is that so?"

"Yes, Your Regal Highness. However, I may have my office arrange a time for me to take a regal tour of their charity. I think that in the spirit of today, that would be quite appropriate. Don't you?"

Amazed by Olivia's deft handling of the situation, all Cassandra could do was laugh.

His Highness Edward sat on the soft beach as the clear blue water crashed before him. Edward's concentration was momentarily broken when his iPhone rang. Despite the unknown number, Edward answered the call. "Hello?"

"Hi, Daddy! It's Sammy!"

"Sam," sighed Edward. "How are you, buddy? I miss you."

"I miss you too. Joey and I are in…Where are we, Joey?"

"Monaco," the prince said in the background.

"We're in Monaco. It's really nice. Have you been here, Daddy?"

"I have," Edward said gravely. "Are you ready to come home?"

"Yeah." Samuel sighed. "I miss you and Mommy. Is she with you?"

"No," replied Edward. "She's at the palace."

"Oh. Well, tell her I called. I have to go, Daddy. I love you."

"I love you too, Sammy." Edward hung up the phone with a heavy sigh. No matter what Margaret did, she did give him a perfect little boy. Even though he was barely speaking to his wife, he was intent on doing whatever he could to protect his son. Edward stretched before making his way back to Port Agnes House. However, as he started up the beach, he saw Prince Robert coming towards him.

Prince Robert wore a black bathing suit and clutched a towel. He caught Edward's gaze, but did his best to avoid it. However, he could manage a small, "Hello."

Edward ignored him.

"I know you heard me," Robert called after him.

Edward turned to his in-law. There were few people in the world that Edward hated, but Prince Robert was now at the top of his list. He hadn't confronted Robert before because of Princess Sophia. Since he and Princess Sophia had been friends for so many years, Edward found it beneath him to cause a scene that could result in one of them ending up in traction. "Let's not do this, Robert."

"Look, Ed, I'm sorry," muttered Robert.

Edward couldn't believe what he was hearing. "If you were truly sorry," he said in a low voice, "you wouldn't have screwed my wife."

Robert took a deep breath. "It wasn't like that…"

Edward raised his hand. "Don't. I don't want to hear you profess your love for my wife. It was sex. That's all."

"It was more than that, Ed. On some level, you know that."

Edward had heard enough. "And you know that she's married to me. You have a wonderful wife who would do anything for you. Why throw it all away for something you know you will never have?"

"Ed, life isn't that simple."

"So you thought you'd complicate my marriage and yours, Rob? Do you get off on that?"

Robert threw his hands into the air. "Look, forget I said anything."

"I can't," snapped Edward. "I never will. Tell me, what did Sophia say when you told her of your…deed?"

"That's none of your business."

"You haven't told her, have you," asked Edward.

Robert cast his eyes heavenward. It wasn't as if he hadn't tried, but it seemed that Princess Sophia wanted to be left in the dark.

"You know, you're a coward, Rob. For all of the attention and adulation that's heaped onto you, you're nothing but a little man who hides behind the women in his life." Edward shook his head in disgust as he brushed past the prince.

Prince Robert watched Edward walk inside, but he didn't feel angry or even upset. He felt guilty because Edward was the first person put him in his place.

10

The middle of September brought with it not only a change in season, but the return to life as normal in the kingdom. The King opened his government, Prince Joseph, and His Regal Highness Samuel returned from their tour abroad, Lord Walter's relationship with Daisy deepened, and the Princess of Kemp awaited the results of her newest pregnancy test.

Port Agnes House was officially closed for the year and the entire regal family returned to life at Andover Palace. In the private state apartments where Princess Sophia and Lady Margaret resided, the tension was rife. Sophia refused to even walk in the halls if Lady Margaret was in the vicinity. Meanwhile, Lady Margaret did everything she could to see Robert, although Sophia stuck by his side as if nothing had happened. Yet for some reason, Margaret didn't trust Sophia. Her cousin was cruel, but in the last few days, she was remarkably controlled. The last time they'd spoken was at Cassandra's tea party, but Margaret kept herself on her guard because she could only speculate as to what surprise Sophia was cooking up.

The King sat in his official office at Andover Palace with a wide grin on his face. In the next twenty-four hours, Count Matthew Hall was scheduled to return to the Kingdom of Andover. While the Count was flying from Amsterdam on a private jet, it wasn't the regal jet. On the advice of his advisors, King Michael decided to save that extravagance for after their wedding, which was only seven short months away. Before the wedding, Count Matthew would stay at his parents' mansion in Kemp Forest. This way, they could still see each other every day, but Matthew would be able to keep his profile low until the wedding. The wedding, Michael thought to himself. He hadn't been this excited in years and he couldn't wait for his dream to come true.

"Your Majesty, His Regal Highness The Prince of Kemp requests an audience with you," Glenn announced.

Prince Alexander made his way into his father's lush office. Since becoming the King of Andover, this office was where Michael spent the majority of his day. Alexander loved this office, and he couldn't wait to make it his own. "Father, how are you?"

"Very well, Alexander. Would you like a drink?"

Michael poured two tumblers of amaretto.

Although Alexander hated the liquor, he drank it dutifully. "I came here today because I have a proposition for you."

"Go on," the monarch said as he sat behind his desk.

"I know you'll be very busy in the next few months planning your wedding," he choked. "I thought that as heir to the throne, I could be of service. What if I were to assume some of your duties until after the wedding?"

Michael couldn't believe what he was hearing. There sat his eldest child, the heir to the throne, and he just offered to install himself as the King of Andover. Over the last eight years, Michael had seen Alexander's naked ambition. But in this moment, he knew that the prince had gone too far. If Michael had ever said something to that effect when his mother was Queen, he wouldn't have survived the initial conversation. Biting his lip, Michael replied, "That won't be necessary."

"It makes sense…"

"Alexander, I have the entire regal household at my disposal. They will plan the wedding."

Alexander placed the crystal tumbler onto the oak table. "Dad, you and I both know that a wedding can consume people. Why don't you let me help?"

"If you want to help, you can help the chef with menu. As for my duties, I am more than capable of performing them without assistance," Michael snapped.

The Prince of Kemp stood with fury. "I don't even know why I try with you. All you ever do is belittle me to the point of ridicule! Why do you always push me away?"

"Son, calm down. I will not stand for your melodramatic antics."

"Then let me help."

The King carefully eyed his son. Ever since Alexander's birthday, Michael assumed that he and his son were growing closer. However, he should have realized that Alexander was probably planning a corporate coup to assume his position as the King of Andover. "Alexander, you have more than enough duties to keep you busy. If you'd devote more time to those than trying to unseat me, you'd be much happier."

"Unseat you? That's not what I'm doing," replied Alexander.

"Then what are you doing, Alex? Be honest with me."

The Prince of Kemp rolled his eyes with frustration. "Do you ever stop to realize how hard it is to be your son? I mean, really? It's not easy, Dad. There are times when I feel that you'd want nothing more than to get rid of me."

The King of Andover was shocked to hear what his son's accusation. Everything Michael had done over the past thirty-one years had been for country, crown, and his children. To hear this from his eldest child was a literal slap in the face. "I'm sorry you feel that way…"

"Are you? When you ascended the throne, you, Helena, and Joseph moved into the palace and I was left to fend for myself at Kemp Castle! How do you think that made me feel?"

Michael seized his son by his shoulders. "You are acting like a petulant child. You are fully aware of how this family works. When your grandmother was the Queen, I lived in Kemp Castle for twenty-eight years and when she was my grandfather's heir to the throne, I was raised there. Do you think your argument makes you special? I've been there, Alex. I know how you feel…"

The Prince of Kemp walked away from his father. "No you don't. When I was growing up there, it was wonderful. But when you moved into the palace, it was as if you placed me in exile."

“Then what do you want? Shall I come to the castle more often? Tell me what you want, Alexander.”

“Forget it, Dad; I’m sorry I came.” And with that, Alexander left his father thoroughly confused.

“It is with our profound wishes that we open the newly renovated Princess Fiona Aquatic Center,” Princess Sophia smiled.

With Lord Walter’s assistance, they cut a large blue ribbon. Photographers snapped their picture as reporters stood by with their microphones.

“Some day,” Lord Walter said to Princess Sophia.

“It is,” she said. Today, the princess was in an unusually good mood. Ever since she’d climbed out of bed, she felt as if anything was possible. Even though these sort of regal events didn’t thrill her, she was delighted to see that the turn out was quite large. “What are you doing for lunch,” Sophia asked.

“I’ll probably have lunch at Blake Manor. Would you like to join me? The chef is to prepare a delicious quail and pheasant meal.”

Sophia let out a small smile. “That sounds lovely, Walter. Thank you.”

“Your Regal Highnesses, may we have a picture,” asked a waiting photographer.

After five minutes of pictures, Sophia turned to her cousin. “I’ll have my driver drop me off around two?”

“That’ll do. Do you think Prince Robert would like to join us?”

“No,” she replied quickly. “He’s with his father today. Hider insisted that they have a father son day. Walter, may I ask you something?”

“Sure.”

“Well,” Princess Sophia said in a low voice, “why don’t you live at the palace?”

"I like my privacy," he replied, seriously. "Living in the palace can be stifling. Why?"

"I just wanted to know… Is that why you barely came to Port Agnes House this summer?"

Walter nodded. "Partly, but I needed to make sure Maggie was all right."

"I see."

After studying the princess for a moment, he said, "Are you all right?"

"Yes," she stated emphatically.

"Excuse me, Your Regal Highnesses. Sir," Jasper said to Walter, "someone would like to have a word with you."

Walter excused himself as he walked towards Daisy. He was aware that she would come to this event. It was the first time since her run-in with Princess Sophia that Daisy had been seen in public with the lord. By Walter's estimation, it was too long. And, he reasoned, maybe it was time for him to buck regal tradition and follow his heart.

"Your Regal Highness." Daisy performed the requisite curtsy.

Jasper took a step back.

"Miss Herman, you look ravishing," Walter said.

"Thank you. Guess what? I have a surprise for you."

Walter was impressed. "Surprising a member of the regal family, Miss Herman? Will I need my security detail in place?"

"No," she said, wistfully. "I'll be by tonight."

With that, Daisy drove off away in her Toyota Prius.

From her vantage point, Princess Sophia could see the entire exchange and she instantly recognized that woman. Although she hadn't made a big deal about it at Port Agnes House, Sophia was suspicious about this woman's motives.

Was she a spy or was she in love with Lord Walter? Sophia wanted to know who this woman was, but she didn't want to seem like a middle aged busybody. Granted, she did care about Walter and seeing him unhappy was the last thing she wanted. After all, her own marriage was still in tatters even though she tried to keep up appearances. Unable to resist the chance to interfere, Sophia had her secretary fetch Jasper.

"Yes, Your Regal Highness," he said with a bow.

"Jasper, who was that woman with Lord Walter?"

"Her name is Miss Daisy Herman."

Sophia chewed on this piece of information. "Just 'Miss'? She's not a first or second peer?"

"Not that I'm aware of."

"Is she a danisi or a countess?"

"I wouldn't know, Ma'am."

Sophia thanked Jasper for his help. She made her way towards her waiting car. Walter stood nearby, talking with the executive director of the Princess Fiona Aquatic Center. "Your Regal Highness, may I have a moment," she asked.

"What is it?"

"Who was that woman?"

"I'm not doing this here," he replied quickly.

Sophia followed him to his car. "Walter…"

"Will you stop," he whispered. "Just leave it alone."

With that, Sophia watched the car drive away. Although she knew that she shouldn't meddle, but she simply couldn't help herself.

"I can't believe you did that." Hider Lawson cleaned his glasses with a silk handkerchief. Although he was seventy-eight, he still had a flair for life.

Prince Robert sat across from his father in the study of his house near Kemp Castle. This ten room country house was where Robert was raised, but he rarely visited his father these days. Despite that, they were still close. Much of Robert's time was spent performing regal duties on behalf of the King, but when he did get the chance he spent time with his father.

"Dad," Robert muttered, "it's over."

"But you slept with your wife's cousin? Robert, I didn't raise you to do things like that. Yes, I understand that as a man you have needs, but to act in such a careless manner? What if Lady Margaret gave birth to the child?" Hider swallowed a spoonful of his turkey soup.

Robert moved the food on his plate. "The whole damn thing is over now..."

"And what about Princess Sophia?"

"The princess acts as if nothing has happened."

Hider knew that this was a terrible sign. "Has she told the King?"

Robert crossed his arms. "The King knows everything. But my wife barely speaks to me."

"Can you blame her," Hider interjected. "You're lucky they haven't started divorce proceedings."

Robert leaned back in his chair. "Look, I don't need a lecture. I'm very aware of the brevity of the situation. I messed up."

"Be careful, Robert. Those people aren't like other people. They live by their own code of ethics."

"They're not that bad, Dad."

Hider leaned closer to his son. "Get on their good side. Do whatever you have to do, but fix this situation."

"I will," Robert stated. "Anyway, let's talk about something else, shall we? How's business?"

"Mother, I can't stay long because Walter's expecting me at Blake Manor for lunch. Do you have the book?"

Cassandra opened the worn copy of *The Andover Peer Review* that lay on her desk. "Herman, you say? Well, let's see. Now, I don't know anyone with that last name, but that doesn't mean that they aren't important, Sophia." Cassandra turned the heavy pages with great care. Once she reached the H's, her face fell. "I'm sorry, dear. There are no Herman's in *The Andover Peer Review.*"

"I knew it," Sophia crowed triumphantly. "When will he learn?"

"Who's that, dear?" Cassandra took a long sip of her personal drink. "When will who learn?"

Sophia let out an exasperated sigh. She sank into the damask chair in her mother's private study within the confines of her private suite. "Walter. I don't know why he's so attracted to painfully common women."

Cassandra sniffed. "Princess Fiona, may she rest in peace, always said the same thing. We always worried about Walter's taste in women. Granted, when he lived in New York and dated those women, it was deemed merely acceptable since he wasn't in the kingdom and he was out of the regal glare. However, now… Let's just say that he should behave in an appropriate manner."

"I don't understand what's wrong with the men in this family. Michael's marrying a man, Joseph has a thing for vapid models, Walter loves those common women, and my husband can't keep his dick in his pants."

"Sophia," exclaimed the former monarch. She nearly choked on her drink, which made her cough for dear life. "I've never heard you speak in such a way! You are a princess!"

Sophia glared at her mother. "I know that, Mother." The princess let out a frustrated groan. “I’m so tired of… Never mind.”

“Sophia, talk to me.”

“I’ll be late for lunch.”

“Darling…”

“Mother, I don’t have time. These past few months have been very trying for me. To be honest, I wouldn’t mind flying to some country where no one knows me and they didn’t want to know me.” Sophia picked up her Tory Burch hand bag. “Goodbye.”

Cassandra watched as her daughter stormed out of her suite. It was true that Sophia had been through a lot in the last few months, but they rarely spoke of such matters. To Cassandra, talking about one’s personal life was a sign of weakness, which is why she was so hard on the Princess of Kemp. It was unacceptable to be so open with one’s feelings, Cassandra stated to herself. However, in that moment, she wanted nothing more than for her daughter to open up to her for the first time in her life.

“I can’t believe him,” Alexander said. He threw his knife and fork down in a fit of rage. No matter what he tried to do, his father continually pushed him away. Well, Alexander thought, enough is enough!

The Princess of Kemp sighed to herself as she ate her Andover salad. She’d heard all about Alexander’s failed attempt to help his father and, quite frankly, she was sick of listening to him. “Alex, you know why he said what he said.”

He shot his wife a terse look. “Are you on his side?”

“No,” she shot back. “Leave him alone. He’s a busy man.”

Alexander instructed the butler to clear his plate. “Another scotch, Ben. Why do people always make excuses for him? No one ever gives me a second thought.”

Olivia sipped her iced tea. "That's not true. Everyone loves your father; the kingdom has been a great place to live since he's been the monarch. Alexander, you have to start being reasonable."

"Are you finished," he asked. "Did you get the results of that pregnancy test?"

She demurred. "They were negative."

"Why would I expect anything else," he spat.

"What's wrong with you," asked the princess.

He sucked his teeth. "Everything. My father hates me and my own wife can't even get pregnant. I knew my father should've made you take a fertility test before the wedding."

Olivia recoiled in shock. This was news to her. There was never a time during her engagement to the Prince of Kemp when she was asked about her ability to have children. The fact that she and Alexander hadn't had sex until a few weeks ago was a source of quiet comfort for Olivia. Thankfully, they'd managed to pass that hurdle. Olivia assumed that the reason they couldn't get pregnant could be her fault or her husband's. But now that her husband blamed their fertility issues on her, she was livid. And to think that the regal family even discussed subjecting her to a fertility test made her skin crawl. "Are you serious," she cried. "A test?"

"Oh, get over it. It's standard procedure," Alexander groaned.

"Couldn't it be your issue?" challenged Olivia.

The look her husband shot her was death defying. "How dare you speak to me like that? I am His Regal Highness The Prince of Kemp, son of His Majestic Regal Highness The King, grandson of Her Regal Highness The Dowager Queen, and the great-grandson of King Henrik."

Olivia couldn't stop the tears from flowing. "That doesn't absolve you from something that may be your fault!"

"This conversation is over!"

"Far from it! We've just started making love because you couldn't perform sexually. I've been willing and able," she seethed.

"Go to hell, Olivia."

"What's gotten into you? You have been all over the place lately. I can't continue to worry about your mood just because you're ego is so damn fragile." She took a deep breath as she stared into her husband's eyes. "If you've ever loved me, please stop this right now."

Alexander averted her gaze. The only thing he felt at this moment was hatred for everyone; even his wife. "Maybe this just isn't working," he moaned. "Maybe we are too young and too self involved to make this marriage work. I don't know anymore…"

"How can you say that?" Olivia's heart was pounding. After everything they'd gone through since their wedding, she couldn't imagine giving up this life or this man. "Alex, I love you."

"But you think I don't love you," he spat.

Olivia bit the inside of her cheek. "I don't know," she replied honestly. "The signals are terribly confusing."

The Prince of Kemp shook his head. Had the last year of his life been a sham? Or were external factors influencing their relationship? He could vividly remember the day they fell in love. Unlike most love stories, it happened on a cold March day. He was waiting for his driver, and she was waiting for her taxi. They had known each other for years, but seeing her in such good spirits while standing in the wet winter weather reassured the prince. In that single moment, he knew that Olivia was a woman who could deal with any situation.

But this was different. Their marriage had been mostly smoke and mirrors. To the outside world, they were the pinnacle of a happily married couple. And while they had many happy times, the bad times always erased the memories of those days of laughter. The prince walked towards his wife. He placed a firm hand on her trembling shoulder. "I do love you," he sighed. "You know that."

"Then why is it so hard," she asked. In the past few months, Olivia had no idea whether or not she and Alexander would survive. She loved him more than anything, but the idea of losing this wonderful life she'd managed to obtain was more than she could bear. "Can we start again?"

"We should try. But first things first: We need to produce an heir. Once you have our first child, everything will be fine. Then we can focus on the bigger picture."

Olivia gave her husband a quizzical look. This was the side of Alexander that worried her. He would become very introspective and secretive, but he would never reveal the true nature of his plans. "What does that mean," she asked, tentatively.

Without a word, he planted a passionate kiss on her mouth. And, there in the study, they made love on the oak floor.

Princess Sophia's lunch with Lord Walter ended sometime before four o'clock in the afternoon. Sophia decided to walk through the woods of the estate, while Walter attended to business in his office. Upon her return to the manor, Sophia spied that same woman from Port Agnes House and earlier today in the foyer with Lord Walter. The princess instructed the household staff to ignore her obvious invasion of privacy, as she listened in the shadows.

"But Wally," Daisy whined, "why can't you bring me?"

"Because it's a regal event and it won't be right in the eyes of my family. Also, the King doesn't know about our relationship…"

"Still? Wally, when are you going to tell him? I love you. Don't you love me," she whispered.

Walter kissed her forehead. "Of course I do. However, one must be aware that one cannot simply make grand gestures at regal receptions without clearing them with the right people."

Daisy placed her hands on her supple hips. "Then when will you tell the King?"

"In due time."

"You said that before, Wally! I won't wait around forever."

"Your Regal Highness," Jasper called. "His Regal Highness Prince Joseph's office is on the line for you."

"I'll be right there. Daisy, I must take this call. Will you wait here?"

Daisy watched as Walter bounded down the corridor.

"I never thought I'd see you again," stated Sophia. She came around the corner with an imperious stance. "What are you doing here?"

"I… Your Regal Highness…" Daisy managed a weak curtsy. "If you'll excuse me."

Princess Sophia approached the young woman. "Are you going so soon, Miss Herman? His Regal Highness asked you to wait. Surely you wouldn't go against the wishes of a regal family member, would you?"

"I don't want to cause any trouble," Daisy replied quietly.

"I couldn't have guessed that. Why else would you have asked Lord Walter to take you to a regal reception? It seems to me that you want nothing more than to isolate him from the rest of his family." Sophia cast an evil eye towards Daisy as she said, "I'm sure he will have no use for you in a few days. To be honest, I'm surprised it's lasted this long."

"Ma'am, I don't mean to be rude, but this doesn't concern you!"

"Oh, it does. When it involves you carrying on with a regal family member in a regal residence, it more than concerns me. Let's not even mention the fact that this would be considered social suicide for you if someone found out."

Daisy crossed her arms. "I'm not afraid of you. I love him."

"Yes," sniffed Sophia. "I'm sure you do. However, Lord Walter does this sort of thing quite often. You may think that you're special, but nothing could be further from the truth. After a while, he'll move onto someone else."

"That's not true," Daisy huffed.

"Do you really think Lord Walter would give up Blake Manor, his Regal Expenditure payments of three million dollars per annum, and the many entitlements of regal life for you? You have no breeding or social standing of note." Princess Sophia let out a small laugh. "And to think he'd mention this trite relationship to the King? You may not be the right sort, but I doubt you're *that* inept."

Walter returned to the foyer to find his cousin towering over Daisy. He instantly moved between them. "What's going on here?"

Unable to speak through the lump in her throat, Daisy ran out of the house.

Sophia stopped her cousin from running after her. "Let her go," suggested Sophia.

"What did you say to her," he yelled. The staff walking through the corridor quickly dispersed. "I'm speaking to you, Sophia."

The Princess Sophia waved away his concerns. "Walter, I did you a favor. That woman is no good for you. For one thing, she's painfully common!"

"This has no bearing on you," he said through gritted teeth. "You have no right to dictate who I can and cannot see."

"Get over it, Walter. We all know this is your pattern. Besides, even if you did fall in love with her, you couldn't marry her. And if you can't get married, what's the point?"

Walter shook his head. Sophia's flip statement was shocking at best. "How can you say that? Your own marriage is barely viable."

Sophia felt as if she'd been knocked over. In the weeks following Lady Margaret's accident, many people speculated over the true nature of the event, but no one had ever spoken to her like this. "Leave my marriage out of this," she said softly.

"I will not. You did everything right: You perform your regal duties in service to crown and country; you married the dashing, wealthy young man from the right sort of aristocratic family; and you put forth delusions of happiness. But then he cheats on you for God knows how long with your own cousin! And to top it all off, it happened right in front of you! Tell me how can you be so self-righteous about the sanctity of marriage when your own husband threw it out of the window?"

Princess Sophia did her best to hold back her emotions. In that one moment, Walter had summarized her entire existence over the last twenty-one years. She didn't feel any malice towards her cousin. What she felt standing there in the hunter green foyer of Blake Manor was sadness over the fact that her husband had deceived her and she had yet to face that heartbreaking fact. However, in that same moment, she knew what she had to do next. After thanking Lord Walter for his hospitality, she was driven back to Andover Palace.

Lord Walter spent the rest of that day calling Daisy, to no avail. Maybe Sophia was right, he thought. Walter always knew that he would never give up his regal entitlements, no matter how wonderful the women seemed to be. But Daisy was different, he told himself. As the day turned into night, he decided that maybe it was time to be honest with the rest of the world, including his family. Walter ordered Jasper to arrange a meeting with the King for sometime next week. It's time, Walter reasoned in the loneliness of his bedroom.

"Dad? Are you busy," asked Joseph.

"Not at all," Michael replied. "Come in."

Prince Joseph closed the door to his father's private suite with great care.

He rarely disturbed his father at this time of night, but the prince felt he needed to speak with him. During his European tour, Joseph began to re-evaluate the state of his life. In the last year he'd graduated from the International University of Monaco, danced the night away to the delight of the Andover press and the horror of the regal family, and been the most visible face of the kingdom abroad. Yet, in the last few months, the prodigal prince had changed. Maybe it was due to the fact that he was responsible for Samuel's wellbeing for so long. Whatever the reason was, Joseph knew that he had to speak with his father in order to come to terms with the brevity of his new decision.

"What's on your mind, Joseph?" The King poured a glass of cognac for his son. "Is everything all right?"

"I think so. I'm sorry I missed the summer at Port Agnes House."

"It may have been best that you were away with Samuel." Michael still wished that many of the truths that were revealed this past summer were never revealed. "I'm sure your grandmother will tell you every sorted detail."

Joseph placed his tumbler on his knee. "I don't want to know," he laughed. "Besides, there's something I want to tell you."

"Yes?"

"While I was on the regal tour with Sam, I began to think about the state of my life. I love you and the whole family, but just being a prince isn't that fulfilling. I wouldn't give it up for anything, but shaking hands and cutting ribbons can only be interesting for so long."

Michael eyed his son carefully. Of his three children, Prince Joseph was the one who always spoke his mind and connected with people. Michael knew that this was a skill Joseph acquired from Katherine. "Go on."

Joseph sighed. "The thing is, everyone seems to have something here. Alex is next in line for the throne, he has Olivia and he manages the Kemp Castle estate. You have the whole kingdom and Matthew. Everyone in this family has something, even Helena! She has Derek. But I just feel like I'm flitting around in the wind. Do you understand," asked the prince.

The King gave his son a knowing smile. "I do. But it's natural. Once you find your place in Andover, you'll be much more content. You can't be so hard on yourself, Joseph. You've just graduated from university. Maybe you'll meet someone soon or find your calling… Once you do, life will change."

Joseph sat on the arm of his father's chair. The smell of his father's slightly musky cologne reminded him of life in Kemp Castle, which seemed to be a million midnights ago. "I know what I want to do, Dad." The prince took a moment before saying, "I want to join the armed services."

The King couldn't believe what he'd just heard. Prince Joseph never showed an interest in anything beyond the next good time. Joining the armed services would be a big blow to the life his son was accustomed to. "Are you sure this is what you want," asked Michael.

Joseph shook his head firmly. "Dad, I need some point to my life. Being the errant prince is only fun for a few months. Anyway, I've been back in the kingdom for over a year and I haven't done anything important."

"Son, if you need to prove yourself, there are other ways. You have the polo team…"

"Dad, you know what I mean. Being a champion polo player isn't the most important aspect of my life. I really want to join the armed services, Dad. Alex did it; so did Walter. It's only six months of my life," pleaded the prince.

Michael couldn't deny the passion in this Joseph's words. Unlike Alexander, Michael always worried that Joseph would turn into a drunk or womanizer because of his apparent lack of direction. But now, his son was taking the initiative to change his life and Michael was very proud. "Joseph, if this is what you want, we can meet with Patricia Ali, Lieutenant Major Huckley, and the Head of Andover's Armed Services, Matt Parsons. They will be the best people to guide you through the process." Michael leaned into his son. "Is this what you really want?"

"Yes," he replied emphatically.

"Good. Then we'll sort it out."

Joseph gave his father a hug. "Thanks, Dad. So, when's Matthew coming?"

11

The Great Scandal erupted the day before the King's Reception. This event was the highlight of the autumn calendar because ten men and ten women from the kingdom would be given peerage titles of first or second peer or Dane or Danisi, which would allow them to enter the vaulted world of Andover's aristocracy. It also meant that they would be eligible to marry a regal family member. Although the King selected the men for this honor through his own private process, the Dowager Queen's summer tea party was her vetting process for the King. This process was not taken lightly by anyone within the kingdom. A title from the King was worth its weight in gold in any situation. It also meant that the regal family thought you were good enough to be in their presence.

No one actually saw the Great Scandal erupt. In hindsight, it simply happened. There was no warning from the press. The palace seemed wholly surprised by the item when the morning papers were delivered to the regal family. Had anyone been aware of the item, someone may have been able to perform damage control. However, like so many great moments in history, no one realized the true brevity of the situation until the damage was complete. The story read:

A REGAL SCANDAL!

By Gavin Shaw Martinez, Editor in Chief

> *A source from within Andover Palace has revealed a shocking truth! Our reliable source from within the regal household has told us that Her Regal Highness Lady Margaret of Andover's riding accident resulted in the loss of an unborn child.*
>
> *The palace swiftly locked down the regal family's summer residence, Port Agnes House, after the incident, citing Lady Margaret's privacy. Yet our source has told us that Port Agnes House was locked down*

because of Lady Margaret's miscarriage. The daughter of the late Princess Fiona and cousin of the King was allegedly three months pregnant. Simple math reveals that the child was not her husband's, His Highness Edward of Andover, as he was in the Sahara Desert at the time!

One must wonder how the regal family could keep such an explosive secret! The values they allegedly put forth each and every day are only sullied by this indiscretion on the part of Lady Margaret. Her wild antics have graced the page of this paper before, but this is the most shocking thing she has ever done!

Who is the father of this child? Will he ever come forward? Will Lady Margaret and her husband recover from this, the ultimate deception?

Andover Palace has yet to comment on this breaking story.

The Sentinel will have the details as they become available.

If you have any information, please e-mail me:
gmshaw@sentinel.ad

"I want whoever is responsible for this piece of salacious gossip brought before me this instant," exploded King Michael. His face was filled with rage. Despite his carefully crafted regal image, in this moment, everything he'd spent a lifetime creating seemed to slip away.

The news of Lady Margaret's accident was enough to tear apart his family. The King also realized that the entire kingdom could come after him. After all, he was an unelected official. However, when news of a scandal of this sort came to light, it was impossible to ignore the repercussions. The King hadn't seen the regal family as of yet, but they were all ordered to an emergency meeting in his private suite. He was even flying in the Prince and Princess of Kemp on the regal helicopter due to the enormity of the situation.

The King turned to the Head of Household for Andover Palace, Marcy Hawke. "I want every member of staff interviewed by the Andover Secret Police, you, and Glenn. I want each statement signed and delivered to me. Until everyone is dealt with, no one leaves the palace. Is that understood?"

Marcy's voice quivered. "Yes, Your Majesty. I can assure you that we will find the responsible party…"

"Just do it," snapped the monarch.

Glenn ushered Marcy out of the office, before returning. "Is there anything I can do, Your Majesty?"

The King shook his head. Michael spent his entire life in duty to the kingdom and scandal had never followed him. Margaret's antics had always been a cause of concern for his mother's generation, but he simply thought his cousin was trying to find love under every man she could find. He knew he would have to deal with her.

"Get that editor of *The Sentinel* on the phone. Now," growled the King.

"This is Gavin," the cocksure editor said moments later.

"This is His Majesty The King."

Gavin choked on his apple. "Your Majesty… I didn't expect to hear from you."

The King grimaced at his cavalier tone. "Who gave you that ridiculous story?"

"Ridiculous?" Gavin laughed. "You wouldn't be speaking to me if that story were so ridiculous, now would you?"

“I am ordering you to give me the name of the responsible party, Mr. Shaw.”

Gavin blanched. “No can do, Your Majesty. It was an anonymous tip from someone employed by the regal household. Guess there’s a rat in the palace,” he laughed.

The King slammed down the phone. He had to get to the bottom of this. Margaret’s accident was very close to being forgotten. But there were two marriages at stake. Michael sat behind the chair in his private study. He placed his head in his hands as he tried to come to terms with this untimely incident. A second later, his iPhone jolted him back to reality. It was Matthew. “I can’t talk.”

“I figured as much. I just heard. I’m sorry.”

“Thanks, Matthew. What are the people saying?”

Matthew sighed. “I don’t know. I haven’t been outside and I had my parents turn off the news.”

“I’ve ordered every television and radio to be seized within the palace.” Michael let out a primal grunt. “Why is this happening?”

“I don’t know, Mike. Just remember that I love you. I’ll see you tomorrow.”

“I love you, Matthew. Goodbye.”

“Your Majesty,” interrupted Glenn. “Their Regal Highnesses are here.”

The regal family walked into Michael’s private study. Although the room was the size of a three bedroom apartment in the best part of Andover, it still felt small to the regal family. Princess Sophia sat as close to Michael and Cassandra as she could, while Lady Margaret stood near the door. The tension in the room was palpable as Michael thought of what he should say next.

“Words cannot express how ashamed I am at this very moment. I have never asked a lot from any of you. My mother and grandfather were Andover’s monarchs, so I’m very aware of the limitations placed on every aspect of your private lives. I am not blind to the scrutiny and intrusion that is a daily part of regal life. In my eight years as the King of Andover, I have never once asked any of you to go above and beyond the call of duty. To be repaid in this manner is abhorrent. We are now all aware of the true reason behind Lady Margaret's accident. As unfortunate as it is, it does not excuse this leak," King Michael stated icily.

The Dowager Queen raised her bejeweled hand. "Dear, that atrocious story stated that it came from within the regal household. Surely the staff must be dealt with and disciplined!"

"They are being dealt with as we speak," Michael replied tactfully. "However, I do not believe that the story was leaked from a member of the staff."

Shock ran through the regal family. Could such a vicious story have made its way from one of them and to the desk of *The Sentinel*?

"That's preposterous," Cassandra exclaimed. "None of us would *do* such a thing! It violates everything that we stand for!"

The King glared at his mother. "Mother, the people in this room were the only ones to know what truly happened to Lady Margaret this summer. For someone to reveal that she was carrying a child that wasn't Edward's couldn't have come from a member of staff." His cold brown eyes scanned the room. "I think we all know that."

"Dad, this is ridiculous," the Prince of Kemp replied. "Why would anyone do that to Margaret?"

"I don't know." Michael lowered his voice. "But I will find the culprit." The King straightened his tie. "You all may go now," he said.

The regal family quietly left the King to his own devices.

As Michael stared out of the window of his study, he couldn't stop thinking about the source of this leak. If it had been from a member of the palace staff, surely it would have been quite obvious. However, if it were a member of the regal family, it would make his task much more complicated. Could it have been Edward or Robert? Or even Sophia. She hated Margaret more than anyone. Could she really be blamed for leaking the truth behind her husband's escapades to the press in order to ruin Margaret's reputation?

Michael let out a fierce scream. The secret was out. Now was the time for true damage control. At tomorrow's reception, he intended to play the part of Andover's monarch. It was truly a part to play and no scandal, whatever the size, would change that.

"How could you," screamed Prince Robert. "Of all of the manipulative things you've done, how could you do this?" He threw a sixteenth century vase to the floor of the lavish state apartment he shared with his wife. Rage filled his body in a way he'd never experienced before. He felt betrayed. Now the whole world knew he was the other man, but no one knew. His child was gone. Robert wondered if anyone would ever discover the truth, a scenario he found terrifying.

Princess Sophia stared at the shattered vase. In some ways, she thought, that vase represented her marriage. How could Robert think she could do such a thing? "I didn't even know the baby wasn't Edward's," she countered snidely.

"Come off it, Sophia! You knew…"

"I did not!" She clenched her fists until her hands went numb. "You never told me! She never told me! Michael never told me! Edward never told me! How was I supposed to know?"

Robert charged towards his wife. "Do you actually expect me to buy your ingénue routine? I know how much you hate Margaret…"

"I may hate that insipid shrew, but I did not tell the press. I may have wanted to, but I didn't! I wasn't raised like that. I know how to keep my feelings to myself," she screamed. "I didn't ask for any of this, Robert! If this is anyone's fault, it's yours!"

"Mine," he snapped. "I didn't leak that story."

"You didn't have to sleep with *my* cousin! Of all the women! How do you think that makes me feel? I have to see that woman every day walking around the palace like she owns the damn place. For years, I've had to listen to her tales of woe. Nothing is ever her fault. She finally finds Edward and then she cheats on him not once, but twice! Margaret isn't sane, Robert. But you just had to sleep with the one person in the world that I can't stand," the princess seethed breathlessly.

Prince Robert could feel his body tensing up. He knew he was equally culpable for what was transpiring, but in twenty-one years of marriage, he'd never heard his wife speak in such a way. "Sophia, I'm sorry…"

"Like hell," she sniffed.

"What do you want me to do? It's out now!" Robert threw his hands up in the air. "I'm sorry I screwed up!"

Princess Sophia pulled out a handkerchief with the regal crest from her pocket. Dabbing her eyes, she looked at her husband with fury. She'd never hated him before, but she wanted to see him dead. "You're right about that. How many people know that the child is yours, Robert?"

"Michael, the doctor, Margaret, and Edward."

She studied his well worn face. He was beginning to show his age, she thought ruefully. "Who else?"

"My father," muttered Robert.

Princess Sophia felt her stomach tie into a thousands knots. "Do you think your father would do…"

"No! My father has never uttered one word of what happens behind the palace walls to anyone," Robert stated adamantly. "He'd never hurt me."

Robert knelt at Sophia's feet. He kissed her soft hands.

Princess Sophia yanked her hands from his with disgust. "Don't touch me," she spat. "I can't be around you right now." She stormed down the corridor and into her bedroom suite where she remained for the rest of the day.

"Am I interrupting," Cassandra cooed. Lady Margaret and His Highness Edward's housekeeper left Cassandra in their spacious sitting room. Margaret was crying, as Edward rubbed her back. The atmosphere in the room was filled with sorrow and regret.

"Shall I go," asked Cassandra.

Edward shrugged. "Margaret?"

"I...don't care," she cried. "Why is this happening to me?"

Cassandra sat at the edge of a lilac sofa. "Darling, it's simply dreadful. I don't think anyone of us gave the story to the press. No, I think it may have been one of the staff," reasoned Cassandra. "They'd have the most to gain."

Margaret shot her aunt a cold look. "It was probably Sophia."

The Dowager Queen was taken aback. "The Princess Sophia? She'd never betray the confidence of the family..."

"She hates me," Margaret interjected. "She always has..."

"I don't think she'd do something like this," Edward said.

"He's right." Cassandra twisted the diamond watch on her wrist. "Listen to me, Margaret. There's no use crying about this."

Margaret looked at Cassandra with shocked, blood shot eyes. "How can you say that?"

"Listen to me," Cassandra demanded. "The story is a rumor right now. The palace hasn't confirmed anything. As far as the public knows, you've had a riding accident; that's all."

Lady Margaret dried her tears. She sat up and looked at her aunt with great interest. In Margaret's mind, Cassandra was a daft old woman with too much money and power, but this was the side of her aunt she rarely saw: the operator.

"I know the King will issue a statement revealing that the story is false. Tomorrow, you will make an appearance at the reception. You will smile, wave, and be the life of the party. Edward, be sure to support her. The only people who will ever know what truly happened will never say anything. Deny the story if anyone ever asks." The Dowager Queen clasped her niece's hand. "My dear, don't make this an issue. Simply let it go."

The King's children sat in Prince Joseph's private suite at Andover Palace. In all of their years as the monarch's children, they'd never seen something so shocking. Michael was very good at keeping the exploits of the regal family at bay, but everything seemed to be out of his hands.

"I should've known Margaret would be the weak link," Alexander huffed.

Prince Joseph stretched out on his king sized bed. "Well, I feel bad for Sam. Can you imagine what people will say about his mother?"

"She should've kept her legs closed," Alexander replied callously.

"You're such a pig!" Helena couldn't believe her brother. "Alex, it happened. Let's be glad that it's over."

"Well," added Joseph, "Dad's regally pissed. I'm glad I won't be around to see how that plays out."

Alexander let out an exasperated sigh. "Don't tell me you're jetting off to Europe again."

Prince Joseph sat up. "No. Actually, nothing's definite yet, but Dad and I are having a meeting in a few days to discuss it."

"What," Helena inquired.

"I'm going to join the armed services for a few months."

The Prince of Kemp gave his brother a tight hug. "I'm so proud of you for finally getting your life together."

"I figured it was time," Prince Joseph replied wryly.

"Be careful, Joey! I need you," joked Helena. "It'll be weird knowing that you're here but not."

Joseph was delighted by his sibling's reactions. "It's only for six months. I bet you won't even miss me."

"I guess we'll have to see," Alexander retorted dryly.

For Immediate Release by Order of His Majesty The King

From the Office of His Majesty The King's Personal Secretary

Andover Palace, Christoph Road, Old Andover, Andover, 2819OA

> *In response to the story printed in today's Sentinel, Andover Palace has issued this statement.*
>
> *Her Regal Highness Lady Margaret of Andover suffered a terrible riding accident this summer from which she has fully recovered. Furthermore, she was not expecting a child at the time.*

With regards,
Andover Palace

12

The day after the Great Scandal, the palace flew into action for the King's Reception. Preparations were under way as if nothing had happened, which is precisely what the regal family demanded. Despite the onslaught of media attention raised by the article in *The Sentinel*, the palace's press release was enough to stop the story. Many of those opposed to the monarchy wanted nothing more than to keep the incident alive for two reasons: to show how corrupt the regal family was, and to show that they would do anything to manipulate the truth. However, the mainstream press deemed the story a fabrication by *The Sentinel*, which was more than enough to satisfy the King.

Although the true culprit of the leak remained a mystery, the Andover Secret Police deemed that no one within the regal household was responsible. As Michael had suspected all along, it seemed likely that someone within the regal family let something slip, thus causing the biggest scandal in the last five years. The King wanted whomever was responsible for this scandal to be brought forth, but on the advice of the Dowager Queen, he simply let it go. However, he knew within his heart that he'd been betrayed. Now, more than ever, he intended to expose the traitor within his midst.

But today was a special day for the King. Today, Count Matthew Hall and his family would make their first official appearance at a regal reception since the announcement of their engagement. King Michael relished this opportunity to be publicly photographed with his new fiancé in a very public setting. As Michael prepared for the big night in the privacy of his suite, he felt happier than he had in a very long time.

Slap!

His Regal Highness Lord Walter rubbed his face. Daisy's hand left a sizable imprint, but the strength of her furious expression caught him by surprise.

"What on earth," he exclaimed.

"Why aren't you taking me, Wally," she cried.

Walter let out an aggravated sigh. He'd told her multiple times that he couldn't take her to this regal event. "Daisy, don't make this any harder than it already is."

"I've been more than patient!" She paced through his private sitting room at Blake Manor. "Ever since we've met I've put up with the rules of your life. But what about me," she wailed.

"Just… Please, stay here. I'll be back tonight…"

"You want me to stay here by myself while you mix it up with Andover's elite? How do you think that makes me feel," she countered.

Walter threw his hands into the air. "What do you want me to say? Damn it, you knew this was my life when you first met me! I'm a member of the regal family! I can't change that no matter what I do. There are certain duties one must perform…"

"Don't," she said, cutting him off. "I've heard this all before. You're a victim of circumstance…"

"In a manner of speaking," he replied sharply. "Did you think we would have a fairy tale ending?"

Daisy let out a high pitched scream. "I don't know! I don't even know how we ended up like this!" She sat on an old marble card table. "I've turned into one of those whiny women I read about in magazines. I'm not that woman, Wally."

Walter began to rub her tense shoulders. "I know… I know," he said calmly. "Will you wait for me? I promise, it'll get better."

"I don't believe you. Ever since Her Regal Highness Princess Bitchiness tore into me, you've been siding with her." Fire filled Daisy's eyes. "Why do those people matter more to you than I do?"

“They’re my family,” shouted Walter. “Damn it, Daisy! I can’t give up my entire life for someone I met a few months ago. Look around you! My entire life is in the walls of this house. My family’s been very good to me. Granted, there are many rules and traditions that I’d rather not adhere to, but I understand why they’re in place. And if you want us to work, you’ll have to understand those rules too.”

She rose from the table and stormed into the adjoining room. Daisy pulled on her trench coat and scarf in a mad rush.

“Stop,” sighed Lord Walter.

“You’ve had more than enough chances to tell the King about us. I deserve respect. Goodbye, Wally.”

Walter tried to stop her, but she raced by him, and down the halls of Blake Manor. He ran after her, but by the time he reached the foyer, she was gone. Rage filled the lord’s body as he watched her drive away. She’ll be back, Walter told himself.

He returned to his bedroom to prepare for the reception. However, something in the back of his mind told him that the only woman he’d ever loved was gone forever.

The regal family sat in the Crimson Room before entering the Throne Room where the King’s Annual Reception was to be held. Outside of official events, the Throne Room was rarely used. Its purpose was still as important as it had been many years ago, however tradition tended to fade over the years, in spite of those who tried to preserve it.

Princess Helena glanced at herself in the mirror of the Crimson Room with great admiration. Whether it was a psychological or physical need, the princess couldn’t live without her new eating regime. Luckily for Princess Helena, the drama surrounding Lady Margaret for the last few months was enough of a distraction for the press; they barely noticed that the princess was alive. If only they'd paid this much attention to me before, Helena thought ruefully.

"Is that Mother's tiara," Prince Alexander asked his sister.

She gave him an apathetic glance. "I think so. Oh, Alex, isn't it wonderful? I just love these nights in the palace. Don't you?"

"You're in a good mood," he replied with a raised eyebrow. "Are you high?"

"Oh, please. I have never done that!" Princess Helena turned her gaze to the mirror. "I just think life is wonderful right now."

Prince Alexander couldn't believe what he was hearing. His sister was always ready to quip about something negative. It was his favorite thing about her! This positive mood made him wonder if he was going crazy. "How can you be so carefree in the middle of a scandal?"

"That?" Helena rolled her eyes. "I don't concern myself with such nonsense. Whatever goes on between Lady Margaret and Edward is none of my concern."

"Are you going to ignore me all night," Prince Robert asked his wife. He moved his bow tie in order to breath.

"No," Princess Sophia replied coolly. "Once we're in front of the public, I'll be the perfect wife."

Moments later, the regal family was ushered into the Throne Room. The twenty guests receiving peer titles were seated in the first two rows, while Andover's aristocracy filled the remaining eighty seats. Since the reign of King Henrik, one hundred guests were deemed the absolute maximum in this exclusive room.

The King of Andover was the last to enter. Everyone stood with a low bow as he made his way onto his throne. With his monarchical adornments in hand, he began the solemn ceremony of welcoming twenty new peers into Andover's polite society. Among the recipients were Derek Sharpe, a member of

Prince Joseph's polo team and Princess Helena's new love interest. Although they hadn't seen much of each other over the past few months due to Derek's enrollment in the armed services, the princess wanted to be with him more than ever. However, it was Prince Joseph who suggested that his father's bestow upon Derek the title of second peer in case things turned serious with Princess Helena. The King was never one to go against his own instincts, but he knew that this formality was harmless. If Derek and his daughter didn't work out, at least he was a member of the right set.

After the reception, the party retired to the State Dining Room for a lavish dinner, followed by dancing and drinks in the State Ballroom.

"Thank you, Daddy," Helena cooed.

The King turned to her with a smile. "Darling, you should thank Prince Joseph. It was his suggestion."

"Joey? Really?" The princess grabbed a glass of champagne from a passing waiter. "I didn't see that coming."

"Nor did I."

"Your Majesty," called Cassandra. "Darling, it was a moving reception! Don't you agree, Helena?"

Helena smiled. "Yes, Grandmother."

"Now, I was speaking with Mr. Sharpe and he seems quite taken with you. I think it stands to reason that I would have my reservations about you giving him a peerage title, Michael, but he's a nice young man. It's not his fault his mother married outside of her social world, but there's always one woman in a generation who feels the need to throw tradition on its head." Cassandra grimaced. "Why can't people simply accept the world for what it is?"

"How much have you had to drink," Michael whispered.

Cassandra let out a bubbly chortle. "Not nearly enough! If you'll excuse me, Countess Masoli is here with her daughter. I haven't seen them in ages!

Helena, you should meet them. Come along dear!" With that, Cassandra gently led the princess towards her waiting guests.

Michael put down his tumbler of amaretto when he saw Glenn approaching him with Mary Walsh, his late wife's sister. He'd instructed Glenn to have Mary brought to him as soon as dinner was over. "Your Majesty," Mary said with a great curtsy. "It's an honor."

"Thank you, Mrs. Walsh." Michael waited as Glenn took a respectable step back. "Where's Ted?"

"He's with Prince Joseph and the Princess of Kemp." Mary gave the King a small smile. "It was a lovely reception. I remember when your mother made me a peer. I don't know how it happened. But I think my sister's impending marriage to you had something to do with it," she recalled with a laugh.

The King nodded. "My mother has a way for making situations happen. I'm very glad you came, Mary. I wanted to speak to you before the wedding plans picked up. What do you think?"

Mary shook her head. "Honestly? I think it's time. You've been alone for long enough. Katherine would not have wanted you to be alone. Besides, we both know that she'd be elated."

"Mary, I wanted to tell you that Matthew and I never did anything…"

"I know," she interjected. "You loved her. Despite the circumstances surrounding your marriage to Katherine, I know you were faithful."

Michael studied her for a moment. "How do you know that?"

"Sometimes it's easy to see. I could always tell that you two were in love."

"Count Hall," called Michael as Matthew walked past them. "Have you met Mrs. Walsh? She's the late Princess Katherine's sister."

"How do you do," Count Matthew said.

"Very well," answered Mary. "I hope you and the King have all the happiness in the world. If you'll excuse me…"

Matthew watched with trepidation as Mary walked towards her husband, Ted. "Did I say something wrong," asked Matthew.

"Not at all, Matt," the monarch replied. "Mary's never been one for small talk. That's where she and Katherine differed. Are you and your parents having a nice time?"

Matthew beamed from ear to ear. "The best. I've never been to the reception ceremony before."

"That's because you were born into the titled class," joked Michael. "Yours comes with birth, not social contribution. Have my children made an effort to be civil?"

Matthew took a sip of his gin cocktail. "The Prince of Kemp has been civil at best. Princess Helena was cordial, but Prince Joseph has been very warm."

The King took this in before saying, "Prince Joseph is like his mother. The other two are their own people. Come, I want to introduce to the Minister of Government."

"You look terrible," muttered Lady Margaret.

Lord Walter finished off his drink. "I've had a long day."

"Well," she said in a low voice, "at least the entire kingdom isn't speculating about your personal life."

"Is your husband even talking to you," asked Walter.

"What do you think," she shot back. "My life is hell."

"No one told you to… Never mind, Maggie." Walter ordered the waiter to bring him another drink. He didn't want to argue with his sister in public, but he wasn't in the mood for one of her parties of sorrow, especially when she brought this upon herself. Unlike him, Margaret seemed to invite drama into her life.

Margaret stiffened at her brother's apparent lack of compassion. "Walter, don't turn on me. The King isn't speaking to me, Princess Sophia has ignored every overture from me, Prince Robert refuses to be in the same space as me, and my own husband looks at me with contempt. I need someone on my side."

"Maggie, what happened that day is a travesty. But what did you expect? Michael only has so much power," he whispered. Walter took his drink from the waiter as his mind drifted towards Daisy. In this moment, he wanted nothing more than to share it with her. He ordered Jasper to track her down, but it seemed that she didn't want to be found. Now, he might possibly have to wait an eternity to ever see her beautiful face again. "Look, you have everything. If you want to throw it away, it's on you."

"I can't believe you're saying this! I've always stood by you!" Lady Margaret could feel her face clench out of sheer fury. Her brother always tried to play the martyr, but she knew he was full of secrets. The only difference was, he knew how to clean up his messes, while hers always exploded in her face. "Walter, please..."

Walter avoided his sister's pathetic gaze. "If you need to stay at Blake Manor until this dies down, do it. You'll have all the privacy you need without the rest of the regal family glaring at you."

Margaret let out an exasperated gasp. "You want me to admit defeat? Walter," she seethed over the orchestra, "that's what they want. Just because we're Princess Fiona's children and not Aunt Cassandra's, they feel we should stay in Blake Manor and keep to ourselves! I will not leave the palace and let them win!"

Suddenly, everything seemed to make sense. Walter caught his breath as he took a step back. "Oh my god is that why you've done...everything..."

Margaret gave her brother a steely gaze. "Done what? I haven't done a thing," Margaret snapped before flouncing off towards the bar.

Walter watched his sister as she stormed off. He knew her all too well, which is why he always found it highly dubious when she cast herself in the role of the victim. Margaret, Walter knew, was a very smart, conniving woman who could hurt anyone – including herself – to get what she wanted. The story in yesterday's paper was most likely true, although Walter shuddered to think that Margaret had actually become pregnant with another man's child while Edward was in the Sahara Desert. However, the more he wanted to ignore the facts, the more it all made sense to him. She would do anything to prove to the Dowager Queen, the King, and Princess Sophia that she was just as good as them. If that meant going to extremes to prove her point, Walter knew that Margaret was more than capable of doing it. In that moment, Lord Walter began to suspect that Margaret was responsible for so many things, but the one thing he thought she was behind was too disgusting to even consider.

His Highness Edward left the reception for a few minutes to put His Regal Highness Samuel to bed. His son was full of questions because, as Edward suspected, he'd seen the newspaper reports from yesterday, even though the palace did everything they could to stop that occurring. The one thing no one considered was that Samuel had easy access to his parents' iPhones, which during the bedlam, were left unattended. Edward did his best to tell his son that the story was false, but he knew his son was too smart to believe that lie.

Once Samuel was asleep, Edward decided to take a walk near the palace lake. By the moonlight, the palace looked like a Gothic nightmare from the mind of a great nineteenth century novelist. During the last days of summer, just before autumn officially began, Edward thought that the palace grounds looked ideal. Growing up outside of the walls of Andover Palace, Edward had spent his life wondering what went on beyond the gates, but now that he knew, he longed for life on the other side. While life with Margaret had been one dramatic incident after another since he returned to the kingdom, his main focus was his son. Spiriting Samuel away from this place and its denizens was still in the forefront of his mind, but he still lacked a plan to carry out the plot.

Edward sat on the bank of the lake. The cool air made him feel at peace.

Above, a flock of night owls sang a song of yore. As soon as Edward closed his eyes, a familiar voice said, "Crap. I didn't know you were out here." Edward turned to see Prince Robert standing behind him with his hands in his pockets. Robert had one of the best media images of anyone in the regal family. Many said that he was as dashing as Cary Grant with the charm of John F. Kennedy. However, in this moment, Edward thought that he looked like a disheveled has-been.

Edward walked away from the lake. "It's all yours."

"Can we talk," asked Robert. The prince approached his mistress' husband with great trepidation. "Please."

Edward crossed his muscular arms. "What?"

Prince Robert searched the sky for the right thing to say. "I'm sorry," he stammered. "For everything."

"Is that supposed to make me feel better? Or, is it supposed to make you feel better," challenged Edward.

"Edward, I…"

"I really don't want to hear it, Rob. Your pithy excuse for an apology doesn't absolve you from what you and my wife have done." Edward clenched his fist to stop them from flying into Robert's perfectly formed nose.

"Look, I want us to be okay. I just want to put this behind us," Robert stated. Before all of this occurred, he and Edward had been reasonably close. Robert had asked himself many times why he'd even slept with Margaret, but at the time, it seemed like a great idea. Had he known the pain it would cause, he would have avoided her at all costs.

Edward couldn't believe what Robert was suggesting. Although he hadn't spoken to the prince since Margaret's accident, he knew he couldn't avoid him forever. The kingdom was only so big. "Robert, you're asking the impossible of me right now. My son just read that his mother was pregnant with another man's baby. How do you think he'd feel if he – and the rest of the kingdom – learned that Princess Sophia's husband has been sleeping with her cousin for the past year? How could you betray me for so long? I thought we were friends."

"We are! God, when you married Margaret I felt as if I finally had someone to connect with in this world." Robert tried to contain his rising emotions. "I never meant…"

"For me to find out," finished Edward. "I know. Rob, I'm not going to take the moral high ground, but you deceived me. I opened up to you about my issues with Margaret when all along you were sleeping with her. It's disgusting," snapped Edward.

Robert avoided Edward's gaze. "I don't know what else to say."

Edward laughed at the irony of Robert's words. "Then don't bother. If you'll excuse me, I have to return to the reception."

As Edward made his way towards the illuminated palace, Robert said, "For what it's worth, I think it's best the baby was lost. At least this way, we can all start anew."

"Some silver lining," muttered Edward. And with that, he returned to the regal celebration.

"It was a lovely reception, Michael," noted Cassandra. Bramble and Voltaire lay at her feet as she removed her mother of pearl necklace. "I do wonder what happened to Robert and Edward."

Michael leaned down to pat Voltaire on his head. The night had been a great success. All traces of yesterday's scandal were a distant memory. Even though Michael knew it was best to move on, he was very much aware that most people in the kingdom were still speculating about the veracity of the statement in yesterday's newspaper. "Mother, it's a non-issue."

"Well," began Cassandra, "I'm very curious to have the culprit exposed!"

“I think that little piece of filth has caused enough damage to the family for one lifetime. Don’t you?” Michael helped his mother remove her diamond ring. “Besides, we must focus on the plans for the wedding.”

“I wouldn’t seat Princess Sophia and Prince Robert anywhere near Lady Margaret and His Highness Edward.”

Michael shot his mother a terse glance. “Leave it alone, Mother. I want to invite the Halls to spend Christmas Eve with the entire family.”

Cassandra was puzzled by her son’s sudden show of generosity. In the years since becoming the King of Andover, Michael kept all family holidays between the immediate family members. “Darling, what do you mean?”

“The Halls will join us for lunch on Christmas Eve, as well as Prince Christian and Prince Erich’s descendants.” Michael bit his lower lip. “With all of the nonsense surrounding the family at the moment, I think it’ll show the rest of the world that we are actually committed to the notion of family. Besides, I want the other branches of the family to meet Matthew before the wedding.”

Cassandra started for her dressing room as she said, “I do think it’s a lovely idea. Now, it will require a lot of planning. But that’s why we have a staff of over two hundred! Those details will entertain them to the hilt!”

“Mother,” the King called after her. “May I ask you something?”

“Of course,” she answered.

“Why didn’t you encourage me to enter the armed services?”

Cassandra returned in her dark green dressing gown with silver trim. “I didn’t think it would interest you. Your father was the driving force behind that. Come to think of it, my father wanted you to be a great military hero, but I resisted. Andover has never been in a war! To think that the heir to the throne would risk his life in a pointless regiment made me cringe.”

“Why did Aunt Fiona allow Walter to join?” Michael leaned against a vintage armoire that belonged to his father, His Regal Highness Duke James.

Cassandra let out a flustered moan. "Darling, why does this matter now? It's almost one-thirty in the morning and I need my sleep."

"Mother…"

Cassandra climbed into her king sized feather bed. "Walter wasn't the heir to the throne. And he needed direction. Fiona and Nicholas thought it would be the right fit for him. However," she sighed, "I wonder if it was worth it."

"He's trying," the King reminded his mother. "Walter didn't even want to return to Andover."

Cassandra motioned for the dogs to climb onto her bed. After taking a sip of water, she replied, "As you know, duty comes before self, Michael. Why are you full of questions tonight?"

"No reason." The King kissed his mother on the forehead. "Good night."

13

As autumn continued its assault on the Kingdom of Andover, the Prince of Kemp grew restless. He was bored with life as he knew it, although he didn't know why. His relationship with his father was still strained, but Alexander developed a plan that would ensure he would become Andover's monarch faster than anyone realized. Meanwhile, his marriage to Olivia had taken a turn in an unexpected direction. She still wasn't pregnant and the thought of being a childless monarch was beginning to wreck havoc on his personal life. There was days where the barely spoke to each other. The Princess of Kemp spent most of her time at the stables with her horses or with her cousin, His Highness Edward, at Andover Palace. To top it all off, she was seriously considering becoming the patron of a fertility charity. The Prince of Kemp only found out about his wife's secret plans because his private secretary alerted him to the meeting on the princess's diary.

Although Olivia pretended that the patronage was entirely innocent, Alexander had his doubts. He instantly assumed that she was somehow going to use this charity as a way to showcase their issues like a desperate European reality television star. The thought of having their intimate lives splashed across a glossy magazine made the young prince cringe. However, he knew all too well that he could not alienate his wife at this moment in time. He would need Olivia's devotion to sustain him until his plan came into effect. When the time was right, they would have everything. But until that penultimate day, Prince Alexander had to do whatever he could to play the role of the perfect prince.

As he sat in his private study at Kemp Castle reading the annual report concerning the castle's estate, his wife came to the door. She was dressed in a new riding outfit. Lately, the Princess of Kemp had been on a shopping spree every day of the week. The press was beginning to pick up on her ten thousand dollar shopping trips, but Kemp Castle quickly put an end to their suggestions that the princess was being irresponsible with the money her husband received from the Regal Expenditure. The castle quickly issued a statement that the princess had a three million dollar trust fund which was the source of her discretionary income. As she stood in the doorway, Alexander couldn't help but notice how cold she looked. He realized that he hadn't done a thing to reassure his wife that everything would work out because he had his own doubts about the state of their life.

"Would you like to come for a ride," asked Olivia. A riding crop dangled from her left hand. "You've been cooped up in here all day."

"I'm all right," he said weakly.

The Princess of Kemp rolled her eyes. Shutting the door behind her she said, "What's wrong now?"

"Nothing, Olivia. I have a lot on my mind."

"You always do," she snapped. Ever since their last fight, they hadn't made love. And since the King's Reception at Andover Palace, they'd barely spoken. "I think I'm going to spend a few days in Cyprus with my parents."

Alexander looked up from his report. "Why," he muttered. "You have everything you need here."

Olivia tried to ignore the irony behind his words. She still managed to smile in public, but her heart was bleeding. The princess didn't know if she'd ever get pregnant, but the longer she and Alexander slept apart, the more she worried that they would eventually split up. Maybe, she reasoned, he would miss her if she went away for a few days. But this wasn't the response she was expecting. "I have everything except happiness," Olivia stated.

Alexander's eyes grew dark. "You are an ungrateful…"

"Insulting me will not help your cause," she spat. "Besides, my brother and sister will be in Cyprus with my parents. They're renting a yacht…"

"Why don't you use the regal yacht? I could come."

"I want to go alone," she snapped. "I need to get away from the confines of your world for a while. I need to be around people who don't expect me to be a princess every minute of the day."

"Then why the hell did you bother marrying me?" Alexander could feel himself starting to lose control of his emotions. He could barely read his wife most of the time, but now she had become impossible. "If you want out of this, just say so. I'll have my father authorize a divorce. You'll be free from all of this. Is that what you want?"

Olivia remained silent for what seemed an eternity. There were plenty of times over the past few weeks when she dreamt about what life would be like if she were her old self. Yes, she did love Prince Alexander. She always would. However, she couldn't deal with the many codicils that came with this man. She wanted nothing more than to be the Duchess of Andover one day. But at what price, she asked herself. "I won't talk to you when you're like this."

"I'll take that as a yes," he retorted.

The Princess of Kemp took a deep breath. If this fell apart, she knew her life's ambitions would end before her eyes. "It's a no, Alex. I'm not going anywhere. Deal with it," she stated. Olivia started for the door with newfound confidence. "I'll have my secretary put my holiday on your schedule. When I get back, things will change."

Patricia Ali, Lieutenant Major Huckley, and the Head of Andover's Armed Services, Matt Parsons, sat around the large conference table in the State Banquet Room in Andover Palace. Today's meeting was arranged by the King's office with regards to a matter of great security. No one knew what the King intended to say, but he'd never called a meeting such as this before, which only meant that it was of national importance.

When the clock struck noon, the King of Andover walked into the banquet room with his youngest son, Prince Joseph of Andover. They took their seats at opposite ends of the table as the King said, "Ladies and gentlemen, what we are about to discuss is of the utmost confidence."

"Of course, Your Majesty," cooed Patricia Ali, the Minister of

Government.

"His Regal Highness The Prince Joseph would like to join the armed services for a period of six months. I have given his request great thought and I do believe that he would benefit from such an experience," stated the monarch.

"That's wonderful news," Matt Parsons smiled. "We could use a man of your caliber in our midst, Your Regal Highness."

Prince Joseph took the compliment in a gallant manner. "I only hope to live up to your expectations. Following in the footsteps of Their Regal Highnesses The Prince of Kemp and Lord Walter, it is my goal to achieve success in my own right."

"Lieutenant Major," began the King, "the prince's security will be of great importance to me."

"Your Majesty, we will do everything in our power to keep His Regal Highness safe. However, there are risks associated with the armed services that one cannot foresee." Huckley folded his arms. "Will security be an issue?"

The King pursed his lips. Lieutenant Major Huckley was a man's man, which irritated Michael more than anything. "The palace does not want the prince exposed to unnecessary danger."

"But I still want to be treated like any other solider," added the prince.

"With all due respect, Sir, that will be impossible," added Patricia Ali. "As a member of the regal family, your safety will be an issue."

Prince Joseph turned his attention to his father. "Does this mean I won't be able to participate?"

"Not at all," stated Michael. "Son, could we have a moment?"

After the prince left the room, Michael said, "I want the same courtesy extended to Prince Joseph as it was extended to the Prince of Kemp."

The three official guests exchanged defeated glances.

"Sir, this is not outside of our normal field of expertise, however, I would hate for the prince to have unrealistic expectations of what he'll be able to do," retorted Lieutenant Major Huckley.

"Lieutenant Major, I expect you to make the proper allowances for Prince Joseph. If joining the armed services is what he desires, then it shall be. If there are any questions to the contrary, have them directed to my office. Now if you'll excuse me, I have other business to attend to," King Michael said with great finality.

"Will I be able to go," Joseph asked as he walked down the corridor with his father. "Will I?"

"Once the small details are sorted out, you'll be a man of the armed service," Michael assured his son. "Joey, are you sure this is what you want?"

Joseph nodded. "This is what I need."

"Very well. Son, I have a meeting, but I will see you later. Have a good day." With that, Michael disappeared into the vast palace.

The invitation for dinner with the regal family came shortly before Count Matthew Hall was scheduled to meet his father at the family financial advisory firm. He hadn't expected this invitation, partly because the King made it very clear that they were to keep a low profile until their engagement party. The King's Reception was the first time they'd been photographed together, but this event was to be the ultimate test: An entire meal alone with the regal family. Matthew still couldn't believe that after more than three decades, his dreams of marrying the only man he'd ever loved were actually coming true.

Matthew re-read the invitation which was printed on thick cream paper with the regal crest in the center. In a few months, he reminded himself, this life would be his. The thought almost made him sick to his stomach. It wasn't because he didn't love Michael, but because he was very aware that nothing would ever be the same again and that truly frightened him.

The Count promptly responded to the invitation before leaving his parent's house. Outside, a throng of paparazzi snapped his photograph as he climbed into his three-year-old Range Rover. He deftly maneuvered the car through the front gates, down the back roads, past Blake Manor, and onto Route 12 which led to Old Andover. As Matthew approached the city, he began to realize that this would be the last time that he was able to come and go as he pleased. He knew that Michael wouldn't keep him inside the palace for the rest of his life, however, regal life was much more structured than this. Hell, he may never own a second of his personal life again. Being the consort of the King meant structure, duty, and support, no matter what the personal cost. A woozy feeling swept through Matthew's body as he parked his car in front of his family's financial advisory company, Hall & Pratt Finance.

"And what would you like us to do about your house in the Netherlands," asked his father, Count Patrick Hall.

Matthew shrugged. "I guess we could rent it out. The income would be nice."

"Do you really need the rent," joked Patrick. "Matt, you're going to marry the King. On top of that, you'll also receive money from the Regal Expenditure, which is six million dollars a year. Why don't you just sell the place?"

"I love my canal house, Dad. Selling it would be like losing something," Matthew said.

Patrick gave his son a crooked smile. "Son, you won't need it. Besides, even in this market, you'd be able to get at least market value."

"Then I should wait until I can get more than that," stated Matthew with great earnest.

Patrick leaned closer to his son. "Are you having doubts?"

Just then, Matthew's cell phone rang. It was his mother, Countess Sally Hall. "Hi, Mom."

"Matthew, are you with your father," she asked breathlessly.

"Yeah. Why?"

"I have a table at Cabo! Come right away!" With that, Sally snapped her phone shut.

"Mom has a table at Cabo."

Patrick groaned. "Not again. I think she's taking this whole mother-in-law to the monarch thing too far. Is the press waiting for you?"

"Probably. They followed me here. Can we take your car?"

"Of course," nodded Patrick.

By the time Matthew and his father joined Sally at Cabo, there were fifteen photographers snapping their pictures while they ate lunch in the main dining room. The private dining room was booked by a visiting American billionaire, Charles Montgomery, IV, which meant the soon-to-be husband of the King had to dine with the people. While Matthew loathed the attention, his mother lapped it up. Matthew studied her for a few moments before deducing that she seemed more intent on him marrying Michael than anyone else in the kingdom. Hell, it was all she wanted to talk about.

"I went to Georgina Smith's for a wedding ensemble. She's going create an outfit that will be the toast of the wedding," she cooed. Sally took a gulp of her martini. "Someone from the palace told me that I'd have to have my dress approved. Is that so," asked Sally.

Matthew shrugged. "I guess. It would be terrible if you wore the same designer as the regal women."

Sally sniffed. "I doubt it. They'll probably have all of their dresses handmade in Paris or New York! Oh, I've spoken with your sisters. They will be at the wedding and this Christmas Eve event. The King is kind."

Matthew shifted uneasily. The stares he was receiving were bordering on intrusive. It was at the point now where people were snapping his picture with their camera phones. One patron even instructed the waiter to bring him the exact meal as Matthew. And now, his own mother was acting like a fifteen-year-old girl who was invited to Cassandra's tea party. Matthew could feel himself beginning to sink into an unknown funk, much to his dismay.

"Sally," Patrick said in a low, grave voice. "People are staring."

Countess Sally Hall scanned the room. "Oh, that's nothing. After all, we will be the in-laws of the King. People will look to us by default. Isn't that so, Matthew?"

"Mother," he stated, "could you please stop? You're embarrassing me."

"That wasn't my intention," she huffed. "For goodness sake, I can't help if people are gawking at us. Matthew, this is your life now."

"And what if I don't want it," Matthew said quickly. He didn't even realize the severity of this statement until the words fell out of his mouth. The Count felt as if he'd betrayed Michael in a single moment of frustration. "I didn't mean that," he told his amazed parents.

Patrick gave his son a concerned look. "If this isn't what you want…"

"I didn't mean it, Dad." Matthew cut into his duck. He chewed the moist meat as he stared at his plate. "I've been under a lot of stress. When I was in Amsterdam, I had an anonymous life. But now…I'm the main attraction."

Sally shook her head. "It isn't so! I was terrified before I married your father. But my mother assured me that I'd be happy. And I still am."

"But Dad isn't the King. This is huge…and I think this is the first time it's actually hit me."

"Matt, it would be ill of us to give you advice," Patrick noted. "I was very good friends with His Regal Highness Duke James. He was a great man. He loved his son very much. I don't think being the Queen's husband changed him, although many people wanted him to defer to her. If the King is anything like his father, you'll be fine."

"Dad, I don't know." Matthew took a deep breath. "What if I can't handle it?"

Sally placed her hands on her son's. "Listen to me, Matthew! This was meant to be. After everything you and Michael have been through over the last thirty odd years, it's time for you to take your rightful place in his life," Sally retorted. "You deserve this!"

"You're right," reiterated Matthew. "I'm just being silly. After all, they're just people with titles, aren't they?"

"Thank you for meeting with me. Please, have a seat." The Prince of Kemp showed his guest into a small room outside the confines of Kemp Castle. The Prince assumed his seat at the head of the table with great importance. "I trust you've received the file I sent to your office."

"I have. However, I do have many questions, Your Regal Highness."

"Very good." The Prince of Kemp lowered his voice as he narrowed his eyes. "We must proceed with the utmost caution until such a time where we can move forward. Don't you agree?"

"Yes, Sir," replied Patricia Ali.

"Good." His lips curled with delight as he said, "I'm glad we're of the same thought, Ms. Ali. Now, let's begin."

14

Her Regal Highness Princess Sophia lay in her gargantuan bed, while Prince Robert slept beside her. In the months following Margaret's accident, Princess Sophia wanted nothing more than to make her cousin and her husband pay for their crime. Yet, somehow, none of it seemed to matter anymore. It was as if by a sheer force of nature that she didn't care what happened to Margaret; the only thing that concerned her was the state of her marriage. No matter what, Sophia loved Robert and that was a fact that would never change.

Princess Sophia stepped into the running shower with great care. Her schedule consisted of three regal engagements throughout the kingdom before dinner with Andover's ambassadors from the United States, Brazil, and France. This would have been too much for any other member of the regal family, save the King, which is why she relished her role. Her stamina alone made her the ideal candidate to show everyone how viable the regal family was in today's world.

Sophia walked into her dressing room to find that her personal stylist had laid out her outfit for today: A classic Chanel suit with a matching hat and Manolo Blahnik heels. As she put on the venerable outfit, she caught sight of Lady Margaret walking with Samuel and his dog, Austin, on the grounds. This was a rare sight, she reminded herself. Margaret loved to shirk her responsibilities off to anyone she could. These days, that task fell to Prince Joseph, which Sophia found revolting. The fact that Lady Margaret could have as many children as she wanted and never seemed to want them, while people like Sophia couldn't have children, made the princess angry each time she thought about the sheer irony of the situation. However, whatever malice she held for Margaret had subsided, even though they hadn't spoken since the accident.

Princess Sophia emerged from her dressing room as Prince Robert arose. He gave his wife a small smirk. To Robert, life was back to normal, although the guilt he felt refused to abandon him. "Good morning," he said.

"Hello. I didn't mean to wake you."

Prince Robert walked towards his wife, kissing her on the forehead. "You didn't. I couldn't sleep."

"Guilt," Sophia asked sharply.

"Probably," he replied. "What time are you attending that breakfast meeting with the environmental commission?"

Sophia fastened an emerald necklace that belonged to Duchess Mary around her neck. "Ninety minutes. I wanted to have coffee and brioche with my mother before I left. What are your plans for the day?"

"Your brother arranged for me to attend an all day seminar about investing in renewable energy abroad." The prince admired his wife. "Fascinating stuff," he joked.

Princess Sophia failed to find the humor in her husband's words. "If the King didn't think it was important, he wouldn't have sent you as the regal representative," shot the princess.

"I know…" Robert acknowledged. "I'm grateful he's speaking to me again."

"My brother can be forgiving in his own time, Robert."

"Can I ask you something?"

"What," Sophia said.

Robert sat on their bed as he said, "Do you want to go away for our anniversary? It'll be twenty-two years in two weeks."

Sophia was surprised that he'd remembered when she'd forgotten all about their wedding anniversary. Each year, Robert did his best to surprise her with trips to a remote island or a rare gift from some unknown corner of the world. She didn't expect anything from him this year, but the fact that he'd managed to remember their wedding anniversary made her even more grateful for this man, in spite of everything.

"What do you say?"

Sophia shrugged. "I'm not sure. I will have to check my diary. I do wish you could have given me a bit more notice."

"Sophia…"

"I'll see what I can do." Then, it hit her. "Why don't we throw a party?"

"Where?"

"Here! We could host a small dinner party in the palace or at your family home. I have to go, but have your secretary run it by my office." Sophia grabbed her purse before meeting her secretary outside of her bedroom.

While Prince Robert was in the shower, he realized that life as he knew it was slowly getting back on course. Yes, he still had a long way to go with Sophia, the King, and the rest of the regal family, but everything would be fine from now on.

"Which is why, I will seek a second term as the Minister of Government for the Kingdom of Andover in next year's election," announced Patricia Ali.

The King turned off the television with clear exasperation. While he could not express a politic allegiance in a kingdom where he still wielded a considerable amount of power, the King wanted nothing more than for Patricia Ali to simply step down. He was growing quite tired of her policies, instigations, and general foolhardy approach to running his kingdom. Michael knew that restraint was important right now. Even though he couldn't openly say that he loathed Patricia, he could do whatever he could to ensure she wouldn't be elected for another term.

A few minutes later, the King met with the palace planners in charge of organizing his wedding. During his first marriage, Michael was told to turn up to the chapel because his parents, Princess Fiona, and the Dowager Duchess Victoria were handling the many details. This time would not be like his first marriage, which is why he finally decided to take an active role in the wedding plans. After deciding the final menu for the reception, the King's private secretary, Glenn, briefed him on the rest of his day.

"You have an appointment with Prince Joseph in one hour, but before that, there's something I feel you should know, Your Majesty."

The King nodded. "What is it, Glenn? I do hope it's good news."

"It concerns the Count, Sire."

Michael sat up in his chair. In the three years since he began dating Matthew, Glenn had never come to him with this sort of news. On a typical day, a statement such as this would involve Lady Margaret or one of his children, but not Count Matthew. "For goodness sake, what is it Glenn? I do not have all day…"

"Sire, it is probably nothing, however, there are bloggers…"

The King shot Glenn a confused look. "What on earth is a blogger?"

"I assume it is someone who keeps a running commentary of life or a niche market, Sire." Glenn continued, "The Count and his parents were dining at Cabo yesterday afternoon. A few people overheard the Count say that the regal family are people with titles."

Michael looked confused. "I don't understand."

"Sire, the bloggers seem to think this shows no respect for the monarchy as an institution or the regal family."

"That's preposterous. Have any of the newspapers run this story?"

Glenn shook his head. "No. I've checked the papers and the palace press office staff have called their contacts. No one outside of the blog world has given this story a second thought."

The King bit his lower lip. "It's a non-issue. I appreciate your need to brief me, Glenn. If you'll excuse me…"

Glenn left the office as Michael dialed Matthew's phone number.

"Hi, Mike," said Matthew.

"Hello, Matt," he said kindly. "Did you say that the regal family are people with titles?"

Matthew felt the floor drop from underneath him. "Only to my parents."

"Apparently, something called bloggers heard you. It's all over the Internet."

"Michael, I'm sorry. I didn't…"

"I know," interjected Michael. "Thankfully, the legitimate press has ignored the story. I suspect it has to do with Lady Margaret's incident... In the future, it's wise to use the private dining room at Cabo. You'll be a member of this family soon enough; you shouldn't be dining amongst the people."

Matthew could feel the sweat encompassing his body. He'd never heard Michael yell, but this was worse, reasoned Matthew. If Michael had simply yelled at him, he would have known how to react. However, Michael's calm demeanor threw Matthew. Was this what he had to look forward to for the rest of his life? Because if it was, Matthew noted, it truly petrified him. "I'm sorry Mike. I truly am. My mother made reservations, but the private dining room was booked by that American billionaire. That's why we were in the main dining room."

"Matt, I'm not angry. Things like this happen. However, we must do all we can to ensure that they won't happen again. Which is why," Michael added, "I will have my office draft a retraction of misunderstanding in case the story explodes in the next day or so."

"Do you think that's necessary?"

"It may not be necessary, but one must always be prepared."

"Yes, that sounds lovely. Tell me, has this business been good to you," asked Princess Sophia. She couldn't have cared less as her focus fell on Princess Helena. As of late, her niece was more concerned with her newest boyfriend, Derek Sharpe, 2nd Peer and less with her regal duty. While Helena's addition to this morning's breakfast meeting was last minute, the King must have sensed that his only daughter needed some sort of focus in her life. After politely excusing herself, Princess Sophia approached Princess Helena. "Are you enjoying yourself?"

"Of course, Aunt Sophia." Helena poked the omelet on her plate. "I'm having the time of my life."

Sophia sat next to her niece with great concern. "You've been in an odd mood for months. Is everything all right?"

Helena placed her fork down with great care. "I'm fine," she said in a tempered voice. "I'm a bit tired, but it will pass."

"Is something amiss with your new beau?"

"No," she said sharply.

"Helena, I'm concerned about you. I can't remember the last time I saw you eat anything. That coupled with your new figure…"

Princess Helena couldn't believe what her aunt was saying to her. After the months of her minimal food diet, someone was finally taking an interest in her wellbeing. While this should have elated Helena, it only angered her. "What are you trying to say?"

"Calm down," ordered Princess Sophia. "Come with me."

The princesses made their way to a private holding room. Princess Helena stood near the door as Princess Sophia wagged her finger at her. "If your father could see you, he would be ashamed."

"My father doesn't care," shot Helena. "He's more concerned with everyone else. You're the first person to realize that I've lost weight. No one else cares. Except Derek."

Princess Sophia took a deep breath. "Darling, your know father cares about you. However, his situation precludes him from taking a more active role in your day to day life."

"Then why was he able to make Joseph's wish to join the armed services come true," snapped Helena. "We all know what type of woman Margaret is, but he still protects her." Helena began to feel lightheaded. "I don't want to talk about this anymore. I just want to be left alone. Excuse me."

"You wanted to see me, Aunt Cassandra?" Lord Walter asked as he sat in an early twentieth century chair in Cassandra's private tea room.

The Dowager Queen was surrounded by her yapping dogs. A fresh tea service sat on the marble table that had been a gift from her late husband. She poured herself a cup of tea before saying, "I've heard that you've had a visitor at Blake Manor a majority of the summer."

Walter couldn't hide his disgust. This literally smelled like Princess Sophia. "Why couldn't Sophia…"

"This has nothing to do with my daughter," snapped the former monarch. "A very kind person from within Blake Manor informed me. They are concerned for you, Walter."

"There's no need," sighed Lord Walter. "I know what I'm doing."

Cassandra shook her head. "Walter, your parents always feared about your taste in women. When you lived in New York City and Luxembourg, you were free to date whomever you chose because of the distance. However, it's time you dated women from within the proper circle."

"With all due respect, my personal life does not concern you, Aunt Cassandra." This had been Walter's life since returning to Andover after the death of his mother. How he loathed his family's intrusion into his private affairs.

"It does," bristled Cassandra. "The affairs of this family concern me deeply. After your mother died, I swore that I would look out for you and your sister. Granted, you are adults, but I do worry about you."

Walter crossed his legs as Voltaire sniffed his ankles. "Whatever occurred with Daisy is a non-issue. Besides, she's gone."

"Oh?"

"As you can see, it doesn't matter."

Cassandra strongly disagreed. "It always does. Now, I would like you to meet Countess Masoli's daughter, Danisi Samantha Masoli…"

"Aunt Cassandra…"

"She's the right kind of woman," interjected the former monarch. "Samantha was educated in Paris, she's artistic, and she's an expert horsewoman. Now, I've arranged a cocktail reception at Blake Manor which Samantha will attend. I do expect you to be on your best behavior."

Walter folded his arms in defiance. This woman had done everything she could to run his life over the past few years and he'd had enough. "I won't do it. I will find someone in my own time."

"Is that so? Walter, you're forty-seven! When will you find a wife?"

"A wife," laughed Walter. "The marriages within the family haven't been successful – to say the least! Why would I even want to bother with that sham of an institution? I won't do it and I won't pretend to be interested in that woman."

"Now you listen to me, Walter! This has gone on long enough," snapped the Dowager Queen. "You will attend the cocktail reception. You will date women of the right class."

"And if I don't," he challenged.

Cassandra stiffened. She placed her tea cup on its saucer with great care. "We'll have to bring the matter before the King. I'm sure that's not what you want, is it?" The Dowager Queen gave her nephew a pert smile. "I didn't think so."

***

Lord Walter stormed out of Cassandra's tea room. He felt trapped inside this vicious game of duty and appearances. The only person on his mind was Daisy. Although they hadn't spoken to each other in months, he wanted nothing more than to find her, make love to her, and know that everything in his world was right again. If she finds out about this cocktail party, it will destroy her, he worried once more. Walter hated the way Cassandra intruded into his life, but she did have a perfectly valid point. However, Walter had spent the majority of his adult life running away from the things he knew he should do, but he could never deduce why.

Somehow, Walter found himself outside of Margaret's state apartment. He hadn't been to this part of the palace in years. Mainly because his sister and Sophia never invited him over to their palace sanctuaries, yet they always showed up unannounced at Blake Manor. He rang the bell twice. A moment later, the butler opened the door.

The butler bowed. "Your Regal Highness."

"Good afternoon. Is Lady Margaret in?"

The butler disappeared around the corner of the lavish state apartment as Lord Walter became lost in the opulence of his sister's home. When Walter moved back to Andover after his mother's death, the Queen offered Lord Walter a state apartment of his own. However, Walter knew that he would never have a moments break from the task of being a member of the regal family. Walter jumped at the chance to live at his childhood home, Blake Manor, which was close enough to the palace, but with regard to location, it was a world away. Walter walked around the soft lilac reception room when Lady Margaret walked in. She greeted her brother with a kiss, before ordering the butler to prepare lunch for two.

"I can't stay long," he murmured. "I was in the palace to see Aunt Cassandra, so I thought I'd see you. No regal events today?"

"No," she smiled. "Edward has one at the airport. It's some new plane or something like that. I don't know. I wasn't listening. But I have two events tomorrow and then a dinner for an arts charity." Lady Margaret reclined on a love seat.

The butler reappeared. "Lunch is served in the Drawing Room."

Lady Margaret led the way. "I was telling myself that I should go to Blake Manor to see you, but life has been quite stressful as of late."

"Is it getting any better," inquired Walter.

"I suppose. Edward's the only one speaking to me." Upon entering the Drawing Room, she sat at the table and began eating the poached fish.

Walter examined his sister. She looked much older than she was, but he realized it was simply stress. Margaret had always been the pinnacle of youthful energy, but in this moment it seemed as if she was bearing the weight of the world on her shoulders. And with the rest of the regal family avoiding her, he could tell that she was barely hanging on. "Can I ask you something," Walter sighed. "It's something important."

"I suppose."

"Do you think the reason I can't make a relationship work and you do what you do has to do with our parents?"

Margaret sat up with great earnest. Ever since the death of their mother eight years ago, she and Walter rarely discussed her. She quickly realized that whatever was troubling him – whatever was behind this impromptu visit to her state apartment – was huge. "Why do you ask," she choked.

Walter bit into his fish. He hated being in this situation, however, ever since his talk with Cassandra, he wanted nothing more than to get this topic out in the open. "Think about it: While we were growing up, Mom and Dad were too busy to even take care of us. For most of the school year, the nannies oversaw our daily lives and the cooks ensured we ate."

Being the eldest of Princess Fiona and Lord Nicholas' children, Margaret remembered their unique parenting methods with great scorn. "I remember," she replied coolly.

"Maggie, they were never really there for us. We spent most of our time with Aunt Cassandra and Uncle James at Kemp Castle." Walter shifted in his chair. "I don't know, but maybe it's because we never had real role models to show us what a healthy marriage was that we are such losers at love."

Margaret couldn't help but bristle at her brother's innuendo. "I'm no loser in love, Walter. My husband adores me!"

"I didn't say that he didn't. But we all know about your past."

"Well," she snapped. "I suppose anything's possible. But it doesn't matter."

"I think it does. Maggie, do you remember when Constance died? Mom and Dad barely made it back for her funeral. And after that, they spent most of their time arguing and blaming each other for her death."

Walter tried to hold back his raw emotions. He hadn't thought about their younger sister in years. Lady Constance was only fourteen when she died in a boating accident one summer at Port Agnes House. The police ruled the death accidental, but that didn't stop Princess Fiona for blaming everyone within the regal household for not doing enough to save her little girl. Walter and Margaret were shocked by their sister's death and the only person who pulled the entire regal family through the tragedy was Cassandra. Life didn't get any better for Walter and Margaret after Constance's death because it led to more week long fights between their parents, which always resulted in them being shipped off to Andover Palace, where the current monarch, Queen Cassandra, lived.

Lady Margaret stared into space. The death of her sister has very traumatic. What Margaret always found infuriating was that Sophia was supposed to be on that boat too, but she'd changed her mind at the last minute. Had it been Sophia instead of Constance, maybe, Margaret thought, her family life would have been a happy one. "Walter," sighed Margaret, "I wouldn't waste another minute thinking about Mom, Dad or the past. It's not healthy."

"And ignoring it is?"

"Walter! Please. I don't want to think about it."

Lord Walter finished his glass of white wine. "Do you think that Michael and Sophia have been luckier in love because Aunt Cassandra and Uncle James were actually good parents?"

Margaret bristled at the statement. "I don't. Anyway, it's not like Uncle James and Aunt Cassandra were ideal parents. She was off on official business most of the time and James was by her side. Michael and Sophia are just as screwed up as we are; they just know how to hide it. Anyway, why were you meeting with Aunt Cassandra?"

"You know what? It doesn't matter. Thanks for lunch."

As Walter rose to leave the room, Samuel rushed in and nearly knocked him over with his governess, Eloise Nnanna behind him. "Sorry," Samuel cried breathlessly.

"I'm so sorry, Your Regal Highnesses," cried Eloise. The governess rang her hands with great agony.

"What is it, Eloise? We're having lunch," bit Margaret.

"Ma'am, the school called me to pick His Regal Highness up early because…"

Eloise tried to find the right words, which only infuriated Margaret. "For heavens sake, Eloise, just say it," snapped Margaret impatiently.

"I got into a fight," pronounced Samuel.

Margaret couldn't believe what she was hearing. "What? Why?"

"Eloise, why don't you walk me out," Walter suggested.

Margaret waited until her brother and the governess left the Drawing Room before exclaiming, "You were in a fight?! Samuel! What will the King say?

How could you?!"

Samuel threw himself onto the soft sofa. He shot his mother a defiant look with his big brown eyes. In every way that mattered, he was his mother's son. "I don't care," he shot back.

"Who did you fight?"

"Josh Rogan. He's an ass."

"Sam!"

"Mom, I'm ten. I know a lot of bad words." Samuel slid from the sofa to the floor. "You're the reason I had my fight," he shot back defiantly.

Margaret was thrown by her son's statement. She rarely made appearances at his school except to drop him off or pick him up, so why was he fighting about her? "Why," she asked with great concern.

"Because Josh called you a slut."

Margaret nearly collapsed at her son's candor. She'd been called many things in her time, but a slut as never a word anyone had said to her face. Well, remembered Margaret, Sophia once called her a slut, but that was years ago. Why, wondered Margaret, were the children at her son's school, a school she had to pay over twenty-five thousand dollars a year to, calling her – the King's cousin – a slut? "Sam, why… How…"

"Because," Samuel groaned, "the kids in my class were saying that the story in the paper was true. I said it wasn't. That's when Josh called you…"

"I get it," interjected Margaret.

Samuel kicked off his shoes onto the ancient Persian carpet. "Am I in trouble?"

"No… Just go to your room. Your dad should be home soon."

"Yes, Michael. Edward and I will handle it. Goodbye." Margaret placed the silver phone on its cradle. She turned her attention to Edward, who was drinking an ice cold beer.

"Where's His Majesty tonight?"

Margaret took her husband's beer. "I don't know. He's in the car."

Edward stroked his wife's arm. "What are we going to do about our son?"

"I don't know."

"What did Michael say?"

"He told us to handle it. Thankfully," added Margaret, "the school is bound by a long standing confidentiality agreement with the palace." Margaret took a long sip of Edward's beer as she looked around their bedroom. "I thought this incident was behind us."

Edward shook his head. He knew that the story would remain an issue for the rest of their lives. "Margaret, we'll just have to live with it. Besides, Sam was defending your honor."

She laughed at the irony. "That's your job. You did nothing when the story was leaked."

"I couldn't. We both knew it was true."

Margaret moved towards the open window. Although she felt that her relationship with Edward had improved in recent weeks, he would never let her forget her sin. "So? The public doesn't need to know. Besides," she said turning to her husband, "Josh Rogan be the last one to cast stones."

"What do you mean?"

"His mother, LeAnn, has three children by just as many men! She's no pinnacle of virtue."

Edward rolled his eyes. "You're missing the point..."

"I'm not," she snapped. "That woman's son is the last person to call someone a slut. I'm glad Sam set her bastard son straight. That'll teach them to mess with me."

"Maggie, it's over. Let it go."

"I can't."

"We'll have to." Edward tried to gather his thoughts. "We'll need to punish our son for a few days to be sure that he understands the severity of the situation. I think that'll be sufficient enough, don't you?" He began to massage his wife's back with great affection. "Why don't I take Samuel out of the kingdom for a few days?"

"Hmm?"

"My aunt Fran and my uncle Thomas…"

"Olivia's parents?"

"Yes," he said. "They're going to Cyprus for a few days and renting a yacht. My dad's going as well, so why don't I take Samuel? Olivia will be there, so he won't be alone."

Margaret smiled. "Is Alexander going? I mean, I can't imagine the Prince of Kemp on a rented yacht."

Edward averted his gaze. Olivia usually confided in him about the inner workings at Kemp Castle, but she hadn't said anything in the last few weeks. While he found it odd, Edward realized that things weren't well in the heir's castle. "I don't know, Maggie. Things… Well… It can't be easy being four hours away, let's leave it at that."

"Fair enough," reasoned Margaret. "Edward," she sighed fruitlessly. "Do you ever think things will be normal again?"

"Maggie," surmised Edward, "we're beyond normal."

15

The Princess of Kemp surveyed the suitcases that sat in the corner of her private suite in Kemp Castle. After today's event for Count Matthew Hall, she was off to Cyprus with His Regal Highness Samuel and his father, His Highness Edward. The last few weeks had been especially stressful for the princess, but she had to remind herself from time to time that she did have real, blood relatives within the regal family. After all, her mother Danisi Fran Green and Edward's father, Count Grayson Miller, were brother and sister. To add more intrigue to the mix, Lady Margaret and Edward were second cousins due to the fact that they shared the same great-grandmother, Georgia Marsh, 2nd Peer. However, Olivia constantly felt as if she were adrift in this family with her spastic husband as her only connection to the outside world. The fact that they hadn't spoken to each other over the past few days wasn't helping their situation. On top of that, the princess wasn't pregnant, the prince was losing patience, and he was dead set against her going off to Cyprus for what he viewed as a frivolous trip. No matter what he thought, she reminded herself, she needed to get away because if she didn't, she didn't know if she would make it until the end of the year.

"Alex," she called on her way to the waiting car.

"What," he bellowed from the library.

Olivia wandered into the comfortable, homely library. She always loved this room because her husband hadn't turned it into a cold, soulless room. The library was kept to the same intimate standard as it had been in King Michael's twenty-eight year residence at Kemp Castle.

Alexander sat by the crackling fire with a pen in one hand, a cup of coffee in the other, and a leather journal on his knee. His eyes caught the sight of his lovely wife in a seasonal dress with a shawl that deftly covered an emerald pendant. "Where're you off to," he asked.

"The palace."

He glanced at the grandfather clock in the center of room. “That’s not for another five hours. Are you lying to me?”

“No,” she retorted. “I’m having a drink with Edward. I have to leave now if I’m to make it on time.”

“Olivia,” he called after her. “Can we talk?”

She wasn’t in the mood for another one of his meaningless statements of love. During the last few days, he’d snapped at her more than usual, but for no apparent reason. These were the moments when she was glad that she hadn’t brought his child into the world, although a child might be the one thing to finally change her husband once and for all. Yet in this moment, she didn’t want to entertain his ego. “What is it,” she demanded to know.

Alexander placed his china coffee cup on the floor. “Look, I know I’ve been impossible lately. I’m sorry. It’s just that… Something big may be in the works, but I can’t say anymore than that. If you stay with me,” he whispered, “everything will be as it should.”

The hairs on Olivia’s arms stood at attention. The princess thought that her husband’s words should have calmed her or assuaged her in some way, but they provided the opposite effect. She looked into her husband’s eyes for any sign of life, but they were remarkably cold. The man she’d fallen in love with was gone, Olivia realized sadly. But whoever this man was, she was terribly frightened of him.

Count Matthew Hall joined the regal family in the Music Room for lunch. The affair was just as everyone expected: quietly restrained, with an air of dignity, and underlying tension. The Count seemed oblivious to the drama around him. He stood nervously between His Majestic Regal Highness The King and Princess Sophia with a glass of wine in his hands.

“Matthew,” began Michael, “is a very good tennis player, Sophia.”

"Is that so," she smiled weakly. "Then we'll have to play. The tennis courts here at the palace are so lovely in the spring."

"We could always go to the club," added Matthew.

Princess Sophia gave him a curious look. "The club? Count Matthew, I don't play sports in public. What would people say?" And with that, Princess Sophia excused herself.

"Did I…"

Michael patted Matthew on the back with great care. "No... That's my sister. She's a traditionalist."

"I see. What else should I know," Matthew asked wearily.

Michael instructed the butler to bring him another glass of amaretto. The King scanned the room in an attempt to break down the dynamic of the regal family. In all of his years as Andover's monarch, Michael had rarely thought about how the small incidents of life culminated in this assortment of personalities. Yes, he thought, they all seemed to be able to pull themselves together for the good of the public, however, in their most intimate moments, their lives could have been those of anyone in the last thousand years. "The only thing to know," Michael sighed, "is to never take sides. They'll try to pull you to one side, but resist. It's the only way."

"Can we talk," Margaret whispered to Robert.

Prince Robert continued to stare out of the oversized window that looked onto the front court of Andover Palace. He remembered the many times he'd been driven past the gates of this isolated world of privilege, yet somehow, these walls felt like a gilded prison. "That's not a wise idea, Margaret." Robert looked over his shoulder to see Princess Sophia engaged in conversation with Princess Helena and the Princess of Kemp.

"Look, Edward and Samuel are going to Cyprus tomorrow. I thought… You should come over." Margaret gazed into Robert's deep brown eyes with endless hope. This was her last chance at love, she reasoned, and now was the time to finally snare the man she always wanted.

Robert took a step back. "No. This is over, Margaret," he sighed. "It's beyond over."

"You can't…I love…"

Robert could see the desperation in her face and the determination in her soul, but this was something he couldn't deal with right now…or ever. "I have to go."

Margaret watched with helpless frustration as Robert joined his wife. Sadness filled her body because she knew within that moment that everything she'd done to be with Robert was for naught. And, she reasoned, she had done everything possible. Margaret stormed over to the butler and ordered another drink.

Seeing his sister in such a state, Lord Walter joined Lady Margaret at the bar in the corner of the Music Room. "Are you all right?"

"No," she slurred. "But I'll be fine. Life will go on." The alcohol from the vodka burned her throat with utter delight. "Walter, after everything I've done, I still don't have Robert."

"What do you mean?"

Margaret averted her gaze. "You know…The whole thing. I did what I thought was right, but nothing I've ever done has turned out right. I'm broken," she choked.

Walter listened to his sister's ramblings with great concern. He had his own worries about her mental stability. However, in this moment, the last few weeks made perfect sense. "It was you," he stammered.

"What?"

"You…leaked the story to the press, didn't you?"

Lady Margaret almost lost her footing.

"Maggie…"

"Walter," she spat, "mind your own business."

"Are you enjoying yourself," the Prince of Kemp asked Count Matthew Hall.

"I am. Everyone's been so kind."

Prince Alexander bit into a fresh plaice and asparagus hors d'oeuvre as he tried to read Matthew. Alexander may not have shared the same moral fiber as his father, but he was very protective about the people within his personal world. The young prince knew that the image of the regal family was paramount to everything else. It was their image, Alexander reasoned, that had kept them in good favor since the beginning of the last century. "Yes," remarked Alexander, "my family enjoys making people feel welcomed. Tell me, Count Matthew, what type of music do you enjoy?"

"I'm open," smiled Matthew.

Alexander tried to suppress a haughty smirk. "Well, His Majesty enjoys the classical works and opera. It can be very dry at times, however, if the King demands it, so it must be."

Matthew couldn't understand Alexander's sudden fascination with him. Matthew decided that the best thing to do was simply go along with Alexander's line of questioning with the hope that someone would appear to save him from the heir to the throne. "The King and I have similar tastes," Matthew stated. "We should be fine."

"That's until he's called away for a tour of six African countries or he must cancel a dinner engagement with you to tend to the needs of his government." Prince Alexander chewed on a second hors d'oeuvre. "Regal life is quite demanding."

Matthew finished his glass of wine. He couldn't tell if Alexander was trying to advise him or scare him away, but he refused to let anyone intimidate him, which is exactly what he suspected Alexander of doing. "Your Regal Highness," Matthew said, "I am well aware of the duties His Majesty must undertake as Andover's monarch."

"Are you?"

"Yes."

"Are you prepared to be second in line for my father's time and affection?"

"Time, Your Regal Highness, is something that I can handle. However, His Majesty's affection towards me is something I've never had to doubt. If you'll excuse," Matthew replied bitingly.

"I hope you told her where to get off," Sophia snapped. She was on her third glass of champagne, but she still felt fine. Sophia made a point to caress her husband's arm because she knew Margaret was staring at the couple.

Prince Robert led his wife to a quiet corner of the Music Room. They sat on a alabaster sofa as he said, "It will never happen again, Sophia."

"And if it does, I cannot take you back, Robert. You do know that, don't you?"

He shook his head.

"Good. I don't know why she doesn't move out of Andover and to Hong Kong or somewhere. Her presence is no longer welcomed in the kingdom," sniffed Sophia.

Robert squeezed Princess Sophia's hand. "Why don't we just forget about her? I've been thinking…Why don't we have a house built for us? That way, we can escape the prying eyes of the palace…"

"I'm not leaving," interjected Sophia. She narrowed her cold eyes. "I didn't tell you to sleep with my cousin," she said in a low voice. "If I were to move out of the palace, it would cause suspicion. I've done nothing wrong."

"Why don't you think about it…"

"There's nothing to think about," Sophia snapped. "I am fourth in line for the throne. My life is in service to assisting the King with his duties as Andover's monarch."

Prince Robert stared into his wife's eyes with great concern. He'd heard this speech about her duty to crown and country throughout their marriage and it was finally beginning to annoy him. "What about our duty to each other as man and wife," he challenged.

"Robert," she said in an imperious tone, "you knew what you were getting into when you married me."

As Sophia walked away, Robert pulled Matthew aside. "Do you know what you're getting yourself into," asked the prince.

Matthew gave Robert a confused look. He wasn't sure if the regal family was trying to give him helpful advice or dissuade him from marrying Michael in some odd attempt to preserve Princess Katherine's memory.

"I think so," responded Matthew.

"They put this damn kingdom before everything else. All of them," Robert spat. "I hope you have the stomach for it."

"What's that supposed to mean," Matthew asked, annoyed by Robert's tone. "Why are you and the Prince of Kemp so intent to ruin this day for me?"

Robert rolled his eyes with extreme boredom. "You don't get it. Once you say I do, your life will no longer be yours. They take it away from you when they invest you as the Duke of Andover. Your life will become a series of schedules, meeting, regal events, official receptions, days at the openings of golf clubs, photo opportunities with the government…" Robert moaned out of sheer agony at the state of his life. He placed a hand on Matthew's back. "Matthew, I know what it's like. I'm married to the King's sister. Can you imagine what it's like being married to the King himself? It'll be a trillion times worse."

“Your Highness,” Matthew began, “the King and I will be very happy together.”

Robert released a guttural grunt. “Fine, but I’ll ask you in a year from today and let’s see if you still feel the same way. Deal?”

“So,” Alexander sighed. “When are you going into the armed services, Joey?”

Joseph looked up from the piano and gave his brother a terse look. He’d been minding his own business, however, it seemed like Alexander had already annoyed most of the people in the Music Room and it was now his turn to suffer through a conversation with his big brother. “I don’t know,” he sighed. “Dad will tell me when he finds out.”

Alexander sat next to his brother on the piano bench. “You’ve always played the piano better than most.”

“Is that your pithy attempt at a compliment?”

Alexander ignored Joseph’s biting remark. “I’m trying to be nice.”

“What do you want?”

“Nothing. Sometimes I miss my brother.”

“You know where I am.” Joseph began to play a piece by Chopin. “Besides, whenever I call Kemp Castle to arrange a meeting with you, you’re always busy. I have a life too, Alex.”

Alexander placed his drink on the grand piano. “Well, you’ll probably start basic training after the New Year. That’s when I started.”

Joseph glared at his brother. Even though he’d tried to connect with Alexander since returning to the kingdom, Joseph found it increasingly hard to find common ground. They were too different to ever have a true brotherly relationship. Although this fact should have disturbed Joseph, he was at peace with the notion.

"Alex, I don't know. I guess I'll go when they want me to go."

"Are you going to miss Dad's…ceremony," snorted the Prince of Kemp.

"No," sighed Prince Joseph. "I'm sure they'll let me go to my own father's wedding."

"Ceremony," corrected Alexander.

"Wedding," Joseph insisted without looking up from the piano keys. "By definition of the Marriage Equality Act, the union between two people of the same sex is classified as a wedding in the Kingdom of Andover."

Alexander was surprised by his playboy brother's knowledge of Andover's law.

"I do know a few things," Joseph added. "I'm not as vapid as you seem to think I am."

"I don't think you're vapid, Joey."

Joseph held the keys to take in the final chords of the song. The prince stood with great confidence. "Yes, you do. You always have."

"Sophia, may I have a moment," asked Walter.

Princess Sophia excused herself from her conversation with Princess Helena and the Princess of Kemp about the newest fashion houses in New York as she walked to the south corner of the Music Room with Lord Walter. "What is it, Walter?"

Walter looked around the room before saying, "I think I know where the leak came from."

Princess Sophia looked intrigued. It was assumed by many that she was the cause of the leak regarding Margaret's accident, but nothing could have been further from the truth. Luckily for Sophia, the people that mattered seemed to believe her. "Where," she asked with great interest.

"The horse's mouth."

Sophia's eyes grew wide. The thought that Lady Margaret could do something that vile made her ill. When Sophia thought about the agony, stress, and ultimate grief it caused the regal family, it made her want to hurt the culprit. Now, with Walter's belief that Lady Margaret had been the cause of the leak made her crave revenge. How, Sophia thought, could one person do something so disgusting?

"Are you sure," asked Sophia.

Walter nodded. "She denied it, but it makes sense. I mean, she's been acting like she's done the most altruistic thing in the world. I didn't know she wanted Robert so much."

Princess Sophia averted her cousin's gaze. "I did."

"What are you going to do?"

"Nothing now, but I'll get to the bottom of this. If she did what you believe she did, I will not let her get away with it."

"How long will you be gone," Princess Helena asked her sister-in-law.

The Princess of Kemp tried to suppress her delight to escape her life within the kingdom. "Ten days in the sun. I can't wait."

"It must be nice having your entire family around without the drama."

"Oh, there's always drama with my family, but you don't want to hear about that."

Princess Helena smiled. "Thank you. I don't."

"Helena," called the Dowager Queen. "Come here! Your father and I need a word!"

"What is it," asked Helen as she approached her grandmother and father.

"Now, I've heard rumors that you're seeing this Derek Sharpe," Cassandra announced.

Helena blushed. She and Derek had been seeing each other ever since he was created a second peer. Needless to say, she was enamored with this dashing young man. Yet, not everyone in the regal family shared her enthusiasm with her boyfriend. Even though no one had expressed their distaste verbally, Helena could feel it all around her. "Grandmother," the princess said, "must we talk about this now?"

The King gave his daughter a kindly look. "Helena, how do you feel about Mr. Sharpe?"

Princess Helena shrugged. She had yet to truly give her relationship with Derek a title, due in part because they'd only been able to meet at Derek's apartment in Old Andover, which wasn't deemed proper by the officials within the palace. "Dad," began Helena, "I don't know."

"Honey, the only reason I ask is because we need to know where you two stand. Sooner or later, people will begin to ask questions," the King stated. "The holiday season is coming up, the wedding isn't that far away, and if Mr. Sharpe is on your arm, we need to figure out his role within your life."

The cold, clinical nature of her father's deduction left Helena feeling withdrawn. "But I'm not sure," she said truthfully.

"Do you see yourself marrying this man," interjected Cassandra. "If you are, that changes everything!"

"Grandmother! I don't even know if I want him to bring me coffee! How am I supposed to know if I want to marry him?! I'm only twenty-five!"

"Yes, but when I was your age, your grandfather and I were already married," Cassandra exclaimed.

Helena folded her arms with disdain. "Dad, must we do this now?"

"No. However, this topic isn't going to dissipate anytime soon, Helena. For your sake, we need to know what to make of Mr. Sharpe before you two proceed any further."

Princess Helena withdrew from the conversation, but she didn't feel at peace with the topic at hand. Even though she was terribly fond of Derek, she wasn't ready for anyone to place a title on their relationship. Suddenly, Helena remembered where she was. Unlike the other twenty-something women in the kingdom, she didn't have the high powered career or the freedom to date and sleep with as many men as possible. Anyway, the thought of being so free with her body made the young princess want to vomit. But there was a part of her that did want to know whether or not she and Derek could blossom into more. However, it was that same yearning that made her dread the possibility of true happiness. Her weight loss was due to her strict eating regime. What would happen, she worried, if she couldn't keep up this routine? Would Derek leave her? Would she ever find a real boyfriend who could become her husband? Those other girls were lucky, Princess Helena reminded herself. But the sad irony of her situation lay in the fact that all of those high flying twenty-something women would give it all up to be her.

"Did you enjoy the dinner," Michael asked Matthew in the comfort of his private sitting room.

Matthew wrapped himself in a black cashmere blanket as Michael held him with all of his might. The wind blew past the giant oak tree outside of Michael's window with great authority. In that single moment, Matthew felt more secure than he had in a very long time.

"I did," Matthew replied. "The dinner was lovely. However, the more I'm around the Prince of Kemp, the more I think he has it in for me."

Michael kissed Matthew's forehead. "He doesn't. Alexander is special."

"No," laughed Matthew. "I'm serious, Mike. I think your son would like nothing more than to see me on the next flight to Amsterdam."

"Stop that," ordered Michael. "Whatever the Prince of Kemp thinks is inconsequential. I love you and we will be wed in the spring. If he can't handle it, that's his problem, not ours."

Matthew considered these words before saying, "But then I had a very odd conversation with Prince Robert."

"What did the dashing prince say?"

Matthew turned his gaze towards Michael. "Nothing…just about how your life is about duty and the crown… How every minute of my life will be planned for me… The Prince of Kemp also said that I'll be second when it comes to your time and affection."

"Is that so?"

"Mike…"

"Matthew, they were completely out of line. I don't know where they get off saying that to you, but they know nothing of the details of my life." Michael grabbed his lover's hands with great strength. "Look, this is new for me too. In the eight years that I've been the monarch, I haven't had to share a minute of my life with anyone."

"Do you have doubts?"

"If I were to say that I didn't, I'd be disingenuous. What's important is that we work as a cohesive team. As long as we do that, no one can upend us."

"Then why would the princes say that to me?"

Michael rubbed his eyes. "Robert's miserable in his own life and my son has no sense of boundaries. Let's leave it at that."

"Agreed," Matthew nodded. He looked at his watch before saying, "Well, I'd better leave now. It's almost two o'clock in the morning."

Michael shook his head with great abandon. "Stay here."

Stunned by Michael's statement, Matthew replied, "But I thought you wanted to wait until after the wedding."

Michael gently kissed Matthew's soft lips. His hands grazed Matthew's hard chest. "Matt…just stay…"

With a slight nod of his head, Matthew allowed the King to make passionate love to him for the first time in months.

16

Lady Margaret returned to her state apartment after saying goodbye to her husband and son before their trip to Cyprus with the Princess of Kemp, only to find Princess Sophia waiting in her reception room. Lady Margaret watched as Princess Sophia walked through her reception room as if she owned everything in it. Annoyed by her cousin's presence, Margaret snapped, "What do you want?"

"That's no way to talk to someone who ranks above you in every way that matters," Sophia sighed.

Lady Margaret stormed over to Princess Sophia with purpose in her stride. "Get out. I don't have time for you."

"Actually, I came to see Edward…"

"He and Samuel are on their way to the airport. You can see him in ten days," Margaret replied.

Sophia started for the door before stopping in her tracks. Although she hadn't come to speak with her cousin, this was the perfect time to finally express her utter contempt for the woman who stood before her.

"He's not here," Margaret wailed. "You can go."

Princess Sophia closed the door to the reception room and ordered the waiting valet to keep out all visitors. "We need to talk."

"I have nothing to say to you."

"Very well. I have a lot to say to you. You may want to sit down."

Lady Margaret stood in front of the roaring fire. She hated when her younger cousin acted as if she were the Queen of Andover. It made her sick to her stomach to think that Sophia had done nothing worthwhile in her entire life, yet everyone seemed to worship her as if she were a saint. "If you want to order someone around, go to your own state apartment," Margaret challenged. "Say what you will, and then get out."

"I want you to leave my husband alone. He told me what you said to him last night. I think it's wholly unacceptable that you would do something so cheap and tawdry at a reception thrown by His Majesty," Sophia sniffed. "It only shows your true character."

Lady Margaret laughed in Princess Sophia's face. "You think you're God's gift, don't you? How dare you judge me, Sophia? You're no more than an ice queen. Why do you think Robert came to me?"

"You're easy," retorted Sophia.

"I'm sensual. I love the human form."

"Tell it to someone who doesn't know you're a whore, Margaret."

"What language. I'm sure His Majesty would cringe to hear you speak in such a common way," bit Margaret.

"And I wonder what he would do if he were to ever discover that *you* leaked the story about your accident and the miscarriage to the press."

Margaret spun around on her heels. How did Sophia know about that? Walter, Margaret instantly deduced. How could he betray her like this? "You don't know anything," Margaret wavered.

"I know how utterly desperate you are to have my life! You covet everything I have! It's just sad!" Princess Sophia clenched her fists in order to keep her anger under control. After a lifetime of loathing Margaret without verbalizing it, Sophia knew that it was now or never. "But why would you put your family through that ordeal? Just to get back at me?"

"It has nothing to do with you, you narcissistic bitch! Not everything in this kingdom hinges on the whims of Princess Sophia! God," screamed Margaret. She could feel the years of hatred for this woman overflowing within her. "How dare you come into my home and accuse me of something so reprehensible!"

"Because I know you. You either did it to spite me or to gain sympathy for yourself."

Margaret flashed her cousin a twisted smile. “Well, the princess isn’t as simple as she appears.”

“How could you,” choked Sophia. “Why would you put the family through that scandal?”

“Does it matter?!”

“Yes!”

Margaret let out a primal scream. “I did what I had to do. I would be better off with Robert. You and I both know that!”

“He’s my husband…”

“But you’ve never loved him like he needs to be loved.”

“Oh, come off it! You’ve been sleeping with him for a year! You have no idea what he really wants or needs. You’re just a desperate, over the hill woman with too much time and money on her hands,” seethed Princess Sophia. “You cannot have my husband.”

“I already have. And,” Lady Margaret sneered, “he made love to me in ways you could never imagine.”

Princess Sophia tried to restrain her mounting anger. “Did you honestly believe that leaking that story to the press would solve anything? If anything, it only made Robert more committed to <u>our</u> marriage. He wants nothing to do with you!”

“That’s not true.”

“It is. He barely looks at you, Margaret. No one in the family, except for your brother, your husband, and son, will even talk to you! We all know what sort of woman you are. And, to be frank, it’s embarrassing.”

“How dare you sit there in judgment of me? You have had just as much to do with this as I did. You made me leak that story!”

“What?” Sophia recoiled at the thought. “I had nothing to do with that,

Margaret!"

"But you would have done it sooner or later. I did it for both of us." Lady Margaret began to pace the room with fierce determination. "You would have done it… Why not let Robert go? He would be much happier with me…"

"You're crazy," gasped Sophia.

"Why do you always win?! It's not fair," shouted Margaret. "All of my life I have had to sit by and listen to everyone extol your virtues. You are far from perfect! Why should you have Robert and everything else?"

Sophia tried to find the right words to bring her cousin back to reality. "Margaret, it's over. The leak doesn't matter anymore. You have a husband who loves you, and a son who adores you. Why can't that be enough?"

"It was," Margaret whispered. "But now, it's not."

Sophia started for the door. "Margaret, Robert doesn't love you. Whatever happened between you was physical, not emotional. Edward would die for you."

"It wasn't supposed to be like this," Margaret called after Sophia. "No. It was supposed to come out that Robert was the father of the baby…then he would have left you and Edward would've left me… That's when Robert and I would have been together!"

Sophia looked at Margaret. In that single moment, Sophia felt terrible for her, but she didn't want to make things worse by making it seem as if she were condoning her cousin's slightly psychotic behavior. "I have to go…"

"Get out," snarled Margaret.

Sophia opened the door to the reception room as she said, "I'm sorry, Margaret…"

Margaret raised her hands in disgust. "Go..."

Tears began to roll down Lady Margaret's face as she finally realized that everything she'd done in a misguided attempt to win Robert's love was in vain.

She dried the tears on her smooth face as she wondered what she should do next. Nothing for now, she decided. However, it was time for her last chance at happiness.

His Highness Prince Robert of Andover walked down the corridor that linked the private state apartments to the main artery of Andover Palace. The household staff bowed as he made his way towards Michael's official office. Whatever this was, Robert thought, was of great importance, and that's what worried him.

Upon entering the King's office, Robert was surprised to see the Prince of Kemp scowling in a chair across from the King of Andover's immense desk. He bowed before them. "Your Majesty; Your Regal Highness."

"Sit," ordered Michael. The King sat behind his desk with an expressionless grimace. "I am deeply disappointed in you two."

Alexander rolled his eyes. "What else is new?"

"That's enough, Alexander."

"Dad, if you made me sit in a car for four hours to listen to what a disappointment I am, I'll go now."

"You're not going anywhere," Michael snapped. "Now sit down."

The Prince of Kemp sat down like an insolent child. "I have better things to do..."

"As do I," Michael said angrily. "At last night's dinner, I expected everyone to make Count Matthew feel welcomed. In a few short months, he is to be my husband and any disrespect to him will be seen as disrespect to me."

"I'm sorry," Robert said, "but what's this all about?"

Michael took a deep breath. "You and my son told the Count separately that I wouldn't have time for him due to my position as Andover's monarch."

“Michael,” Robert stammered, “I didn’t mean anything by it. Last night was a bit difficult for me.”

“If you didn’t make your life so difficult, you wouldn’t wind up in these situations,” countered the King. “And as for you, Alexander, what do you have to say for yourself?”

Alexander crossed his arms defiantly. He didn’t know why his father was being overly defensive about some man he wanted to marry. To Alexander, this was a pointless exercise in his father’s use of monarchical power. “What do you want me to say, Dad? I’m sorry? I was simply making sure that Count Matthew was right for you.”

“Is that so,” asked the King, suspiciously.

“Of course, Dad. If Matthew can’t understand the reality of the union he is about to enter into, then he might want to rethink his place within your life,” Alexander cooed.

The King eyed his son with great care. “Be that as it may, you had no right to speak to him in such a manner.”

“My apologies,” the heir to the throne sighed. “Is that all?”

“You may go.” Michael waved them out.

As they walked down the corridor, Robert said, “What was that all about?”

The Prince of Kemp shook his head. “Who knows? But if this is what it’s going to be like with Matthew was my new stepfather, I’m not looking forward to it, Uncle Robert.”

Robert lowered his voice. “If he makes your dad happy…”

“Oh, my dad’s happy, but I think this whole incident is a mistake. Can you imagine what the European royals must think about the King of Andover marrying a man,” Alexander retorted. “It’s embarrassing.”

Prince Robert bit his tongue. He knew how well Alexander could manipulate people, and he was not going to be the prince's next victim. After twenty-one years within the regal family, Robert decided that keeping quiet was the only smart thing he could do. He was already on thin ice with the King, and to compound that by siding with Alexander or speaking out of turn to Matthew would further complicate his life. With that, Prince Robert bade Alexander goodbye and returned to his state apartment.

Princess Helena flushed the toilet in Derek's two bedroom apartment in Old Andover. Although she was less than twenty minutes away from the palace, she felt like she was in another world. Derek's apartment was nothing like the princess had ever seen. The first seventeen years of her life were spent in Kemp Castle, while the past eight were spent in the calm, protective walls of Andover Palace. While her mother's sister lived in a large mansion, this was the first time Helena had ever been in an apartment. Needless to say, she was bewildered that anyone could live within the confines of four walls within a building with hundreds of other people they didn't even know. The sheer size of the apartment stunned Helena the first time she'd stepped into it, but this was the third time she'd been to Derek's apartment and it still bothered her.

The Princess of Andover washed her hands thoroughly with the bar of soap. After drying her manicured hands on a towel she'd smuggled in her purse from the palace, Princess Helena returned to Derek, who was strumming his guitar in the living room. She looked around for a safe place to sit.

"What do you want to do," he asked quietly.

Princess Helena gave her boyfriend a light smile. "We could go to Cabo. I love their egg and Brie salad. I use to eat their lobster and Gouda salad, but then the papers wrote about it and everyone started eating it. Did you know that the chef at Cabo made that salad just for me? You see, when he started out, he worked at Port Agnes House and then he would work at Kemp Castle for a few weeks when a lot of the staff had off. Anyway, that salad was his gift to me, but everyone had to have it." She exhaled before saying, "What do you want to do?"

"Your Regal Highness," he said, "I don't know if I can do Cabo today."

"Why," she asked bewilderedly. "It's the best luncheon restaurant in Old Andover. Unless you want to go to Blake Manor... Lord Walter's cook is terrific."

Derek placed his guitar on the floor and moved towards his girlfriend. "Look, I 'm not in the same financial situation as you."

She stared at him blankly. The one thing Princess Helena had been taught by her mother and Princess Fiona was to never discuss money with anyone. The five million Andover dollars she received each year from the Regal Expenditure was hers in lieu of her duties in support of the King, but she had further trust funds from her grandfather, His Regal Highness Duke James of Andover, her mother, and her mother's family. Princess Helena also had financial interests in many publicly listed organizations, some of which she wasn't even aware of. "Derek, money doesn't interest me."

"I don't mean any disrespect, but that's because you have it."

She crossed her feet at her ankles. "I don't want to talk about it," she replied firmly.

"Princess, my mother's parents didn't leave her a lot of money when they died. Most of their estate went to taxes and stuff like that. I basically live on credit cards."

"But," began the princess, "can't you get those taxes back?"

He shook his head. "It doesn't work like that."

"But Derek, you're in *The Andover Peer Review.*"

"So?"

"So, that means you have money. Everyone in there has money."

Derek averted her innocent gaze. "Not everyone. Besides, I shouldn't even be in that book because my mother refused a title."

“But the King made you a second peer! Surely you can do something with that! Why don’t I call His Highness Prince Robert? His father owns a shipping company – or something like that – so maybe he can give you a job…”

“I have a job,” Derek snapped.

“Playing polo with Prince Joseph? Derek, that doesn’t pay when you’re not playing!”

Derek stood up in a huff as he walked towards the window overlooking the main road that led to the chic downtown district of Old Andover. “Maybe we should just call it off for today. I have a lot to do.”

Helena was confused by Derek’s sudden change in mood. What she couldn’t understand was why he was so concerned about money. Everyone she knew had it. After all, Derek was a friend of Prince Joseph, so by proxy, he should have had some money. If Derek didn’t have any money, then how did he manage to meet Prince Joseph? “Derek,” she said in a soothing tone, “why don’t you let me pay for lunch? I’m simply famished. The car is waiting outside, so we can leave now.”

“Not today. I need to be alone.”

Resolute in the fact that he didn’t want to be around her, Princess Helena picked up her vintage Hermes Birkin handbag. “Send me an e-mail when you’re in a better mood. Goodbye.”

“Goodbye, Your Regal Highness.”

Princess Helena walked out of the apartment building to the waiting executive Lancia Thesis. The one good thing about being in this part of town, was that the paparazzi seemed to be oblivious to the fact that she was seeing Derek. That, or they simply didn’t care. Either way, the princess craved this moment of total freedom.

She ordered the driver to take her to Cabo as she instructed Bertie, who sat up front with the driver, to reserve a private dining room at the restaurant. After a moment of quiet contemplation, Helena dug her iPhone from her bag and called Prince Joseph.

"Hey," he said. The sound of barking dogs filled the air.

"Where are you," she inquired.

"I'm at the palace with Grandmother. What's up?"

"Can you meet me for lunch at Cabo? I need to talk to you."

"Fine. I'll be there in a few minutes."

His Regal Highness Prince Joseph entered the private dining room to find his sister typing away on her iPhone. "Spreading gossip," he joked.

"No," she said, putting her phone down to greet him. "Do you remember that girl Courtney Marshall? We met her a few years ago at one of Grandmother's garden parties."

Joseph sat down and began flipping through his menu. "No… Why?"

"Well, I've heard from Danisi Rachel Collins that Courtney is going to marry some X-List Hollywood actor. Needless to say, her parents are furious. I can't blame them. Why would she marry an actor of all people? I mean, to be tabloid fodder when you're a member of the regal family is one thing, but to seek it out? The thought makes my skin crawl. Anyway, I was simply reading about the actor she's going to marry." Helena took a deep breath. "Thanks for meeting me."

"Sure. Grandmother was crushed that you didn't want her here."

"That's not true! I needed to have a moment alone with my brother," Helena stated. "What are you having?"

"The goose."

Helena waved over their private waiter. "I'll have the egg and Brie salad. His Regal Highness Prince Joseph will have the goose breast. We'll also have a bottle of champagne." The waiter disappeared. "Tell me everything you know about Derek Sharpe."

Joseph let out a hearty laugh. "I should've known. You only want my endless streams of knowledge!"

"No," teased Helena, "it's not true! But I need to know everything."

"Helena, it's not proper. I shan't divulge what I know."

Helena sat up. "So you do know something! I knew it!"

"Helena, I'm not going to play gossip girl with you. You can play that game with Grandmother or Aunt Sophia." Joseph poured himself a glass of water. "Why do you care all of the sudden? I thought you were totally smitten by Derek."

Helena nibbled on a piece of bread. "I was…I mean, I am. But he got all weird when I suggested that we come to Cabo for lunch. Then he goes on this tirade about how he isn't rich! I didn't ask him for a flow chart regarding his finances, I just asked him to lunch!"

"Helena, Cabo isn't exactly cheap."

She furrowed her brow. "That's what he said. It's not my fault I've never had to pay for a meal…or anything else. Is it?"

"No," Joseph sighed. "But the one thing I've learned by being away from Andover is that we are the lucky ones."

Helena groaned. "Don't get all save the world on me! I'm not in the mood to feel bad about who I am."

"I'm not asking you to feel bed. But that egg and Brie salad you're so fond of is one hundred and thirty dollars, Helena."

"So?"

"That's like a days work for some people," explained Joseph. "Derek was probably put off by the prices."

"I told him I could pay," she exclaimed. "But he turned me down."

The waiter returned with the champagne, poured it, and left the young regal family members in peace.

"I think Derek's just very proud."

"I was only trying to help! God, this is annoying."

"What is?"

"The fact that my power and position can get me anything, except the respect of the man I could actually fall for." Helena twisted a strand of her hair. "It sucks."

"Helena!"

"Joey, how did you meet Derek?"

The young prince took a sip of his champagne as he tried to recall the events of so many years ago. "I met him during a riding competition the year before I left for Monaco. He was really nice, we got along very well and we had a few mutual friends. When I formed my polo team, I had to have him on board."

"But you never knew he had no money?"

Joseph cringed at the talk of money. Like his sister, he had been brought up never to mention his financial position under any circumstances. His father had taught him to say that if anyone ever asked him if he were rich simply to say, 'I'll have to look into that.' "Helena, you asked him about money?"

"No," she replied quickly. "He brought it up. So, tell me what you know."

Joseph played with the butter knife as he said, "From what I know, Derek was put through private school by his grandparents, but they stopped paying for his education when he graduated from high school. Other than that, I don't think his parents were especially well off. He's just an average guy."

"That's what I feared," the princess responded truthfully.

"Mother, do you have a moment," asked the King. He walked into her tea room where she was reading a novel by Jane Austen.

"Of course. Have a seat. Would you like for me to call for a tea service?"

"No."

Cassandra observed her son with great care. He looked very tired, more so than in the past. However, Cassandra was aware how being the monarch of Andover could wear on a perfectly fit person. "Darling, I must say that I enjoyed the dinner last night. Count Matthew is a delight."

Michael gave his mother a tight smile. "I'm glad you feel that way. My son and brother-in-law seem to feel otherwise."

"What did they say," she inquired.

Michael recounted the tale from earlier this afternoon as Voltaire and Bramble sniffed around his feet. The King took a deep breath before adding, "Do you think I haven't prepared Matthew for the realities of regal life?"

"Michael, there's no true way to ever prepare someone for life within the palace," reasoned the Dowager Queen. "Since we were born into this life, we have been taught by example on how to operate within our world. For those who marry into this family, there are a different set of rules. Your father use to say that he had to reconcile the part of him that wanted to go out with his hunting friends, and the part of him that had to support me in my duties as the Princess of Kemp, and then as the Queen of Andover."

"Mother, it seemed easier with Katherine." Michael stopped himself before it sounded as if he loathed being with Matthew. "What I meant to say was that with Katherine, there didn't seem to be a lot of pithy observations from other members of the family."

The Dowager Queen nodded in agreement. "That's true. Yet I don't think it has anything to do with Katherine being more prepared than Matthew. One could argue that Katherine was left to her own devices. However, at that time you were the Prince of Kemp, which allowed you more time to teach her the ways of regal life. As the monarch, everything is different," said Cassandra.

This statement was the one thing Michael continually told himself that didn't matter. He was resolute in the notion that he loved Matthew more than anything, but things had changed since his last marriage. Michael was no longer the heir to the throne; he was the King of Andover. No longer could he take two months off to tour the world; each and every day was spent in the daily routine of duty and expectations. Michael began to seriously wonder if he could implement a new spouse into the equation, or if he was being too ignorant to the potential problems that lay ahead.

"Son, you will be the first monarch since King Henrik to marry whilst on the throne. Thankfully, I had twenty-five years with your father before I ascended the throne. I have no doubt that you and Count Matthew will find a way to make your marriage work."

"Thank you."

Cassandra held her slender hand to her lips as she said, "Why don't you take the Count to the regal performance of that musical next week?"

"Do you think it will be seen as too soon for the people?"

"It should be fine. Besides, it's time you two were seen in public together."

"But *The Last Five Years* isn't exactly a jubilant show," noted the King.

Cassandra nodded in agreement. "I think it'll be a smart move for you. Show the world how happy you two are... And it should dispel whatever fears others may have about your relationship."

Michael left his mother in her tea room, before ordering his secretary to make the necessary arrangements for next week's regal performance at the Duchess Victoria Theatre in Old Andover. Feeling on top of the world, Michael decided that it was time to stop worrying what his son or brother-in-law had to say about his union, because he was resolute in the fact that this marriage would change the world forever. What's more, the King realized more than ever how much he loved Matthew and the eighth of April couldn't arrive soon enough.

His Regal Highness Lord Walter stood in the midst of his dressing room as the bespoke tailors from Hutton & Company, dressers to the male members of the regal family for over one hundred years, examined the evening suit that gently clung to his mid-sized frame. Despite the fact that Walter missed Daisy a little less with each passing day, he was beginning to look forward to tonight's cocktail party. The household staff of Blake Manor was busy preparing for the party below, as the head tailor from Hutton & Company, Mr. Zachary Cole, said, "What do you think, Your Regal Highness?"

"It fits well. Thank you." Walter gave them a small smile. "Will that be all for today, gentlemen?"

"If Your Regal Highness wishes," Mr. Cole replied.

"Very good. That'll be all. Thank you." Walter wandered into his bedroom, as Jasper instructed the tailors on what to do next.

In the privacy of his bedroom suite, Walter collapsed on his king size four poster feather bed. He closed his eyes, when Jasper knocked at his door to inform him that Princess Sophia was waiting in the Green Drawing Room. Walter quickly dressed and took the back staircase to find his cousin waiting patiently on the sofa.

Princess Sophia wore a sleek silver gown that was a one of a kind creation by her personal fashion designer, Clifford Pennington. His designs were all the rage due to the fact that he'd dressed the princess for evening and special occasions for the past six years. The princess looked up as her cousin offered her a glass of Merlot, which she politely declined.

"You're a little early for the cocktail party. Did your mother send you to ensure it went off without a hitch," he asked wryly.

Princess Sophia laughed. "I suppose. I received an invitation this morning, but I was in the area, so I thought I'd come by early and relax."

Walter sat in a chair directly across from Sophia. "Is that all?"

"You were right about Margaret," she blurted out. "I really do think she leaked that story to the press. I even confronted her about it, and she didn't deny it."

"Wow," Walter moaned. "I didn't think you would do that."

Sophia uncrossed her legs. She rarely confided in Walter to this degree, but he was becoming a stable force in her life, especially since she'd discovered her husband and cousin's blatant deception. "Walter, I had to say something. Sometimes I think Margaret does what she does because she thinks I'm a pushover. Well," the princess stated, "I am not."

Walter finished his glass of Merlot. "What happens next?"

"I don't know," sighed Sophia. "Maybe she'll join Edward in Cyprus."

"Sophia, I don't know what to say. It's hard being caught in the middle of all of this, but I don't want to see your marriage fall apart because of Margaret's manipulative tendencies."

"Thank you. Speaking of marriage, whatever happened to that woman… What was her name?"

"Daisy," Walter said softly. "The last time I saw her was after you tore into her. I haven't seen or heard from her since."

Sophia bit the inside of her cheek as she gazed out of the large window. To some degree, she felt truly terrible for the way she behaved upon discovering that Daisy and Walter were seeing each other. What if that was Walter's one chance at love, Sophia wondered. However, she was all too aware of the social conventions and regal duties that bound them together, thereby limiting the pool of acceptable romantic partners. "If it's any consolation, I am sorry," the princess finally said.

He couldn't believe what he was hearing. In the forty-seven years that he'd known his cousin, this was the first time she'd ever apologized to anyone, especially him. "Thank you, Sophia," he said with great warmth. "However, I'll be all right."

"Yes, you will," she smiled.

Walter poured himself another glass of Merlot. "Who else has Aunt Cassandra bullied into attending this cocktail party?"

"I think it's just you and me. She said it was an intimate gathering for fifteen, which means that it should end by seven-thirty or so." The princess rose as she said, "I'm going to retreat to a bedroom in the East Wing until tonight."

Lord Walter watched as his cousin left the room, but thoughts of Daisy were now on his mind. Yet, he didn't miss her. He was livid with her! How could someone who claimed to love him so very much run off without so much as a courtesy letter to inform him of her whereabouts? He'd spent the better part of the last few weeks using every tool at his disposal, but it was all for naught. In that moment, Lord Walter decided that it was time to push Daisy out of his life for good because he had a lifetime of happiness ahead of him.

The cocktail party at Blake Manor was underway a few minutes past five-thirty in the evening. A queue of expensive, yet eco-friendly cars dropped off the crème de la crème of Andover's proper society. The fifteen invited guests included Countess Masoli, and her daughter, Danisi Samantha Masoli, who was to have a formal introduction to two important members of Andover's regal family: Princess Sophia and the man the Dowager Queen wanted to be Samantha's future husband, Lord Walter. Events such as this were quite common in the kingdom, but the invitations were quite difficult to come by. In order to be invited, one had to have some sort of connection with a member of the regal family; however it never ensured entry into their exclusive world. Tonight, Cassandra spent more time than usual preparing the guest list because if all went to plan, Walter would have a family in a matter of years.

The guests were led through the vast, impressive foyer, down the corridor, and into the Official Reception Room of Blake Manor. Although Blake Manor was originally built as a regal residence by King Henrik for his youngest daughter, Princess Fiona, it was still intended to host official functions. As the household staff of the manor served the fifteen guests, Princess Sophia and Lord Walter were announced before entering the room and being introduced to their guests.

The majority of Princess Sophia and Lord Walter's lives were spent hosting affairs of this kind. While they always performed their duties with the grace of a regal family member, they secretly wished they would end before they began. The princess caught herself glancing at her watch as she made her way down the reception line; however, her perfect smile never vanished from her face. As for Lord Walter, he was as charming as could be, despite the fact he wanted nothing more than to go for an early evening ride around the grounds of Blake Manor.

"And how long have you been in the kingdom," Lord Walter asked Danisi Samantha Masoli as her mother, Countess Masoli, stood to her right.

"I came back from Paris three years ago, Your Regal Highness," cooed Samantha.

"That's quite nice," smiled Walter. "I spent quite a bit of time there with my parents in my youth. Yes, Paris is a very special city to me."

Samantha couldn't help but smile. "It does hold special memories for me, Sir."

"Your Regal Highness," Countess Masoli chimed in, "you have a lovely home."

Walter was a bit flabbergasted by the way in which the countess intruded into their conversation. It was a known rule within the kingdom that one was not supposed to speak to a member of the regal family until addressed by said family member. However, during the last few years, people seemed to become much more lax with that tradition, Walter reminded himself. Even though he refused to embarrass the overeager Countess Masoli because he was too polite, he didn't want to offend a friend of the Dowager Queen. That, Walter reminded himself, would be a fate worse than death.

"Thank you." Walter signaled Jasper for another drink. "My grandfather, the late King Henrik, built Blake Manor as a home and wedding present for my mother and father. This home holds many special memories for me."

"I can see why," Countess Masoli responded quickly.

"Tell me, Danisi Masoli, what are your interests?"

Samantha pursed her lips. "I have a love for horses. Right now, I work with a charity that specializes in the promotion of sports as a rehabilitation technique…"

"She also sits on the board of The Farringdon Art Museum," interpolated the Countess.

"Yes," Samantha demurred. "I do that as well."

"Very interesting." Walter looked up to see Princess Sophia chatting with an old friend. "Please enjoy the evening," he smiled. "If you'll excuse me."

"How is she," asked Sophia once Walter reached her.

Walter tried to suppress his smile. "Danisi Samantha is very interesting. The Countess is…Let's just say I can understand why she's a friend of your mother's."

Sophia simply nodded because she knew all too well what Walter meant by that statement.

As the party began to wind down, Lord Walter instructed Jasper to bring Samantha to him. "Yes, Your Regal Highness?"

"I would like to have you as my guest on a ride through the hunting grounds of Blake Manor next weekend."

"Shall I bring my own horse?" asked Samantha.

Walter let out a soft chuckle. “We have plenty in the stables. Now, I will have my office contact you with the details.” He extended his hand towards his guest. “It was very nice to meet you, Danisi Masoli.”

“Thank you, Your Regal Highness.” Samantha shook his hand as she performed a flawless curtsy. “Good night.”

“I think now is the time to initiate the first phase of our plan.”

The Minister of Government, Patricia Ali, folded her hands. “Your Regal Highness, is this what you want?”

“Yes. It’s time, Ms. Ali. Are you having second thoughts?”

“No,” she replied. “We’re in this together.”

The Prince of Kemp raised his crystal tumbler of cognac with purpose. “Minister, you won’t regret this partnership.”

17

A week later, November came to Andover with a great storm that grounded all flights in and out of the island kingdom. Although this storm could have been a public relations disaster for the kingdom, the King's announcement that acts of nature were the consequences of life seemed to provided stressed travelers with a sense of hope.

As the rain slapped the windowpanes of the Smoking Room at Andover Palace, Princess Helena paced the room with great anticipation. This was the first time Derek had visited her at the palace. While the press made a few overtures about the nature of the visit, Princess Helena had Bertie release a statement that Derek's visit was merely official and nothing more. However, as Helena waited for Derek to be seen into the Smoking Room, she couldn't help but feel ill.

"Mr. Derek Sharpe, 2nd Peer," the valet announced.

Derek bowed, as Bertie curtsied. "May I get you anything, Your Regal Highness," asked Bertie.

"No, thank you."

Bertie left with the valet.

Derek couldn't take his eyes off of the dark blue room with thick damask drapes. "My whole apartment could fit in here twice!"

Helena managed to give him a weak smile. "Oh, I've always loved the Smoking Room. Actually, no one smokes in here anymore. The Dowager Queen banned smoking in the palace twenty years ago. But this room is my favorite. Please, have a seat."

Derek fiddled with his tie, and shifted uncomfortably. "So, what's up?"

"Where is this going," she blurted out. "Derek, I need to know."

Derek did his best to catch his breath, but the wind was already knocked out of him. "I…don't know…"

"But that's the problem! My family expects certain things from me and my brothers. I'm second in line for the throne, which means I have to be serious about who I spend my time with," Helena revealed.

"What is this? I thought we were having fun…"

"Having fun is a night at the palace with the King of England. Derek, where are we going? Are we going to be serious? Do you want to marry me?"

"I haven't even thought about any of that. It's totally out of my realm of thought," he said truthfully.

"But it's within mine. If this isn't going anywhere, I have to know now. If it is, then it's a different story."

"How so," he asked cautiously.

Princess Helena began to pace the room as a million thoughts flew through her head. "You'd have to meet my grandmother and aunt before we went any further. After that, you would meet the rest of the family. However, you'd meet my father last. I don't know why, but as the monarch, he will only receive you once he knows this relationship is going somewhere. Then, the palace will release a statement saying that we're officially seeing each other and where it goes from there is up to us. But if we were to get married, we'd have to get permission from my grandmother, my father, and the Minister of Government." Helena stopped in her tracks. Derek sat in the chair near in the center of the room looking like a suspect in custody. She walked towards her frightened beau with great concern. "Derek?"

"What?"

"Is something wrong?"

Derek shook his head as he said, "Yes… I can't do this. I mean, a relationship should be allowed to blossom in its own time without all of those rules and conditions."

Princess Helena tried to put on a brave face. "But Derek," she exclaimed, "it's not nearly as intimidating as it sounds! Ever since King Christoph ruled, this is how regal life has been!"

"But are the rewards worth the journey," he asked.

Princess Helena suddenly felt sick. In all of her dreams, this wasn't how her first true love was supposed to turn out. "Derek…" Helena's voice broke off. No matter what her heart told her, she already knew how this incident would play out. "You don't want me, do you?"

"You're great, Your Regal Highness. It's me… I'm not from this world."

"So?"

"I wasn't even brought up to think this world was a possibility. I'm sure that some men would jump at the chance to be your husband and live a regal life." Derek took Helena's soft hands in his. "It's just not me."

Princess Helena pressed a discrete button in the arm of the sofa. A cold look came over her youthful face as the Smoking Room doors flew open. "The servants will show you out."

Derek rose to his feet and followed the waiting valet out of the palace.

Tears filled the princess' eyes as her heart broke in half. It didn't matter to Princess Helena that Derek didn't come from the same background as her or that they were still getting to know each other. How she felt about Derek was unlike how she'd ever felt about any man before. But the fact that he refused to even consider changing his point of view to have a life with her made the young princess want to crawl into bed for the next hundred years.

"Your Regal Highness," Bertie called from the doorway.

Princess Helena turned to her with mascara stained cheeks. "What, Bertie?"

"You are expected in the Sun Room for lunch with the Dowager Queen and Prince Joseph."

Princess Helena dried her eyes as she stormed down the endless corridors of Andover Palace and into the Sun Room where her grandmother and brother were playing with Cassandra's dogs.

"Helena," exclaimed Cassandra, "you look a fright!"

"Thank you," snapped Helena.

"How did things go with Derek," asked Joseph earnestly.

Helena shook her head. "It's over."

"What's over?" Cassandra sat Voltaire on her lap. "Did I miss something," she asked as she stroked the dog.

Helena proceeded to inform her grandmother and brother about her futile attempt to get Derek to become a permanent part of her life. "I only wanted to be happy," wailed Helena.

"Darling, don't make a fuss! These things *happen*. Now, granted, they've never happened to *me*, but they do happen." Cassandra took a satisfied sip of her special drink. "You'll have to be aware of the sort of men out there. Not all of them want to be a member of our illustrious family."

"Grandmother," Helena seethed, "it's not about that! I followed your advice and now look at me! I'm no better off than I was last year."

"Helena, this isn't the time to point the finger of blame. Now," the former monarch sighed, "you will be fine. I pray you won't make a scene at the regal performance tonight…"

"I'm not going," Helena interjected.

Cassandra placed Voltaire on the floor as she leaned into her granddaughter. "You have no choice in the matter. I'm sure His Majesty wouldn't appreciate his daughter making a scene on an official night."

"She's right," Joseph reasoned. "Helena, if you want, I'll remove Derek from the polo team."

Helena gave her brother a weak smirk. "No…I'll be okay. Eventually."

"What you need," Cassandra rambled on, "is someone from *The Andover Peer Review*."

"Derek was in that book and look where it got me!"

"That's not what I mean, Helena. Please, stay with me. That Derek Sharpe was someone who wasn't raised to want to be the spouse of a regal family member. You need someone who was raised in that mode. It's that simple!"

Joseph gave his grandmother a dubious glance. He knew that Cassandra could do a lot more harm than good for the sake of the regal family. He just hoped his sister wasn't a casualty of the greater good. "Grandmother, why don't we let Helena process this before we start planning the rest of her life," Joseph suggested.

"Very well," Cassandra sighed. "I was only trying to help."

His Highness Prince Robert drove to The Hunting Lodge with the heaviness of the world on his shoulders. Ever since his affair with Lady Margaret was exposed within the regal family, he made a decision to stay away from the place where he'd conducted the affair. The Hunting Lodge was Robert's private retreat from the regal family and regal life, but he knew within his heart of hearts that he had to sell it in order to move on with his life. Besides, he and Sophia were slowly getting their marriage back on track and this show of solidarity for their union could only enhance his standing with the rest of the regal family.

Robert steered his BMW X3 through the rain and down the narrow country lane to the dirt drive that led to The Hunting Lodge. There it sat, a brick and timber framed cottage that he'd fallen in love with so many years ago. However, the wonderful memories of the past turned to the cruel realizations of the present and suddenly the cottage looked more foreboding than it ever had before.

He unlocked the door to find the cottage as he'd left it so many months ago. The living area had been tided by his maid, while the kitchen smelled of old cheese. Robert rummaged through the refrigerator until he found the offending piece of diary, which he threw out of the window, and onto the soft grass near the lake. With a heavy sigh, the prince observed the cottage for the last time.

A knock on the door made him jump out of his skin. As he started for the door, he didn't know why he hated having visitors here, but that's how it had always been. He pulled open the door to find his father, Hider Lawson, standing there with a black trench coat wrapped over his body.

"Come in," Robert said quickly.

His father removed his coat before sitting on an old oak chair. "I can't believe you're getting rid of this place."

"Dad, I told you not to come in this weather."

"I had to. Rob, what's this all about?"

"I need to let go of the past. Sophia's giving me another chance. I need to make a clean break."

Hider examined his son with great care. "Is this what you want or a regal directive?"

"To be honest, the regal family hasn't said anything about my selling The Hunting Lodge. Actually, they're just starting to speak to me again."

"How can they just ignore you? You're the King's brother-in-law," exclaimed Hider. "Rob, I don't know why you tolerate their behavior."

Robert rubbed his eyes as he reclined against the rough wall. "It's not their fault. I don't know what I was thinking, but I should have known better. And the worst thing is, I didn't think I would get caught."

Hider released a deep grunt. "Son, it's your life. I just don't think selling The Hunting Lodge is a wise move. Why don't you let me buy it from you? I'll hold it until you come to your senses."

“Thanks, Dad, but I need to rid myself of this place.”

Hider clambered to his feet as he put on his coat. “Well, I have to get back to the office. If you change your mind, let me know.”

“I will.” Robert ushered his father to his car, gave him a tight hug, and watched him drive off.

“I thought he’d never leave.”

Robert froze in his tracks. His mouth turned dry as Lady Margaret entered the living room from the bathroom. She was dressed in nothing but a small towel. Her eyes twinkled in the afternoon sun that made its way through the torrential rain. He slowly backed away from her. “What are you doing here,” he stammered.

“I know you still want me,” she cooed. “We’ll have to be more careful this time, Robert.”

“How did you get up here? I thought you were…”

“Shh… I’m here now and that’s what matters.” Margaret moved towards Robert. She placed her hand on his crotch. “Come on. We’re so good together.”

Robert smacked her hand away. “Get out, Margaret.”

“What?”

“Leave. Now,” he ordered.

“No,” she said defiantly.

“Fine.” Robert whipped out his iPhone and dialed a familiar number. “Sophia, it’s me. I wanted to let you know that Margaret broke into The Hunting Lodge… I’ll handle it.” He placed the phone into his pocket and gave Margaret a cold stare. “Just go.”

Margaret clutched her stomach with the flair of a dramatic actress. In that single moment, she felt as if her world were falling apart in front of her. She loved Edward, but her love for Robert was something deeper. It was, to her mind, the love she’d been seeking her entire life. How could he reject her in her moment of need? "Don't you love me," she cried.

"Get dressed," he demanded.

"I won't! I've given you everything! How can you treat me like a common whore?"

Robert seized her by the shoulders. He gazed into her eyes, but he couldn't see the woman who once enraptured him to the point of no return. In this very moment, she looked broken. "That's not how it is and you know it. Our spouses have given us a second chance! I intend to make my marriage work," Robert said with great conviction.

Margaret freed herself from his grasp. "You're really going to be unhappy for another one hundred years with that ice queen?"

"I love my wife."

"Don't say that! It's not true!"

"It is! I always have! This…was a moment of weakness." Robert grabbed his car keys from the nearby table.

Margaret tried to wrestle the keys from his hand, but her attempt to make her lover stay was futile. She fell to the floor, sobbing as she'd never done before. "Please…it was more than that. You and I…we were real."

"Goodbye, Margaret."

"No!" Margaret released a primal scream as she watched Robert drive away. Her breathing became labored as she continued to grab her stomach. Whether the pain was imaginary or not didn't matter. Nothing mattered, she told herself. How was she meant to go on when the only man she'd ever loved more than life itself rejected her for that insipid Princess Sophia?

Margaret pulled herself from the floor. She started for the bathroom when she caught her reflection in the mirror. How unkind the years had been, she thought ruefully. Lady Margaret wiped the tear stains from her face because she knew this was no way for a regal family member to behave. No, she thought, this was no way to behave. Just because Robert rejected me, she said to herself, didn't mean this was over. No, Margaret told herself, this was not over.

The Duchess Victoria Theatre in Old Andover stood as a beacon to the burgeoning artistic community in the Kingdom of Andover. This theatre was first established over ninety years ago by the then Duchess Victoria of Andover as a way to introduce the best of theatre, opera, and symphonies to the people of the kingdom. Ever since its founding, it had been an unmitigated success. Quite often, the regal family would attend a performance of the best new show. There were even times when a regal family member would show up for a matinée to the surprise and elation of the actors and patrons. Tonight's performance of *The Last Five Years* was eagerly anticipated by everyone in attendance. However, the presence of the entire regal family as well as a few international celebrities – each vying for a photo opportunity with the King – ensured that the press would be in full force tonight.

The car containing Her Regal Highness Lady Margaret was first to arrive. Although her husband and son were still in Cyprus with the Princess of Kemp, she decided that making an appearance without her family would be the best thing for her image at this moment in time. Despite the events that transpired between her and Robert at The Hunting Lodge, Margaret was resolute in the fact that she was meant to achieve greater things, whether or not she had to drastically alter the course of her life. The photographers went wild over her dress by a new Andover designer, C.P. Jude, but her personal secretary whisked her into the theatre before anyone could ask those pesky questions regarding the riding accident at Port Agnes House all those months ago.

"What a turn out," Prince Joseph whispered to his sister, who was unusually quiet. "Helena, are you here?"

"Yes," she murmured. "I'd rather be at home than attending this silly show."

Prince Joseph patted his sister on the head. “Hey, Derek's an ass. If he can’t see what a catch you are…”

“Don’t patronize me, Joey. I’m not in the mood.” Princess Helena tossed her brother a dirty look as the chauffeured car came to a stop in front of the illuminated theatre. The door to the car swung open as the flashbulbs nearly blinded the prince and princess. As they waved to the screaming crowds before entering the theatre, a reporter called out to Helena, “Do you have any comment about what happened today?”

She turned to the reporter with a terse look. Her relationship with the press had never been good, although they’d stopped calling her Princess Porky once she started her diet of little to no food. Right now, she wasn’t in the mood to entertain whatever issue they decided to make up in order to get a rise out of her. Princess Helena whispered something to Bertie before walking into the theatre behind her younger brother.

“I knew she was crazy,” Princess Sophia muttered to Prince Robert as their car pulled up to the theatre. “You can’t trust her.”

“I didn’t know it would go this far,” Robert said adamantly.

Sophia cast a disapproving glare over her husband. “What did you think would happen? She would let you use her and then slink into a corner? That’s not how Margaret operates. She’ll do whatever it takes to get what *she* wants and woe to everyone else.” Sophia pulled at the drop diamond necklace around her neck. “I can’t believe you could be so naïve.”

Prince Robert gazed out of the window at the screaming crowds. “How many times do I have to say I’m sorry?”

“Until I forgive you,” she retorted.

Princess Sophia and Prince Robert walked onto the red carpet to the delight of the crowds. In spite of all of the turmoil affecting their personal lives over the past few months, they were still the most beloved regal couple in the land. Although Margaret had leaked the story about her accident, she wasn’t callous enough to mention Robert, much to the relief of Sophia and Robert. This meant that they could go about their lives in public as they always had because no one would ever be the wiser.

Princess Sophia and Prince Robert walked into the theatre as the car containing Count Matthew Hall came to a stop at the foot of the red carpet. Matthew stepped out of the car in a daze. This was the first time in his life that he had ever been subjected to the frenzy of public sentiment. He had no idea what they thought of him or his upcoming marriage to the King of Andover, however, he stood resolute in the fact that this would be his life from now on. The Count was met by a junior member of the King's office, Danielle Wallace, before he stepped onto the red carpet.

"It's very nice to meet you, Count Matthew," Danielle said breathlessly.

"Thank you. What happens now?"

She glanced at her clipboard. "I'll walk you into the theatre and to the reception room before we meet His Majesty in the Regal Box." Danielle began to lead Matthew down the red carpet as she said, "After the performance, you will have a backstage tour with His Majesty before leaving for a quiet reception at the palace."

"That's a lot," he joked uneasily.

"Where's the King," called a reporter.

"Who made your suit," screamed an overeager fashion journalist.

"Don't respond, just smile," advised Danielle.

"Why is he here," Prince Alexander pouted to the Dowager Queen as their car drove towards the theatre.

Cassandra rolled her eyes at her grandson's childlike petulance. "Alexander, sometimes you can be quite annoying," she said breezily.

"That was uncalled for, Grandmother."

"Is it? Your father has already told you how much the Count means to him, yet you continually throw meaningless tantrums. Your brother and sister are just fine with the news!"

Alexander folded his arms with marked defiance. "I'm not my siblings."

"Isn't that a shame," she countered.

"Grandmother, why are you taking my dad's side? This whole marriage is an embarrassment to the kingdom!"

Cassandra pointed a long finger at her grandson. "Now you listen to me, young man! Your father has sacrificed more than his fair share of happiness in duty and service to country and crown. He shouldn't be asked to give up a second chance at love. If you cared about him as much as you say you do, you could keep your thoughts to yourself and let him be."

Alexander froze as his grandmother tore into him. He suddenly remembered everything Princess Sophia told him regarding the real reason why his father married Katherine all those years ago. That's not my problem, Alexander thought angrily. "I can't help the way I feel," sniffed Alexander.

"I'm not asking you to," she countered. "But I'm telling you to support your father and his soon-to-be-husband in public. Nothing more."

As soon as their car came to a stop, a security officer opened the door and helped out the Dowager Queen. She waved to her adoring public, as the Prince of Kemp changed his scowl into a tightly controlled smile. They walked into the theatre as the final car arrived, the car containing His Majestic Regal Highness The King and Lord Walter.

"I'm glad the cocktail party went well," Michael told his cousin.

"I am, too. Samantha is a great woman."

"Walter, I do want to see you happy. But I have to ask you one question."

"What?"

Michael bit his lip before asking, "What has become of Miss Daisy Herman?"

Walter was stunned to hear her name come from Michael's mouth. "To be truthful," Walter finally said, "I haven't spoken to her in months. I'm moving on with my life."

"I'm glad to hear it."

"How did you find out about her," Walter inquired.

The King simply gave him an all knowing smirk as he stepped out of the car, flanked by his bodyguards and his personal secretary, Glenn. Walter followed behind his cousin with great admiration. Walter was grateful that Michael had let him handle his relationship with Daisy in this own way. In that very moment, Walter began to see the King of Andover in a completely different light.

18

The ninth of November, His Regal Highness Lord Walter's forty-eighth birthday, was marked by a quiet dinner at Blake Manor which was attended by the entire regal family. The talk revolved around whether or not Walter would eventually marry Danisi Samantha Masoli. She was the chief candidate for Walter's wife, but he was still unsure was to whether or not she was the one.

Meanwhile, the tenth of November, proved to be a turning point in the relations between members of the regal family and their proven enemies, the press. The first story from the tenth of November was splashed on the front page of *The Pass Observer* with the trashy headline: "*I Dated Princess Porky – Derek Sharpe's Story*". To the horror of the regal family, the salacious story revealed the true nature of Derek's relationship with Princess Helena and what he perceived as her desperate attempt to get him to marry her.

"Daddy, how could this happen?!" Princess Helena cried on her father's knee.

The King stroked her head tenderly. "Helena, why did this happen?"

"I don't know, but," she sniffled, "it's not my fault! I only wanted to know where we were going, but… How could he betray me?"

Michael asked himself this question. It was one thing to reveal details based on pure conjecture about members of the regal family, but to invade the privacy of the King's daughter was a step too far. "Don't worry," Michael said in a low tone, "I'll fix this."

"I'm so humiliated. I thought…"

"I know," the King responded sympathetically. "However, he is a less than an honorable man."

"He only did this because he's poor," she retorted. "He got a peerage and then he betrayed me!"

"Helena…"

The young princess stood up and threw herself onto her father's bed. "I want to kill myself!"

"You stop this right now," the monarch ordered. "Helena! Listen to me!"

She turned her tear stained face towards her father's stern expression. "What?"

The King sat next to his daughter with great concern. "I don't want to hear you speak in that manner again. Is that understood?"

"Why does this always happen to me? I was falling in love with him." She wiped her eyes with the back of her hands. "This is all Grandmothers' fault."

"What does she have to do with this?"

"She made me rush my relationship because she thought it wasn't right for us to date for so long without making some sort of announcement about the state of our commitment. That's the only reason why I asked him about it!"

"Is that all?"

"No… I didn't know he was poor when we met, but then he always worried about money. I'd want to go to Cabo and he'd decline because it was too expensive. I don't even know what that means," she wailed. "Then when I called him to the palace to talk, he said that he could never be a part of this world and all of that crap." Princess Helena buried her face into her hands. "How could I have been so foolish?"

"Mother, may I have a word?"

"Yes, Your Majesty?"

Michael stood across from his mother, who was writing in her journal in the study within her private suite. She placed the fountain pen down with great care.

"Mother, what did you say to Helena about her relationship with Mr. Sharpe?"

Cassandra recounted the conversation she'd had with her granddaughter. "I was only trying to help," she said innocently. "I didn't know he would turn on her! This has never happened to us before!"

She was right about that, Michael realized. This was, to Michael's mind, the biggest breach to regal life in the last hundred years. "Be that as it may," the King said sternly, "I have a young woman who is utterly humiliated in my bedroom. It breaks my heart to see my daughter in this kind of pain. After all she's been through, she doesn't deserve this."

"I know," demurred the former monarch. "Did you read the story?"

"Unfortunately. I had to."

Cassandra pulled a copy of that morning's *Pass Observer* from her desk drawer. "He said that the princess was, 'Too self-involved to care about the pain of the average man. Her world consisted of expensive three hour lunches at Cabo and careless shopping excursions at the expense of the palace and tax payer. Princess Helena's concern for the everyman is severely lacking. When she discovered that I could not conform to her world, she banished me from the palace.'"

Michael ordered his mother to stop reading. "I don't need to hear that trash again. He paints the princess as a vapid socialite."

"Which she is not," corrected the Dowager Queen.

"I'm still curious as to how people can buy this everyman routine. We are all equal. It's not Helena's fault she has a lifestyle that some people envy," snapped the King.

"I agree, Michael." Cassandra placed the newspaper in her desk drawer. "What are you going to do?"

Before Michael could respond, Cassandra's attending valet opened the door with a deep curtsy. "Excuse me, Your Majesty; Your Regal Highness. Your

Majesty, your personal secretary has requested to see you."

"Show him in."

Glenn ran into Cassandra's private study, gasping for air. "The Minister of Government is giving a press conference on Channel 3. We just got word from her office."

Michael and Cassandra turned on the television as Glenn dutifully waited outside. The King and the Dowager Queen watched in earnest as the Minister of Government took her position at the top of the decorated podium.

"With regard to today's events concerning a story about Her Regal Highness The Princess Helena's relationship with Mr. Derek Sharpe, I must express my view on the matter…"

Cassandra turned to her son with fear on her face. "What is she doing?!"

Patricia continued: "The way in which a member of Andover's regal family could cast aside a member of the public in such a careless manner is abhorrent. As the ruling family of the Kingdom of Andover, the regal family has a duty to behave with the utmost respect to their public. The Princess Helena did not express a modicum of compassion for Mr. Sharpe.

"Subsequently, I have offered Mr. Sharpe a role in my government in the Department of Social Policy. His story has truly raised an issue that many of us in Andover rarely discuss: The differences between us and the regal family. With that said, I would like to address another issue that one could say is in direct correlation with Mr. Sharpe's story.

"As we know, His Majesty is set to wed Count Matthew Hall on April 8th of the upcoming year. While this is a joyous occasion for the regal family, as well as the kingdom, one must wonder if we will have to pay for the Count's lifestyle. As the spouse to the monarch, Count Matthew Hall is entitled to six million dollars per annum from the Regal Expenditure, which is funded in part by the taxpayer. The Count comes from a wealthy aristocratic family; the King is worth five billion dollars. Why must the taxpayer continue to fund the expenses and extravagances of the regal family in light of Princess Helena's callous behavior towards a member of the public?

"I urge the people to consider my comments. These issues will be a part of my re-election campaign next year. I hope that we can systematically end the social divide within the kingdom, as well as stopping the Count from profiting from the Regal Expenditure. This money should be used for the public good.

"Thank you, and good day."

The Dowager Queen sat up in shock. In all of her life, she had never heard an elected official speak out against the regal family, or the way in which the Regal Expenditure operated. This woman had spoken out against the King, Princess Helena, and the future spouse of the monarch, Count Matthew. The Dowager Queen couldn't believe the lengths this Patricia Ali woman would go to in order to secure her position as Minister of Government. Cassandra had never truly cared for the woman, but now, she wanted nothing more than to see her pay for her betrayal of the regal family.

Michael stared at the television screen as commentators on Channel 3 began to dissect Patricia Ali's speech. By Michael's estimation, something had to be done and fast. This woman had single handily turned a story that could have simply died in the days to come into a social and political nightmare. Michael had supported Patricia's bills and signed the majority of them into law. Without his support, her government would fall apart. He knew the power he wielded over this woman, which made him question the true reason behind her speech. Something wasn't right, he told himself. Until he found out what it was, he had to deal with a public relations nightmare. The entire regal family would need to work together to set this right because if they didn't, their entire way of life would be threatened. Michael knew that he had to do whatever it took to pull the monarchy through this time. However, in this very moment, he knew that the time to act was now.

The King of Andover instructed Glenn to put out a letter to the entire regal family ordering them to remain quiet about Patricia Ali's earth shattering speech. Princess Sophia continued to call her brother with the fear that her entire world would crumble around her, but he reassured his younger sister that he would handle this debacle.

In the twenty minutes following Patricia Ali's speech, Andover Palace, Kemp Castle, and Blake Manor were inundated with phone calls from the Andover press, as well as monarchist reporters from around the world asking for a statement. "No comment," was all the regal residences had to say. For the King, this was the worst kind of disaster because it was out of his control and he, like the rest of the regal family, was caught completely off guard. Had the King actually seen this coming, he may have been able to stave off the resulting worry from the regal family, but that was not meant to be.

Alone in his private office, Michael held his head in his hands. Defeat, it seemed, had swept through the body of this powerful man. Right now, the only person he needed to speak to was his mother. Michael ordered Glenn to send word for the Dowager Queen to join him in his private office.

"Michael," she cried upon her arrival, "this is terrible! I've never seen anything like this! The press is reporting that Patricia has blindsided the kingdom and other members of the press are saying that she's right, but then some believe that she's overstepped her bounds by criticizing you…"

Cassandra lowered her weary soul into a chair near her son's desk. In all of her eighty-three years on earth, she'd never lived through a time as trying as this. Maybe, she thought, she should never have abdicated. If Cassandra were still Andover's Queen, Michael and Matthew would be free to live under the radar for a few years…at least. Yet, at this time, the only issue that mattered was the one at hand.

"Mother, we need to maintain a cool thought process."

"That vile woman had no right to speak out against us," growled Cassandra. "One could have her beheaded for treason!"

"I won't disagree with you," muttered Michael. "However, what's done is done."

"Then what are you going to do?"

Before Michael could respond, Glenn called the office to say that Patricia's main opposition, the leader of the Andover Libertarian Coalition, Daniel Harris, was preparing to give a speech on Channel 3.

"Good afternoon," began Daniel, "I would like to address the concerns my opponent, Minister of Government Patricia Ali, expressed regarding the Regal Family of Andover."

"Oh, God," moaned Cassandra.

Daniel continued: "Ever since King Christoph founded the Kingdom of Andover over one hundred and thirty years ago, the regal family has played an integral role in the development, strength, and international stability of this great kingdom. My party and I are shocked by Ms. Ali's statements that the regal family consider themselves above the every day man.

"My party has collected data that suggests that the regal family is the number one supporter of charitable organizations, excluding those they support as regal patrons. Last year alone, the regal family donated more than one hundred million dollars to various causes throughout the kingdom and abroad. My opponent has failed to mention this in her tirade against the regal family. While I do not know what transpired between Her Regal Highness The Princess Helena and Mr. Derek Sharpe, we cannot judge her for the way in which their relationship has ended. As many of us know, what happens between couples is very hard to decipher.

"With regard to her statements concerning Count Matthew Hall, his role within the kingdom and the Regal Expenditure, my party finds her intrusions into the private financial affairs of the regal family shocking. The Regal Expenditure is administered with the dividends from the King Henrik Bank and Trust, which the regal family owned until the first depression eighty years ago, and in return for a sixty percent interest in the bank, the government would pay those of the regal blood, and the monarch's spouse, a payment in kind for their services to and for the kingdom. Had it not been for this arrangement, many of Andover's early citizens may not have survived the first depression.

"My party and I hope that before the next election, the people of Andover will see Patricia Ali's party for what they truly are. Thank you, and good day."

Michael turned off the television. "I can truly say that I didn't expect Daniel Harris to be so kind."

Cassandra sniffed with great indignation. "Well, he's right! That Patricia Ali woman must be dealt with, Michael!"

"I know."

"Are you making a speech? I think you should."

"I will," he said calmly. "I'll order Glenn to send for a camera crew."

Cassandra shook her head with disbelief. "Be sure to reassure the kingdom that Matthew will be treated as any other monarchical spouse. They need to know that."

"Did you have to deal with this when you became Queen and Dad became the Duke of Andover?"

"Of course not," she scoffed. "Back then, people were much more accepting of life as it was. That Ali woman is nothing but a divisive figure, Michael. She'll do anything to undermine you, us, and the kingdom. For all we know, she wants to turn Andover into a republic."

Michael sat in the chair next to his mother. "That won't happen," he replied. "Mother, do you think this is happening because I'm marrying a man? If Katherine were alive, I don't think this would be an issue. Do you?"

Cassandra avoided her son's gaze. She knew he was right because Michael's marriage was still a bone of contention for some people within the kingdom, although those who mattered were fine with the fact that their monarch was gay. “I do think it may be a source of that Ali woman’s vitriol,” sighed Cassandra. “Be that as it may, we must deal with it as it comes. Michael, you are a fine monarch. We will win.”

“Your Majesty,” Glenn said with a knock on the door.

“What is it?”

“Count Matthew Hall is on the line?”

“Fine. Glenn, call Channel 3 and have them send a small crew to my official office.”

“Very well, Sire.”

“Mother, could you excuse me?

With a nod, Cassandra followed Glenn out of Michael’s private office.

“Hello, Matt.”

“Michael,” Matthew said, his voice shaking, “there are so many reporters outside of my parents’ house. It’s ridiculous.”

“I know. The press has called every regal residence. I’m thinking of moving everyone to Port Agnes House until this dies down. That includes you and your family,” Michael stated.

“Mike…”

“I will fix this, Matt. Don’t worry.”

Matthew let out a frustrated sigh. “Why is this happening?”

“I don’t know. Patricia Ali is very unpredictable. Why she’s so negative towards you is beyond me.”

“You should rescind her invitation to the wedding.”

“I can’t. As the monarch, I am not allowed to express a political view. And despite the next election, she will be at the wedding.” Glenn opened the door to Michael’s office to inform him that the press would be at the palace in thirty minutes. "Darling," continued Michael, "I have to go."

"All right. Mike, I'm sorry if I've caused you any undue stress."

"Matthew," Michael replied sternly, "you've done nothing wrong. I love you."

"I love you. Goodbye."

"I hope Michael knows what he's doing," Princess Sophia stated as she paced through the Crimson Room.

At Michael's request, every member of the regal family was in the Crimson Room for his live broadcast to the kingdom. The Prince and Princess of Kemp were noticeably absent because their residence was four hours away, however the King instructed his son and daughter-in-law to watch his live address and not to say a word to the staff.

"How are you doing," Prince Robert asked Princess Helena.

"I'm so humiliated," she admitted.

"That Patricia Ali woman is abhorrent," Cassandra interjected.

Lady Margaret shivered at Cassandra's blunt statement. "Aunt Cassandra, you shouldn't say such things."

"It's true, Margaret," insisted Cassandra. "That woman has no respect for tradition or the laws of the kingdom. I don't know why the people voted her into power in the first place!"

"She was a fresh voice," noted Edward. "That's the problem with a pseudo-democratic system when the monarch is Head of State."

"Are you defending her," challenged Cassandra.

"Of course not," Edward responded. "I think the Minister of Government does whatever she can to keep her party in power, despite the repercussions. She acts for the moment, not for the future interest of the kingdom."

“Which is why we have a monarch as Head of State,” Princess Sophia stated. “It keeps the entire kingdom from slipping into entropy.”

“I wouldn’t say that,” Margaret snapped.

“I didn’t ask you,” bit Sophia.

“Stop it,” ordered Cassandra.

Prince Joseph turned up the volume on the television. “Here we go,” he sighed.

“And now, live from Andover Palace, His Majestic Regal Highness The King…” Channel 3’s lead anchor announced gravely.

In the next moment, the camera showed King Michael standing before his desk with a solemn expression on his face. No more was the jovial monarch; he was gone, possibly forever.

“Good day,” he began. “The recent events of today have brought many issues to light, which affect each of us in a different way. One is not immune from what one could consider small or even trivial news in the world we live in today. Each new revelation must be met with the utmost importance in order to distill its true importance.

“Many of you may be aware of the two speeches give by opposing political parties regarding the role of the regal family in today’s world. While the regal family is legally obliged not to engage in the political world except for the monarch’s right to refuse to sign a bill into law, it is important for the kingdom to know that my speaking with you today does not involve a political angle.

“Furthermore, the recent story in today’s press concerning Her Regal Highness The Princess Helena is a matter which is being dealt with internally. It is the wish of Princess Helena for her privacy to be respected at this time.

“With regard to the matter of Count Matthew Hall, he will be a member of the regal family as His Regal Highness The Duke of Andover. The last Duke of Andover was my father, His Regal Highness The Duke James of Andover, a title which he held until his death eight years ago. As stated in the Kingdom of Andover's Constitution in Section 7, Part 43, Paragraph 1, the spouse of the monarch, will be styled as the Duke or Duchess of Andover and receive the appropriate fee as per the Regal Expenditure. The Count will receive six million dollars per annum, as per the law, and this comes from the dividends of the King Henrik Bank and Trust, not the public coffers. Anyone who may doubt the veracity of this statement is free to consult the constitution. The role of the monarch's spouse is to support the monarch in their duties, as well as their own. Lastly, the monarch's spouse is the only regal spouse to receive funding from the Regal Expenditure. The other spouses married to regal family members, including the Princess of Kemp, are financed by their regal spouse.

"I thank you for your time this afternoon. Good day."

"The press is on our side," cheered Prince Joseph. "The bloggers and reporters are saying that your speech single handedly saved the kingdom and put Patricia Ali in her place."

Michael gave his youngest son a weary smile. In the ensuing hours since his speech, the palace was once again under attack by the press to get a copy of his speech in order to dissect every word. However, Michael rarely wrote down any of his speeches, which left the task of transcribing his live speeches to a lowly member of the palace's press office. The King reclined on his bed, as Prince Joseph sat at its foot.

"Dad, are you all right?"

"I'm old," Michael replied. "It's been a long day."

"Yeah, but Helena's better."

"Good. Joey, do you still want to join the armed services?"

Prince Joseph bit his lip in the same manner as his father. "I guess. It is frightening to think about. What if I die out there?"

“You won’t die,” Michael said quickly. The sheer thought of losing his son while he was serving the kingdom – and his own father, the King – made Michael weary each and every time. “I won’t let it happen. If I have to put you on clerical duty…”

“I don’t want special treatment,” Joseph snapped. “Dad, I’m just nervous.”

“Is that all,” the monarch asked softly.

“Yes,” smiled Joseph. “I’m going to bed.”

“Good night, Joseph.”

“Night.”

Across the kingdom, the Prince of Kemp eyed Patricia Ali carefully. “You were very sloppy, Patricia.”

“Your Regal Highness, I had no idea your father would make that statement. Or Daniel Harris!”

“Enough!” Alexander slammed his hands onto the table, silencing the Minister of Government. “Do you know that the majority of people from your own party are now thinking of voting for Harris’ party? This could be a nightmare.”

“I’m aware of that, Sir…”

“What do you intend to do about it?”

Patricia Ali averted his gaze. “I don’t know.”

“Of course you don’t. If everything we’ve worked for so far is thrown away because you were too careless to be smart, we will have a problem,” seethed the Prince of Kemp.

19

In the weeks following the scandals concerning Princess Helena and Count Matthew Hall, life returned to normal in the kingdom. Despite the fears from some within the regal family, the backlash against the Regal Expenditure was slight and only came up on meaningless panel programs which usually consisted of five out of work comedians. To the surprise of many, Patricia Ali's party lost ten percent of their supporters, while Daniel Harris' party gained twenty percent. The Dowager Queen knew that the power of the regal family would forever endure, while political parties barely lasted a decade if they were lucky.

The King managed to exert his control as Head of State by refusing to sign in two of Patricia Ali's party bills into law, which prompted some within the government to wonder if the King was doing this out of spite or because the law wasn't to his liking. Either way, the King's speech placed him firmly at the top of Andover's political world, even though he was still legally bound from expressing a political view. Yet, for a few small moments, the King knew that Patricia Ali's days as Andover's Minister of Government were coming to a quick end.

Meanwhile, life in the palace returned to normal. Princess Helena began to make herself seen in public once more, while Lady Margaret thrust her husband and child into the public sphere with the gusto of a pushy stage mother. For Princess Sophia and Prince Robert, their marriage slowly began to repair itself with the sale of The Hunting Lodge to a local man for three hundred thousand Andover dollars. Although it was billed as a nominal sum, Prince Robert was thrilled to have that part of his life eradicated for good.

In the comfort of the Blue Parlor, Michael sipped his coffee as he surveyed the guest list for his wedding to Matthew. In four months, their union would finally take place to the relief of all those involved with its planning. Guests were coming from all of Europe's royal houses, as well as those of Asia, while the President of the United States and his wife had confirmed their invitation weeks ago. Michael looked up and smiled at Matthew, who had just arrived for his first regal breakfast.

"How many people are coming to the wedding," asked Matthew.

Michael handed him the list. "I believe there will be two hundred people at the wedding and a thousand people at the reception."

Matthew nearly fell out of his chair. "That many, Michael?"

Michael shrugged as he ordered the maid to refill his coffee cup. "It's a regal wedding. People from all over the world are coming to support our union. To be honest, it's a great honor."

"I should've known it would have been a big deal," Matthew stammered.

"I do hope it's all right with you. If it's not…"

"Don't be silly," smiled Matthew. "Who doesn't love a big party?"

"Oh, that reminds me, is your sister Kate coming to the Christmas Eve luncheon? I've had responses from your parents, and your sisters Suzanne and Nancy."

Matthew nodded. "I don't know why she didn't send a response, but she spoke with my mother the other day and she'll be there with her husband James and their daughter, Clara."

"Very well. They'll get to meet my entire family. My office has just informed me that the descendants of Prince Christian and Prince Erich will be there."

"This is the first time I've ever heard you mention them. Why don't you ever talk about them?"

Michael took a long sip of the piping hot coffee. He rarely spoke about his grandfather's brother's families because he hadn't been brought up to think about them with any regard. While his mother was Queen, she invited them to Christmas Eve luncheon, but they rarely mingled with the rest of the regal family. Michael found the entire day quite odd, so once he became the King of Andover, he simply stopped inviting them, much to Cassandra's chagrin. However, with his upcoming marriage, Michael decided that now was the time to bury whatever animosity that may exist between the different branches in the family with the hope that all was not lost.

"They live around the world," Michael said solemnly.

"Are they coming to the wedding?"

"As far as I know, yes."

"Will you tell me about them?"

Michael shifted in his seat. As the King of Andover, he wasn't use to people asking him to explain himself, yet when Matthew did it, he never felt as if he was being put on the spot. "What's there to tell," he began. "I don't know them that well. For reasons only known to them, King Henrik and my mother, Princes Christian and Erich moved out of Andover and to other parts of the world. Rumor has it that Prince Christian and Prince Erich disliked Duchess Victoria – their sister-in-law – so much that they left the kingdom. She wanted her daughters to be at the fore and not have to share the spotlight with Christian and Erich's children. Needless to say, my mother rarely discusses her uncles. Anyway, their descendants are still in the line of succession. There aren't many of them left today simply because they didn't have a lot of children or live very long."

"Who will be here on Christmas Eve," asked Matthew.

"From the Prince Christian branch we'll have His Regal Highness Vincent and his father, Mark, His Highness of Andover, who is the widow of Her Regal Highness Sylvia of Andover. Also, Her Regal Highness Elmira will be in attendance. Now, you should know that her lineage is very…interesting…"

"How so?"

Michael leaned in and whispered, "Her father is Lord David, Prince Christian's only son. Her mother is Her Highness Ilsa, who is the sister of Edward's father and Olivia's mother."

"Are you serious," Matthew asked with wide eyes. "Her mother is Edward and Olivia's aunt?"

"Yes," nodded the monarch. "She's Edward and Olivia's first cousin, Samuel's first cousin once removed through her mother and Margaret and Walter's second cousin through her father, Lord David."

Matthew couldn't help but cringe. "That's a too incestuous."

The King nodded. "Be that as it may, that's the way it is, Matthew."

"What about Prince Erich's descendants?"

"His great-granddaughter, Her Regal Highness Frances is married to His Highness Richard and they live in Italy with their son, Jason who is the 1st Marquis of Westport. Frances and I have never gotten along. We have very different views of the world."

"That's all very interesting," Matthew smiled. "There's so much to learn."

"Christmas Eve is in three weeks, so you'll have plenty of time to become acquainted with the regal family tree." Michael glanced at his watch and stood up quickly. "I have to attend a regal event in Lord's Pass in ninety minutes. I'll see you soon," Michael said as he kissed Matthew passionately.

Matthew watched as the King marched out of the room with a regal air. As Matthew took in the lush environs of the Blue Parlor, he began to feel very much at home.

The Dowager Queen stepped out of the car with the help of her longtime driver before entering the main hall of Kemp Castle. Although the Dowager Queen lived in Kemp Castle for twenty-seven years before she ascended the throne, she rarely came to the castle these days. While the best memories of her life were captured in the walls of this castle, there were some moments in time she wish would simply vanish from her collective memory. However, she still felt at home at the castle in spite of the many renovations paid for by Michael when he moved into the Kemp Castle. Alexander, on the other hand, had kept Kemp Castle in the same fashion as when his parents resided there. Cassandra assumed that for some reason, Alexander was trying to maintain a link to the past and his mother.

The attending butler led Cassandra down the long corridor to the Drawing Room where the Princess of Kemp was waiting to have lunch with her husband's grandmother. As she welcomed the former monarch to her home, Olivia informed Cassandra that Alexander would be along in a few moments.

"Very well," Cassandra smiled. She placed her drink order before turning her attention to the future Duchess of Andover. "My dear, how are you getting on these days?"

"I'm quite well, Your Regal Highness. I feel that being away in Cyprus was a real chance for me to reconnect with myself."

The Dowager Queen took a sip of her drink. "In my day," she sniffed, "one had to face their problems at home instead of running off to some island." Cassandra placed the crystal glass onto a nearby table. "I do suppose that times have changed, as they always say. Did the Prince of Kemp have any objections to your little jaunt abroad?"

Olivia managed to give the Dowager Queen a weak smile. In the many months since Cassandra told her that she was replaceable, Olivia had done everything in her power to become pregnant and save her marriage at the same time. However, it was proving harder than she thought. She was still without a child, her husband was pushing her away, and she wanted nothing more than to run for her life. The single factor that kept her content within her marriage was the notion that she would become the Duchess of Andover whenever Michael passed on. That, Olivia reasoned, was reason enough to stay in her loveless marriage.

"My husband is very supportive of me," lied Olivia. "The cook is preparing braised rabbit with a country style stew for lunch."

Cassandra wrinkled her nose. "That's very traditional, dear. With all of the money the regal family spends on a chef for Kemp Castle, one could do better than rabbit and stew."

"I thought it would be nice as the weather is much cooler. We are in the beginning of December."

"I am aware of that," bristled Cassandra. "I'm not a doddering old fool!"

Olivia turned red at Cassandra's biting remark. "My apologies."

"Yes! Now, the lunch will suffice. My dear, have you given any more thought to our conversation earlier in the year?"

Olivia nodded. "Your Regal Highness, the Prince of Kemp and I…"

"Grandmother," Alexander called as he walked into the Drawing Room. "You look ravishing."

Cassandra rose to give her grandson an affection hug. "My dear, we were just talking about you."

"Is that so," he asked.

"Your wife was telling me about the lovely lunch the cook is preparing. I can't wait." Cassandra gave the Princess of Kemp a withering glare. "How was your meeting?"

"Long. I do wish people could do what they were supposed to do. It would certainly make my life easier," remarked the prince.

The Princess of Kemp said, "Darling, who was at your meeting?"

"No one important… It was just more of the same, really."

"Well," began the Dowager Queen, "every meeting is important. That's what my father use to say. I live by that edict. If one spent their time at unnecessary meetings, the world would simply dissolve into an unnecessary state!"

Olivia tried to find the sense behind the statement, but it was lost on her. At least she isn't mentioning my fertility issues, Olivia reminded herself.

The Prince and Princess of Kemp walked with the Dowager Queen to the Conservatory where lunch was being served. They ate in silence until Cassandra said, "When is the baby due?"

Alexander and Olivia gave exchanged a curious look. Neither could quite believe the wherewithal of this woman, but they knew they shouldn't be surprised by the actions of the self professed keeper of Andover's treasured past.

"We're still trying for one," Alexander said firmly. "These things take time."

Cassandra took a long bite of her braised rabbit. "I don't know what's taking so long. The longer you wait, the harder it will be for you to have a child. Alexander, your mother was pregnant with you within a year and a few months of marrying your father!"

"Grandmother," interjected the prince, "you and Grandfather waited eight years before my father was born. Maybe I get it from you."

"I doubt it! For most of that time, your grandfather and I were busy traveling on behalf of my father who was the monarch. Let's not forget that James performed duties with the armed services for four years when we were first married." Cassandra motioned for the attending staff member to bring her another drink. "Besides, those were different times…"

"With all due respect," Olivia replied, "we do lead quite busy lives."

Cassandra gave the princess a kind smile that barely masked her growing annoyance. "I'm sure you do," she cooed. "Alexander, you are aware of how important it is for you to produce an heir."

"I am," he stated.

"If you do not," continued the Dowager Queen, "the throne will pass to Princess Helena upon your death. And if she never finds a husband, the crown will pass to Prince Joseph! But if he never settles down, it will pass to Samuel! The entire regal line will be thrown into chaos! I do hope you understand the brevity of the situation," she said in a low, controlled voice.

Alexander gazed at his wife. "I always have."

Olivia stared back at her husband with great contempt. She couldn't believe that he was trying to put all of their problems on her. If Cassandra had her way, Alexander would divorce her, marry someone else, and continue to pretend that he was the perfect husband. She'd come too far to lose everything now. "I'm sure the Prince of Kemp and I will be able to resolve this issue," Olivia said with great resolve.

The Dowager Queen finished her stew before saying, "I do as well. It would be a pity if you didn't."

"Why does she hate me so much," Olivia moaned once Cassandra was safely on her way back to Andover Palace.

Alexander shrugged with noticeable indifference. "Who knows? The Dowager Queen is very protective of the regal family. I need an heir, Olivia."

The Princess of Kemp could feel her stomach twisting into a thousand knots. While she was away in Cyprus, she had quietly seen a fertility specialist who had flown in from New York to consult with her. It seemed, Dr. Watkins informed her, that the issue was not her fault. He reminded the princess that until her husband received a fertility test, the issue of why she wasn't pregnant would remain unsolved. With this knowledge in hand, Olivia still hadn't told her husband because she feared that he would explode over what he would view as her ultimate deception.

"I know," she finally replied. "We have to keep trying."

"I can't right now," he said. Alexander stood up as he headed for the castle's library.

"I thought we were going to have tea…"

Alexander ignored her protests. "Olivia, I have a million things to do…"

"You've been acting strange ever since I came back from Cyprus. What's going on?"

"Nothing," he lied.

"Liar. Tell me what it's going on, Alex!"

"I'm in the midst of a very important deal."

"Concerning?"

"Issues that do not involve you."

The Princess of Kemp threw her hands into the air. "I do not understand you! You keep me shut out of your life in every way that matters, yet you expect me to simply shut up and accept it."

"You are my wife. I do not need to tell you about everything that involves my personal dealings."

"You do, if they concern me," she snapped.

Alexander grabbed his wife by her shoulders. "Trust me. Please."

"Tell me what's going on."

"If I tell you," he whispered, "you'll be help responsible as well. I'm protecting you."

Those words left a terrible feeling in Olivia's soul. Her husband was usually sulking around the halls of the castle, but as of late, he was much more secretive than before. Why, she continually wondered. If he didn't want her to be held responsible for whatever he was planning, she knew it was to be a great coup of sorts. "What is it?"

Alexander closed his eyes for what seemed to be an eternity. If he informed his wife of the plan he was in the midst of initiating with Patricia Ali, he would risk having her blow his cover or become a willing accomplice. Either way, he reasoned, her life would change forever. However, he still doubted whether or not he could trust his wife. She was the sort of person who could plot a military insurgence without anyone suspecting a thing. In some ways, she was just like her husband. That fact alone made Alexander love her and fear her in the same moment. In that moment, he opened his eyes and decided not to tell his wife about the many details that he and Patricia Ali were beginning to implement.

"Trust me," he said once more. "The less you know the better."

"Do you really believe that," she countered. "What if I knew something that could change everything between us and I kept it a secret?"

Alexander stiffened. "Are you cheating on me? You do know that's grounds for an uncontested divorce. You'll receive nothing from me or the King."

The Princess of Kemp held her steady stance. The terms of her pre-nuptial agreement made no difference to her in this moment. For the first time since their marriage, she had the power. "Of course not," she said.

"What do you know?"

Olivia turned on her heels as she walked through the comfortable library. "Something you don't. Why should I tell you if you won't be honest with me?"

"I don't like games…"

"Neither do I." Olivia made her way for the door as she said, "I just want you to know that I love you, but what your grandmother is so worried about is not my fault."

The Prince of Kemp froze in his steps. If what she was saying was true, their fertility issues were his sin, not hers. How could she know that, he wondered with growing rage. "What did you say," he seethed.

"I'm perfectly capable of becoming pregnant *and* carrying a child to term."

"How…"

"I saw a doctor in Cyprus," she blurted out. For the first time in weeks, she felt free. No matter what her husband tried to do to her, he could never take away the fact that she was perfectly fertile. His fertility was another issue, she reminded herself. "I'm fine."

"You're lying..." He could feel his body tremble.

"Why would I do that?"

"You betrayed me!"

"I did nothing of the kind! I had to know, Alex. I couldn't go another minute without knowing whether or not it was my fault..." She felt out a heavy sigh. "And it's not. I have the doctor's exam results."

"You could have paid him off."

Olivia laughed at her husband's suggestion. "I'm not you."

Alexander's eyes narrowed as he made a beeline towards his ungrateful wife. "After everything I've given to you, this is how you repay me? My family has given you the world…"

"Yes, *your family*. You've treated me like a bit player in the drama that is your life," she screamed. "The reason we haven't had a child yet is not my fault, Alex! It never was!"

Rage continued to flow through Alexander's body as he lowered himself onto the hard maple chair in the corner of the room. His head began to spin with the ease of a child's ball. No, he thought, this isn't happening. If his wife was telling the truth, he was the problem and his reign would be marred by the fact that Princess Helena would become the Queen of Andover, not his first born child. I cannot let that happen, he screamed to himself.

"If you're lying to me," the prince said in a terrifying voice, "you will pay the consequences."

"Get a test," the princess countered. "Let's just put this issue behind us once and for all."

"Give me one reason why I shouldn't ask my father for a divorce…"

Olivia turned her enchanting eyes towards the image of her weak husband. "I'm the only one who has never been able to put up with you. Your own father banished you to this castle and your brother and sister find you more trouble than you're worth. Out of all of the women you've ever dated, I'm the only one willing to put up with the lies, secrets, and your unpredictable mood swings. If you want to divorce me, go right ahead. It will only bring more unnecessary publicity to the regal family in the form of a scandal. You need me, Alexander, and we both know it."

The Princess of Kemp stormed out of the library, while her husband pondered the veracity of her claims. Yes, she was the only woman who could tolerate him. His own family did not seem enthralled with him these days. If he was infertile, it would be a disaster for the kingdom. And if he did manage to divorce Olivia, that wouldn't change the fact that he was barren. Alexander decided that before he moved forward, he had to know the truth. He walked to the telephone at the other end of the library and ordered his office to arrange a private, in-home visit with his general practitioner. As soon as he knew the results of his fertility test, Alexander swore that no one would ever doubt him again.

20

Her Regal Highness Lady Margaret returned to her state apartment with two heavy shopping bags in each hand. She yelled for the butler to relieve her, as she made her way into the Drawing Room where her lunch was waiting. Margaret sat at the table dressed for one with a great sigh of relief. In the weeks following her run-in with Robert at The Hunting Lodge, she had come to find herself in an odd place. While she still loved him and wanted nothing more than to profess her love for him in public, she felt strangely at peace with her life. Margaret often reminded herself that she did have a husband who loved her, a son who did his best to behave, and a lifestyle that was the envy of every woman in Andover. Yet, when the lights were turned out every night, she awoke after no more than two hours of sleep to stare into the empty night sky that seemed to evoke the heaviness in her heart. Somehow, she was still able to perform her regal duties with the same grace as before, despite the fact that Michael was still keeping her at arms length, while Robert and Sophia merely acknowledged her presence in public and private. While these social snubs by her own family would have turned her into a raging queen in the past, she simply ignored them. It was, she reminded herself, the only way to stay sane within the context of this world. Her brother, Lord Walter, offered her a wing in Blake Manor, but she constantly refused. No matter how cold her cousins were to her, Andover Palace was her home too, and for better or worse, she would remain there until her dying day.

"You're home," His Highness Edward called as he joined his wife in the Drawing Room. "I thought you were still shopping."

"I got back a few minutes ago. I didn't want to disturb you."

"I was reading. Not much to disturb there," joked Edward. He studied his wife carefully before saying, "Is everything all right?"

"Fine," she remarked. "Life is fine."

Edward took a piece of asparagus from Margaret's plate. "Have you finished your holiday shopping?"

"For the most part, but I need to find something for Elmira and Frances. Everyone else is accounted for."

"Including His Majesty?" Edward was aware that the subtle Cold War was still permeating all aspects of regal life.

Margaret nodded. "Of course. Michael isn't to blame for everything that's happened. His allegiance is to his sister; I understand that. I know that Walter would do the same thing for me."

"Still," muttered Edward. "We're all adults. Why can't," he cut himself off. "You know what? There are some things I'll never understand about the regal family and this is one of them."

Margaret took in the honesty behind her husband's words. To her, it seemed that everyone who married into the regal family was associated with it or followed it religiously always tried to understand the dynamics of their odd group. It wasn't as if they were completely foreign to the world at large, but their internal politics could make the United Nations quiver. However, Margaret thought, when this is all one knows, it always makes perfect sense.

"Can you believe Christmas is in one week," Edward said, trying to make conversation with his sullen wife. He didn't know why she was so distant, but at least she seemed more present than when he returned from the Sahara Desert and after her accident at Port Agnes House. Edward knew within the recesses of his heart that his marriage would never be the same again because he knew Margaret could never love him as much as she loved Robert.

"It always arrives before I have time to process it."

"Margaret, I was thinking that the day after Christmas we could spend it with my family. If Olivia is available and Elmira is free, we could have a Miller style Christmas," Edward stated. "Sammy had such a good time in Cyprus and I think it would be good for him to be exposed to the other side of his family."

Lady Margaret gave her husband a small smile. “Yes, that sounds nice. However, you must remember that Samuel isn’t like every other boy. He’s an heir to Andover’s throne.”

“He’s sixth in line for the throne,” countered Edward. “Once Alexander and Olivia have children, it will be a non-issue for him.”

Margaret couldn’t believe what her husband was saying. Her son’s place in the line of succession was a great reminder that he could, and possibly would, sit on the throne one day. “A non-issue? We don’t even know if Michael’s children will ever have kids! Samuel could be the King of Andover one day.”

“I doubt it,” Edward replied. “Michael’s children will probably all live to produce ten children each.”

“You don’t know what you’re talking about,” she snapped. “I could very well inherit the throne!”

Edward rolled his eyes because he knew how sensitive the subject of succession was to his wife. Why did I even mention it, he wondered. “Never mind,” he said.

“I guess I now know where your loyalties lie,” sniffed Lady Margaret.

“What is that supposed to mean?”

“You know…”

“Why don’t you just tell me?”

“You will always side with the King because your cousin is married to the heir to the throne!”

“You’re out of your mind,” spat Edward.

“Am I,” she challenged. “You always protect Olivia and the King’s heirs. What about us? Your son matters more than Olivia and her insipid husband!”

“Olivia is my family,” Edward said in a low, angry tone. “That will never change. Samuel may or may not succeed to the throne. As far as I’m concerned, it's a topic that we should just drop. Alexander is the heir to the throne and until we know otherwise, that's how it will be."

Margaret threw her napkin onto her plate of half eaten food. She glared angrily at her defiant husband before storming out of the room.

Here we go again, Edward thought. Why do I put up with this, he asked himself. Margaret always exploded into her infamous moods whenever he disagreed with her or even presented an idea that didn't gel with hers. To him, she was unreasonable most of her waking hours. The only thing he wanted was some sense of normalcy, and if that meant that his son spent time with his relatives that weren't styled His or Her Regal Highness, so be it. In that one moment, Edward decided that enough was enough. He whipped his iPhone out of his blazer before dialing a familiar number.

"Hello," said the bass voice on the other line.

"Dad, it's me."

"Eddie," Count Grayson Miller replied heartily. "It's good to hear from you."

"You too. Dad, I need your help…"

"What did the doctor say?"

The Prince of Kemp stood in the midst of Kemp Castle's vast estate as he watched the farmhands tend to the sheep in the distance. Having lived at the castle for all of his life, Alexander found a small amount of solace in the daily routine that came with being the Prince of Kemp. He took in the uninterrupted views that stretched on for an eternity.

"What did the doctor say," the Princess of Kemp asked again as she stood by her husband's side.

"My father wants us to kill two geese, two turkeys, and two pigs for Christmas Eve lunch and Christmas Day."

The Princess of Kemp gave her husband a curious look. She was aware that Alexander's fertility results were in because the doctor came by the castle after breakfast. However, once her husband received his results, he walked off without a word. Now that she'd found him, he wanted to talk about poultry and pigs. "Is that so," she sighed.

"I told him that it will be fine. There are thirty geese kept near the lake, eighty turkeys, and twelve pigs. Actually, I'm surprised he wants a pig. My family doesn't eat pork, but Their Regal Highnesses Elmira and Frances are big fans of it. One must make their guests welcome," Alexander noted with his usual brand of detachment.

"Alex…"

"I bought Joseph a vintage pocket knife set for his time in the armed services. My father gave one to me, so I thought I'd return the favor. It actually helped," he continued.

Olivia couldn't take this anymore. "Alex! What did the doctor say?"

He averted her gaze. "I'm fine. If you think I'm lying, have your doctor examine my test results. My sperm count is fine, as is everything else. Are you satisfied?"

Relief swept through Olivia's soul. This was the news she'd been waiting to hear about ever since their confrontation in the library a few weeks ago. However, her victory felt remarkably hollow. "Then," she asked carefully, "why haven't we had a child?"

"I don't know. We just started having sex a few months ago, so we must give it time."

"Then we should try at least four times a week. I know I can get pregnant…"

"But what if we can't have a child together," the Prince of Kemp said suddenly.

"What?"

"Olivia, what if we're not meant to have a child together? This could be the universe's way of telling us to move on with our lives."

"Do you want to leave me," she asked in a hushed tone.

The Prince of Kemp held her hand as he'd never done before. He gazed into her eyes with the same amazement he had when they first met. "No," he replied. "But my grandmother has a point. If I can't produce an heir, then the entire regal line is in jeopardy."

Olivia froze. "What are you saying?"

"I don't know. I think we need to do everything we can to have a child. All we need is one and everything will be fine."

"And if we don't?"

He didn't answer the question because he knew it would not be in the best interest of his wife. No, he thought; let's let life go on as it is. Everything is going to be fine, he said to himself once more. But this time, he tried his hardest to believe it.

"Elmira will stay in the Lake Suite, Frances and Richard will stay in the Winchester Suite, Mark will have the Burgundy Suite, Vincent is in the suite near Princess Helena, and Jason will stay in the suite next to Prince Joseph. Well, that's that," Cassandra said cheerfully.

The King eyed her list detailing the sleeping arrangements of his distant cousins with great indifference. As the monarch, these were the tiny tasks he hated doing that his mother seemed more than happy to perform.

"I suppose the Hall's will leave after lunch," added Cassandra.

"Count Matthew will spend the night here and proceed to his family home on Christmas morning."

Cassandra's eyes lit up in amazement. "Now, will he stay in the Wesleyan Suite as before?"

"Mother, he'll stay in my private quarters."

"Michael," she exclaimed. "Do you think that's wise?"

The King bit his lip. "Mother, he will be my husband in a few short months. This isn't one hundred years ago. The Count will stay with me and that's final."

"Whatever you wish," she stated. "Dear, are you all right?"

"I'm fine," he said shortly.

"Don't lie to your mother."

"I'm tired. I have to meet with Patricia Ali in one hour before government closes for the holidays and I can't stand the woman."

"Neither can I! I find her vile."

"I also have to worry about Joseph's time in the armed services being leaked before my announcement. To be perfectly honest, I don't want him to go."

"But he wants to go," Cassandra reminded her son.

"I'm aware of that, Mother," snapped Michael. "He's my youngest child.

"I know how much you love your children, but they're adults now."

"Well, we both know how parental concern can alter the course of a child's life."

"What's that supposed to mean," asked Cassandra.

"Never mind."

"Michael, I did what I had to do all those years ago. Had I let you marry Matthew back then, it would have been a travesty! The line of succession would have been in doubt! We all knew that you would have had to give up your right to the throne and Sophia would be the Queen of Andover. Your marriage to Katherine was the right thing at the right time."

The King always loathed it when his mother defended her actions from so many years ago. He was at peace with the fact that life was as it was, but he couldn't quite reconcile the fact that he had to give up Matthew for more than thirty years. "Mother, I didn't say you did something incorrect. I understand that I had to make a sacrifice for the kingdom."

"Good," bristled the Dowager Queen.

"If you'll excuse me, I must prepare for my meeting."

Princess Sophia sat in the Official Meeting Room within her state apartment as she picked through the merchandise in order to select her Christmas presents. The princess rarely shopped in public because she found the whole affair too taxing and intrusive. She always wondered how Lady Margaret could put up with the people staring at her as if she were a side show star. In the weeks since Robert phoned her about Margaret's sudden appearance at The Hunting Lodge, Sophia couldn't help but feel sorry for her cousin. She wondered if Margaret was that lonely, depressed, and desperate to make such a blatant plea of Robert's affection.

"Your Regal Highness," called the attending valet.

"What is it?"

"His Highness Edward is here to see you."

"Send him in," she replied with complete surprise. Although she knew Edward was as blameless as she was in the affair between Lady Margaret and Prince Robert, Sophia hadn't seen her dearest friend in a long time. She told herself that it was for the best, but in all honesty, she needed Edward in her life.

Princess Sophia rose to greet her best friend, as the valet closed the door behind him. "Edward," she said gleefully. "This is the best surprise."

Edward gave her a tight hug. "Well, it's about time the stalemate between us came to an end."

Sophia led him to the plush sofa in her office. "I wouldn't call it a stalemate… It was just an uncomfortable situation."

"Well, your husband and my wife…"

"Could we please not discuss that," sighed Sophia. "I don't want to re-live the past year."

Edward nodded in agreement. "Are you ready for Christmas?"

She motioned to the vast array of merchandise laid out in her office. "I suppose. Are you?"

"I am looking forward to it. Listen," he said in a low voice, "there's something I need to tell you."

The tone of Edward's voice made Sophia undeniably nervous. The words he'd just uttered were never followed by deep admissions of anything good, which only made Sophia fear for the rest of his statement.

"What is it?"

"I'm filing for divorce," he blurted out. In that moment, Edward felt as if the events of the past year had been erased. His soul felt lighter, and the world actually seemed to possess the ability to be a great place once again.

Princess Sophia gasped out of pure shock. In the entire history of the regal family, there had never been a divorce. "You can't be serious! Edward…"

"Sophia, I can't do this anymore."

"What do you mean?"

"I can't stay married to Margaret! I can't put with her constant scheming and the fact that she won't let me have any say in the way we raise our son." Edward ran his hands through his strawberry blonde hair. It had been years since he'd ever expressed his true feeling about being married to Margaret, and it felt great. "I can't do this anymore."

"Why are you telling me this? Have you filed the papers?"

"No," he admitted. "I've informed my father to find the best possible attorney for my case."

"Edward, you can't do this," warned Sophia. "It will undermine everything the regal family stands for!"

"And what's that? Lies and deception," countered Edward.

"That's not fair," Sophia snapped. "Margaret is not a representative of the regal family as a whole or our illustrious history! If you divorce her, it will open up all of our finances and private affairs for the world to scrutinize!"

Edward was unmoved. "For the past eleven years, I have been faithful, dutiful, and the pinnacle of regal restraint. I haven't done a thing to embarrass the regal family in any way…"

"I know…"

"But I can't continue to live like this, Sophia. It's too much."

"Edward, there must be something you can do. Why don't you take a lover? I'm sure Margaret would jump at the chance to have one of her own…"

"Sophia," he sighed, "this isn't easy for me."

"Then don't do it! You can't get a divorce now because of everything we have planned! The King is getting married in April! If you get divorced before then, it will be a travesty. Can't you wait until then?"

Edward knew that his oldest friend had a valid point. Michael had been good to him, despite his initial reticence towards Edward and Margaret's relationship. Upstaging the King's wedding would only sour any relationship he might be able to salvage with the regal family; if not for Edward's sake, then for his son's. "I suppose," he replied. "But I am going ahead with this, Sophia. I'll wait until Michael and Matthew's wedding to file for divorce, but I won't wait forever."

“Have you thought about how this will affect Samuel?”

“Of course I've thought about how this will affect my son! I will ask for a closed divorce in order to keep the records sealed. I don’t want anything from Margaret…”

“But she’ll probably take whatever she can get from you out of spite,” reasoned Sophia. “She’s that kind of lady.”

“Be that as it may, I just want my son to have a normal life… I need to be free of that woman.”

Sophia thought about this for a moment before adding, “This *is* Samuel’s life. He’s from the regal blood line. That will never change. Being normal is something that will never be a part of Samuel’s life, Edward.”

“You sound like Margaret.”

“Well,” bristled Sophia, “if it’s one thing Margaret knows, it’s that being born into the regal family is very different from marrying into it. You look at the world in a very different way, and, in turn, the world treats you as if you’re not human.”

“My son deserves to have a childhood, not afternoons spent performing regal duties.”

Sophia couldn’t contain her frustration any longer. “It’s a part of who he is! I may not care for Lady Margaret, but I do know that she would never let you, or anyone else, stop her son from claiming his place in the line of succession. She will do whatever it takes to keep him in the regal fold. Besides, he is the King’s cousin’s son, so he has – by default – regal duties to perform.”

“He can always abdicate his place in line for the throne…”

“Edward,” moaned Sophia. “Samuel’s only eleven. I don’t think it’s time for us to think about that. He may never even succeed to the throne, but his place in the line of succession is necessary. If you fight Margaret on that issue, you may very well lose.”

"Are you siding with her?"

"No! But she will have regal law and tradition on her side." Sophia shook her head with great compassion. "If you divorce her, I will support you. I know how terrible Margaret has been to you, and you deserve better. But promise me that Samuel won't become collateral damage."

His Highness Edward took in Princess Sophia's concerns. "I'll try."

"Do more than try," pleaded Sophia. "We both know that if certain things come out during your divorce, my life could be ruined. I need you to ensure the divorce will be amicable and swift. Can you do that…for me?"

The only thing Edward could do was smile at his friend, because he didn't know what the next few months would hold for him. He could fully understand her worries when it came to his impending divorce, but he knew he couldn't make assurances about things that were beyond his control.

His Regal Highness Lord Walter of Andover picked up the small box tied neatly with a satin crimson bow. Lord Walter touched the bow as thoughts of Danisi Samantha Masoli raced through his mind. She was the first woman in his entire life to actually excite him. While he couldn't truly forget Daisy, he was smitten by Samantha's willingness to experience life as it could be with him, instead of what it would be like in the presence of the King and the rest of his family. In the weeks since the cocktail party, Walter and Samantha had spoken on the telephone every day and exchanged quietly romantic notes that could have been seen as the beginning of something more. Even though it may have been considered too soon for such displays of affection, Walter knew that if he didn't let Samantha know how fond he was of her, she may have found another man to love her in the way he thought she needed to be loved.

Walter glanced at the clock again. In less than twenty minutes, Samantha was supposed to arrive for a late lunch before she departed for Paris for Christmas with her parents and skiing in the Alps for the New Year. He tried to convince her to spend New Year's Eve with him in Andover, but she refused to cancel her prior commitments because it would have been seen as "callous and inconsiderate". Yes, Walter thought to himself, he wanted to spend his life with this woman.

"Presenting Danisi Samantha Masoli," pronounced Jasper.

Samantha stepped into the Grand Rose Room. She was dressed in a red dress with a pair of black high heels by Andover's hottest cordwainer, Avi Emanuel. "Your Regal Highness," she said with a curtsy.

"Danisi," he cooed. Walter took his hand in hers, before instructing Jasper to leave them alone. "You look delectable."

She laughed with bashful elegance. "Thank you, Sir. I'm sure you say that to all of the women you know…"

"No," he said quickly. "Samantha, I don't." Samantha gazed into his weary eyes. "I didn't mean to offend you."

"You didn't… I…" Walter remembered that he still held the box in his hand. He led Samantha to the sofa near the large French windows. "I've never done this before."

"Oh?"

"Samantha… Here. This is for you."

She took the small box from his large hands with great interest. Samantha knew she must have made quite an impression on Lord Walter. However, until this very moment, she did not know how deep that impression ran. "Your Regal Highness," she said breathlessly. "You shouldn't have…"

"Please. Open it."

Samantha carefully untied the crimson ribbon and opened the box to find a priceless diamond necklace glistening in the soft winter light. Samantha gasped with shock. "Your Regal Highness…"

"You can call me Walter…"

"Walter, this is too much."

"Don't worry," he smiled as he fastened the gift around her neck. "It's nothing. Really."

Samantha fingered the necklace as an innocent smile crossed her face. "Thank you. I feel terrible that I have not brought anything for you."

Walter placed his hand on top of hers. He could feel her pulse racing, which matched his. "Samantha," he said in a low voice, "these past few weeks have made me happier than I ever thought was possible."

"I feel the same way."

"Please accept this gift as a token of my affection for you."

"I will."

Walter leaned in and gently kissed Samantha's full lips. Their tongues danced in unison as passion swept over them. Walter closed his eyes as he ran his fingers through her cascading hair. In that single moment, Walter felt more at ease than he ever had before. "Are you ready to eat," he asked.

She simply nodded in response to his question.

Walter rang a silver bell. In a moment, the attending butler entered the Grand Rose Room. "We are ready for our meal."

"Very good, Your Regal Highness," the butler replied.

"Walter," Samantha said as the butler left them alone, "are you happy with me?"

"I am. I've never felt this way, Samantha."

"Me neither," she admitted. "I wish I could spend a part of the holidays with you, but I have my commitments."

"Don't worry. When it comes to family obligations, I completely understand. Now, let's eat."

***

"Your Majesty, may I present the new budget for the government's next fiscal year," said Patricia Ali.

The King watched as the Minister of Government placed the thick document before him. As was customary in the Kingdom of Andover, he'd received the new budget three days before this meeting in order to review it and sign it. However, during the past few weeks, his relationship with Patricia Ali had fallen to new lows. Their weekly meetings had become routine with Patricia doing her best to keep the King's attention while he glanced at the clock above her head. How he loathed her. Ever since her speech, the mood within the kingdom had turned into one quite unknown to the regal family. No one had ever challenged their rule, which made this situation quite uncomfortable for the King.

"This new budget has been increased by thirty percent, is that correct," asked the King.

"Yes, Sire" she said unflinchingly.

The King folded his hands as he placed them on his desk. His eyes narrowed as he said, "I must keep the best interest of the kingdom in mind, Ms. Ali, which is why I will not sign this budget into effect."

"But Your Majesty, my party thinks this will be the best thing for the kingdom."

"The best thing for the kingdom? That's a very sweeping statement during these precarious times, don't you agree?"

"The two branches of the government have already passed this budget, Sire."

The King maintained a steady gaze on the woman in front of him. "Ms. Ali, this new budget is not sound. You may forget, but I did study law and finance while I attended the University of Andover and fulfilled my duties as the Prince of Kemp in support of the Queen. A year to year increase of thirty percent is too extreme to ask the taxpayer to bear. The Consumer Growth Index has set growth at four and a half percent this year. In the best interest of the kingdom, I would suggest this budgetary increase to be that of no more than four and a half percent."

"Your Majesty," fumed Patricia, "government closes today! If this budget doesn't pass before five o'clock, I will be stuck with last year's budget for the entirety of the next year."

"I am aware of that," the King replied. "These are the issues one must deal with as the minister of <u>my</u> government, Ms. Ali."

"I must beg Your Majesty to reconsider…"

"Ms. Ali, I urge you to return to your office and propose the new budget to the branches of government before it closes for the holiday season. That will be all," the King said with great finality.

Patricia Ali gathered her belongings as the attending valet escorted her out of the palace.

The King sat in his great chair as he replayed the events of this meeting. In truth, he could have handled Patricia in kinder manner, but he no longer felt anything where she was concerned. That woman had tried to bring down his daughter and fiancé with one of her inane speeches about absolutely nothing. Hell, thought the King, she tried to ruin the monarchy and everything his ancestors had spent their lives creating. There were times in the past when Michael doubted whether or not the institution of the monarch could endure for another hundred years, but he knew within his heart that the way in which the regal family operated in the eyes of their people and the world was unlike any of today's ruling families. The Regal Family of Andover was an institution unto itself, which made it even more unique in the context of the world. For Patricia Ali to try to undermine the regal family, her own boss, and the kingdom as a whole made him sick every time he thought about her speech.

The King rose and started for the door that led from his office to the secret corridor that deposited him in his private suite. On his journey to his inner sanctum, his mind drifted towards next year's election. Although the King was fully aware that he couldn't express a political opinion, he knew that by rejecting Patricia's budget, the government would know that the King did not support Patricia Ali. If anyone tried to say that the King was doing this in order to spite the woman who'd spoken out against the regal family, Michael knew what to say.

He entered his private office and sat in the leather chair behind his simple, yet refined birch desk which held his personal stationary. The King began to draft a letter to the government stating that he didn't support Patricia's budget due to the enormity of the budget increase, its adverse affect on the people, and the simple fact that it outpaced the Consumer Growth Index. The King finished the letter, folded it twice, and placed it in his secure desk.

The King walked towards the window which overlooked the grounds of the palace with great delight. If he had his way, Patricia would be out of office before the next election. Yes, Michael thought gleefully, next year will be wonderful.

"It's a no go," Patricia Ali seethed to the Prince of Kemp.

The Prince of Kemp could hear her car idling in the background as she went on about the King's efforts to sabotage her government. "What else can you do," he snapped. "Go back to the government with the new budget and pass the damn thing, Patricia."

"With all due respect Your Regal Highness, it's not that easy…"

"It is," he interrupted. "The only thing you have to do is redraft the damn thing, get the houses to approve it, bring it back to the King, and it will be done. Don't make this harder than it has to be."

"This will only complicate all of our hard work," insisted Patricia.

Alexander rolled his eyes. If he had known that Patricia would be such a ditherer, he never would have enlisted her in his coup for the Kingdom of

Andover. To the prince, she was becoming a liability. "Patricia," he snapped. "Just do it! If you don't, everyone will lose confidence in you. Stop wasting my time and do not contact me until it is done." With that, the Prince of Kemp ended the call with the Minister of Government.

The Prince of Kemp sat in his office as thoughts of the future whirled through his head. If everything went to plan where Patricia was concerned, his policies would be implemented in the government, which in turn would lead to his succession to Andover's throne. Yes, the plan was quite ambitious, but Alexander knew in his heart that his father was not the right person to run the kingdom. Even though Alexander was legally barred from expressing a political view in public, he didn't see what was so wrong with using the Minister of Government to express them for him. However, Patricia was beginning to show signs of weakness. The Prince of Kemp knew how badly she'd botched her speech about the King's impending marriage to Count Matthew Hall; however, her attack on Princess Helena did not sit well with the prince. Attacking the King was one thing, but using his sister's personal agony as a political maneuver was going too far in the Prince of Kemp's mind. If Patricia could regain the trust of the people of Andover, their plan might stand a fighting chance, but it seemed less likely that they would ever trust her, let alone re-elect her.

Alexander closed his eyes as he pondered what may happen if Patricia ever decided to turn against him in order to save herself. Luckily for Alexander, he always had a plan. If Patricia did betray him, he would deal with her in due time. The Prince of Kemp did not view himself as above doing what needed to be done in order to preserve the monarchy. He didn't care if the King or the Minister of Government stood in his way; he would have everything he'd ever dreamed about and restore Andover to the glorious kingdom it was before his father became its monarch. To Alexander, now was the time to be patient because in the next few months, his ultimate plan would come into full effect, and the kingdom would be his.

***

"Your Majesty, the Head of the Andover Secret Police is here to see you," Glenn said somberly.

Michael put his cup of tea down with great irritation. He wasn't scheduled to see anyone for the rest of the day and he was truly looking forward to a moment alone. The King let out a small sigh as he placed the tea cup onto its saucer. "Show him in."

Kerr Ellison, the Head of the Andover Secret Police, bowed as Glenn ushered him into the King's Official Office at Andover Palace. Kerr was a lifetime member of the secret police, having served as its leader under Queen Cassandra. "Your Majesty," began Kerr, "I thank you for taking the time to see me. Normally, I wouldn't make such an appearance, but I thought it was best."

The King eyed Kerr carefully. Throughout his reign as the King of Andover, Michael had come to rely on Kerr's unwavering judgment and innate ability to protect the regal family as well as the people of Andover. The King always saw Kerr as the biggest source of safety within the kingdom, which is why he decided to allow this impromptu meeting. "Mr. Ellison, have a seat. What seems to be the problem?"

Kerr sat erect in the Chippendale chair across from the King's desk. "Sire, it concerns His Regal Highness The Prince of Kemp…"

"God," moaned Michael. "What has he done now?"

"As per your instructions a year ago, we have performed light surveillance on the Prince of Kemp, the Princess of Kemp, and Kemp Castle."

Michael distinctly remembered ordering Kerr to perform this task because he sensed that Alexander may be up to something that didn't quite sit well with him. What it was, Michael had no clue and the staff at Kemp Castle wasn't talking. However, with the Head of the Secret Police in his corner, Michael received periodic reports regarding the inner workings of the castle. "What have you found," asked Michael.

"The Prince of Kemp has been in almost daily contact with the Minister of Government in what seems to be a plot to gain control of the government and the throne."

The King felt his entire body go into shock. Alexander's grand ambitions were known to everyone in the regal family, but no one took him seriously. Michael suddenly worried if his callous indifference towards what Alexander was planning may have been the worst thing for the entire kingdom. Suddenly, everything seemed to make sense with Alexander's moods, Patricia's blatant defiance of His Majesty, and her lack of respect for the regal family. "How long has this been going on," asked the King.

"For a few months, Sire."

"Why am I hearing this now?"

"At first," explained Kerr, "we thought this was merely two parties expressing their views towards each other. However, ever since the Minister's speech concerning Princess Helena and Count Matthew, we have begun to believe that there may be a conspiracy of sorts brewing. Based on a conversation between the Prince of Kemp and Ms. Ali transcribed today, we have reason to believe that something is amiss at Kemp Castle."

Kerr presented the King with a thick dossier which covered Alexander and Patricia's telephone conversations and secret meetings over the last few months. If Kerr's suspicions were right, the entire fabric of the Kingdom of Andover could be at risk. And for what, wondered the King, Alexander's dreams of grandeur and Patricia's overeager political ambitions? Whatever the true reason, the King knew that action was the most important thing right now.

"What do you think should be done," the King asked Kerr Ellison.

"I would advise His Majesty to increase security at the palace and place the Prince of Kemp and Ms. Ali under constant surveillance."

"Is that not a bit extreme," countered the King.

"With all do respect Your Majesty, I believe this is the right course of action. I would also advise that action be taken to protect Count Matthew Hall."

Michael nodded in agreement. However, if Michael were to use public funds to protect someone who was not a member of the regal family, it would produce a backlash throughout the kingdom. "How much will it cost to initiate a security force around the Count until the wedding," asked the King.

"I cannot say off hand, but I would assume that if four men were assigned to him it would cost about twenty thousand dollars a week."

"That's all right. Send the bill to my office and I will pay for Count Matthew's security detail.

"Very well," said Kerr.

The King paused for a moment as he took in the enormity of the situation. The King was fully aware of his son's ambitions and if those ambitions meant claiming the throne through whatever means necessary, he had to be stopped. "Mr. Ellison," began the monarch, "should I worry about the state of my own… mortality."

"Sire, I wish not to think of such things."

"In your professional opinion…"

"In my professional opinion," began Kerr, "being cautious is the best thing right now. My duty is to protect the monarch from harm, which I intend to do."

The King rose and shook Kerr's hand. "Thank you, Mr. Ellison. I appreciate your dedication to the kingdom."

"It's my pleasure, Sire. Once again, thank you for meeting with me on such short notice."

Kerr bowed as Michael said, "It was my pleasure. Have a pleasant day, Mr. Ellison."

"Thank you, Your Majesty."

Alone, Michael thought about the events which had transpired with Alexander since Michael announced his engagement to Matthew. Alexander had been much more quiet, withdrawn, and secretive lately, but Michael never dreamed that his son was plotting against him. As Michael read the many notes and transcribed conversations between Patricia and Alexander since the surveillance of the Prince of Kemp had begun, chills ran down his spine. Suddenly, everything made sense. Life, as Michael knew it, was over. Now, his son was his most potent enemy. That thought alone, made Michael's heart break in ways he didn't know were possible. If Alexander was plotting some sort of regal takeover with Patricia, it could spell the end of Andover's monarchy. The Prince of Kemp will not succeed in this coup, Michael told himself.

Michael locked the dossier in his desk. His entire life with Alexander flashed before his eyes. He wondered when Alexander had gone from his little boy to a potential participant in treason with Patricia Ali. Was it Katherine's death, Michael's ascension to the throne, Michael's signing of the Marriage Equality Act, or Michael's engagement to Count Matthew Hall? Whatever it was, Michael realized, Alexander was no longer his little boy – his son was now his sworn enemy.

21

The snowfall reached Andover just after midnight on Christmas Eve. By sunrise, six inches of snow had fallen, but all roads leading to the palace were cleared for the invited guests.

As was tradition on Christmas Eve, the regal family hosted their annual lunch for their extended family and invited guests. Hours after lunch, the regal family would distribute gifts to every kindergarten child in Andover before a nighttime reading of *The Night Before Christmas* by the King. After that, the Dowager Queen would read *The Tailor of Gloucester* to all of the children of Andover in the warmth of the palace's Great Hall. Lastly, the King would make his ten o'clock holiday speech to the people of his kingdom. The King always looked forward to his annual speech because it gave him a chance to address the many issues faced by the kingdom throughout the year.

Morning quickly turned to afternoon as the King's dresser finished tying His Majesty's tie. "What are your plans for the holidays," the King asked his longtime dresser, Dennis Highsmith.

"I will spend the holidays with my wife and children, Your Majesty," replied Dennis.

"Quite nice," the King smiled. "I always think people should spend their holidays with their families." Michael eyed the tie in the mirror and nodded with great satisfaction. "Thank you, Dennis."

"Your Majesty," Dennis said with a bow before he left the monarch alone.

Michael walked out of his dressing room into his private sitting room when a knock interrupted his peace of mind. Glenn ushered in the Dowager Queen before leaving them alone. "Yes, Mother?"

"Elmira, Frances, Richard, Vincent, Mark, and Jason are on their way to the palace. It will be so nice to see them once more," sighed Cassandra. "I do wish

I could get away to see them…"

"Mother, you have all the time in the world. Go see them," Michael replied.

"I would, but I have duties," she nodded.

"That sounds like an excuse to me."

"Michael," exclaimed Cassandra. "I'd never!"

The King released a dark laugh. "Oh Mother, relax. After a lifetime of duty and service to Andover, you deserve some time away from the kingdom."

"I suppose, but my heart is with Andover." Cassandra poured herself a glass of gin before saying, "When are Alexander and Olivia due to arrive?"

Michael shrugged. "In time to receive our guests, I assume."

"Michael," began the former monarch, "is something amiss?"

"What do you mean?"

Cassandra cast a disapproving glance at her son. She knew all too well that there were things as Andover's monarch that he kept from her, just as she'd kept things from him when she was the Queen. However, she could sense that there was something wrong with the kingdom.

"Mother," sighed Michael, "don't worry."

"Son, I know something's wrong with you. In the days since government closed for the holidays, you've barely spoken to anyone! Not even Matthew! Dear, you can talk to me…"

"I can't," he said quickly. "I just can't."

"Then why was Mr. Ellison here to see you that same day?"

Michael stared at her blankly. "It was a private matter. I have ordered a security detail of four guards from the Secret Police for Matthew until the wedding. And before you start, I am paying for this out of my own pocket."

"Well," surmised Cassandra, "I suppose that is all right. After all, he will be seen in public with the regal family much more as the wedding approaches, so it only makes sense." Cassandra studied her son with great interest. She couldn't help but feel that Michael was keeping something more from her. But it was a private matter between the King and Mr. Ellison, which meant that it did not concern her. However, she refused to back down. "Son, what else is there?"

"Nothing."

"Michael…"

"Mother, please! Not today! I have a full day and I won't get any peace of mind until late tonight. If you don't mind, I'd like to be alone before I must receive our guests."

The Dowager Queen bristled at her son's demand. "Well," she sniffed, "I'll leave you alone."

With that, Cassandra made her way out of the King's private quarters and down the corridor to her own suite. She reminded herself that becoming angry with Michael would be pointless. Yet, if she were able to help, it might make life easier for everyone in the palace.

"Grandmother! Merry Christmas Eve," Joseph called as he came around the corner, followed by the Dowager Queen's dogs Voltaire, Bramble, Maisie, Yonkers, and Edison.

The Dowager Queen gave her grandson a light hug and slipped her arm through his. "Joseph, it is lovely outside. Why don't we take a walk around the grounds?"

Moments later, they braved the freezing weather as the former monarch's dogs pounced through the fresh snow.

"Joseph," began Cassandra, "have you seen your father?"

Prince Joseph bit his lip. Like everyone else in the regal family, he'd barely seen the King in the past few days. To Joseph, his father had truly become the man behind the curtain. “No,” sighed Joseph. “Have you?”

“Briefly...just now… Something isn’t right,” stammered Cassandra.

Joseph picked up Yonkers. “What do you mean?”

“It’s not like your father to shut himself away, turn away guests and become sullen. In the past few days, he hasn’t spoken with anyone from the regal family or Count Matthew. I know something is wrong,” she insisted.

“Grandmother, I don’t think we should concern ourselves with Dad’s problems.”

“We shouldn’t?”

“Not really,” reasoned the young prince. “He has a lot on his mind. Maybe he needs some time to process life in its present form.”

Cassandra scoffed at the notion. “Be that as it may, he’s the King and he has certain responsibilities that must be carried out.”

“Which he’s done,” Joseph said in defense of his father.

They approached the frozen lake, which the dogs ran to cautiously. Joseph cleared off a bench and helped his grandmother as she sat down. The sunlight twinkled off the lake and turned it into a glistening jewel in Andover’s crown.

“Did you know he’s paying for the Andover Secret Police to guard Matthew,” whispered Cassandra.

“Why are you surprised?”

“It’s not…proper,” Cassandra said haughtily. “Darling, it’s not something that’s ever been done before!”

Joseph couldn’t help but laugh to himself. In spite of his grandmother’s ambition to move with the times, she was still very much a woman of her own generation. The world they lived in today had changed vastly in less than a decade. For Joseph, he could see how much trouble his grandmother had reconciling the past with the future, but he could also see his father was caught between the two worlds.

"Grandmother, you know as well as I do that there are people who wouldn't mind if the King never married a man. I think my dad should protect Matthew. Besides, if he spends his own money, what's the big deal? Anyway, Matthew will have his own security team when he marries the King in April."

Cassandra shivered in the brisk air. "I suppose you have a point. I just wish I knew what was going on with your father."

"Whatever it is," sighed Joseph, "I'm sure he can handle it."

"Your Regal Highnesses," a maid called as she rushed across the frozen terrain.

"Yes," smiled Prince Joseph.

"The guests have arrived."

"Well," Cassandra sighed as the maid returned to the palace, "it's time to be happy."

Princess Sophia sat in the Crimson Room with only her thoughts to keep her company. Prince Robert was on his way back from his father's house for the afternoon luncheon, while the rest of the regal family took their time to receive their extended family members. Unlike the rest of her family, Sophia always enjoyed re-connecting with Prince Christian and Prince Erich's heirs because it reinforced the fact that the regal family existed beyond the confines of Andover Palace.

The calm princess paced the room as thoughts of Edward's admission to her from days ago ran through her head. Despite her urge to go right to Michael with this news, she'd managed to keep it to herself because it had nothing to do with her. For Edward to confide in his oldest friend was a sign of trust that Sophia didn't intend to breach in order to hurt Lady Margaret. Besides, Sophia reminded herself, this divorce may not happen at all. Yet a small voice from within the princess reminded her that Edward was a good man who had been yanked around by Margaret one too many times and he had most likely had enough.

"Sophia," Margaret gasped as she stood in the doorway of the Crimson Room.

Princess Sophia turned to see her cousin standing there in a green cocktail dress with their grandmother, Duchess Victoria's diamond, ruby, and emerald necklace fastened around her neck. Sophia had always coveted that piece of fine jewelry, but it was left to Princess Fiona, who in turn left it to Lady Margaret. There was little chance that Sophia would ever touch that necklace again.

"Hello," Sophia said softly. "You look…well…"

"As do you." Lady Margaret breezed past her cousin and poured herself a glass of orange juice. She really wanted a stiff drink, but she didn't want to hear Sophia's judgmental comments about her alcohol consumption.

The two women stood on opposite sides of the Crimson Room without any idea of what to say to each other. Finally, Sophia said, "Where are Edward and Samuel?"

"They'll be here in a few minutes. Edward's teaching Sam how to tie his own tie."

"My," smiled Sophia, "how quickly they grow up."

"Yes… And Robert?"

Sophia cast a terse eye towards Margaret. "He's coming from his father's house."

"Oh. Sophia," Margaret said after a while, "how long will this go on?"

"What?"

"This stalemate between us? We are family…"

"I'm aware of that," snapped the princess. "I'm also painfully aware of the fact that you had an affair with my husband for the better part of a year."

Margaret placed her crystal tumbler onto a marble tabletop. "I made a mistake…"

"Margaret, don't," stated Sophia. "If you were ever sorry, you wouldn't have slept with him… After everything you've done to me over the years, finally owning up to your fallacy now is too little, too late."

"My fallacy," Margaret replied in an exasperated tone. "What about you?"

"What about me," challenged Princess Sophia.

"You walk around the kingdom like you're the pinnacle of all that is right and virtuous," bit Margaret. "You couldn't even keep your own husband pleased in the bedroom. I wouldn't have had to sleep with him if you'd been any kind of wife."

Princess Sophia did everything she could to stop herself from slapping Lady Margaret. This is why I hate her, Sophia reminded herself. Sophia loathed Margaret for the plain fact that she never took responsibility for the pain she inflicted on other people. For some reason, Margaret was the victim and the rest of the world was the villain. "I do not need marriage advice from the likes of you," spit Sophia. "You didn't even know who fathered your own son!"

"How dare you!"

"How dare I? You have some nerve, Lady Margaret! The day you take responsibility for the melodramatic operetta that is your life, maybe then we can have a cordial relationship. I can barely stomach the sight of you."

"Well," challenged Lady Margaret, "it finally seems that we have something in common."

At that very moment, Prince Joseph, the Dowager Queen, Princess Helena, the Prince and Princess of Kemp, Lord Walter, Prince Robert, His Highness Edward, and His Regal Highness Samuel entered the Crimson Room engaged in delightful conversation. The animosity between Sophia and Margaret still infused the air; however, no one thought it was right to mention this issue. By the time the King entered the room, the family was alive with chatter about the holiday season.

"Everyone," called the King, "it is very nice to see all of you. I do hope that we can put aside the issues of the outside world and enjoy this holiday season Now, Glenn will inform us of the time line for today's events."

"Thank you, Your Majesty. Your Regal Highnesses will receive Their Regal Highnesses in the Official Reception Room for light drinks. Next, Count Matthew Hall's family will be received before the start of Christmas Eve luncheon in the State Dining Room. Once luncheon is completed, Your Regal Highnesses will retire with your guests to the Drawing Room for drinks and dessert. Once the Halls have departed, save for Count Matthew, the evening will commence as it has before," said Glenn.

In that moment, the regal family followed His Majestic Regal Highness The King Michael into the Official Reception Room where they stood in order of precedence to greet their distant relatives. As Glenn opened the door to usher in the descendants of Prince Christian and Prince Erich, Michael's face lit up with more joy than he'd experienced in days.

"Your Majesty, hello," Her Regal Highness Elmira said as she curtseyed before the King.

"Your Regal Highness," the King replied. "It's very nice to see you again. I do hope you enjoy spending the holidays in Andover."

"Thank you for the invitation," responded Elmira. She took in the sights of the Great Hall for the first time in what seemed to be a lifetime. Although she was ninth line for the throne, Elmira rarely visited the kingdom, but she still felt a small sense of duty whenever she returned to the palace. "You look well."

The King gave his distant cousin a wry smile. "It's age."

Elmira gave Michael a knowing nod as he moved further down the reception line. As the regal family became better acquainted with their distant relatives, a feeling of familiarity settled over the room.

"Tell me, Vincent, are you seeing anyone," inquired Cassandra who stood next to Vincent and his father, Mark, His Highness of Andover.

Vincent nodded in agreement. "We've been dating for a while."

"Is it serious," asked Cassandra. She waved to the attending valet to bring her another one of her special drinks. "I think it is so important to know whether or not a relationship has a future…"

"Vincent's still young, Ma'am," responded Mark.

"That means even more," insisted the Dowager Queen. "In my day," she went on, "if you weren't serious about someone from the beginning, you didn't waste your time! Now, it seems as if people date someone just because they need something to do!"

Vincent could feel the tension rising between his father and his late mother, Her Regal Highness Sylvia's first cousin once removed. This was the first time Vincent had ever been to the Kingdom of Andover. While his mother was alive, she insisted that her son have a normal life away from the rigorous world of Andover that her own mother, Lady Sharon, despised. Despite the distance between his father and the rest of the regal family, Vincent began to wonder if he could adjust to life in Andover. There were plenty of times when he was at home on the Upper East Side of New York City or at Yale when someone would discover that he was a member of Andover's regal family, but he always downplayed his connection to the King. After all, Vincent and the King were only second cousin's once removed and they hadn't met officially. However, Vincent began to wonder what his life could be like if he ever returned to the Kingdom of Andover.

"Well, Vaughn and I are quite serious, but we are studying, so we won't get married anytime soon," stated Vincent.

"Besides," interjected Mark, "Vincent plans to go to law school."

"Why," questioned Cassandra. "He's a member of the regal family. He shouldn't work! After all, Sylvia left him a ninety million dollar trust, Mark! A trust to which you are a beneficiary. My cousin was very generous."

Mark quickly downed his gin and tonic as he listened to Cassandra ramble on about the past. When he first proposed to Sylvia, he wasn't aware of her ancestry. They were students in Rome, but their love soon blossomed into a love affair. When Sylvia took Mark home to meet her mother, Lady Sharon, he was shocked to discover that they were members of Andover's regal family. Although they wanted a small wedding, Princess Fiona and Lord Nicholas attended their wedding as well as Prince Erich's daughter, Lady Rebecca and her husband, His Highness William. With such important guests, their wedding was besieged upon by reporters from around the world which is why Mark always tried to keep his distance from the regal family. With Vincent's premature birth eight months after the wedding, Mark and Sylvia moved to New York City where they lived a quiet, yet philanthropic life until Sylvia's untimely death a few years ago. In the years since his wife's death, Mark avoided the kingdom, but he knew his son wanted to know his extended family.

"I loved Sylvia very much," sighed Mark. "If you'll excuse me, Cassandra…"

"What was that all about," Cassandra asked breezily.

Vincent shrugged. "I don't know. My dad took my mom's death very hard. With me away at Yale, he's lonelier than before."

Cassandra digested Vincent's words. "I understand. Besides, death is the inevitable mistress that creeps into all of our lives at one point or another. Well, Vincent," smiled the Dowager Queen, "have you met Prince Joseph?"

"Mom," His Reverence Jason Hamilton, 1st Marquis of Westport said to Her Regal Highness Frances, "this is so cool." The eleven-year-old looked around the Official Reception Room with wonderment because he'd never seen a sight such as this in his entire life. He lived with his mother and father, His Highness

Richard, in a rambling villa in the hills of Florence, Italy. "Did you grow up here?"

Frances shuddered. "No. When I was born, my father, William, lived in Spain. But we did come back from time to time to see the family."

"Frances," called Michael as he approached her. "It's so nice to see you."

"When the King commands your presence, one cannot object," Frances noted dryly.

Michael nodded gingerly. "I suppose not." The King forced a tight smile as he tried to find the right words. As monarch, it was his duty to make people feel at home, however, for some reason, it all seemed quite difficult today. "Jason, have you met Lady Margaret's son, Samuel?"

"Not really."

"Sam," Michael called as the young boy rushed across the room.

"Hi, Mike," smiled Samuel.

"Have you met Jason, 1st Marquis of Westport?"

"No," said Samuel. The young boy extended his hand. "How do you do?"

"I'm okay," replied Jason, for whom the formality of regal life as still new.

"Do you want to come to my state apartment? My dad just bought me the new Dragon Quest game and we can play with my dog."

"Can I, Mom," asked Jason.

Frances gave her son an approving nod as he ran off with Samuel. She gave Michael a tight smile. "Princess Sophia told me that you are to marry Count Matthew Hall."

"Yes. I'm very excited," responded the King.

"Michael," Frances began, "I am happy for you. However, I don't think it's right."

The King took a step back. In all of his years as Andover's monarch, no one had ever spoken to him in this direct manner. As a guest of the monarch, Michael knew that Frances was overstepping her boundaries. "Is that so," he asked.

Frances crossed her arms. "My religion does not recognize a union between two people of the same sex. I don't want Jason to be confused..."

"My dear cousin," Michael sighed, "in this kingdom, a union between two consenting adults is perfectly legal, regardless of religious doctrine."

"I have my beliefs..."

"I respect your beliefs, Frances. However, you are tenth in line for the throne. I expect you at the wedding."

Frances held her tongue as she tried to process the orders demanded by His Majestic Regal Highness The King. "And if I don't," she asked defiantly.

"Don't," responded the King. And with that, he made his way across the room.

"How's regal life treating you," His Highness Richard asked Prince Robert.

Robert thought about the past few months before responding, "I can't complain."

"I don't know how you do it," muttered Richard. "The pomp and circumstance is enough to make one vomit."

Prince Robert gave his distant in-law a careful glare. No matter what Robert thought about the monarchy, he always knew that they had been good to him. Michael and Cassandra had always accepted Robert as Sophia's husband and as a regal family member, despite his recent fallacies. Richard's ignorant statement prompted Robert to say, "You don't know a thing about regal life, Richard."

"I think I do..."

"If you did," the prince interjected, "you'd understand the reason behind the pomp and circumstance. I've lived in this world for twenty-two years now and in spite of what you may think, the King does whatever is necessary to protect the family."

"Well," Richard said haughtily, "it's all so unnecessary."

Without word, Robert joined his wife who was making small talk with Princess Helena.

"Robert, what's wrong," asked Princess Sophia.

Robert took a glass of water from a passing butler before saying, "Richard's an ass."

"What did he say," asked Princess Sophia.

"It doesn't matter."

"I feel like we're on display," Princess Helena muttered. "This is strange."

"Well," Sophia said as she eyed the guests, "this is the first time the regal family has been together in years. We must relish this moment."

Princess Helena cast a careful eye over the crowd. She felt quite detached from her own family, which made mingling with their extended family an uncomfortable chore. The only thing she wanted to do in this moment was escape to her suite until Christmas morning. "If you say so, Aunt Sophia," sighed Helena.

"What time are the Halls arriving," Robert asked his wife.

She checked her watch before saying, "Soon. Helena, go mingle with Elmira. She's quite interesting from what I remember."

"Lucky me." Helena turned on her heels as she walked towards the small wet bar where the Princess of Kemp and His Highness Edward were speaking with Elmira. "Hello," she said pertly.

"Your Regal Highness," Elmira replied with a small curtsy.

"We're family, there's no need for that," snorted Helena.

"That's what we were just discussing," Edward stated.

"What's that," Helena asked.

"The fact that Elmira is mine and Olivia's first cousin through her mother and is your second cousin once removed through her father."

Helena took in this news with great curiosity. "Wait, are you telling me that you're related to Alexander <u>and</u> Olivia through blood?"

"Yes," Elmira replied. "At least they're not related like Margaret and Edward who are second cousins."

"In their defense," Olivia added, "they didn't meet until they were adults."

"That's still…odd," Helena remarked. "When get married, I don't want their cousin to be my cousin or my cousin's cousin."

"When my parents, Lord David and Her Highness Ilsa, were married it was a different time," Elmira stated firmly.

"Besides, no one planned for two cousins to marry into the same family," Edward noted.

"Still," Helena shuddered. "I need a drink. Excuse me."

"Hello, Margaret," Michael said.

Lady Margaret gave her cousin a tight smile. This was the first time Michael had spoken to her in months.

"How are things with Edward?"

"Fine… Why?"

"I wanted to be sure that your marriage was back on track. This family doesn't need another scandal between now and the wedding, don't you agree?"

"Of course," she answered honestly. "I think it's best if we all move on."

"I'm glad to hear it."

"Besides, there are plenty of people around the palace who need to focus on their own lives…"

"Maggie," he said forcibly, "I will not pick sides."

"I didn't ask you to," Margaret gasped.

Michael could feel his blood begin to boil. No matter what he thought about Margaret and Robert's affair, he refused to cast blame because he didn't have all of the facts. He could easily see why Robert was smitten with Margaret and why Margaret couldn't refuse a man like Robert. However, Michael was fully aware of how Margaret operated. She was one of the most cunning people he'd ever met. "Maggie, let's just enjoy the holidays. Life has moved on, hasn't it?"

"It has."

"Then what's the issue?"

"There isn't one."

"Good. Let's look forward to a peaceful new year."

The State Dining Room was bathed in the soft glow of candlelight which was accented by the tastefully decorated table. The table itself looked like a Christmas dream that could have only been conceived within the confines of Andover Palace. As the regal family entered the great dining room, a roaring fire welcomed them and they greeted Count Matthew Hall and his family.

"Are you enjoying yourself," Prince Joseph whispered to Matthew's youngest sister, Nancy Hall, who was sitting to his right.

Nancy gently bit into a piece of rustic style bread. "I am, Your Regal Highness."

Prince Joseph smiled at her stoic formality. "There's no need for all of that. In a few months you'll be my step-aunt or something to that effect."

"I suppose you're right," she smiled. "This is all too real. I still can't believe that my brother is going to marry your father."

"It's about time," Joseph noted. He looked around the crowded dining room as everyone chatted heartily. He didn't know what his time in the armed services would entail, but he was fully aware that the few months he spent in public service would be nothing like his life in Andover Palace. "Personally Ms. Hall, I think your brother is a great guy."

"You do?"

"Of course," Joseph said as the attending waiter refilled his wine glass. For a moment he caught Nancy's face in the candlelight and swore that they'd met somewhere a lifetime ago. "Have we met before?"

Nancy shook her head. "Not that I recall. But it's possible we could have met at an event of some kind over the years."

"Maybe," smiled the prince. "Well, once the union is official, we'll have to go out on the town to celebrate. Have you ever been to Hart & Sons?"

"I wish," Nancy sighed. "The waiting list to get into that club is three years long and that's with a recommendation."

"Luckily for you, I know people," Joseph cooed. "We should go one day."

Nancy lifted her water glass as she said, "Your Regal Highness, I'm flattered, but I am twelve years older than you and my brother is set to wed your father…"

"I know, but we can have fun, can't we?"

Walter watched as the dining room staff cleared the table for the start of the soup course. As was tradition in the palace, every meal was conducted like a piece of theatre; nothing was ever out of place and everything seemed to appear as if by magic. Although Walter sometimes thought life in the palace was too formal for his tastes, he did enjoy the ease with which he fell into old routines and habits. While he insisted that life at Blake Manor be a bit more relaxed than it was at

Andover Palace, Kemp Castle, and Port Agnes House, there were times that the Lord secretly craved the fuss. To his right sat Count Matthew Hall, who was already gazing at the King as if no one else in the world mattered. Why Cassandra and Michael had decided to seat Matthew next to him was a mystery to Walter. However, given the fact that Lord Walter had barely sustained a full conversation with the Count, he was fully aware that he had to make an effort and making small talk over the next two courses before he turned his attention to Frances, who was seated to his left, was a very easy task that suddenly felt Herculean.

"Tell me Count Matthew, have you had a proper tour of the kingdom as of yet," asked Walter stiffly.

"From what I've been told, Your Regal Highness, I will receive one before the wedding."

"That sounds nice," Walter replied. "There's nothing like seeing the kingdom through the eyes of the regal family. It's a completely different world. I do hope my cousin has impressed upon you the brevity of the situation you are about to enter."

Matthew digested Walter's words with great caution. After the small debacle with Prince Alexander and Prince Robert and their "helpful words", Matthew was very reticent to listen to another diatribe about regal life. Even though this was a world totally new to Matthew, he wanted to experience it with his husband, minus the jaded views of those already entrenched in the day to day minutia. "His Majesty has been very helpful, Your Regal Highness," said Matthew.

Lord Walter instantly sensed the defensiveness in Matthew's tone. The last thing Walter wanted was for Matthew to become his enemy before they'd even had a proper chance to dislike each other. "Count Matthew," Walter said calmly, "you and the King have my support. I only wish you the best. We all know how much the King loves and adores you, which is why I have no doubt in my heart that you two will be happy for many decades to come."

"That's the nicest thing anyone has said to me since the news of the engagement."

"I'm not like everyone else," whispered Walter. "There's a reason I live at Blake Manor."

The Count laughed at Walter's wry joke. Maybe Walter wasn't that bad after all, Matthew thought to himself. "I've heard that Blake Manor is beautiful. I do hope to spend some time there."

"Everyone else does. Whenever you want a weekend away from the palace, just drop by. If I'm not in, the staff will see to your every whim."

"Sir, may I ask you something?"

"Yes?"

"Do you think the Kingdom of Andover will accept me as their Duke?"

Walter was taken aback by Matthew's insecure question. In the eight years since he returned to the kingdom, Walter rarely thought about what it meant to the regal spouses to be accepted by the people. Walter had already lost Daisy to his own fears of her not being the right kind of person to introduce to the King, yet Matthew had the approval of most of the regal family, but he was still petrified about what the Kingdom of Andover would think about him as the monarch's spouse. "I don't know," Walter sighed. "One can never assume what will be. The only advice I will relay is for you to enjoy what is and leave the posturing to the press."

The King reached for his tumbler of amaretto as Vincent recounted his tales of life in New York City. No matter how far Michael traveled on official tours or official duties, he always longed for the footloose world of Manhattan. To Michael, that was a world unlike any other and he envied Walter for the years he'd spent in that great city. Vincent began to regale the King with tales of his first year at Yale, as the King watched Alexander with great intensity. Throughout the day, Alexander hadn't said much to anyone, although he did hear him bark at the Princess of Kemp on their way to the dining room. Michael had an innate feeling that all was not well his son's marriage, which only compounded the fact that his son was involved in collusion and treason with Patricia Ali. Thankfully, Patricia's new budget as dictated by the King was rushed through the government before it closed for the holidays; however, Michael was still on guard where his son was concerned. Whatever Alexander was planning, Michael knew more than ever that it was time to deal with this problem once and for all.

"You've done quite well for yourself," Michael responded lightly. "I am very proud of you, Vincent."

"Thank you, Your Majesty."

"Please, we're family. Call me Michael."

"Okay…"

"Tell me about your girlfriend. She seems like a very interesting person."

"Her name is Vaughn Phillips and she comes from a very old moneyed family that has interest in everything from railroads to timber to oil and banking."

"I see," said Michael. "I suppose she's what one would call an heiress of sorts."

Vincent nodded in agreement. "I guess. Anyway, she's a History of Art major. This summer she's interning in Congress before traveling throughout Asia before we start our third year of Yale."

"That sounds lovely. I do hope that you enjoy yourselves." Michael tasted the soup before him before asking, "Vincent, does Miss Phillips know who you are?"

Vincent raised an eyebrow. "Huh?"

"Does she know that you're a member of Andover's regal family?"

"No," said Vincent quickly. "I haven't told her. Besides, it's not important."

"Why do you say that?"

"Michael, I'm eighth in line for throne and I don't know the first thing about…all of this…"

"All of this," Michael replied, "is in your blood. You are of the regal blood, Vincent. However, the fact that Miss Phillips is unaware of your true ancestry may work to your advantage in the long term."

"How so," Vincent inquired.

"For starters, you'll always know that she fell in love for you for who you are, not what you are."

"You have a point," sighed Vincent. "She just thinks I'm another trust fund kid from the Upper East Side, which is what I am…kind of…"

"You're more than that," the King noted. "You are a direct descendant of King Christoph, the founding father of the Kingdom of Andover. Vincent, if you have time this summer, why don't you spend it in Andover? I think it would be good for you to become acquainted with this side of your history. How does that sound?"

Vincent gave the King a sly smile. "Not too bad, Your Majesty."

The staff cleared the dishes from the second course in less than one minute as the families engaged in polite exchanges before they were to shift their conversation to their other dining companion for the afternoon. The goose, turkey, and ham were laid before the families as the attending staff members served generous portions to everyone with great skill. As soon as the staff refilled the empty wine glasses, the King turned his attention to Count Patrick Hall.

Michael's history with Count Patrick was vast. His father, His Regal Highness Duke James was Count Patrick's hunting partner. Michael saw Patrick often in his youth, but when the families discovered Michael and Matthew's relationship all those years ago, it seemed as if an impenetrable blockade was forged. This was the first time he'd seen Count Patrick since Duke James' funeral eight years ago and that exchange was formal and devoid of emotion.

"Are you enjoying yourself," Michael asked stiffly.

Patrick nodded. "I can't thank you enough for opening your home to my family, Your Majesty."

"I want Matthew to know his family is welcomed in the palace; this will be his home, too."

"The last time I was in this dining room I do believe that President Carter was still in office."

"That was a while ago," noted Michael. "What are your thoughts on the wedding, Count Patrick?"

Patrick eyed Michael carefully as he cut a piece of goose breast. To Patrick, Michael was the epitome of a monarch – fair, benevolent and, above all, imposing. The memories Patrick had of the King were of Michael as a little boy and then a young man running through the halls of Kemp Castle and Andover Palace. With all of the unspoken history between the regal family and Patrick's family, Patrick's relationship with the Duke suffered, but Patrick was committed to supporting this union wholeheartedly because it could only be a beneficial thing for his family and the kingdom.

"The union? Sire, I believe that you and Matthew will be very happy together. I'm looking forward to the wedding."

"Very good," said Michael. "Now, tell me, what is it that you do?"

"Why aren't you married," Prince Alexander asked Elmira, bluntly.

She nearly choked at the Prince of Kemp's intrusive question. "Excuse me, Your Regal Highness…"

The Prince of Kemp raised his wine glass with great care. "Come now, you're not exactly unattractive. I'm sure the men of Amsterdam must find you somewhat appealing…"

"Are you insulting me or hitting on me," she shot back.

"I can assure you it's not the latter," smiled the prince. "Is there any reason you're not married? From what the Dowager Queen has told me, you're not a lesbian, are you?"

"No," she retorted. "I love men."

"Then why don't you have a husband," asked the prince. From across the table, Alexander could see his wife giving him a careful glare, but he didn't care. He was bored, irritated, and ready for some excitement other than mingling with Matthew's family and his extended line of cousins.

Elmira bit into an artichoke before she said, "I don't feel that having a husband or the cliché notion of a family does anything to enhance one's life. In my opinion, Your Regal Highness, it only perpetuates the myth that a woman's place is in the home tending to children and her husband. Frankly, it's not a fairy tale I'm keen on living."

The Prince of Kemp was struck by Elmira's stark honesty. Never in his entire life had he ever heard someone speak out against the institution of marriage. "Are you telling me that you're just as happy without a husband and children as you are right now?"

"Yes. Besides, most of my friends are divorced or re-married. That doesn't exactly help the cause of marriage, does it?"

"No," the prince responded, "I don't think it does."

The Dowager Queen took a deep breath between finishing her goose while regaling Countess Sally Hall with her stories of yore. "Needless to say, that was the *last* time I ventured to a public motion picture theatre! As soon as I returned to the castle, I ordered my staff to create a home cinema," laughed the Dowager Queen.

The Countess smiled broadly. In the months since the monarch's announcement that he and Matthew were to wed, Sally could barely believe the amount of publicity her family had received. Now, this lunch with the regal family in the State Dining Room was too much for Sally. She sipped a glass of Chablis. "That was very clever, Your Regal Highness."

"Now, I've always wondered why one would want to be subjected to the perceived ills of the outside world if everything they need is in the comfort of their own home," she laughed.

"I… That's indeed something to ponder."

"It is," Cassandra smiled. "Now, tell me, who are you wearing to the wedding?"

Sally dreaded that someone would mention this all day long. It was custom in the kingdom that no one could wear the same designer dress as a member of the regal family at any official function. That meant Sally had to venture far and wide to find a suitable dress as the mother of the future Duke of Andover. "Oh, that's still to be decided," she said softly.

"So it is," smiled Cassandra. "Countess, do you have any concerns regarding the union between our sons?"

"No," Sally said.

"Good," the Dowager Queen proclaimed. "It is a relief to know that you're on our side. I still find it truly barbaric that some people within the kingdom refuse to allow the King to be happy. After all, it is a basic human right, is it not?"

"Of course," nodded Sally. "I was lucky to find Patrick all those years ago. I assume your marriage to the Duke was filled with happiness…"

The Dowager Queen stiffened as she poked her food gingerly. Since the death of her husband eight years ago, the people rarely mentioned him in front of her. The Dowager Queen was fully aware that Countess Sally Hall was merely trying to make pleasant conversation, however, the subject of her late husband on Christmas Eve was something best left alone. "Countess," Cassandra sighed, "marriages are very unique with regard to the way in which one views them during, and after, the union. I do believe that one can find happiness with their spouse, yet it remains to be seen how much of our memories are clouded by the harsh reality of the day-to-day lives we once shared with them."

"Ma'am, I didn't mean to offend you…"

"I'm aware of that, Countess." Cassandra took a deep breath, forced a pert smile onto her face and said, "Tell me, do you enjoy the ballet?"

Christmas Eve luncheon ended one hour later. The Halls returned to their family home, while Count Matthew joined the King in his private suite. The rest of the regal family dispersed to their own corners of the palace while the staff prepared for the Christmas Eve readings performed by the Dowager Queen and His Majesty The King to the kindergarten children of Andover. While the children were regaled with Christmas tales, their parents and select guests were invited to a champagne reception in the State Ballroom.

In his private suite, the King took Count Matthew into his arms. No matter what was happening in the palace or the kingdom, the King wanted this moment to mean everything to Matthew. "Did you enjoy yourself," Michael whispered as they lay on his obscenely soft bed.

"I did," he replied lightly. "My family did, too. I think we'll be all right."

"Was Lord Walter civil?"

"He was. Actually, he's a very interesting guy. Today was the first time I've actually had a real conversation with him. I like him," Matthew said. "Are you all right, Mike?"

Michael gave Matthew a small smirk. Even though they'd only reconnected three years ago, Matthew still knew him better than anyone else in the world. "I can't get into it," stated Michael.

"Why?"

"It's a matter of security," Michael said flatly. "Trust me, I wish I could tell you everything that was going on."

Matthew chewed on this for a moment before asking, "Is this why I have four men tailing me?"

“Matt, I told you that it was necessary. I can’t get into the specifics…”

“I know…”

“However, your security means the world to me. You have to trust me, Matthew.”

“I do.”

“What happens for the rest of the night?”

“Well, I’ll read to the children after the Dowager Queen and then give my live broadcast before joining the reception and turning in for the night…with you…”

Matthew placed his head on the King’s chest with quiet appreciation. Never in his entire life had Matthew felt so at peace than he did in this moment. To be honest, it didn’t bother him that he had a security detail, but it was a normal part of regal life that he would have to become accustomed to sooner or later. However, in this single moment with the most powerful man in the kingdom, Matthew couldn’t help but thank the universe for sending Michael to him after so many years apart.

“I think my sister, Nancy and Prince Joseph will get along just fine,” sighed Matthew. “It seems that they go to the same nightclubs.”

“Really? Can you imagine if they married…”

“No,” laughed Matthew. “That would be too strange.”

“Speaking of strange, what do you think of my extended family?”

“They seem nice enough.” Matthew replied.

Michael nodded. “Vincent’s great, but I’m worried about Frances.”

“Why?”

“She doesn’t support our marriage because of her religious convictions.”

“What do you mean? The regal family has always taken a nondenominational view on religion…"

"Of course we have. However, now that Frances lives in Italy, she's converted. She even threatened to boycott the wedding."

"What did you say?"

"I told her in no uncertain terms that if she didn't attend, there would be trouble for her."

"Mike…"

"I had to," interjected the monarch. "If we don't present a united front at all times, it leaves us susceptible to the whims of people like Patricia Ali. I will not have the kingdom suffer because of Frances' beliefs. Besides, she's a minor member of the regal family with no real power or responsibilities. Once my children have children, Frances will continue to move down the line of succession until she's irrelevant."

"Wow," Matthew said, after taking in everything his fiancé had just said. "I've never heard you say that before."

"Does it frighten you?"

"No… But it is Christmas Eve, Michael. Let's just let it go and enjoy ourselves."

"…Merry Christmas to all, and to all, a good night."

The King of Andover placed the ornate book in his lap as the children before him clapped with joy. They clutched the gifts the regal family had given them before the Dowager Queen read them the story of *The Tailor of Gloucester*. A moment later, the King made his way through the corridors into his Official Office, where the news crew waited. A make-up woman powered his face lightly, while Glenn briefed him on the small details of tonight's broadcast.

Michael glanced at the typewritten sheet before him. Unlike many monarchs throughout the world, he wrote his own speeches. He felt that it lent an air of authenticity to his position as the King, while showing the rest of the kingdom and the world that he actually had a brain. The director of the broadcast alerted him that they were going live in thirty seconds. Michael stepped onto the raised platform which was placed in front of a window overlooking the grounds of Andover Palace.

"…Three, two, one," the director said calmly.

"Good evening," began the King. "I speak to you tonight from Andover Palace as festivities are carried out throughout the kingdom and the world. As we remember the true meaning of the holiday season, I urge each and every one of you to reach out to someone whose values are different from yours. In today's world, the smallest issue can divide us, yet if we were to look at the bigger picture, we would see that we are, for all intents and purposes, the same. By accepting our differences and overcoming them, we can reach a new state of clarity as a kingdom.

"In the new year, it is my hope that the Kingdom of Andover will rise to new heights. The regal family and I wish each and every one of you a fruitful new year. With the end of each year gives rise to the endless possibilities of the next. Please accept them with the strength, will, and determination that is the backbone of this celebrated kingdom.

"From my family to yours, may you all have a safe holiday season… Good night."

22

January 12

820 Fifth Avenue

Apartment 10

New York City, New York, 10065

USA

Andover Palace

The Office of His Majesty The King

Old Andover, Andover 1000OA

Dear Michael,

I would like to thank you for your hospitality over the Christmas season. I had the time of my life. Being back in New York has felt like home, however, I cannot forget the many interesting pieces of family history I learned from you, the Dowager Queen, and Prince Joseph. I would love to spend part of the summer at Port Agnes House. Also, I think that it may be time to tell Vaughn the truth about my family.

I have to finish packing for my next term at Yale.

With fondest regards,

Vincent

Michael smiled as he placed the letter in his private desk. In the weeks since the regal family had reunited over the Christmas season, Michael and

Vincent had grown quite close. To Michael, Vincent represented the lifestyle he may have had, if he had grown up as an heir of Prince Christian or Princess Erich, not as the heir to the heir of King Henrik. Such was life, Michael reminded himself. The King made a note to himself to reply to Vincent's letter within the next twenty-four hours, as he deemed that acceptable within the realm of his regal duties.

The King walked out of his private suite, down the corridor, and into his Official Office. There, Michael was met by Kerr Ellison. Kerr briefly informed the King about the developments concerning the Prince of Kemp, but nothing of great importance had occurred. Tomorrow, Michael was due to re-open his government after the quiet holiday season.

"The Prince of Kemp will be in attendance tomorrow," Michael told Kerr. "I think it will be wise if he and Patricia Ali are kept under tight surveillance. Tap her office phone if necessary."

"Your Majesty," Kerr sighed, "it would be in a catastrophe if she found out."

"I'm not worried about that, Mr. Ellison. That woman and my son are plotting against me. Whatever they have planned could bring down not only me, but the entire regal family, and the kingdom. Mr. Ellison, they are threats to national security."

Kerr nodded respectfully. "As you wish, Sire."

Michael remained in his office for three hours following his meeting with Kerr Ellison. Yet, no matter how hard he tried to focus on the task at hand, Michael's mind drifted to Alexander. Over the course of the holiday season, he and Alexander had barely spoken, much to his chagrin. If Alexander was plotting against him with Patricia Ali's assistance, this would be a first class nightmare. If the rest for the kingdom discovered Alexander's association with Patricia, it would have dire consequences.

"Michael," Cassandra called as she entered his office. She was followed by her yapping dogs and her attendant. The attendant placed Cassandra's drink on the nearby table along with several thick binders before leaving them alone. "I saw Kerr Ellison leaving. I don't recall you having had so much contact with him before…"

The King gazed out of the large windows onto the frozen lawn beyond. "What can I do for you, Mother?"

"When I first met Countess Sally I said to myself, 'This woman probably cares more about having a regal connection than the welfare of her son!' Luckily, I was wrong. Now, we all know how rarely I'm wrong, but Countess Sally is a hoot. We had the loveliest time chatting on Christmas Eve. Well, we've decided to meet for tea today to refine the guest list for the wedding," Cassandra exclaimed.

"I'm happy to hear you two are getting along. What do you need from me?"

"I need the list of visiting royals and dignitaries who will be in attendance because I need to incorporate them into the overall plan for the wedding."

"Andover Chapel only seats two hundred people, Mother. Besides, my office is handling the visiting VIPs. That has nothing to do with me."

Cassandra took a sip of her special drink. "You haven't been yourself for weeks."

Michael eyed his mother cautiously. Even though she was away on official engagements for the better part of his childhood, they were always close. In spite of the moments in time when they refused to speak to each other, there seemed to be an unbreakable bond between these two people who had both been born to rule the Kingdom of Andover and no one else would never know the cost of that position. "I'm tired," he lied.

"Michael, tell me why Mr. Ellison has been visiting you? I'm sure there's something I can do to help…"

"There isn't," snapped the King. "Mother, I appreciate your concern, but this cannot be resolved by talking about it *ad nauseum*."

"Well," bristled Cassandra, "you are in a mood. When you act this way, you remind me of your father."

"As you know, there are certain matters that I cannot discuss with anyone. Mother, please. Let me handle this in my own way."

"Fine," she retorted. "However, I must beg you not to let it affect your interactions with everyone else. You must open government tomorrow, Joseph's leaving for the armed services after the wedding and he'll need your support. Let us not forget that you have two other children who need their father and a kingdom that relies on you for strength and direction."

"Are you finished?"

The Dowager Queen shook her head with great indifference. Whatever was plaguing her son was beyond her realm of comprehension, which only compounded the fact that Michael was slowly withdrawing from his family. As she walked through the corridors of Andover Palace to her tea room, Cassandra thought about her twenty-eight years as the Queen of Andover. Yes, she recalled, there were plenty of times when she knew of events that would change history forever, but she was unable to speak about them to anyone. Michael was in the same position, she told herself, and it pained her to see him in so much agony.

In the comfort of her tea room, Cassandra examined the list of visiting royals and dignitaries delivered from His Majesty's Office. Due to the size of Andover Chapel, not everyone would be admitted to the service, but the reception would be one for the ages.

"Your Regal Highness," Sally cooed as she curtsied before the Dowager Queen.

"Countess, please have a seat." Cassandra ordered the attending butler to pour their tea before leaving them in peace. "You look wonderful. Is that vintage Dior?"

"It is," smiled Sally.

"I met him in Paris while I was touring France. He was a true gentleman," Cassandra recalled, fondly. "How is your family?"

"Very well, Ma'am. My husband and daughters had a wonderful time on Christmas Eve."

"I've received their cards of thanks. Do you have your final guest list?"

Sally pulled out several pieces of heavy cream paper from her Valentino purse. "Exactly sixty people for the wedding and one hundred for the reception, as we've discussed before."

"Yes, quite nice," said Cassandra. She examined the list with deft precision. "Who is this Mr. Jeffrey Carlyle?"

"Oh, he and Matthew dated for a few years. They met in Hong Kong and moved to Amsterdam, but they've been broken up for five years."

Cassandra sat in silence as she processed the news. It wouldn't be out of the ordinary for a former lover or spouse of a soon-to-be member of the regal family to attend a regal wedding, but she didn't think it would sit well with the King. After all, having Matthew's former boyfriend at his wedding could only compound Michael's sullen spirit. "Darling," tutted the Dowager Queen, "I must run Mr. Carlyle by the King to ensure he is at peace with his presence at the wedding."

"I understand. Ma'am, I wanted to ask you about the press."

"Press?"

"I've been contacted by the Quest Broadcasting Network and the Independent Broadcasting Channel about doing a series of interviews leading up to the wedding which will culminate in a live broadcast of the regal event," beamed Sally. "What do you think?"

The Dowager Queen pursed her lips. The idea of having news crews at her son's wedding made her sick to her stomach. Unlike many of the regal family's counterparts in other corners of the world, they had never invited the cameras into their daily lives or private moments. When the regal family performed official duties, the press kept a respectable distance and no interviews were given that involved issues outside of the task at hand. No one in the history of the regal family had ever given a personal interview and that's the way everyone wanted it. Cassandra always thought it was bad enough when the news crew from the public television channel, National Broadcasting Network infiltrated the palace to broadcast live from His Majesty's Official Office. But having those people invading the King's wedding day? "Absolutely not," Cassandra exclaimed.

Sally sat up with a bolt. She'd heard how blunt Cassandra could be from other women in her circle, but she'd never experienced it firsthand. "Excuse me," she gasped.

"Countess, I will not have the press harassing the regal family on His Majesty's wedding day!"

"The controllers of both networks have assured me that they will use the utmost discretion…"

"No," Cassandra said firmly. "If we were to allow those…people…into our personal lives even once, they would assume that they have free reign to harass us at every available moment. We've resisted the advances of the press over the last one hundred years in order to keep ourselves sane and free from their scrutiny."

"With all due respect, Ma'am, this is my son's wedding, too."

"The Count will be a member of this family in less than three and a half months, Countess. I'm thinking of his interest as well. For his sake, do not allow those people into your life. Your family will never have a moments peace."

"I think you're being very dramatic…"

"I am not!" countered the Dowager Queen. "Countess, look at the rest of the world if you don't believe me! You'll see I'm right! The press will become a hindrance to life as we know it. Let's face facts, the reason they approached you instead of the palace was because they knew we would refuse their request outright."

"And what if I want a memento from the day?"

"The palace photographer will take plenty of pictures. Besides, those wedding videos I've seen are quite tacky, wouldn't you agree?"

Sally shifted uncomfortably in her seat. "I suppose you're right."

The Dowager Queen gave her new friend a tight smile. "Countess, you'll see that everything will be fine. After all, your son is marrying the King."

Lady Margaret stood in front of the palace as she waited for her car. Unlike most days, Lady Margaret wanted to drive into the countryside of Kemp Forest alone. However, alone for Lady Margaret meant an unmarked security car following her, however, that didn't faze her. She pulled her iPhone from her oversized Prada bag to check the time. As she waited in the crisp winter air Lady Margaret noticed Countess Sally Hall being escorted from the palace by a courtier. Margaret did hear that the Countess was meeting with the Dowager Queen, but the specifics of the meeting did not interest her. Hell, Margaret thought to herself, most things concerning palace life didn't interest her anymore. Maybe it was an effect of being the family pariah, but it actually felt good to be blissfully ignorant about palace politics.

"Countess, hello." Margaret extended her hand with cheerful exuberance.

"Your Regal Highness." Sally performed the requisite curtsy as she shook Margaret's hand. Sally pulled her cashmere wrap around her as the cold air blew past them.

"Lovely weather," said Margaret. "I trust you had a fruitful meeting with the Dowager Queen."

The Countess merely smiled. "You could say that."

Lady Margaret eyed Sally carefully. She quickly deduced that Cassandra was the source of her frustration. "Don't worry; the Dowager Queen is very strong willed. If you didn't know any better, you would think she still ran the whole damn kingdom."

"Ma'am, I… Let's just say that I couldn't agree with you more."

Margaret offered her a soft smile. "Well, don't let her get to you. The King is in charge, not her." A valet finally arrived in Margaret's vintage Maserati. As she stepped towards the idling car, Margaret called to Sally, "Have a nice day and don't let that old woman get you down." With that Margaret drove away, and as she watched Sally from the rear view mirror, she knew her good deed for the day had been accomplished.

"Thank you for dinner, Walter," Samantha sighed.

They walked through the fresh snow at Blake Manor without a care in the world. Ever since Samantha returned from her Christmas vacation, they had been inseparable. Although they had yet to spend the night together, Walter enjoyed this quiet, uncomplicated relationship. With Daisy, Walter felt constantly on his guard that she would do something unpredictable at a moments notice. Now, Walter felt as if he'd been given a second chance at life and love.

"Samantha," Walter finally said, "I don't know about you, but I want to slowly introduce you to the rest of the regal family, including His Majesty."

Samantha stopped dead in her tracks. Suddenly, this was all too much for her, even though the thought of meeting the King frightened and elated her. "Walter, do you think it may be too soon?"

"No," he said adamantly. "Look, we've only been together for a few months, but it feels right, Samantha. I feel so calm around you."

"I do, too." Samantha took his hand in hers. "To be honest, I never thought this would happen to us."

"What do you mean?"

“Well, you do have the reputation for being a playboy and I never thought that we would last.”

“Really?”

“But being away from you and the kingdom made me see how much I want to know you… In every way...”

“Then meet my family.” Walter hugged her tightly as they made their way back to the house. “I know it’s old fashioned, but when we date someone, they have to meet at least three family members. It’s the vetting process.”

“How romantic,” she replied dryly.

Walter led her through the back entrance of the manor and into the Drawing Room where a great fire was roared. “Like I said, I know it’s old fashioned. But once you have their seal of approval, you can meet the King.”

Samantha kicked off her snow boots as she and Walter relaxed on a plush sofa. “What happens if someone doesn’t like me?”

“That won’t happen. The Dowager Queen is fond of you, and from what I can tell, Princess Sophia thinks your tops.”

“Did you just say tops?”

“I was listening to Cole Porter this morning. Anyway, I do want you to meet Lady Margaret and maybe Prince Joseph. What do you say?”

“If anyone had told me last year that I would be in Blake Manor with His Regal Highness Lord Walter, I would have laughed out loud. But, to be honest, I’m glad my mother and your aunt conspired to have us meet.”

“Me too.”

“And,” she added, “I haven’t been this happy in a very long time.”

Walter gave her a passionate kiss. He hadn’t felt this way about anyone in years; not even Daisy. Walter knew in that he wanted to spend the rest of his life with Samantha. After everything he’d been through in the last few years, Walter knew that it had all been worth it. He broke their passionate kiss to gaze into her soft eyes once more. If every day could be like this, he told himself, he would want nothing else for as long as he lived.

Princess Helena walked through the familiar halls of Kemp Castle while the staff prepared dinner for herself, her brothers, and Princess Sophia. She was noticeably anxious due to the fact that her twenty-sixth birthday was two days away. Getting older never scared her, but for some reason, turning twenty-six seemed to be a fate worse than death. By the time her mother was eighteen, she was already married to her father. Needless to say, Princess Helena felt behind the curve. She didn't want to have a birthday party this year, so her father planned a quiet birthday lunch in the private dining room at Cabo. That would be enough for her, especially after the year she'd had.

As Helena walked through the discrete door that connected the private suites of Kemp Castle to the state rooms, she noticed the portrait of her father and mother hanging above the fireplace in the Grand Hall. During Princess Helena's childhood, the oil portrait was above the Grand Staircase. However, a new portrait of the Prince and Princess of Kemp hung there with great prominence. She studied the portrait for a moment before deciding that she didn't think Alexander was good enough to become Andover's new monarch. Helena knew she would never address this view publicly, but she thought it quite often. In Helena's mind, Alexander didn't have the simple people skills or the likability factor that was needed for the role of King of Andover. Helena knew Alexander well. He was cold, prickly, standoffish, and the first person to jump down your throat if he felt threatened. He'd probably behead the locals, Helena thought wickedly.

"Helena," the Princess of Kemp called as she marched into the Grand Hall. "We've been looking all over for you."

The icy princess smirked at her sister-in-law. No matter how long Olivia was married to her brother, Helena would never respect her as his wife or the future Duchess of Andover, Consort of the King. There was something Helena couldn't quite verbalize, but she felt like Olivia was nothing more than a pretender to the throne.

"You've found me," she replied dryly. "You forget that I know all of the secret passages in this castle."

The Princess of Kemp gave her a warm smile. "Shall we have dinner?"

"I suppose."

Olivia followed Princess Helena through the discrete doors back to the private suites of Kemp Castle. "What would you like for your birthday?"

"Nothing," Helena sighed. "I have everything."

Olivia bristled at her sister-in-law's admission. "I suppose I can't argue with that statement. Maybe we could have breakfast…or something…"

"Possibly, but you'll have to check with my secretary."

"Helena," Olivia sighed, "I'm trying to be nice."

Princess Helena stopped in her tracks. Did this woman know who she was talking to, Helena wondered hotly. "Olivia, I know you're trying to be nice. You're my brother's wife, but that doesn't mean that I have to be nice to you. Your only purpose is to produce an heir for my family – that's all."

"How dare you…"

"Oh, get off your pulpit, Olivia. That's the main purpose of the Princess of Kemp. My mother knew it, so did my grandfather. Your role is to support the heir to the throne in every capacity."

"How can be you so vicious," stammered the prince's wife. "No wonder Derek Sharpe wrote that story about you! You are cold…"

Princess Helena rolled her eyes with irritated disgust. "Me? I am who I am and I've never apologized for that. You haven't had the life of me and my brothers. You have no idea what we've been through, Olivia."

"Yeah," she choked, "but I know how to be human and kind."

"Kind? At least I'm no phony! You walk around this castle like you own it and the way you suck up to my grandmother is sickening. We all merely tolerate you because you're Alexander's wife," shouted Helena.

Olivia felt herself falling ill with fury. In the year and a half since her marriage to Alexander, Olivia had managed to keep her relationship with the entire regal family cordial and friendly, but Princess Helena had never been kind to her. "Tolerate me? You're the saddest member of the entire family! The whole kingdom feels sorry for you! You're almost twenty-six and no man has ever expressed any interest in you…"

"Watch yourself…"

"No! You think you can saunter into my home and insult me? Honey, I've done everything in my power to be nice to you, but it's impossible!"

"How dare you! I am the daughter of His Majesty The King and don't you ever forget that! You, my dear, are fully expendable!"

"Enough!" Princess Sophia shouted from the door of the Drawing Room. Behind her stood the Prince of Kemp and Prince Joseph, their mouths wide open at the spectacle before them. Sophia charged over to the two princesses with fire in her eyes. "That is *quite* enough! What is going on? What will the staff think?"

"I don't care," snapped Helena. "She deserves it."

"Helena, stop this," ordered Alexander. "What's gotten into you?"

Princess Helena crossed her arms defiantly. "Me? Nothing, Alex. I was in the Grand Hall minding my own business when your wife started harassing me. She then proceeded to tell me that she's just being nice," mocked Helena in Olivia's soft voice.

"That's not what happened," Olivia snapped coldly.

"Whatever. Alex, thank you for having me tonight, but I'm going home." Princess Helena turned on her heels and barked at the attending valet to fetch her full-length mink coat and bring around the car.

"Helena, stay," insisted Joseph.

Without a word, Helena snatched her coat from the valet and stormed off.

The remaining party stood in silence for an eternity. Finally, Joseph said, "Guys, this is weird, so I'm going to head home, too."

"Joey," muttered the Prince of Kemp. "Stay…"

"This is weirdly uncomfortable."

Princess Sophia agreed. "Alex, you need to tend to your wife. Olivia, thank you for your hospitality… Good night."

"What was that all about," seethed Prince Joseph.

Princess Helena sat coolly at the table in her dressing room as her brother watched her with marked disappointment. On the ride from Kemp Castle, Helena's mind went blank due to the fact that she didn't want to recall tonight for as long as she lived. "Nothing," she sighed, as she removed her diamond earrings. "If you'll excuse me, I need my sleep. We have to accompany father to tomorrow's opening of government."

Joseph shook his head with great contempt. "Look, I know Olivia can be a bit much, but you shouldn't have made such a scene at the castle."

"Joey," snapped Helena, "you don't get it. It will be the tenth anniversary of Mom's death in a few days and Alex's wife thinks she can run around as if she's the one and only Princess of Kemp."

"Is that what's bothering you?" Joseph followed his sister into her dusty pink bedroom. Ever since the death of their mother, Joseph and his siblings rarely discussed Katherine. For Joseph, it was easier to keep the pain inside, rather than admit it to the rest of the world. He never knew how Helena felt about Katherine's death, especially in the proceeding years when the comparisons to mother and daughter were unkind at best. "Helena, Mom would probably love Olivia."

“I don’t think so. Don’t get me wrong, I’m glad Dad’s found Matthew, but that Olivia is all wrong for Alexander.”

“That’s not for you to decide.”

“I’m his sister! I have a right to voice my opinion!”

“But not in the middle of Kemp Castle!”

Helena threw a terse glare towards her brother. “Get over it, Joey. We were in the private part of the castle! It’s not like I made a scene in front of the staff. Besides, she deserved it.”

“Look, I don’t know what else to say.”

“Good. I’m tired…”

“You should call Alex to apologize.”

“Why? He never should have married her. Besides, he’s been so cold and distant lately, I don’t even know what to say to him.”

Joseph nodded in agreement. “That’s Alex. But you should try to be amiable towards Olivia. She will become the Duchess of Andover and mother to the future monarch of Andover sooner or later.”

“Yes, and I’m sure that will make her quite jubilant,” sniffed the princess. Helena lowered her eyes as she walked towards the oversized windows in her private suite. “Can you believe it’s almost been ten years since Mom died?”

“No… It seems like yesterday…almost…”

“I know.” Princess Helena removed a vintage watch from her wrist with great care. This Cartier watch was the last birthday gift her mother had given to her before succumbing to pneumonia on a cold January night so many years ago. “The press always compared me to her…they always said that you were her son, but I was most certainly Duchess Victoria’s great-granddaughter because of my size. I’ve always tried to take it in stride, but it hurts, Joey. Sometimes I think that if Mom were still here, we could have a mother-daughter spat that would make everything okay again. But I'll never be able to tell her how much I love her…or anything else…again. Do you want to know something?"

"What?"

"After she died, I could smell her… In my dreams, mostly or if I closed my eyes and concentrated very hard, I could smell her. Sometimes, I could see her face. But now it's all fading. When I was in the Grand Hall tonight, I noticed for the first time that Alexander moved the portrait of Mom and Dad and replaced it with one of him with Olivia…"

"He is the heir to the throne…"

"I know," she sighed. "But it was all too real…" Helena brushed away the tears as they began to stream down her face.

Joseph moved towards his sister to comfort her, but she kept him at bay. "Helena…"

"I'm fine. I need to rest."

Joseph left his sister's private suite with a heavy feeling in his stomach. While he didn't agree with Helena's behavior tonight, he understood how she felt. He was very close to his mother as well as his father, which always caused a slight rift between himself and his siblings. Katherine's death had hit Joseph hard, but he somehow managed to deal with the pain. But there were times in the last ten years when he hadn't handled his motions well and acted out. Hell, thought the prince, his entire university education in Monaco was spent acting out, which prompted his father – the newly crowned King of Andover – to order his son to straighten up or suffer the consequences. Alexander thought Joseph should suffer, but Michael always forgave his children, especially Joseph. Now, in the cold light of a winter's night, Joseph wondered what would happen next for the regal family. He reached for his iPhone and dialed Alexander's private extension.

"Hello?"

"Alex, it's me."

"Joseph… What can I do for you?"

Prince Joseph shifted his weight as he sat on the edge of an eighteenth century end table in his private suite. "I wanted to apologize for Helena… She's going through some stuff."

"Joey," interjected Alexander, "she's always going through something. It's her thing."

"Alex, it's not like that…"

"She was cruel to my wife."

Joseph searched the dimly lit room for guidance. "At the end of this month, it will be a decade since Mom's death,"Joseph stated quickly.

"I'm aware of that."

"Can we forget that tonight happened?"

Alexander paused for a brief moment. "I don't know. That damage is done. Good night, Joey."

"Who was that," Olivia asked meekly. She walked into her husband's bedroom wrapped in a full-length silk nightgown.

Alexander placed the phone on the cradle without looking up. "Joseph."

The Princess of Kemp slid onto Alexander's bed with great care. Her eyes were red from crying, which didn't seem to faze Alexander. "What did he say?"

"Nothing," he replied crisply. "I wish you and my sister could get along."

"It wasn't my fault," insisted the princess. "Your sister has had it in for me for as long as I can remember. I haven't done anything to her, except try to be nice…"

Alexander removed his evening clothes and tossed them onto a nearby Chippendale chair. He climbed into his large bed as he said, "Just leave her alone."

"Are you taking her side?"

"No. She's my sister. You're my wife. I won't take a side."

"But you are," gasped Olivia. "What have I done to deserve this? Your sister hates me and you – my own husband! – won't even defend me!"

The prince shook his head with great annoyance. "If you're going to keep up these inane histrionics, go to your own bedroom, Olivia. I have a long day tomorrow."

Olivia let out a defiant huff as she stormed towards the door. "You'd better be nice to me, Alex. If you don't want the whole world to know about your meetings with Patricia Ali…"

"What?" The Prince of Kemp could feel the color drain from his face. His wife seemed quite content with herself as she stood in the doorway wrapped in the warm, devious moonlight.

"You heard me," she countered. "You're not the only person who knows more than he lets on."

"You know nothing."

"You don't know what I know," she said forcefully. "Now it seems that whatever you have planned may be bigger than anyone knows. I'll keep my mouth shut if you do two things for me: Keep your sister away from me, and participate in IVF treatments."

The Prince of Kemp couldn't believe what his wife was saying. How could she be so cunningly deceptive? "IVF?"

"It stands for…"

"I know what it stands for," he snapped. "I will not! The King would never allow it…"

"He never has to know. You need an heir and you need me to keep my mouth shut. I need to become the Duchess of Andover. You see, you have a lot to gain and even more to lose." Olivia walked over to the bed and kissed her husband on the head. "Think about it." With that, she sauntered into her adjoining suite.

Alexander stared out of the window of his suite for over an hour. If Olivia knew anything about what he and Patricia Ali were planning, she could ruin everything. No, he reminded himself, they'd been careful while concocting their plan. Alexander was fully aware that there would be casualties; if Olivia happened to be one, so be it. When he married her, he did love her, but that everlasting love had slowly grown into eternal contempt. To Alexander's glee, his wife had made a juvenile move in the art of sabotage: She'd exposed her end result which was to be the Duchess of Andover.

As the clock struck half past two in the morning, Alexander finally allowed himself to fall asleep. But as he passed the realm between consciousness and delirium, the heir to the throne knew what he had to do in order to fully enact his carefully planned coup. People would get hurt, he told himself, but every war needed a martyr.

"Daddy, I don't need a lecture," groaned Princess Helena. She quickly turned her back as she picked up her purse from the table. "Besides, Olivia's too sensitive anyway. I didn't mean what I said… She's making a big deal out of nothing."

The King shook his head with grave disbelief. He felt like he was the matron of a boarding school instead of the ruling monarch of his own kingdom. The Prince of Kemp had called him at five o'clock this morning to relay his version of last night's events to His Majesty. Although Michael wanted nothing more than to forget about this unimportant incident between his daughter and daughter-in-law he was fully aware of the fact that he had to say something in order to show the world that he cared about everyone in his family. "Helena, what set you off?"

Princess Helena glared at her father. "She did. That's all. Dad, I don't want to talk about this anymore. Besides, we'll be late for the opening of government. You know it's my favorite time of year."

"It is?"

"Of course," she smiled. They left the princess' plush private suite and walked down the corridors of Andover Palace to the idling town cars in the forecourt. "The ceremony makes winter worth living. I still can't believe that Alexander would be so petty as to call you at dawn to report my run-in with Olivia."

"Darling, I do think you should apologize."

"Why?!" Helena could barely hide the incredulously tone in her voice. "I was being honest! She is expendable. She's not even pregnant with an heir, yet she walks around like we owe her something. If I remember my history lessons, she owes *us* something."

On the ride to Andover's Government Complex in the heart of Old Andover, Michael couldn't get Helena's words out of his mind. Olivia and Alexander had yet to produce an heir, even after a year and a half of marriage. The King fully understood that most young couples wanted to take time to know each other. However, the Prince and Princess of Kemp had access to limitless funds to ensure their lives went on without interruption. With everything he knew about his own son's deception, the King surmised that it may not be the worst thing in the world if Alexander and Olivia didn't have children.

"Mother, what do you know about the Prince of Kemp's marriage," the King asked his mother.

She fiddled with her gloves as she pursed her lips. Since the death of his father, Michael always rode with his mother to the opening of government; it was their personal tradition. "Why, their marriage simply confuses me, Michael."

"What do you know?"

"The Princess of Kemp was in tears last summer because she and Alexander weren't even…making love," she said in a low voice. "How can one have a baby when they don't even try?"

"She told you that?" Michael couldn't believe the candor with which Olivia had spoken to Andover's former monarch.

Cassandra nodded gravely. "Yes. Now, I'm not one to gossip, but I don't know what to make of my grandson's marriage. I did tell her that it was her duty to produce an heir. I hope my insistence that she *try* has led them to *try*."

"Did you hear about Princess Helena's argument with the Princess of Kemp?"

"Joseph told me on our morning walk," smiled the Dowager Queen.

"So that's what you two discuss every morning," the King joked dryly.

Cassandra touched her son's arm. "Michael, if the Prince and Princess of Kemp do not have children in due time and Alexander dies without an heir, the crown will pass to Helena."

"I'm aware of that, Mother. But would it be a terrible thing if that happened?"

"Michael! How can you say that?"

"Alexander hasn't been the most popular member of the regal family as of late..."

"He's better than Lady Margaret," scoffed the Dowager Queen. "Michael, he's your son!"

"Mother, I'm not going to fight with you. If Alexander doesn't have a natural, legitimate heir, the crown will pass to Princess Helena. It's the law."

The Dowager Queen nodded in agreement, although the thought alone made her pray that an event such as that would happen after her death. "Son, the throne has passed from the first born child of every monarch since my father ascended the throne on the death of his father, King Christoph. It's the only way to keep the regal line in tact. I am very sure that the Prince and Princess of Kemp will have an heir."

"And if they don't?"

"Well," thought Cassandra for a long while, "you'll have to deal with that when the time comes. After all, if they divorced it wouldn't be the worst thing in the world...especially if his new wife produces an heir."

The opening of Andover's government was a festive official occasion with the pomp and circumstance of a million important events to keep the world enthralled until next year. As the regal procession reached the gates of the government building, a crowd of eager citizens and members of the press shouted to the passing cars. When the procession finally reached the front of the alabaster monument to law and order, the regal family emerged from their chauffeured cars with the King leading the way.

The King was led to his private regal suite where his attendants dressed him in his official ceremonial robes. As he listened for Patricia Ali to announce his entrance, Michael thought of the ease with which Cassandra could suggest that Alexander find a new wife to sire his heir. Twenty years ago, Michael recalled, his mother wouldn't have dared to make such a suggestion. Times are changing, he reminded himself.

"His Majestic Regal Highness The King Michael of Andover," pronounced Patricia Ali.

Michael stepped onto the balcony built high above the hall of governors. His eyes fell upon a screen at the back of the law which projected his speech.

"It is my hope in the coming year that the Kingdom of Andover achieves new heights of success. As the kingdom votes for a new Minister of Government at the end of this year, I encourage everyone to exercise their right to vote. No matter what the outcome of the election, the regal family will continue to support the initiatives of the Minister of Government. I know I speak for the entire regal family when I say that a new dawn has come." Michael picked up a gavel, which prompted everyone in attendance to rise. He banged it three times on the podium in front of him. "I officially open my government for the New Year."

"Don't you think your speech was a little biased, Dad?" The Prince of Kemp's eyes darted around his father's private office.

"Are you worried what the Minister of Government will think," the King suggested blithely.

Alexander choked on his orange juice. "Excuse me?"

"My speech wasn't biased. I plainly said that I would – and the regal family would – support the new Minister of Government, no matter who wins the election. Do you have a preference," Michael asked his son.

"No," he responded unflinchingly.

Michael smiled to himself as he watched his son squirm with obvious discomfort. Maybe this would finally put an end to Alexander's very dubious interaction with Patricia Ali once and for all. "By the way, I spoke with your grandmother about the Princess of Kemp."

Alexander let out an irritated huff. "Why? Dad, just leave well enough alone."

"Alexander," the King snapped. "When you call me at five o'clock in the morning on the day I have to open government, don't expect me to leave well enough." Michael lifted his water glass ever so lightly as he said, "Why didn't you tell me about your…romantic issues…with your wife?"

"It was none of your business," replied Alexander. "Anyway, that's in the past. My wife and I are fine."

"Is she pregnant?"

"We're trying. Dad, let's drop it."

The King folded his hands. "Son, if an heir isn't produced in the next year or two, I'll have to make Princess Helena the heiress presumptive to the throne."

"You can't do that," protested Alexander. "Olivia and I are trying…"

"Keep your voice down," warned Michael. "You and your wife need to have a natural, legitimate heir in order to secure the line of succession."

Alexander bit his lip. "You're right. You're always right."

"Don't patronize me, Alexander. Oh, and if you could keep your meetings with Ms. Ali down to a minimum, I would appreciate it. If you're seen cavorting with her the divorced head of my government outside of official events, people may get the wrong opinion."

The Prince of Kemp froze as he watched his father walk out of his office. If his father knew this much about his relationship with Olivia and Patricia Ali, the prince didn't stand a chance. As it stood right now, Alexander and Patricia were in the midst of their plan to eventually take over the kingdom. However, he now had to kowtow to Olivia's demands that he – the King's son – submit himself for IVF treatments. Alexander quickly deduced that his own power would be moot if Princess Helena succeeded him to the throne. No, Alexander told himself, that will never happen. In that moment, Alexander pulled his iPhone from the inside pocket of his jacket. *Now*, was all he typed, but the prince knew it was all he needed to say.

The Princess of Kemp and His Highness Edward galloped along the snowy horse trail at Kemp Castle with skillful grace. Edward brought his stallion, Fred Go-Lightly, to a stop near the edge of the estate where it turned into farm land. He tied the horse to a tree, while Olivia dismounted her horse with great ease. Edward pulled a flask from the inside pocket of his coat and took a swig before handing it to his cousin.

"Thank you for coming," Olivia stated quietly.

"I love riding in the dead of winter. Why couldn't we talk in the house," he asked.

Princess Olivia shook her head. "We can't. Did you hear what happened here last night?"

"I did and I'm staying out of it, Olivia."

Olivia gnashed her teeth with intense frustration. It already seemed that everyone in the regal family knew about the blow-up at Kemp Castle. Olivia naturally thought it was the doing of Princess Sophia and Princess Helena, although she knew her own husband could be a gossip when it suited him. Still, Olivia couldn't shake the feeling that her status within the regal family was on tenuous ground. The King had spoken to her briefly this morning, which made it only obvious to her that he was either siding with his precious daughter or staying out of their juvenile war. "Eddie, it shouldn't be this hard, should it?"

"I don't know. Margaret and I haven't been the same since this summer. To be honest, I'm terrified that I'll come home one day and she and Samuel will be gone."

"She wouldn't do that to you…"

"You don't know the half of it," he groaned. "Are you miserable with the Prince of Kemp?"

"No… There's just so much pressure on us to have a baby from a lot of people in the family."

"That's what this institution is all about," surmised Edward. "The family has to produce heirs to continue with the line of succession to ensure their dominance over the kingdom. It's a classic anthropological example of the alpha male asserting his place in the world."

"Are you saying we're nothing but animals?"

"Olivia," he scoffed. "I've known you since you were born. If you wanted to have Alexander's baby, you would've had it already."

Her Regal Highness Lady Margaret sat in the comfort of her private state apartment as the snow began to fall. Her last encounter with Matthew's mother, Countess Sally Hall, had prompted her to rethink her allegiances within the regal family. If Cassandra was already upsetting Sally before the wedding, it was only a matter of time before the two women went to war over their sons. For Margaret, this was a golden opportunity to soften her public image and play the role of the mediator between the two branches of the regal family; she would be the savior.

"Your Regal Highness, Countess Sally Hall is here to see you," pronounced the attending valet, who showed her into the Margaret's Music Room.

Sally curtsied. "Your Regal Highness."

"Countess, please have a seat. I'm sorry that we didn't have a chance to speak the other day."

Sally removed her chinchilla coat and gloves. "I understand, Ma'am. To be honest, I'm afraid I let my emotions get the better of me that day."

"Why don't you tell me what happened? I'm sure I can provide some sort of insight into what occurred between you and Dowager Queen."

Sally proceeded to recount her meeting with Cassandra that involved inviting the press to the regal wedding and Cassandra's reaction. "Needless to say, it's a non-issue now," sighed Sally.

Margaret thought for a moment before she said, "Countess, why should the Dowager Queen have so much influence over your decisions? Granted, she is my aunt and His Majesty's mother, but she is no longer the Queen of Andover."

"What are you saying," the Countess asked cautiously.

Margaret summoned the attending butler to bring a pot of coffee for herself and the Countess. "You are still a private citizen and you will always be one until Count Matthew marries the King. Until then, you have complete control over your personal life. The Dowager Queen revels in her need to control everyone and everything. Countess, what do you think?"

"I've had time to think about it, and I do agree with the Dowager Queen. If I invite the press into my life, they'll never leave. It's bad enough that they're camped outside of my family's estate waiting for a glimpse of Matthew." The Countess rubbed her hands together as she said, "Lady Margaret, I appreciate your concern, but I feel that the Dowager Queen does know best in this situation."

"Do you?" Margaret bit the inside of her cheek. "Why's that?"

"I've already said. It's not the end of the world. We still have a wonderful wedding to plan." And with that, the Countess excused herself to use the powder room.

"Your Majesty," Glenn said as he opened the door to Michael's private office.

"For goodness sakes," muttered the King. He stopped typing a speech he was to give at the King Henrik Center of Economic Studies tomorrow afternoon. "I told you I was not to be disturbed."

"Sire, it's very important." Glenn made his way to the television in the King's office and turned it to the Hourly News Channel. "We may have a problem on our hands."

Tamara Kellison, the lead anchor for the HNC's afternoon newscast, said: "A new subversive group calling themselves The Martyrs of Andover has released the following statement in which they claim His Majesty The King and the regal family were involved in a cover-up concerning the death of the late Princess of Kemp. The Princess of Kemp, Princess Katherine, died ten years ago from - what the palace officials called - a case of pneumonia. However, The Martyrs of Andover claim that King Michael and Andover's former monarch, the Dowager Queen Cassandra, were involved in the death of Princess Katherine, so the King could marry Count Matthew Hall. The Hourly News Channel has contacted Andover Palace; however, they have not returned our calls for a statement. Little is known about The Martyrs of Andover; however, one can be sure that this group will be thrust into the public glare with these earth shattering revelations."

24

The phones rang for the remainder of the day.

After the breaking announcement concerning the death of Princess Katherine, the King locked himself in his private suite, away from the world, the palace, and his family. Silence filled Michael's bedroom as memories of the past flooded through his mind. For Michael, the fact that the Hourly News Channel could report such a vicious, unsubstantiated rumor made him visibly sick. On top of that, Glenn was urging the monarch to release a statement emphatically stating that he had nothing to do with the princess' death. However, Michael resisted. He argued that releasing a statement of that kind would only stoke the flames of scandal, which needed to be put out in the most natural way. The King lay on his bed. He closed his eyes for a brief moment as memories of long ago resurfaced for the first time in years…

"How are you feeling today," asked the Prince of Kemp, Prince Michael of Andover. He removed his hunting coat and draped it over a high backed maple chair. Michael moved towards the Princess of Kemp, Princess Katherine of Andover, who lay in her sick bed, with a small smile on her face. The prince kissed her forehead gently. He sat beside her and grasped her frail hand. Although the doctor said that her pneumonia was incurable, Michael held out hope that everything would work itself out... it had to...

Katherine let out a terrible cough. "I'm all right," she sighed. "Michael...you've been here for three days...Go enjoy yourself."

He bit his lip as he tried to fight back the tears. "Katherine...this is where I belong. You know that..."

"I also know that I don't have much time." She tried to catch her breath. "The doctor has done everything he can...I'm ready..."

"Mary and Ted are waiting to see you."

Katherine attempted to laugh. "When I look my worst, my sister decides to visit."

"Katherine..."

Princess Katherine sighed as she gripped Michael's hand with the remainder of her strength. She studied her husband's face...the small lines around his eyes, the turned-up corners of his mouth...these were the intimate details she wanted to remember forever, because she knew all too well this may be the last time she would ever be allowed to make them her own. "When I'm gone... Michael, you've been the best husband I could have ever asked for. You took a girl who didn't know much about the world and made her into a princess. My dream came true. We have three wonderful children that I love and adore. I know you'll be there for them, as you were for me."

"You'll be fine," insisted Michael.

"Michael, the children will need you. Whenever you become the monarch, be sure to make plenty of time for the children. Helena may need more overt attention, while Joey...Joey...he'll be fine. It's Alexander who worries me the most. Pay attention to him, Michael. He can be as emotionally charged as your father and that will be his greatest weakness. Promise me that you'll do whatever it takes to keep our children happy."

"I will," he replied through warm tears. "I love you, Katherine. I always have..."

"And I you..."

That was the last thing Katherine said to Michael before she died later that afternoon. The flood of memories proved too much for the King who let out a primal scream that filled every corner of his private suite. How could something like this happen after all of these years, he asked himself angrily.

"Your Majesty," Glenn said as he parted the door which separated the monarch's private quarters from the anteroom. "Kerr Ellison is here to see you. He says it's urgent."

Kerr walked into Michael's private sitting room. Michael motioned for him to sit down. "What do you know," asked Michael.

"It seems that The Martyrs of Andover are nothing more than an organization in name only."

"Meaning?"

"They haven't existed beyond today's press release."

Michael took this in for a moment. "What else is there, Mr. Ellison?"

Reluctantly, Kerr pulled a one page brief from his attaché case. "From the intelligence we have been able to gather from our surveillance of the Prince of Kemp and Patricia Ali, it appears that they are behind this press release."

"Where's the proof?"

"Text messages, e-mail, and telephone conversations that point in their direction. What would you like me to do with this information?"

"Nothing." The King folded the brief and placed it in his shirt pocket. "For now, we'll do nothing."

"Are you sure, Your Majesty?"

"I am. I'll handle this in my own way."

Realizing that the King was resolute, Kerr stood, bowed, and started for the door. "For whatever it's worth, Your Majesty, I know you had nothing to do with Princess Katherine's death. We all do."

"Thank you," replied Michael. He watched as Kerr left his private suite before he examined the brief once more. He knew Alexander and Patricia Ali were up to something, but this was too horrible to fathom. Whatever they are planning, Michael told himself, was out of control and, he realized, they had to be stopped.

"What do you mean I can't see the King?" Princess Sophia folded her arms with righteous indignation. Her eyes narrowed as they focused on the haired assistant who was trying to handle the three ringing phones on her desk.

"Your Regal Highness, those are the orders of Mr. Mortimer, who was been ordered by His Majesty. There's nothing I can do!"

"I want to see Glenn," snapped Princess Sophia. Moments later, Sophia sauntered into the small office of the King's Private Secretary, Glenn Mortimer, 1st Peer. "I want to see my brother," demanded Sophia.

Glenn shook his head helplessly. "Your Regal Highness, His Majesty has refused all visitors and phone calls. He is not to be disturbed. These are his orders. Not mine."

Princess Sophia eyed Glenn cautiously. In the eight years that Glenn had worked for Michael, he had always been honest and forthright when it came to mediating between Michael and the regal family. "Is that so?"

"Yes. He doesn't even want to see the Dowager Queen."

"Very well… I'm sorry I've wasted your time." Sophia's thoughts drifted to Michael as she walked back to her state apartment. Ever since the news regarding Michael's supposed involvement in the death of Princess Katherine, the palace had gone mad. Every phone rang incessantly, while the staff buzzed about the implications it may have on their careers. Worse still, the international press had picked up the story and now the whole world thought her brother was capable of murdering his own wife in order to marry his male lover. Sophia couldn't help but blanch at the ludicrous nature of the claims. While something like this may have happened on one of the American soap operas her mother watched, it was far less likely that her own brother would do something so drastic and reprehensible.

As she walked into the foyer of her state apartment, the attending butler informed her that Katherine's sister, Mary Walsh and her husband, Ted, who was also Robert's first cousin, were with Prince Robert in the Drawing Room. "Mary…Ted," she said with a small smile. They exchanged pleasantries before Sophia said, "It's unfortunate to see each other under such despicable circumstances."

"They're horrid," exclaimed Mary. "I'm grateful my parents aren't alive to hear this trash! I want to see the King, Sophia."

Princess Sophia shook her head as she sat in her soft leather chair. "Mary, I was just at Michael's private quarters and I couldn't see him. He isn't seeing anyone, not even our mother."

"Does he think that hiding from the issue will make it disappear," asked Ted.

Sophia gave him a terse look. "No. But we don't know anything about this group… I can't speak for Michael, but I think we should respect his privacy."

"Privacy?" Mary threw her hands into the air with sheer frustration. "Sophia, the tenth anniversary of my sister's death was last month and Michael barely acknowledged it."

"That's not fair, Mary," interjected Robert. "Michael did observe the day…"

"Not publicly," she sniffed.

"He spent three years grieving for Katherine! Isn't he allowed to grieve in his own way?" Sophia countered bitterly.

"You don't understand how distressing this is for me. The King is marrying Count Matthew in April and he's also accused of murdering my sister!" Mary was becoming visibly upset with each passing moment. She poured herself a glass of water before saying, "Sophia, I think I have a right to have a one-to-one conference with Michael."

"It's not up to me," shouted Sophia.

Sensing that this could become an all out shouting match, Robert put his arm around his wife. "Look, why don't we all take a moment to think before we say something that we'll later regret."

"I won't have her tell me that my brother is responsible for Katherine's death," the princess huffed. "How can anyone believe that? Michael loved her! He sat with Katherine for three days before she died!"

"He should have been there with her the entire time," snipped Mary.

"He had the children to look after," quipped Sophia.

"That wasn't an easy time for anyone of us," Robert added. "Mary, Ted, I know Michael didn't kill Katherine. He's innocent and we all know it."

Ted shrugged. "Rob, I know everyone likes to hold Michael in such high regard, but I have to say that the accusation doesn't seem very off base to me."

"What's that supposed to mean," seethed Sophia.

Ted steadied himself. "It all seems too perfect. Katherine dies from pneumonia and then Michael prepares to marry Matthew."

"The two events aren't even connected," yelled Sophia. "How blind are you people? Michael and Matthew didn't even start seeing each other again until three years ago."

"That we know of," Mary said tersely.

Sophia could feel the rage of the past day coming to the surface. This was the first time in her life that she'd heard anyone speak out against the reigning monarch. What made this even worse was the fact that while Michael may have loved men, he was very faithful to Katherine throughout their entire marriage. The love they shared couldn't be faked, Sophia reminded herself. However, in this moment, she wanted nothing more than to lash out at Mary and Ted for even considering that Michael and Katherine's marriage was marred with scandal, lies, deceit, and murder. "Michael is innocent, as is my mother. Princess Katherine was ill, Mary. You know that. These rumors are nothing more than a lazy attempt to undermine the King, the kingdom, and the regal family. Michael would never have done anything to harm Katherine."

"Can you be so sure, Sophia," bit Mary.

"I've had enough of you," Sophia screamed. "This is nothing more than a terrible attempt to sully my brother's reputation and that of the regal family! Mary, how can you believe any of this? You were with Michael when Katherine died!"

Mary averted her eyes towards the fresco of Apollo and Hercules on the ceiling. She could recall all too well the final moments she spent with Michael and Katherine. Mary had never seen her younger sister look so weak and helpless in her entire life. When Katherine left this life, Michael fell apart and they wept in each other's arms for an hour before facing the outside world. Yet, despite the memories of that day, Mary couldn't shake the feeling that someone wasn't telling her the whole truth. "Sophia, I'll always remember the day Katherine died. I would have never of thought that he would have harmed her, but I think it would be careless of me to assume that Michael is innocent because of the love he and Katherine shared."

"What's that supposed to mean?" Sophia took a step towards Mary, as Robert held her right hand.

Mary took a deep breath. "Look, it's an open secret in our circle that Michael wanted to marry Matthew thirty-odd years ago, but Queen Cassandra vetoed the notion."

"So?"

"Michael has always been gay and Katherine was brought along to keep the palace happy. You know as well as I do that their marriage was the work of the Queen, Duke James, the Dowager Duchess Victoria, and Princess Fiona. It was the perfect marriage of convenience."

"Get out." Sophia cast a death defying eye on Ted and Mary. "Now." Mary picked up her Ralph Rucci handbag as she and Ted walked out of the lavish state apartment. "Can you believe the nerve of some people?"

Prince Robert walked to his wife's side and placed his muscular arms around her waist. "It'll be fine…"

"Robert…don't… Please." Sophia wriggled out of his grasp. "I'm going for a walk." And with that, she disappeared down the corridors of the palace.

Prince Robert placed a call to Ted to apologize for Sophia, but Ted assured his cousin that all would be all right – eventually. In that moment, Robert wondered to himself how everything they held dear could turn into a disaster in no time at all. Despite what Robert thought of the regal family and Michael from time to time, he always respected Michael. To think that his own brother-in-law was somehow responsible for the death of Princess Katherine made his shudder with disgust. As the clock struck on the half hour, Robert had a sneaking suspicion that life as they knew it would never be the same again.

For reasons unknown to him, His Regal Highness Prince Joseph was always drawn to the lake at Andover Palace. There was something magical about that particular lake that always made him feel safe, especially on the vast estate that housed the palace. When he was a child, his parents, the Prince and Princess of Kemp, and his siblings would come to the palace every Sunday for brunch with his grandparents, Queen Cassandra and Duke James. Each brunch was long enough that the children would sneak off to remote corners of the palace on their own adventures. When his grandmother abdicated the throne on his birthday eight years ago, his father became Andover's monarch, and his life changed forever. Many people thought this should have been a joyous time for the new monarch and his children, but Princess Katherine's death only two years before still colored their lives.

"Joseph?" Cassandra made her way through the fresh snow with the aid of a valet. She took her grandson's arm, before motioning for the valet to wait for her out of earshot. "I thought you might be down here."

"Grandmother, why hasn't my father released a statement denying these rumors?"

"I don't know," she sighed.

"It's the quickest way to refute these silly accusations," added the prince.

The Dowager Queen closed her eyes. "Joseph, it's a very delicate matter.

A statement may do more harm than good. Besides, your father was speaking with Kerr Ellison a few hours ago…"

"The Head of the Secret Police?"

She nodded. "I'm sure your father has everything under control."

"Except for the fact that he won't see or speak to anyone…"

"Joseph…"

The young prince let out a defeated sigh. "I suppose this is life… I was only thirteen when my mother died. Before she died, Dad insisted that I see her to say a final goodbye, but I didn't want to do it. I guess there was a part of me that thought if I could remember her as she was, instead of how she was in that moment, everything would be different." Joseph let the memories engulf him. "She was so frail. We only talked for a few minutes, but she seemed to know that she was dying…"

"Joseph, you don't have to think about that…"

"But I do. It's bad enough that it's been ten years since she died, but now, these accusations are coming out against my own father. Why are they doing this to us?" A guttural cry came from the prince followed by a raft of tears.

The Dowager Queen gave her grandson a tight hug. "Your mother," she said softly, "was a wonderful mother and wife. The people of Andover loved her very, very much."

"May I ask you something?"

"Yes…"

"Did you and my father have anything to do with my mother's death?"

"Of course not," stammered Cassandra. "Joseph, those are vicious lies! I was very fond of your mother. I remember when she fell ill…that was the Christmas we spent at Blake Manor. It was the third day after Christmas and she insisted on going for a ride because she thought it was a perfect day." Cassandra paused for a moment to recall that day in its fateful detail. "When she came back three hours later, she had a slight cold. She retired to her bedroom for the night, but the next day, she took a turn for the worse."

Joseph nodded in agreement. Although he was fully aware of these events at the time, they had begun to dissipate with each passing season. "I remember… That's when Dad brought her to the palace hospital room…"

"Your mother hated hospitals. The doctors said it would be fine because the palace hospital room was better equipped than most in the world. Princess Katherine had the best doctors in Andover attending to her, but they couldn't tame that damn pneumonia and the medication didn't work." Joseph noticed his grandmother brush away a stray tear as she said, "There was nothing anyone could do…" Cassandra grasped Prince Joseph's hand. "I will always miss Katherine. No matter how much I love Matthew, we both know that he'll never *be* Katherine."

"Princess," Sophia called as she marched down the dimly lit corridor.

Helena turned to see her aunt coming towards her with an obvious mission in her step. "Yes?"

"Have you seen your father?"

"No. He's still refusing to speak with anyone. I'm on my way to the Smoking Room for a cocktail. Do you want to join me?"

As they walked to the Smoking Room, an uncomfortable silence permeated the air. Helena ordered the butler to make her a double dry martini, while Sophia asked for a Bloody Mary. After their drinks were delivered and they were left alone, Helena burst into tears. Stunned, Sophia placed a tentative arm around her niece. "It will be all right," whispered Sophia.

"No…" Helena shook her head violently. She released a piercing wail, which prompted Bertie to poke her head into the Smoking Room to make sure everything was all right. "I… God, I wish I were dead."

"Stop that." Sophia kept a tight grip on her niece's shoulders. "Don't ever say that again, do you hear me?"

The young princess stood up with a grand flourish. She walked to the large window which overlooked the grounds of the palace. In the distance, she could see Edward and Samuel playing with Cassandra's dogs. Despite all of the regal family's issues, Helena still marveled at the fact that Edward never let their issues cloud his relationship with his son. Samuel's lucky, she thought ruefully. "I didn't see my mother before she died." Helena turned to Sophia with tear stained cheeks. "I bet you didn't know that, did you?"

Sophia kept a clam demeanor. "Your father told me…"

"I lied," she interjected. "I couldn't do it…I didn't want to see her." Helena turned her attention to the grounds of the palace as the ghosts of ten years ago began to infiltrate her head. Her mother was always a source of contention throughout much of Helena's life. She loathed being compared to her mother in terms of beauty, size, personality, and coloring. The day her mother died, her father ordered her to see her in her sick room, but Helena couldn't bring herself to see her mother in that state. To be honest, she was relieved she never saw her mother before she died later that day.

Sophia tried to process what Helena was telling her. The problems between Helena and Katherine were known throughout the regal family. However, everyone simply thought that Helena was just being a fifteen-year-old girl and Katherine expected too much from her petulant daughter. Yet this news disturbed Sophia more than she could say. "Helena… Why?"

"I didn't want to see her." Helena released a small sigh, as if she were laughing at a secret joke that was too insulting to be funny. "To be honest, her death was the day of my liberation."

"How can you say that?"

"You don't know what it was like being *her* daughter. Everyone loved and adored my mother. The Princess of Kemp could do no wrong. No… Princess

Katherine was a saint. But to me, she was the biggest hindrance towards me being able to be…free… It was like...I'd spent the first fifteen years of my life living in her shadow and on that day ten years ago, it was gone. It was gone and I could finally feel the sun on my face. But as the years crept on, I realized how much I missed the protection her shadow afforded me. I know I should have seen her, but I couldn't do it." Helena's voice broke off as a second wave of tears began to stream down her face. "And now this… Why is this happening," she demanded to know.

Sophia rushed towards her niece with motherly concern. "I don't know. I don't know who could hate us so much that they could release this damaging story. I do remember the last time I saw Katherine… It was the day before she died. She asked me to look out for you. But…to be honest, I haven't done a very good job of that, have I?"

"I assume that's rhetorical," Helena asked coolly. "Aunt Sophia, you have your own life. Anyway, I'm very aware of how difficult I can be from time to time. I don't blame you. Do you know what's terribly ironic about all of this?"

"What?"

"I didn't see my mother before she died because for me, it was the beginning of my freedom. But I never felt free. And now the very ghost that I've been trying to avoid for the last ten years has come back to haunt me."

"Claudette, my office is shocked by the accusations put forth by The Martyrs of Andover. That's all I have to say about the matter at this moment. Thank you."

Walter turned off the television in disgust as Patricia Ali sauntered into the Government Complex in Old Andover. The entire kingdom was buzzing about the rumors surrounding Princess Katherine's death, but Lord Walter wanted nothing to do with the circulating innuendo. Michael was a popular monarch and he didn't deserve to have this smut infiltrating his life.

"Well," sniffed Margaret, "it seems that our very own monarch may have a few skeletons in his own closet."

Walter glared at her. "He doesn't deserve this, Maggie."

Lady Margaret picked an invisible piece of dust from her cashmere sweater. "Why should Michael always be protected? What if this story is actually true? Have you thought about that Walter?" She could feel her blood pressure begin to rise. "To be perfectly honest, I don't think the press is too far from the truth."

Walter glared at Margaret in order to ensure he'd heard her correctly. Throughout his entire life, Walter had rarely been shocked or surprised by his sister's antics. Yes, she could be wildly unpredictable at times, but for the most part, her scandals were always covered up. "Need I remind you of all of the things Michael and Aunt Cassandra have done for you over the years? Hell, last summer alone Michael saved you and Robert from absolute ruin."

"I didn't ask him to save me," sniffed Margaret.

"She's right." Edward appeared in the doorway with his vicuña coat still wrapped around his fit body.

"What are you doing here," asked Walter.

Edward walked into the Media Room, tossed his heavy coat onto a nearby chair, and poured himself a double brandy. "Samuel had a play date with the boys from his art class, so I thought I'd wait here until I had to get him."

"That's why we have drivers and staff," snapped Margaret.

"Some of us actually enjoy the presence of our son," retorted Edward. He finished his brandy before pouring himself a second glass.

Walter rolled his eyes at the spectacle. He never knew what was going on with his sister and brother-in-law. One minute they were fighting or passionately in love. For Walter, this much drama on the outskirts of his own life caused him to yearn for simplicity. "Why do you agree with Maggie about this whole murder accusation?"

His Highness Edward shrugged. "I know what this family is capable of hiding. Look, I love Michael as much as the next heterosexual guy, but I wouldn't put anything past him if it stood in his way of happiness."

"Wow. I never thought I'd hear something that jaded come out of your mouth, Edward," marveled Walter.

"Walter, you know as well as I do that image is the most important thing in the regal family. You and Maggie know that first hand."

Margaret bristled at her husband's low insult. "You're not being very fair…"

"That's not what I meant," moaned Edward.

"Then what *did* you mean?" Margaret folded her arms furiously as she locked her gaze on Edward.

"I think Michael's role in Katherine's death is irrelevant. It doesn't matter. What does matter is the simple fact that Michael had the means and opportunity to do it *if* he wanted to…well, you know… Besides, Katherine's illness would have been the perfect guise under which to perform the perfect crime."

Walter threw his hands into the air with absolute abandon. "I can't believe you two are behaving like this!"

"Calm down," Margaret sighed. "Edward's being honest…"

"And some could misconstrue your honesty for betrayal. We all know that I've had my issues with being a member of the regal family, but I know Michael. Hell, I've known him all of my life and I know that he wouldn't kill Katherine." Walter knew he had to leave the Media Room before he said something he would later regret. "You two can stay in here until you need to leave, but I'd prefer it if you didn't find me to say your goodbyes." With that, Walter stormed out of the room.

***

As Lord Walter closed the door to his private suite, thoughts of Princess Katherine filled his mind. When Michael married Katherine, Walter was only seventeen. After their wedding, Walter moved to New York City for a few years and lived in Luxembourg until his mother's death, which occurred a year after Katherine died. Even though he and Katherine were never close friends, they respected each other. Within Katherine, Walter saw the strength he lacked and the determination to take on the world with grace and dignity. The only reason he was in Andover for her death was due to the fact he'd returned for Christmas at the urging of his mother, Princess Fiona. Looking back, he was grateful he'd returned for that Christmas because it was the last time he saw Katherine, his uncle, Duke James, and his mother.

"You should get married."

"Don't start, Katherine," Walter joked. His eyes darted around the cold, yet calming hospital room within Andover Palace. This was the reason he loathed being in the palace: You could live your entire life within these walls without ever needing to step into the real world. It wasn't natural, he reminded himself. "You sound like my mother."

Katherine tried to laugh, but she could only manage a small smile. "We all love you. Princess Fiona always talks about you..."

"I didn't come here to talk about my mother. I just want to...do you need anything?"

"I'll ignore that question," she retorted slyly. "You should settle down, find a great woman, and stop running what will never...be resolved."

Walter averted her sickly gaze. No one had ever told him that before, and, to be honest, he didn't like having his own foibles held up for the world to see. "Hey...you need to rest..." With that, he kissed her on the forehead as she drifted off to sleep.

The memories of his last moments with Katherine made him think that she was right after all. His life had been spent running from one party to another, seeking something so illusive it didn't even matter anymore. But now, he knew he had a second chance. In that moment, Walter decided that it was time to propose to Samantha.

In the intimacy of the private dining room at Kemp Castle, the Prince and Princess of Kemp sat in tense silence as Mozart permeated the gently scented air. Ever since the news of Princess Katherine's death broke this morning, the castle had been noticeably silent. Alexander chalked it up to the fact that their geographical location in the northeastern part of the kingdom made them impossible to harass. Besides, the prince noted, it's a four hour drive no one wanted to make. For Olivia, the obvious snub from the regal family made her stomach turn. Until now, she'd always felt as if she were a part of their world, but in this crisis, she was nothing more than a bystander with no power.

"Do you think your father will issue a statement?"

The Prince of Kemp looked from his newspaper towards the attending valet and butler. With a nod of his head, they left the room silently. "Must you say such things in front of the staff? I don't want to deal with their silly rumors."

"What do *you* think?"

"If I were the monarch, I would have denied it this morning. Thankfully, I'm not my father."

Olivia finished her glass of red wine. "Well," she said while cutting into her steak, "that's the truth." Alexander tossed her an irritated glare. Oblivious, Olivia continued. "They could have at least called us! It's not as if we've fallen into an abyss! I find it very odd that your own father wouldn't call you about the rumors concerning your mother's death."

The Prince of Kemp stared blankly at his wife. While she was well intentioned, she had no clue about the power struggles within his family. "Olivia, they're too scared of the public to come out of their gilded cages and refute this story. Hell, it wouldn't be the worst thing in the world if the truth were finally revealed."

It wasn't what he said, but the way he said it that made Olivia sit up and take notice of the cool expression on her husband's face. Now that she thought about it, he didn't seem very perturbed by the breaking news this morning or any of the commentaries throughout the day. He seemed perfectly at ease, which was unlike the man she married. As she tried to gaze into her husband's eyes, an icy chill raced through her body. "Is it true? Alex…"

He wiped his mouth with the cloth napkin and rose from the table. He kissed his wife on the top of her head as he started for the dining room door.

"Alex!"

A dark cloud fell over his face. "Do you want to be the Duchess of Andover," he growled.

"More than anything." Olivia stiffened in her chair. "You know that."

He stormed over to his wife and took her by the shoulders. Alexander didn't know if he could trust her, but he had to take a chance in order to move forward with his plan. Once he told her, she would be culpable. "The Martyrs of Andover is a group I formed with Patricia Ali and a few other prominent, yet dissident members of Andover society." Olivia's eyes grew wide at this admission of guilt. Alexander continued: "My father has done everything he can to bring Andover into the twenty-first century, while single-handedly destroying that made Andover a great kingdom. He's a threat, Olivia. His aim for full modernization of the kingdom through his liberal stance is dangerous. His marriage to Matthew is the biggest threat to the traditions my great-grandfather and my grandmother spent their entire lives building. That story we leaked today is only the beginning."

She could fell herself shaking as his huge hands dug into her skin. She'd never seen her husband in such a state. To think that he was the one responsible for this vicious rumor about his own parents made her sick to the core. If he could do that to his own father, what would he do to her? Even though she knew she should have felt absolute fear in that moment, for reasons unknown to her, she was more drawn to Alexander than she'd been in a very long time.

"Listen to me," he whispered. "You're in this as much as me or Patricia. If you ever breathe a word of this to anyone, I will implicate you as an accomplice and Patricia will verify my claims. Now, are we on the same team or not?"

With a nod of her head, Olivia unwillingly signed a deal with the fallen angel himself.

25

“Will that be all for today?” The King passed a thick fountain pen through his fingers as he glanced furtively towards Patricia Ali. The amount of gall she showed in their weekly meetings was something the King found fascinating. Unlike Alexander, this woman would work against him, while proclaiming to act in the best interest of his kingdom. Yes, Michael loathed this woman, but this new degree of contempt outweighed all else.

Patricia Ali closed her black briefcase, but lingered for a moment. “Your Majesty, with all due respect, I think you should make a statement regarding those rumors about your late wife.”

“That happened nearly a week ago. I see no reason to address those insipid accusations.”

“If you made a statement,” she began, “it would put the kingdom at ease.”

Michael crossed his arms out of sheer annoyance. If it hadn’t been for this woman and his son, he wouldn’t be in this untenable situation. “Ms. Ali, no member of the regal family will make a statement about those rumors. I trust no more will be said on the matter.”

“Then you should have the palace release a statement saying that the accusations bear no merit.” Patricia stiffened in her seat. She rarely challenged the King’s authority, but these were extraordinary circumstances.

The King placed the pen on his desk and picked up a small stress ball Prince Joseph had given him a few years ago. As he squeezed the odd mixture of fabric and gel, he turned his attention to the large oil painting of his grandfather, King Henrik. During Michael’s childhood, he found his grandfather to be a stern, yet kind man in public and in private. His grandfather rarely addressed public rumor, nor had Cassandra. Michael knew that he had to keep the long tradition of monarchical silence. “Ms. Ali, the story is false. I will not waste anymore of my time discussing the matter. My family has been through enough during the past few days and a statement is the last thing on our minds."

"Your Majesty…"

"Enough," bellowed the King. "This discussion is over!"

"I just wanted to…"

"I suggest that you concentrate on your own position, Ms. Ali. Your approval rating is the lowest it's been since you came into office four years ago. The people are restless. The other political parties are circling for your job. I'd suggest that you exert your energy fighting to save your own career rather than interfering in regal matters." Michael kept his eyes on Patricia as she rose and started for the door. She performed a small curtsy before being escorted out of the palace by Glenn. The King sat in his chair with great annoyance as he thought about Patricia's outright betrayal. She wouldn't last long, he told himself. However, Michael was all too aware that he had to play this moment just so or else he would lose everything.

"Hello?"

"Hey, Nancy. It's Joseph."

Her heart stopped. Why was the King's son calling her? Nancy glanced into her bedroom mirror. I look a mess, she thought. She quickly removed the curlers from her hair as she said, "Oh. Hi… How are you?"

"I'm all right. Listen, a little bird told me that you were in Andover. Is that true?"

"I am…" Nancy took a deep breath to stop herself from sounding too enchanted by this dashing prince. "My mother needed a bit of help with the wedding plans, so I came back from Sydney to give her a hand…"

Joseph reclined on his king sized bed. He popped a grape into his mouth with wild abandon. "Then that's good news for me and your mother," he smirked.

"Your Regal Highness," Nancy cooed. "How did you get my phone number?"

Joseph released a hearty laugh. "I have my ways. Look, a few of my friends and I booked the private room at Hart & Sons tonight. At Christmas you told me that you'd never been, so I wanted to know if you wanted to have a night of wild debauchery."

Nancy twisted a long strand of her sandy blonde hair around her narrow ring finger. If Matthew weren't marrying Joseph's father, this could have been the beginning of a fairytale. She would be the lucky maiden chosen by the King's most handsome son to become his wife for all eternity. However, the reality of her situation quickly came to light as a frown crossed her face. "Um… that sounds like fun." Nancy tied her hair into a ponytail. "So, how are you? Is everything okay?"

Joseph rolled his eyes. He was sick and tired of the fact that everyone insisted on checking up on him. After his time with Cassandra by the palace lake, Joseph knew that he would be all right. The rumors were nothing more than a lame attempt to upset the regal family and, quite frankly, it hadn't worked. "Thanks, but I'm fine. We're going to have dinner at Granger's in Old Andover at nine and we'll go to the club from there. Will I see you tonight?"

Before Nancy could answer, her bedroom creaked open. Matthew walked in and sat silently while she finished her call. "Sure. I'll see you tonight."

"Who was that," asked Matthew.

"Your future stepson."

"Which one?"

"The nice one."

Matthew couldn't believe what he was hearing. Ever since the news broke about Princess Katherine, he hadn't heard from anyone in the regal family – not even Michael. He couldn't help but feel left out of the regal circle, but as his mother had told him, "Darling, you're not a member of the regal family yet. Just let this die down." He had, but Matthew still wanted to be kept in the loop. The fact that Joseph had called his youngest sister made him slightly jealous. "What did Joseph want…if you don't mind me asking…?"

Nancy pulled a black lamb's wool sweater over her J. Crew tank top. "It's just a night at Granger's and Hart & Sons with a few of his friends. That's all."

"Oh." Matthew nodded sagely. "I tried to call Michael, but I still can't get through to him. That's why I'm surprised that Joseph called you."

"Matt, I wouldn't read anything into it. Really. Joseph invited me to a club. That's all."

"Still… No one from the palace has contacted me. I hate not knowing what's going on over there. Did Joseph say anything about his father?"

Nancy shook her head. She could see how much her brother loved Michael, but she thought he was making a big deal out of…well, nothing. "He didn't even mention his father. When I asked him how he was doing, he changed the topic. But if you really want to know, why don't you go to the palace to see the King for yourself?"

It wasn't a bad idea, Matthew told himself. If Michael wouldn't make the first move, then Matthew would be the bigger man. With that, Matthew bade his sister goodbye as he left the house, got into his Range Rover, and, with his bodyguards in tow, drove to Andover Palace.

Although he would have rather stayed at the palace, Michael made his first public appearance at the Andover Economic Luncheon for Civil Responsibility in Lord's Pass with great fanfare. Even though he secretly loathed every second of media attention, he was delighted to be able to speak in a public arena away from the questions concerning his late wife. For Michael, even thinking about the past few days made him weary. He would have liked for everyone to forget the story, but it was impossible. The story was still on many blogs and *The Sentinel* insisted on running daily commentaries about Princess

Katherine's life. In the ten years following her death, this was the most attention anyone had given to her life and it didn't sit well with Michael or her sister, Mary. Mary had once again become a source of irritation in Michael's life, but he could understand why she was so agitated over the salacious details with which the press combed through Katherine's life. Thankfully, he allowed himself to forget the last few days as he wrapped up his speech and presented Keith Sao with the Drake Award for Civil Responsibility. After ten minutes of questions, Michael bade adieu to the crowd. On his way to his waiting car, a journalist shouted, "Do you have any comment about your late wife's death? The people want to know!" Michael turned to the crowd with an icy glare, but he knew he had to keep his head down at all costs. The King gave his people a final wave mixed with a small smile as he stepped into the car. His mind raced at a million miles a minute as the regal procession made its way back to the security of Andover Palace.

"Matthew! How long have you been waiting?" The King gave Matthew a long, loving hug as they made their way from the Official Drawing Room to Michael's private suite.

In that instant, all of Matthew's fears and frustrations evaporated into the cold, winter sky. On his way to the palace, he doubted whether or not this move would scream of desperation or loving concern; he banked on the latter. "Not very long… I just wanted to see you… It's been a while."

Michael collapsed on his obscenely soft bed with a heavy sigh. He motioned for Matthew to join him. He kissed his fiancé passionately. "I'm fine."

"But how are you? Really… I know the last few days…"

The King pressed his index finger over Matthew's naturally pouty mouth. "I'm wonderful. Everything's all right."

Matthew searched Michael's eyes for the truth. "Mike…this is me…"

"For a while, I was livid. This entire episode hit me by surprise. No one knew what to do. However, it's dying down. The people have seen that it's a terribly tacky accusation and life will continue as it did before."

"Will this affect our marriage?"

"Look, I'm content to move on with my life. You should know that, Matt."

"Well…do I make you happy?"

The King touched his lover's face ever so lightly. "I'm as happy as I could be, Matthew." Just then, the telephone near Michael's bed rang. "Yes," the King sighed. "Fine… I'll be right there." The King placed the phone onto the receiver. He kissed Matthew once more. "I have to go… I have a regal household budgetary meeting with Quinn Shaw and Amelia Harding. Do you want to stay? Or…"

Matthew rose. "I should get home."

As Matthew drove himself back to his parents' house, he couldn't shake Michael's statement that he was as happy as he could be. Everything will be fine, he assured himself. Yet, as Matthew made his way back to Kemp Forest, he couldn't hide the fact that serious doubts were being to infiltrate his mind.

Granger's was one of the oldest restaurants in the Kingdom of Andover. The Granger family had always been pillars of the kingdom and, early in King Henrik's reign, he bestowed upon the head of the family, Ben Granger, the title of Earl. It was no wonder that for over eighty years, Granger's had drawn the most sophisticated crowd in the kingdom until Cabo opened across the street. In spite of the competition, members of the regal family still frequented both establishments, although each had their favorite.

Tonight, Prince Joseph sat at a quite table in the corner away from the prying eyes of the public as he held court with his friends. The people at Prince Joseph's table ranged from the sons and daughters of the aristocracy, Nancy, and the members of Prince Joseph's polo team, The King's. By all accounts, the crème de la crème of Andover's aristocratic youth set were dining out in a way any photographer would have loved to capture on film.

"Scotty, tell us about the horrid thing Minks told you the other day!" Prince Joseph stated as he polished off another glass of wine.

Earl Scotty Granger, the current owner and de facto head of the Granger family, laughed heartily as he told the story for the third time today.

From his seat, Joseph could see the Prince and Princess of Kemp walk into Granger's, acknowledge the head chef, and make their way into the private dining room. So that's why I couldn't book that dining room, Joseph thought ruefully. Against his better judgment, Joseph excused himself from the table to speak with his distant brother.

"Joseph." Alexander couldn't hide the mix of shock and surprise as his brother appeared in the doorway. "What a nice surprise…"

"I'm having dinner with a few friends. I thought I should at least say hello."

The Princess of Kemp surveyed the scene and decided to make leave the brothers alone. "I'll be in the powder room."

"She didn't have to go," Joseph sighed.

Alexander examined his menu. "What do you want? I'm famished."

"Why haven't you been to the palace since that rumor started?"

The Prince of Kemp lowered his menu. It was just like his brother to jump to conclusions without thinking through his argument, thought Alexander. "Joseph…"

"No. You've been at arms length the entire time. Hell, even Walter came down from Blake Manor for two days to be with the rest of the family."

"How noble of Walter… Tell me, did Vincent or any of the extended family make a trip to the kingdom?"

"No, but at least they called."

"Look, I'm living my own life. My wife and I are doing well and we didn't feel the need to make an obligatory visit to the palace – and for what? So everyone can ignore me?" Alexander took a sip of his glass. "No thank you. Besides, it's not as if Dad wanted to see me."

Joseph sat in the chair next to his older brother. There was something about Alexander that had changed… He couldn't pinpoint the day or time, but his brother was no longer the same man he'd known throughout his entire life. This person was alien to him. "Then you should have come to the palace…"

"I don't need a lecture from you, little brother," spat Alexander. "It's not as if Dad came to Kemp Castle to check on me or Olivia."

"That doesn't make a modicum of sense. Dad and Grandmother were the ones who were attacked in the press. Not you and Olivia."

"Are you finished? My wife and I didn't come here to sit through one of your inane lectures on how I disappoint everyone."

"Is that all you have to say," Joseph asked ruefully.

"Joey, this whole thing may or may not die down. I don't know, and frankly, I don't care."

"How can you say that?" Joseph could feel himself growing very uncomfortable in the presence of his brother. "What did you mean by that?"

Alexander crossed his arms defiantly. "We all know that Dad isn't an innocent…"

"Did…you have something to do with this," whispered Joseph. The skin on his arms began to rise as his breathing became labored. "Alex…"

The Prince of Kemp met Joseph's gaze. His steely eyes quickly fell to the floor as he asked, "Why would you even ask that question?"

Prince Joseph quickly left the room, just as Olivia returned from the powder room. In that moment, Joseph knew more than he ever wanted to know about his brother, the Prince of Kemp.

"Are you sure you don't want to go home?" Nancy pulled her ermine fur coat across her body as a furious wind blew in from the coast.

"No. I promised you a night at Hart & Sons and that's what we're going to have!" Joseph whipped out his iPhone and called Helena. "Come out! We'll be here all night!"

That night, Prince Joseph, Princess Helena, Nancy, and the rest of their entourage danced the night away with an endless supply of Perrier-Jouet, loud music, and pulsating bodies. Joseph spent most of his time dancing with Nancy, who couldn't believe the prince's interest in her. Helena held court at the table in the private room as she ordered everyone to act as if this night would never end. Unfortunately, at four o'clock in the morning, the house lights came up and the regal guests were forced to face the cold winter morning in the glare of the kingdom's photographers.

REGAL EXTRAVAGANCE! KING'S KIDS STEP OUT WITH COUNT'S SIS!

The King's eyes fell on the newspaper headline once again. He was far from pleased about the salacious details listed in the newspaper article recounting his children's night with Matthew's sister. "How did you two spend two hundred thousand dollars last night?" The King didn't feel the need to spare decorum as he tore into Princess Helena and Prince Joseph in the Blue Parlor. "How could you spend that in one night? For goodness sake! I spent the majority of yesterday afternoon sorting out this family's finances and you two do this? What do you have to say for yourselves?"

"To be fair," started Joseph, "we only bought three bottles of Perrier-Jouet champagne. At the time, we didn't know they were that expensive...plus the cost of the room... Dad, it was only one night."

"But it's one night that you two will pay for out of your own bank accounts."

"Dad," protested Joseph. "That's too harsh."

Michael glowered at his son. "It's all ready been done. What were you two thinking?"

"Dad, I have no regrets," announced Helena. "We had a night of fun. So what? It's better than sitting around this crypt waiting for something exciting to happen." With that, Helena returned to her private suite.

"Someone needs to deal with her," Michael snapped.

"Dad, I'm sorry. But Helena does have a point. These past few days have been rough and we needed to blow off some steam. It won't happen again…at least not like this…"

The King couldn't help but laugh at his son's honest admission. "I'll take your word for it, Joseph."

"May I ask you something?"

"What?"

"What are you going to do about that story…the one about Mom?"

"The story is finally dying down because it bore no kernel of truth."

Joseph took a sip of coffee to help the hangover he was still nursing after four hours of fitful sleep. "Good. I ran into Alexander last night at Granger's. Dad, I think he had something to do with that story."

The King steadied himself. He never expected his youngest son to make such a proclamation. "Why do you say that?"

Prince Joseph recounted his run-in with Alexander last night. "…And," finished the prince, "he doesn't seem to have any faith in you, which is weird. It's like he wants you to fail."

"Joseph…let's keep this between us. Could you do that for me?"

"Why? Dad, do you know something?"

"Joey…"

"I won't say anything. Do you think Alex had something to do with that story?"

Although the King never responded to that question, the look on his face only solidified Joseph's suspicions about his brother, the heir to the throne.

"Lunch was lovely." Cassandra cooed as she ordered the maid to fetch one of her special drinks. It wasn't often that her nephew, Lord Walter, hosted lavish lunches at Blake Manor, but Cassandra was pleased to see that he was making a real effort to be charming these days. To Cassandra, that was a good thing because during the last few days, the regal family was getting back to normal, which was welcomed in her eyes.

His Highness Edward dabbed the corners of his mouth. "What's on your mind, Walter?"

"Nothing," Walter lied.

"Come on. This is out of the blue, even for you."

There was something on Walter's mind…something he wanted to shout from the top of Blake Manor, but his regal upbringing curtailed that ambition. "I know the family's been through quite a trying time as of late…"

"That's one way to put it," Cassandra sighed.

"However, I have decided to ask Samantha Masoli to marry me." Walter reached into his trouser pocket and produced an exquisitely cut ruby ring that once belonged to his great-grandmother, Duchess Mary of Andover.

Cassandra couldn't contain her glee as she examined her grandmother's ring. "Walter… Where has this been all of these years?"

"After my mother died, I put it in my safe. Do you think she'll like it?"

"Of course, Walter, she'll love this ring. It is priceless." Cassandra lifted her tumbler. "Have you obtained the King's permission to enter into this engagement?"

Walter bit his lip. "Not yet. Actually…I was thinking about going ahead on my own."

"Oh?"The Dowager Queen began to feel lightheaded as she polished off her second special drink of the afternoon. "Walter, I needn't remind you that to propose and marry without the monarch's consent could cost you your regal entitlements."

"Seriously? Isn't that 'rule' a bit archaic? Walter, I think you should do what you want and shirk regal responsibility," stated Edward.

"Edward," exclaimed Cassandra. "How can you say such a thing? The impertinence…!"

Edward held his ground. He was use to Cassandra's determination to hold onto the past with both hands, but he didn't think her values had any place in today's world; especially when it came to who a regal family member could marry. The whole thing could be down right ridiculous, he thought. "I'm not being impertinent. I think that the restrictions placed on those carrying the style of His or Her Regal Highness can cause a lot of pain for everyone involved, especially when it comes to the issue of marriage."

"Well," bristled Cassandra. "This is our way of life, young man. You were well aware of *that* when you married Lady Margaret!"

"Yes, well, that may no longer be an issue," muttered Edward.

Cassandra and Walter exchanged terrified glances. "What are you saying? Are you giving up," asked Walter.

"I'm tired."

"But a divorce," Cassandra said in a hushed tone.

Edward shifted uncomfortably in his chair. Now, he regretted having said anything. “Please… let’s not make a big deal out of this. Please.”

“It’s ironic isn’t it? I’m ready to settle down and you’re ready to give up, Edward.”

“I’ve tried harder than any of you know,” Edward said quickly.

“Edward, please don’t make any rash decisions you may later regret. And Walter, please speak to Michael…he is the head of the family, after all. Can you two do that…for me?” asked Cassandra.

Both men nodded, albeit unwillingly.

“Mr. Ellison, this is His Majesty.”

“Sire, what may I do for you?”

“I need a dossier on Patricia Ali. They need to be stopped…immediately.”

“Right away, Sire.”

26

Two weeks later, His Regal Highness Lord Walter sat across from his cousin, His Majestic Regal Highness King Michael, in the monarch's private office. It had been a long time since they shared a private meal together that neither knew exactly what to say to the other. For Walter, this meeting was too important because he needed Michael's permission to marry Samantha.

"Michael," Walter began. "I've been seeing Danisi Samantha Masoli for a few months and…I think she may be the one."

The King couldn't hide his surprised expression. Ever since Walter had returned from Luxembourg, Michael had given up hope as to whether or not his cousin would ever get married. It's not that Michael minded or even cared. However, he was not fond of the women Walter enjoyed cavorting with in his spare time. The stories Michael heard from the staff at Blake Manor were salacious enough to make him blush, although, thankfully, these stories never reached the press. "Walter, that's wonderful. I'm very happy for you." Michael embraced his cousin as he asked, "I had no idea you were even considering marriage."

"Well, I think it's time. Samantha is wonderful. I know you'll like her."

The King smirked. "I'll be the judge of that."

Walter could feel the passion he felt for Samantha erupting within his soul. While they hadn't known each other for years like Matthew and Michael or Robert and Sophia, he felt that this union made sense. "Two days ago, I hosted a breakfast meeting at Blake Manor with the Dowager Queen, Prince Joseph, and Lady Margaret."

"And…"

"They vetted her." Walter released a sigh of relief as Michael nodded sagely. "Mike, I've done it right this time. Joseph was has met her before, your mother adores her, and Maggie…well, she was on her best behavior."

"She didn't cause a scene, did she?"

"No. Thank goodness. Mike, with your consent, I would like to propose to Samantha."

The King thought about this for a brief moment. Who was he to deny his cousin the chance of happiness? Michael knew Samantha's parents quite well. They were friends of his parents; Samantha's mother was even the flower girl at Princess Fiona's wedding. "Walter, I've never seen you this happy. If you feel that Samantha is the one…and that she can handle being a member of this family… then you have my consent."

Walter released a hearty whoop as he jumped up from the table. "Thank you, Mike. Thank you!"

"Of course, Walter, but we still have other tasks to perform."

"Such as…?"

"A background check must be run before the engagement is announced to the press and a wedding date is set. I'll have Kerr Ellison perform one right away."

Walter merely sighed at the formality with which the regal family vetted their potential spouses. Nothing got past them, Walter noted wryly.

"Let's have a toast. I think this certainly calls for one." Michael filled their wine glasses to the brim. "To Walter and Samantha: May you two have a lifetime of much deserved happiness."

After finishing his meal with Michael, Walter floated through the labyrinth of corridors to Lady Margaret's state apartment. "Walter," she sighed. Walter stepped into the Music Room to find her alone with the drapes drawn, a cocktail in her hand, and the lonely strings from a symphony filling the lavender scented air. "How nice of you to visit me…"

Perplexed, Walter said, "I thought you had three engagements today."

"I do. I've already performed two of them, and the third is a dinner for someone who did something worthwhile for poor people in some remote corner of the world that I've never heard of…" She finished her cocktail. "What brings you to the palace? You always do whatever it takes to stay away from here, isn't that right?"

He poured himself a snifter of brandy. "I wanted to let you know that I've just received Michael's consent to propose to Samantha."

Margaret closed her eyes in order to process this news. "Walter, I'm happy for you," she said softly. "You deserve to be happy. I remember when Aunt Cassandra gave me permission to marry Edward. It was terrible. I basically had to grovel in order for her to take me seriously. I'd never felt less human in my entire life."

"Michael's not his mother."

"I don't know if that's a good thing or a bad thing." Margaret ran her fingers through her hair with a heavy sigh. "I've got to get away from here. I have to…" A heaviness Margaret had never felt before swept through her body. She suddenly felt queasy; although she knew it wasn't the alcohol…it was something else. "Sometimes I feel as if the whole world is turning against me. It's not paranoia or anything, but it's something I can't pinpoint. There are times when I feel like I can't breathe and then, it's gone. Does that make any sense to you?"

Lord Walter knew that his sister could easily go from friendly to vicious, victim to schemer in no time at all. Whatever she was feeling, he couldn't help her. Besides, he could plainly see that she wanted to take the spotlight away from him and that was not going to happen. "Maggie, go see a doctor…"

"I'm not seeing a shrink," she snapped. "Only common people do that! I'd never air my dirty laundry to a shrink…"

"But you'd do it in the press."

She tossed her brother a vicious glare. "I had my reasons!"

"Look, I just came by to tell you my news."

"Fine." Lady Margaret made herself another cocktail with three times as much vodka. "I think I'm going to go away for a week or so with Edward and Samuel. I need to get out of the kingdom. Anyway, it may show people that I'm serious about my marriage and that I want it to work."

"Maggie, do you think that's such a wise idea?"

"Why do you doubt me," she wailed.

"I'm not! Samuel's in the middle of the school year and you and Edward have full social calendars. Do you really think Michael would approve of you three jetting off right now?"

Margaret shook her head with great annoyance. "I don't know and I don't care."

"Look, I should go. I have to attend a dinner in Port Agnes tonight…"

She studied her brother with great care. Margaret knew her brother was a terrible liar. She could sense the fact that he was keeping something from her. But what, she wondered. "Walter, what do you know? I know there's something you're not telling me!"

"There's nothing to tell," he insisted.

"No! Don't leave… Please… If you know something that I should know, just tell me. Was it something Michael brought up when you saw him?"

"No…"

"Then what," she asked desperately.

Even though Walter knew he should have left at that very moment, the words fell out of his mouth. "I had lunch with Aunt Cassandra and Edward two weeks ago and…well… Edward said that he may not want to continue with this marriage."

Before she knew it, Margaret's legs gave out from underneath her and she fell to the floor with a great flourish. She gasped for air with all of her might. She could feel her heart begin to break into a trillion tiny pieces as the news that her own husband was considering divorcing her raced through her mind. No matter what anyone thought, she loved Edward like she'd loved no other man, except Robert. In spite of everything, Margaret had never given up hope that their fairy tale would have a happy ending, but now she knew that was a fantasy that had crumbled with the slightest touch. Walter rushed to her side, lifted her, and placed her on the plush sofa. "What…did he say…exactly?"

Walter pursed his lips. "Maggie, you should speak to your husband."

"Tell me," she insisted.

"I can't." With that, Walter kissed his sister goodbye and left the palace.

Alone, Margaret could hardly believe that her own husband had confided in her brother and aunt about the state of their marriage. How could he, she thought ruefully. This was unacceptable and this was one incident she would not take lying down. No one makes a fool out of me, she reminded herself. No one… not even Edward…

The Third Annual Children's Literacy Council Reception was the pet project of Their Regal Highnesses Princess Sophia and the Dowager Queen. Each year they held the event at a different regal residence and this year it was held at Kemp Castle. Although the Princess of Kemp wasn't thrilled to have her in-laws and their lackeys taking command of her home for the better part of the day, Alexander insisted that she comply – or else. These days, life within this regal marriage was more tense than loving. They still tried (albeit fruitlessly) to conceive a child. The Prince of Kemp refused to submit to IVF treatments. Now that Olivia knew what her husband was really plotting, she found herself in a very weak position to further exploit her own personal agenda. She felt caught in a endless web of lies, deceit, and power. Although she loathed feeling impotent, she knew she had to smile for the public, as well as the regal family, to assure them all was right in her world. Now, as Olivia sat in the State Dining Room of Kemp Castle, she smiled as Princess Sophia finished her closing speech for the afternoon. The fifty invited guests said their goodbyes before leaving the three regal women alone in the privacy of the intimate Drawing Room.

"Eww," Cassandra exclaimed as she tasted her special drink. "There's too much orange juice and not enough vermouth!" The former monarch handed the glass to the attending butler, who promptly crafted the Dowager Queen's appropriate drink. "That's much better," she sighed. "Tell me, Olivia, how are things these days?"

Olivia smiled pertly. "Wonderful, Ma'am… The Prince of Kemp and I have decided to undergo IVF treatments in order to conceive a child." She couldn't believe she'd just lied to the Dowager Queen and Princess Sophia, but they didn't need to know what really went on at Kemp Castle. Anyway, reasoned Olivia, if she could get these two on her side, then Alexander would have to submit to the treatment.

"Come again?" Princess Sophia couldn't believe what Olivia was suggesting. "IVF? You can't be serious…"

"I said we're considering…"

"Olivia," exclaimed Sophia. "You cannot be that naïve! This is the Prince of Kemp, the heir to the throne of the Kingdom of Andover! If word ever got out that he conceived his child through IVF treatments, it could ruin us!"

"Sophia," sighed Cassandra, limply.

Sophia ignored her mother as she continued her tirade. "It says in the Regal Proclamation that in order for one to be in the line of succession for the throne, they must be legitimate and *natural* children of a regal highness. IVF is not *natural*," huffed Sophia.

"With all due respect, Princess Sophia, this has nothing to do with you," snapped Olivia.

“Like hell it doesn’t!” Sophia braced herself towards Olivia’s blatant disrespect. “This is my family!”

“Sophia,” interjected Cassandra. “That’s enough. Olivia, dear, you mustn’t discuss this…idea…with anyone. We can’t have this getting to the press!”

Olivia could feel these two powerful and influential women pushing her against a wall. If there was one thing she learned from Alexander, it was how to stand up for herself. “Fine, let’s assume I listen to you and keep my mouth shut. Let’s assume that I don’t submit myself and my husband for these treatments. If Alexander and I never produce an heir, then how will the family cope? The throne would eventually pass to Princess Helena and if she doesn’t have children, Prince Joseph would become Andover’s monarch, and if he doesn’t have children, you would become Queen, Sophia. Well, since you and Robert have no children, I suppose Margaret would become Queen…or at least Samuel would become King.”

Those words alone made Sophia nauseous. The thought of having Margaret as Andover’s Queen would spell emanate disaster for the kingdom. “That won’t happen,” croaked Sophia.

“It won’t if Alexander and I go through with this treatment. Think of all of the good things this will show the kingdom about this family. Anyway, this wasn’t my idea, Sophia. It was your mother’s suggestion. She even suggested that I become the patron of an IVF charity.”

The Dowager Queen froze. In all of her years on this wonderful earth, no one had ever had the outright audacity to betray her! How could she, seethed Cassandra. She locked her gaze on the Princess of Kemp. This little upstart was more trouble than she was worth. In the months leading up to Olivia’s wedding to Alexander, Cassandra had her doubts. At the time, Olivia seemed too perfect on paper and now Cassandra knew why. She was a conniving social climber who’d managed to sink her manicured claws into the heir to the throne with her sexuality, impossibly nice demeanor, and deceptive smile. The only thing Cassandra knew at this moment was that something had to be done about her grandson’s wife.

"Mother, is this true?"

Cassandra handed her drink to the butler. "Oh, Sophia, you know how intense I can become from time to time! It was merely a suggestion. Wasn't it, Olivia?"

Feeling the heat and hatred radiating from Cassandra, Olivia merely nodded.

"What I do recall stating was that if Olivia can't have children with Alexander – even with the aid of today's technology – her days as a member of the regal family are finite." Cassandra turned her steely gaze towards the Princess of Kemp. "Isn't that correct, Olivia?"

A second later, Olivia burst into tears and ran out of the Drawing Room.

Feeling caught in the middle, Princess Sophia followed Olivia into the private quarters of Kemp Castle. "Olivia?" Sophia finally found her weeping in her plush bedroom. What startled Sophia the most was that there was no trace of Alexander in this bedroom. Sophia peered through a door that was slightly ajar and saw her nephew's bedroom was just beyond. I always knew their marriage was odd, surmised Sophia. "What's this all about?"

"I've done *everything* I can think of to earn your trust and respect and this is what I get! You all hate me!"

She sounds like Margaret, groaned Sophia. "Melodrama doesn't work with me, dear. Dry your eyes and speak to me like the Princess of Kemp."

Olivia followed Sophia's orders. "You don't even have children and Robert is still a member of the regal family! But you want to kick me out? This isn't fair, Sophia!"

"Dear, this isn't about fair! I've had two miscarriages."

"I… No one told me…"

Sophia brushed off Olivia's pithy attempt at an apology. "I'm only fourth in the line of succession after the King's children. Unless I outlive Helena, Joseph, and Alexander, as well as all of their children, it's very unlikely I'll ever become the Queen of Andover."

"So?" Olivia tossed her silk handkerchief onto the Persian carpet. "Why does that matter?"

Princess Sophia was at the end of her tether with this dense girl. "You are married to the heir to the throne! He needs an heir to assure the world that all is right with the regal family. When Alexander has a child, everyone will see that there is stability amongst us."

"But I've *tried everything*," whined Olivia. "We've even done fertility tests!"

"What have the tests said?"

"There's no earthly reason why we can't have a child together, but we're still childless!"

Sophia touched Olivia shoulder with tender concern. "I understand your worries, Olivia. I truly do. However, my mother does have a point. You need to produce an heir before your clock stops ticking," she said tactfully. "Do you understand?"

The Princess of Kemp nodded as she watched Sophia saunter out of her bedroom. For more than two hours, Olivia sat in the quiet serenity of her bedroom as she thought of ways to retain her place within the regal family, while giving them exactly what they wanted – and needed. Maybe she could work this to her advantage, Olivia thought. If medical treatments are the only way forward, then so be it! The regal family would have to live with it and keep up with the times. Yes, Olivia smiled to herself; she would do whatever it took to secure her place within the family, no matter how many people she offended in the process.

"I can't be easy for her," sighed Prince Robert. He bit into the duck that the palace chef had prepared for his dinner. However, he wasn't hungry and was growing quite restless.

"Robert, it's her duty. I hate to say it like that, but there's no other way to say it without being cruel. When Katherine married Michael, they had Alexander in a little more than a year and a half!" Sophia sipped her champagne as she said, "She has to make some very tough decisions. I just hope Alexander doesn't toss her aside."

"Why would you say that?"

"Where's Edward?!!?"

Princess Sophia and Prince Robert were startled to look up and find Lady Margaret standing in the doorway of the Crimson Room. She looked crazier than an escaped mental patient.

"We're having a private dinner," spat Sophia. "Leave us alone. Please."

"I need to speak with him, you twit! I haven't been able to find him all day! It's important," panted Margaret.

Sophia ignored her cousin. "Robert, shall we have dessert in our state apartment?"

"Sophia! I need to speak with my husband!"

"That's not my problem," countered Princess Sophia. "You are interrupting a private dinner between me and my husband. If you don't mind, would you please leave us alone?"

"Margaret, what's wrong," inquired Robert. "Whatever it is can't be that important."

Margaret let out a hearty chortle. "No? My husband told Cassandra and Walter that he's giving up on our marriage! He probably wants to divorce me!"

Robert couldn't hide his surprise, while Sophia merely shook her head.

"What," Margaret snapped as Sophia stared at her food. "What do you know?"

"Nothing," Princess Sophia lied. "Leave us alone, you nutcase."

"Sophia," murmured Robert.

Margaret walked towards Sophia with hatred in her eyes. "It's okay, Robert. I'm use to her attitude. She's always looked down on me just because her mother was Queen and her brother is King. Good for you, you frigid cow!"

Sophia let out a gasp which nearly caused her to fall over. No one had ever spoken to Sophia in that manner! "Who do you think you're speaking to, Margaret? I out rank you," she reminded her cousin. "Why don't you leave us alone and speak to your husband on your own time?"

"You're doing this on purpose," shouted Margaret. "You put Edward up to this because you want to ruin my marriage!"

"Oh, will you get over yourself? I'm not you! You're the one who sleeps with married men just to spite people who you perceive as a threat," Sophia retorted coldly.

"One day you'll fall from your high horse, Sophia and when you do, I'll be there to kick you as you come crashing down. You've always played the role of the innocent, virtuous princess, but you have *never* fooled me." Margaret's voice dropped an octave. "I can see right through you."

"Get out of here or I'll call security," threatened Sophia.

"What's the matter? Did I hurt your fragile little feelings," Margaret chided spitefully.

Robert banged his fist onto the table. "That's enough! Stop it before the staff run and tell the King! That's the last thing we need!"

Knowing that Robert would no longer take her side, Margaret turned on the heel of her Manolo Blahnik stilettos and stormed out of the room. Prince Robert released a sigh of relief, while his wife crossed her arms in defiance. After an elongated silence, Robert finally asked, "What do you know about Edward and Margaret's marriage?"

"Nothing," insisted Princess Sophia.

"Sophia…"

"He told me months ago that he was going to divorce that lunatic."

"How could you keep that a secret?"

"Robert," she huffed, "I'm not at liberty to divulge the contents of my exchanges with Edward."

"This is me. We can share this secret…"

"No. We can't. I'm allowed to keep Edward's secrets because you and Margaret carried on a year long affair behind our backs. I think this makes us even, don't you?"

Count Matthew Hall took in the sight of the King's private dining room. Although he'd dined in this very room many times before, this was the first time that he felt secure. It's not to say that Matthew thought Michael didn't love him, but he always worried that the foundation of their relationship would dissipate before he was able to realize what happened. With the wedding only a few short months away, Matthew could truly see himself having endless meals with Michael away from the eyes of the press, the family, and the world. In this quiet, personal space, they could be themselves. That thought alone made Matthew the happiest person in the world.

"Is it all right, Matthew?"

Matthew focused on the five page long list before him. This was the final wedding list. *The Sentinel* proclaimed that, by all accounts, this would be the wedding of the century. Although Matthew didn't want to consider such a massive undertaking, he was secretly thrilled with the fuss. It was very true that neither he nor Michael had much to do with the planning of the wedding; Cassandra and Sally saw to that, as did the officials at Andover Palace. The only thing the couple had to do was attend a fitting for their formal wedding wear and turn up on time.

Matthew examined the list for the final time and he noticed one glaring omission. “Michael, why isn’t Jeff Carlyle on the list?”

The King glanced at the list. “I don’t know.”

“Michael, this is important. He’s one of my best friends.”

“Matthew, I didn’t create the list. Our mothers and my office were responsible for the guest list.”

“Michael…”

“Didn’t you date him?”

Matthew nodded. “We dated for five years.”

“Now, tell me again, why would you want your ex-boyfriend at our wedding?”

“We’re friends,” insisted Matthew.

“He’s your ex-boyfriend. To be honest, his presence may create a scandal for the family. Is that what you want?”

“Don’t patronize me, Michael.”

Michael grasped Matthew’s hand. “Look, I didn’t have a thing to do with Jeff’s omission from the guest list. The wedding invitations are going out tomorrow; I can’t do anything, Matt.”

Count Matthew bristled at Michael’s resistance to address this issue. Is this what I have to look forward to, Matthew wondered. “Michael, you’re the King of Andover. You can…”

“For heavens sake, Matthew, why do you want Jeff at our wedding? You left him because you weren’t ready to marry him and now you’re marrying me! How will that make him feel? Look,” the King said, his voice softening, “our wedding day is meant to be a fresh start. I don’t want to move backwards…my life is with you.”

“I know…” Matthew let out a defeated sigh because he knew all too well this was a battle he'd already lost. "What do you think about the amount of time my sister, Nancy, has been spending with Prince Joseph?"

"Why do you ask?"

"Well, I think they've been spending a little too much time together," Matthew stated.

Michael recalled the newspaper headline from two weeks ago, which (in all honesty) made him laugh. "Matt, it's not a problem. I'm glad my children are spending time with your sister. Joseph has told me that they're just friends."

"Nancy told me the same thing, but the whole thing makes me a bit uncomfortable."

"It's not as if members of the same family haven't married different members of the regal family," Michael recalled. "If Nancy did marry Joseph, it wouldn't be the worse thing in the world. It would be a bit odd, but it's nothing we couldn't handle."

"That's not what I'm talking about, Mike. Nancy," he whispered, "is a divorcee."

"Shocking," laughed the King.

"Michael!"

"What? She's divorced! It happens. It is the twenty-first century."

"But no one in the regal family has married a divorcee!"

"Matthew, calm down. Personally, I don't think it's an issue in this day and age."

"You don't?"

"No. We're getting married. I don't care if Nancy's divorced or not, as long as they are happy. Anyway, this is meaningless conjecture. As long as everyone's happy, I'm happy."

"Are you?"

The abruptness of Matthew's question startled the King. The past few weeks had been hard on His Majestic Regal Highness, but he was intent on putting the bad times behind him. "I suppose I am."

"Even after everything that's happened over the last few weeks?"

"Life goes on, does it not?"

Matthew stood up, walked over to Michael, and began to massage his tense shoulders. "You haven't talked about those few days," Matthew whispered as Michael began to melt at his touch.

"There's nothing to discuss." The King turned his face towards Matthew's. "I do wish everyone would stop mentioning it in my presence."

"If you ever want to talk about it…"

Michael gave Matthew a small smile. "Katherine's death was natural. There's nothing scandalous or remotely intriguing about her final days on earth. The only injustice is that the people behind these vicious rumors have not been caught. However, I have the utmost faith in our judicial system. I know these people will be dealt with by the courts, not by me or the regal family."

"Do I have to go to bed now? It's only nine o'clock, Dad!" Samuel stamped his feet as Edward helped his son into his bed. "It's not fair."

Edward let out a defeated sigh. "Sammy, it's already past your bedtime."

"I'm eleven now! Why do I need a bedtime? None of my friends have bedtimes!"

"I'm not their parents. Come on." Edward began to tuck his son into bed. For a moment, he couldn't help but wonder what his life would be like without the small, meaningful moments such as this that made up the basis of one's life. "Did you have a good time at the Children's Charity Dinner?"

"I guess," moaned Samuel. "Kyle Franklin's a moron. He said that he would be a king before me. I told him that he didn't know anything. I hate him."

"Hey. Don't say that."

"Why not? Mom says that all the time. She hates everyone."

"Sam," Edward said forcefully. "That's quite enough. It's time for bed. Now."

Samuel began to fidget as his father made his way to the door. "Can you read me a story? Please?"

Edward knew that Samuel would continue to beg and plead until his demand was met. The boy's father began to read a *Johnny Galactic* adventure novel. By the time Edward read the first two chapters, Samuel was fast asleep. Edward kissed his son goodnight, turned off the light, closed the bedroom door, and stood by the room guarding it as if his life depended on protecting his son. In a way, it did.

As Edward made his way down the corridor of his state apartment, he began to take stock of the decision he'd made in the past few years. He loved Margaret with all of his being when they were first married, but now it seemed as if they simply tricked themselves into a life of absolute convenience. Edward rounded the corner when he noticed Margaret in the Music Room. Why this room was her favorite, he didn't know. Yet he could always find her in there…in her own world. Maybe here was her place of solace, thought Edward.

"Come in," she cooed. Margaret smiled at her husband. She was dressed in a sheer nightgown, which fell to the floor with effortless elegance. "Do you want a drink," she asked as Edward made his way into the Music Room.

He shook his head. "I'm fine."

"Where's Sam?"

"Asleep. I read him a *Johnny Galactic* novel. It always seems to do the trick." Edward felt his breathing become constricted so he loosed his necktie. "The dinner was a success. We raised half a million dollars… Samuel was a hit with the guests."

Margaret grinned. "He takes after you, Edward. I do hope he inherits honesty from someone on either side of his family tree."

"Excuse me?"

Lady Margaret rolled her eyes. "I can see how unhappy you are, Edward. Your face always betrays you. It has misery written all over it…no matter how hard you try to act, it always betrays you." Margaret placed her cocktail on the edge of the grand piano which was crafted especially for her late father, His Highness Lord Nicholas.

"Margaret…"

"Don't insult me, Edward. Walter told me. Do you really want out of our marriage?"

To be honest, Edward thought this moment would never arrive. Instead of feeling furious about Walter's betrayal, he felt relieved. "I haven't been happy for a very long time."

Even though she wanted to scream, Lady Margaret kept a straight face. "Is that so, Edward?"

"Have you been happy? I mean, really happy?"

"I know… I've made a lot of mistakes. I've never denied that, have I? But no matter what I've done, I've always loved you and our son. That has never changed."

He couldn't help but laugh at her selfless exposition. "If that's so, why did you leak that story to the press about your riding accident? You know how much strife it caused this family!"

Margaret couldn't contain herself any longer. "You know why I did that," she shrieked. "I wanted to hurt Sophia and the whole thing backfired in my face."

"Listen to yourself!" Sophia was always a spot of contention between

Edward and Margaret. Now, Sophia was the major, undeniable issue. "Your constant need to seek revenge on Sophia is consuming your life!"

"Stop defending her!"

"She's my best friend! You knew that when we got married." Suddenly, everything seemed to make sense to Edward. A decade's worth of anger, fighting, and jealousy all came crashing down around him with this single realization. "You married me to spite her, didn't you?"

Margaret stopped dead in her tracks. She could feel Edward's eyes burning into her soul. She turned her back as she sauntered to the large window. Seconds later, it began to rain. "How can you…"

"Admit it, Margaret. You wanted her husband. When you couldn't get him, you took the next best thing: Me."

"You're so full of yourself!"

"Admit it, damn it! Be a woman!"

"I will not be talked to in this way…"

"Hell, you would have taken her life if you had the opportunity," Edward snapped coldly.

"Shut up," she screamed. "You have no idea what it was like growing up with that bitch. After she was born, I was forced into the shadows because Sophia was deemed more important by everyone just because her mother was the Princess of Kemp and heiress to the throne. Everyone treated Sophia and Michael like they were a personal gift from the gods. My own parents doted on Sophia. They barely paid attention to me. No… They were always away somewhere fabulously exotic and without telephone service. But whenever they came back to the kingdom, they found time to tell Sophia how beautiful and perfect she was…they did it all the time. Do you know what that does to a little girl?"

"You're three years older than her…"

"So? What does that have to do with anything?"

"It's just that…"

"You don't know," she shot back. "You weren't there! Our grandmother, Duchess Victoria, only cared about Sophia. From the moment of her birth, I ceased to exist in her eyes. Sophia was the only one who mattered and I was an afterthought. When our grandmother died, Sophia got the best jewels and more money in her trust fund than me! I mattered, too!"

"That's enough," Edward snapped. "I've heard this story more times than I care to remember. If they treated you any differently, it's not Sophia's fault."

"Yes it is. She fed their indulgence."

"Get over it, Margaret. Everyone else has."

"Why should I? They still treat me like a third class citizen. Michael lets Sophia get away with murder and I'm always cast as the villain! No one can see her for what she really is…it's like they turn a blind eye to her ways." Margaret exhaled as she added, "When she and Robert were engaged, everyone whispered that he was too good for her. They were right."

Edward refused to believe his wife's apparently drunken ramblings of her distorted past. "That's ludicrous."

"If you say so." She laughed heartily. "I know the truth. So does Sophia. Everyone knows Robert should be with me."

It was as if he'd been thrown into a pit of fire by his closest confidant. The shock that ripped through Edward's body was only replaced by the urge to vomit. His wife had finally admitted what he'd suspected for months. There would never be a moment from this second on when he wouldn't remember the exact words spoken on this very night. His wife was in love with Prince Robert. There was no other way to express this fact. She was probably in love with him when they were wed, even though he was wholly devoted to her. Everything he thought he knew was a lie. This is the end, thought Edward.

"I… I'm sorry… That's not what… I didn't mean…"

"Don't insult my intelligence, Margaret. Even before you two started sleeping together, I knew there was something amiss. I'm just glad to have your confirmation."

"You're taking this the wrong way," insisted Margaret. She could feel her life slipping away with each passing nanosecond. Lady Margaret raced towards her husband and flung her arms around his neck. As she tried to kiss him passionately, he pushed her away. Hurt, she looked into his deep eyes, which suddenly seemed hollow and devoid of love. "Edward… Please…"

"I've tried to save this marriage. But I can't compete – I won't compete – with your twisted need for revenge where Sophia and Robert are concerned!" Edward stepped away from his wife as he tried to take in the brevity of his situation. Anger was the only feeling that coursed through his veins; betrayal beat in his heart. "Sophia is my best friend. You've done nothing over the past year but systematically try to hurt and harm her at every turn!"

"You're taking her side, too?!" Margaret screamed as she threw an eighteenth century vase across the room. It shattered into a hundred little pieces in the marble fireplace. "That's so typical of you, Edward!"

"I'm not taking sides. I'm looking out for the best interest of our son! The more time you spend trying to get Robert into your bed, the longer our son is tormented for your indiscretions! What's worse, the gulf between you and Samuel has grown so wide, you don't even know him anymore."

Margaret refused to listen to any of her husband's accusations. "You're lying…"

"You weren't even there for him tonight!"

"I had another engagement," she snapped.

"You made that one at the last minute! You should have been by his side tonight! It's no wonder he's ashamed of you, Margaret."

The next thing Margaret knew, she was holding her throbbing hand as

Edward looked at her, stunned. Edward hadn't expected her to slap him with such force. However, she was a fiery woman who refused to let anyone dominate her. "Take that back," she demanded.

"Go to hell. I'm a fool for staying with you for so damn long. I should have ended our marriage years ago."

"Why didn't you?"

"Samuel. I only stayed for our son."

"That's so altruistic of you, Edward. However, I'm afraid to tell you that altruism is so last century," Margaret laughed coldly.

"I've had enough. I'm done."

Ice cold tears streamed down Margaret's face. These were the words she'd dreaded hearing since Walter's warning this afternoon. In her mind, if she fought him long enough, they would end up making love and forgetting the strife of the past night. Although it had always worked in the past, she wrongly assumed it would work tonight. The thought of losing her husband made her sick to the core. This can't happen, she told herself. "What are you saying," she demanded to know.

Edward steadied himself. "After Michael's wedding," he began, "I'm going to file for a divorce…"

"No," she cried softly.

"And," he continued, "I am going to request full custody of our son."

In an instant, Margaret's tears came to an end. No one would take her son away from her, she thought to herself. Losing her husband was one thing; she could always find a man to satisfy her needs. However, if Edward took away her son, it would be a fate worse than death. "That will never happen," she stated. Her voice changed from a weeping woman to one of steely reserve. "You know that will never happen, Edward. He's *my* son. He's a member of the regal family. You can divorce me, but you'll never be rid of me. Whether you like it or not, we're stuck together for the rest of our lives because of Samuel. You'll never take him away from me. Never..."

"Then you're in for the fight of your life."

"I won't let you leave me," countered Margaret. "You need me."

"Like hell I do. You need me more than I need you, Margaret. I was no bum when we were married. I still have a thriving career as an archaeologist, a hereditary aristocratic title, and enough money for three lifetimes. I don't need you, Margaret."

With that, she slapped Edward and he stormed out of the room. Fearing that he would walk out of her life forever, Lady Margaret disappeared down the corridors of their state apartment.

As Edward prepared to walk out of the front door, something caught his attention. The sound of stilettos on the marble floor was Margaret's calling card. Against his better judgment, he turned around to see his wife holding her prized pistol. Without a sound, she fired the gun at Edward. Without thinking, Edward moved to the right, causing the bullet to lodge in the thick oak door. Sweat permeated from his body while his life flashed before his eyes. However, the biggest shock came when he saw Samuel and his governess, Eloise standing in the doorway of the Drawing Room with their mouths wide open. Behind them, the butler and on-duty maid covered their mouths out of sheer horror. Lady Margaret soon noticed the crowd and dropped the gun on the marble floor.

"Everything's fine," she smiled.

Samuel burst into tears and ran to his bedroom with Edward and Eloise chasing after him. The boy threw himself onto his bed as the thoughts of the last five minutes ran through his mind. The gun didn't scare him, but the thought of seeing his father dead frightened him more than he could verbalize. "Master Samuel," Eloise called. "It's all right…" She tried to reach out to the boy, but he recoiled at her touch.

Edward asked Eloise to leave them alone. Despite his best efforts, Edward knew his son was inconsolable. He closed the door to his son's bedroom with a heavy heart. When Edward returned to the foyer, Margaret instructed the staff to clean up the mess and keep their mouths shut. Although neither of them said a word, Margaret and Edward knew the end was nigh.

After five minutes of nonstop tears, Samuel picked up the telephone near his bed. Although his mother told him to use it only to call the kitchen or Eloise, he didn't care right now. "His Majesty's Private Suite," the receptionist said.

"This is His Regal Highness Samuel."

"Good evening, Your Regal Highness. What may I do for you?"

"I need to speak to the King." Moments later, Samuel was patched through to Michael's private line. "Mike?"

"Sam… How are you?"

"I'm okay. My mom tried to shoot my dad."

The King arrived at Margaret and Edward's state apartment to find the staff cleaning up the residual mess from the gunshot. He demanded that the butler assemble Edward and Margaret in the Morning Room, where he would be waiting. Upon their arrival, Michael observed the guilty pair. Although Samuel hadn't given him any details over the telephone, Michael knew all too well that the events of tonight were a lifetime in the making. "Enough is enough," declared the monarch. "I have had it with the drama that radiates from this marriage."

"You don't know the half of it," countered Lady Margaret.

"Margaret, someone could have been murdered tonight! Why don't you ever think about the consequences of your actions?"

"I do," she stammered.

"That's crap," interjected Michael. "You've gone through your entire life acting as if someone owes you something, when in fact; the world doesn't owe you a damn thing. I've had enough of you."

Margaret squirmed in her seat. "That makes two of us…"

"You put your husband, son, and staff's lives in danger tonight and for what? Because a petty argument that didn't end your way? Grow up, lady! And Edward, you know how she is… Tell me what happened tonight."

Edward averted Margaret's unrelenting gaze as he said, "I'm considering a divorce. I didn't tell her… She heard the news from Walter…"

"Is it true," the King demanded to know.

"Yes," he sighed.

"This is why I acted the way I did, Michael. It wasn't *my* fault. He pushed me to the edge." Margaret quickly closed her mouth as she met Michael's unforgiving stare.

The King threw his up hands in despair. This was something he would have to deal with tonight. Finally, he said, "You two will sort this out after the wedding – not a moment before."

"What," asked Edward.

"I will not have my wedding spoiled because of your histrionics." Michael stopped mid-sentence as Samuel appeared in the doorway of the Morning Room. The boy carried an overnight bag along with a *Johnny Galactic* novel and his dog, Austin.

"Michael, can I spend the night in one of the guest rooms," asked Samuel.

"Sam," cooed Margaret. "It's all right. Mommy and Daddy had a grown-up fight…"

"You tried to kill him," snapped Samuel. With that, Samuel stormed out of the state apartment with Michael by his side.

As Edward watched his son walk out of his home, his anger turned towards Margaret. "This is over," he proclaimed.

"Why? Because you say it is? That's not how it works, Edward."

"Isn't it?"

"I won't be painted as the bad wife."

"Why deny the truth? I'm going to my father's house."

Margaret watched as her husband strode out of her state apartment. Alone, she began to regret the events of that night. But it wasn't her fault, she reminded herself. She'd been pushed to the limit by Edward and his friendship with Sophia. Sophia, she thought ruefully. All of my mistakes are linked to Sophia, Margaret told herself. Margaret bellowed for her maid to get her assistant on the line as soon as possible. "This is Her Regal Highness Lady Margaret. Yes… I need you to file a flight plan to St. Martin on the regal jet… I want to leave as soon as possible… Fine… I'll be at the airport in two hours." Margaret hung up the phone as a twisted smile crossed her face. She wasn't going to go down without a fight, but a warrior needed to indulge in hedonism before a battle of epic proportions.

27

"Where is Lady Margaret?"

That single question absorbed all facets of regal life in the week following her attempt to shoot His Highness Edward. From the King's office to the scullery maid, the staff was abuzz with the gossip swirling around Margaret and Edward's tempestuous marriage. It wasn't as if the staff didn't regularly gossip about the regal family, but this was different. This story involved shooting, fighting, disappearances, and a heightened sense that all was not well with the regal family.

Away from the glare of regal life, Lady Margaret reclined on a lounge chair facing the Atlantic Ocean. She'd managed to tune out the rest of the world on the beaches of St. Martin, but she knew all too well that her problems were only a plane ride away. No matter, she thought calmly. After the incident, she boarded the regal jet and set off for rest and reflection. In the seven days since she'd been on the island, she'd received a phone call from the King. He simply wanted to inform her that she needed to go through the proper regal protocols to use the jet whenever she decided to return from her little jaunt. When she would return to Andover was unknown, even to Margaret. There was nothing waiting for her in Andover... However, on the beach, she could pretend that nothing mattered, because in this moment, nothing did.

"Sam, it's time to go!" Edward twisted his Rolex watch anxiously. He wasn't use to the morning routine he and Sam had perfected during the past week. His son was notably silent. Edward did his best to make life as normal for Samuel as possible, but the deafening silence that filled the air only reminded them that Margaret was gone. "Sam!"

"I'm here," he moaned.

Edward was irritated to see his son was still in his bathrobe. "Get dressed. I had the butler put your clothes on your bed."

"I'm not going, Dad."

"Samuel, you need to go to school."

"Why?"

"I said so."

"So?"

"Now, Samuel."

With a defiant huff, Samuel marched towards his bedroom. Minutes later, he emerged fully dressed with his shoes in one hand and his leather satchel in the other. "Here." He handed his satchel to his father. "When's Mom coming home?"

Edward led his son out of their state apartment, down the brightly lit corridors, down a flight of triple wide stairs, out of the palace, and into the idling black executive Lancia Thesis. "I don't know."

"Why?"

"Sam... Please. Stop with the questions."

Samuel fidgeted in his seat. His eyes remained transfixed on the gates to the palace as they slowly parted. As the town car turned out of the palace towards the King Henrik Preparatory School, a feeling of dread washed through his body. "This is my fault, isn't it?"

"No," Edward replied firmly. "You have nothing to do with what's happening."

"But… I called Mike. I got you and Mom in trouble."

"Sam, your mother and I…we have our own troubles. We both love you."

"Will you go back to the Sahara Desert and leave me all alone?"

Edward couldn't believe what his son had just asked him. He stared at his forlorn son. By Edward's estimation, he'd never seen any child look as frightened and helpless as his own son did in this very moment. "Sam, I'm not going to do anything like that again. Do you hear me?"

"Do you mean it?"

"Of course I do."

Their Regal Highnesses Princess Sophia and Princess Helena joined the Dowager Queen for tea in her private tea room at Andover Palace. Usually, these gatherings took place after lunch. However, each woman had an event to attend during that usual time, so the decision was made to have an early tea to tide everyone over until lunchtime. Although gossiping was something none of them ever admitted to participating in, the conversation soon turned from the best new fashion designers in Andover to Lady Margaret's breakdown.

"It seems to me," sniffed Sophia, "that she's lost her mind."

"Now," Cassandra said coolly. "Don't be cruel."

"I'm not, Mother. But is it any wonder Edward wants to divorce her after the wedding?" Princess Sophia bit into a freshly baked croissant. "Margaret's simply lost her hold on reality. If she weren't a member of the regal family, she'd be in jail!"

Princess Helena nodded in agreement. "Edward's a great man. Hell, I wouldn't try to kill a man like him."

The Dowager Queen placed her tea cup on the table with a great flourish. She loathed the thought of divorce. Furthermore, she loathed the fact that her daughter and granddaughter seemed to find this situation comical. "We must put Samuel first. The last thing we need is a divorce that keeps us in the papers for years on end!"

"Mother, if a divorce is what it takes to protect Edward and Samuel, then so be it. Besides, Margaret doesn't deserve Edward." Princess Sophia lifted her tea cup to her soft lips. "It is better that Edward divorces her now…it'll be nice and simple."

“Simple? Those things are never simple! Edward may want millions in the settlement and who knows what he may say after it’s all over,” cried Cassandra.

Princess Sophia leaned into her mother and niece. “If he wanted to humiliate us, he could have done it months ago.”

“What do you mean,” chirped Princess Helena.

“He told me that he wanted to divorce Margaret months ago.” A look of shock swept across Helena’s face, as Cassandra covered her mouth with fright. Sophia continued: “Edward’s always been the pinnacle of discretion.”

“You knew all this time,” pouted Helena. “You should have told me!”

“Dear, you cannot keep a secret,” Sophia replied softly.

The Dowager Queen shook her head. She was immensely disappointed in her daughter, and in herself. The issue of divorce, and the secrets being kept within her family, was something Cassandra never enjoyed. During Cassandra’s youth, divorce was something that people did, but not in the regal family. They were above that…or so she’d been taught. If Princess Fiona could see Margaret now, she’d die, Cassandra noted silently. Lady Margaret had always been too feisty for Cassandra’s tastes, but her current scandals were too much for the former monarch to stomach. How much damage would this cause the family and the kingdom, Cassandra worried. “I can’t believe this. Sophia, you should have told me or the King… Did you tell Prince Robert?”

“No,” Sophia stated quickly. “He wasn’t very happy about it, but I had to keep Edward’s trust. After all, Edward needed a confidant.”

“Can you imagine what our lives would be like if you and Edward got married all those years ago,” smiled Princess Helena. “I think you two would have been better than you and Uncle Robert.”

Sophia banished the thought instantly. “Edward’s my best friend. That will never change. Anyway, for some unknown reason, he loves Margaret.”

***

Each year, the men of the regal family attended a special ceremony to commemorate the day when King Henrik established the Andover Securities and Exchange Market. King Michael and Lord Walter had attended this sacred event each year since their fifth birthday. While the event never interested them, they knew it was their duty. However, Michael excused Samuel from this archaic ceremony, much to the young boy's fury. Michael, Walter, and Edward didn't think it would be wise for them to subject him to questions regarding his parents' marriage. No, Michael thought, it was best to have Samuel live his life as normal and attend the event next year.

After the King's ceremonial opening of the market, the men retired to the regal waiting room while their vehicles were brought to the private entrance. The mood amongst the men was quiet, due to the tension between the Prince of Kemp and the King. Although Prince Robert and Prince Joseph talked about the growing rift between the King and his heir, no one dared mention it in this setting. "Your Majesty… Your Regal Highnesses," Glenn said as he entered the room with a bow. "The Minister of Government is making a speech." Glenn wheeled in an old television, turned it on, and left the room. The King narrowed his eyes as Patricia Ali began to speak:

"As the kingdom knows, my duties are to you, the people of Andover. Based on the accusations by The Martyrs of Andover, I believe – along with my governors in government – that the death of Princess Katherine should be investigated to the fullest extent of the law. Therefore, I have formed an investigative committee to look into the true circumstances behind Princess Katherine's death. We must bring to justice anyone who may have had anything to do with her untimely death a decade ago."

"What the hell is this?" Michael screamed as he ordered Joseph to turn off the television. "This woman has no respect for this family! She's conducting nothing more than an orchestrated witch hunt based on scurrilous rumors!"

"Is that so," challenged Alexander. He watched his father, the kingdom's monarch, pace the room like an animal, waiting to murder its captor.

Michael stopped in his tracks. The King could feel himself about to lose control. "I had nothing to do with your mother's death."

"Dad, don't pay attention to Alex. He's working against the family because he hates you and us," Joseph insisted.

"That's crap," Alexander lied.

"Is it? Come on. Tell the truth. You love this," replied Joseph

The Prince of Kemp stood nose to nose with his younger brother. In all of their years as brothers, they weren't very close. For Alexander, being the odd man out was something he'd grown accustomed to a very long time ago. Therefore, it did not surprise him that Joseph painted him as the spawn of Judas and Brutus. "Once again, you have no idea what you're talking about," shouted Alexander. "I do think that something is amiss, but that's all, Joseph."

"Hey," interrupted Walter. "We should keep our voices down or people may begin to ask questions."

Without a second thought, the King stormed out of the waiting room with Princes Joseph and Lord Walter behind him.

Prince Robert lagged behind. He had never felt especially close to his wife's nephew, but he sensed that there was something very off with Prince Alexander. "Are you all right?"

"Uncle Robert, why don't you just go? I'm fine," snorted Alexander.

"Alexander…"

"Go."

Defeated, Prince Robert ordered the attending valet to bring around his car. As he stood in the chilly afternoon air, something didn't sit right with Robert. The ride back to the palace was quite uncomfortable. Why? Robert couldn't quite place his finger on the exact cause of it, but he had a terrible feeling that the Prince of Kemp was spiraling out of control.

***

"Everything, Your Majesty?"

"I want to you to release everything the Secret Police knows about Patricia Ali's involvement with The Martyrs of Andover. Now," ordered the King. This had gone too far, the King told himself. His own son was using whatever means necessary to unseat him and now was the perfect time to beat him at his own sick, twisted game. Michael would have never even considered using these tactics in the past; however, these were unpredictable times. Thankfully, the majority of Andoverians didn't believe that King or the regal family had anything to do with Princess Katherine's death. However, a growing minority believed just that. As the monarch, Michael knew he had a duty to protect the kingdom at whatever cost. And if it meant handing the Minister of Government over as the culprit behind The Martyrs of Andover, so be it. "Tell me you have proof, Mr. Ellison."

Kerr Ellison, the Head of the Secret Police, nodded sagely. "We have enough proof to implicate Ms. Ali, Sire."

"Is it definite or circumstantial?"

"Definite."

"Leak whatever you have to *The Sentinel*."

"Are you sure, Sire?"

"I want that women held to account. If we don't act now, the kingdom may be ruined forever." Michael bit the inside of his cheek. "Do it, Mr. Ellison."

"Yes, Sire. What do you want us to do about the Prince of Kemp?"

The King knew that his son was the key to this entire saga. If it weren't for Alexander, maybe the family would have been spared the last month of pain and agony. However, the King knew all too well that he couldn't expose Alexander as a co-conspirator in this ongoing scandal. To do so would cause reprehensible harm to the Kingdom of Andover. "I'll deal with the Prince of Kemp. For now,

Patricia Ali will have to do."

The Princess of Kemp wandered around the corridors of Kemp Castle out of sheer boredom. Her husband was off with the men of the family, while the women of the family refused to invite her for tea at the palace. Olivia knew that she was still on fragile ground with the Dowager Queen, which is why she didn't tell Alexander about her regal snub. However, being alone in this rambling castle could do terrible things to one's mind. I need something to do, Olivia thought wistfully.

"Your Regal Highness, His Regal Highness The Prince Joseph is requesting to see you in the Yellow Reception Room," announced Ralph Landon, the private secretary to the Prince and Princess of Kemp.

Surprised, Olivia made her way into the main part of the castle. She found the prince sitting in a century old cloth bound chair. "Hello," she said warmly. "Would you like anything?"

"No," replied Joseph. "Is Alex here?"

She shook her head. "I thought he was with you. I never know when he'll be back from his engagements and such..."

"Actually, I'm glad he's gone. Listen, Olivia, I need your help."

"With what?"

"My brother has been acting very odd over the past few weeks. I don't know what it is and he refuses to say anything to anyone. You're his wife...has he said anything to you?"

The Princess of Kemp eyed her brother-in-law carefully. She'd always liked Joseph, but his intrusion into her personal life was not welcome. "Joseph, I don't know what you're talking about." Yes, it was a blatant lie, but she refused to turn against her husband, especially now.

Joseph knew that this task would be more trouble than it was worth, but he refused to give up. He knew that he could break Olivia, but he had to do it gently. "Olivia, I know my brother's been up to no good. I can see it all over his face..."

"You don't know what you're talking about."

"I think I do. Olivia, we could all be in danger."

"That's very overdramatic, don't you think?" Olivia couldn't resist the urge to release a hearty sigh. The last thing she wanted to do was allow Joseph to see the many cracks within her own marriage.

"What's wrong with you?"

"Actually, I'm annoyed. You always think the worst of my husband. But then again, you've always been jealous of him."

Prince Joseph blanched at the suggestion. He never wanted to be the monarch. It was Alexander who was relentlessly ambitious and endlessly jealous; not Joseph. "You know that's not true."

"Isn't it? My husband will be the King of Andover one day. You'll still be a prince who must bow before his brother."

"Do you think that bothers me? I could care less that he is first in line for the throne! What I am concerned about is my family's safety and that includes you."

"He would never hurt me," sniffed Olivia.

Prince Joseph shook his head. He knew that she didn't grasp the enormity of the situation. "Eventually, you will have to choose sides. If Alexander is working against the family, you will be cast out just like him."

"You're insane." Olivia waved her hands in the air as if to clear it of Joseph's insinuations. "My husband would never do anything to hurt me. He's innocent."

"I'm sorry I wasted my time." The prince started for the door, but something refused to let him leave. He didn't know if it was the comfort of being in Kemp Castle or the fact that Olivia seemed terribly oblivious to the true nature of her own husband. Either way, Joseph knew that something had to be done. "Olivia, for your sake, I hope Alex is innocent. If he's not…well, I don't even want to think about what would happen…"

"Edward!"

His Highness Edward spun around to see His Highness Prince Robert walking towards him. Edward released an annoyed sigh at the sight of his wife's lover. Even though it had been months since Margaret's miscarriage, Edward still preferred to not see Robert outside of the confines of regal life. "Robert. What are you doing in Lord's Pass?"

"I was picking up something for Princess Sophia. You?"

"I needed a break from… Never mind…"

"Look," Robert said in a low voice. "I'm sorry to hear about your marriage."

Edward glanced around the busy streets to ensure no one else heard the details of his unsuccessful union. He guided Robert to his waiting car, where they sat in silence. "It's a little too late for that, Rob."

"I am very ashamed of the role I played in all of this…"

Edward didn't want to listen to another minute of Robert's confession. "Well, be glad that Sophia forgave you. She really does love you."

Before Prince Robert could respond, his iPhone sprang to life with a track from an independent band Prince Joseph adored. Robert pulled the phone from his jacket and froze. It was Margaret. Instantaneously, Robert gave the device to Edward, who pressed the answer button. "Robert," she cooed.

"It's Edward." For a minute, he thought she'd hung up, but he could hear her breathing on the other line. "You need to come back to Andover, Margaret."

"I'm having the time of my life! I don't even know when or if I'll ever come back to the kingdom." With that, Lady Margaret hung up the telephone. At that moment, a slender young man with impeccable biceps returned to the lounge chair next to hers and gave her a passionate kiss. I may never come back, she thought gleefully.

His Regal Highness Prince Joseph of Andover couldn't shake the feeling that something was ready to implode. Ever since his visit to Kemp Castle, his sister-in-law's behavior struck him as odd. Olivia was the type of person who would do whatever it took to gain favor within the regal family. Joseph knew for a fact that Olivia was still smarting from her fight with Princess Helena and wanted nothing more than for everyone to forget it ever happened. However, Olivia didn't seem normal. No, Joseph surmised, something was seriously off with her. Whatever it was, Joseph didn't know. Yet, in that moment of reflection in his private suite, he knew that there was one person who would have the answers he sought: His father.

Prince Joseph lingered outside of his father's private suite for five minutes. He knew that the Dowager Queen was already with the King, which meant he shouldn't bother them. Well, regal protocol meant the world to the prince, but his concerns for the future of the monarchy trumped any sense of regal duty he held at this moment in time. He knocked on the door twice, before being admitted into the King's private quarters.

The Dowager Queen gave her grandson a tight hug, while her dogs lay at her feet. The King poured his son a tumbler of amaretto with three ice cubes before saying, "What brings you by tonight, Joseph?"

"Something isn't right," stated Joseph, cryptically. "I mean… These stories about Mom and the timing… It reeks of Alex."

The King studied his youngest son carefully. Prince Joseph's playboy antics were well documented in the press. Where Alexander was sensible, Joseph was footloose. The two were polar opposites, but they were very much cut from the same cloth. Michael could have dismissed Joseph's assertions as mere drivel, but he knew within the depth of his being that Prince Joseph was right in his summation of this grave situation. "Joseph," Michael uttered, "do not repeat that statement to anyone."

"I've already told the Princess of Kemp."

"What did she say," asked the monarch.

"She won't say anything. She either knows exactly what's happening or she's as clueless as they come."

The Dowager Queen finished her special drink as she listened to this exchange. She knew that Olivia was not to be trusted and neither was the Prince of Kemp. Cassandra could finally see that they were most likely in this together, but she felt within her heart that if Olivia could be dealt with, everything would return to normal. "I wonder if Olivia is as inept as she appears."

"What do you mean, Grandmother?"

"No one can be that simple, Joseph. It's impossible. I strongly believe that the Princess of Kemp is aware of much more than we know. I also think it's very possible that she and Alexander may be colluding..."

"That's enough," said the King. He knew far too much to listen to this idle speculation. By Michael's deduction, this entire situation was Alexander and Patricia Ali's creation. If Olivia was aware of her husband's activities, Michael knew that she wouldn't utter one word that would incriminate her husband. "I would appreciate it if you two could keep your suspicions to yourselves."

"Why are you protecting them?"

"Joey, Alexander is too explosive right now. I don't think he can be trusted."

"I knew it," shouted Prince Joseph.

“However,” continued the King, “we must not say one word about this to anyone. Am I understood?”

“Of course, Michael,” nodded the Dowager Queen.

“Joseph? Can I trust you?”

“Yes. But why are you defending him? He’s trying to incriminate you in Mom’s death.”

The King wondered why his other children didn’t express this level of loyalty. “Alexander hasn’t been the same since Katherine’s death. He was never a very emotional boy, but something within him changed ten years ago.”

“Dad…”

“I know him. Granted, our relationship has always been a bit strained, but he’s still my son, Joseph. He’s your brother. If I were to state that Alexander was the sole culprit behind these accusations, this family would never recover. The best thing we can do is leave this alone.”

Joseph didn’t like what his father had just said, but he knew he was powerless to change his mind. “Fine… But what can I do to help?”

The King merely shrugged. “Nothing… Everything will work itself out in due time, Joseph. You’ll see.”

PATRICIA ALI ACCUSED OF BEING A MEMBER OF THE MARTYRS OF ANDOVER.

The next morning’s issue of *The Sentinel* blast that headline from every newsstand in the kingdom. Every morning news program and chat show discussed the story at length, so much so that years later the historians would name this day as the day that Andover came of age. However, nothing could eclipse the story written by Janet Myers:

“*A reliable source has informed this publication that Patricia Ali is a founding member of The Martyrs of Andover. Our source further reveals that she is responsible for the accusations surrounding the regal family's involvement in the death of the late Princess Katherine.*

"*Our source has delivered papers to that show the Minister of Government's signature on papers forming the group. Moreover, there are telephone records which detail her association with people believed to be involved with the group. If this is so, the Minister of Government could face serious charges for being a member of a subversive group, liable, fraud, treason, and conspiring against the regal family.*

"*Phone calls and e-mail messages to Ms. Ali's office were not returned before this publication went to print. Andover Palace has declined to comment on this story.*

"*It should be noted that His Majesty The King has yet to address the claims that the regal family is somehow responsible for Princess Katherine's death...*"

His Majestic Regal Highness The King of Andover walked into the Official State Room of Andover Palace. Before him stood his team of advisors, who had been eating a breakfast prepared by the palace chef. The King took his seat at the head of the table with great ceremony. He'd read the story in *The Sentinel* three times that morning and, in a strange way, he felt at peace with his decision to leak those documents to *The Sentinel*.

"Your Majesty," said Richard Freedman, the Senior Advisor to His Majesty. "We think it would be in the best interest of the palace if you released a formal statement regarding this story."

The King turned his attention to Glenn, who was a member of this special team. "Is that so, Mr. Mortimer?"

"Your Majesty, we feel it would be best for everyone concerned," stated Glenn.

“I do thank you all of your advice, however, I will not comment on this story.”

The team of advisor’s shared a tense look. They knew that the King was a man of his own mind and rarely took their advice. However, these were extraordinary times that called for a break from the King’s usual no comments reign.

“Your Majesty, please listen to what we have to say,” insisted Richard.

“Mr. Freedman, I will not become involved in this scandal,” huffed the King. “This is a matter for the Court of Magistrates to handle; not the palace.”

The Court of Magistrates was the highest court in the kingdom. Laws could be created in the Court, while people who felt they were wrongly accused of a crime could seek their final, ultimate decision. The Court’s powers also extended to cases of treason, which is how Patricia Ali’s actions were viewed by the kingdom.

“Well,” said Claire Hopkins, 2nd Peer, “that may be the best course of action. The palace remains neutral. The last thing we would want is for the King to make a political statement that could disrupt the monarchy. Do you all agree?” Claire’s reasoning was met with generous nods by her peers.

After a moment of conferring, Richard finally relented. “I just fear this could upset the balance of power within government.”

“Ladies and gentlemen,” said the King. “The Court of Magistrates should handle this matter. As Mrs. Hopkins has noted, if the palace were to make a statement, it could be misconstrued and damage this institution. The less sway the family has over the outcome of this investigation, the better.”

Later that day, Tamara Kellison, the lead afternoon anchor for the Hourly News Channel made the following announcement: “Well, it seems as if this day keeps getting more interesting! We have just received a statement from the Court of Magistrates regarding the accusation that the Minister of Government is a member of The Martyrs of Andover.

"The Court of Magistrates has begun a formal investigation in order to deduce Patricia Ali's role with The Martyrs of Andover. Ms. Ali's office has released a statement ensuring that she is innocent and will cooperate with the Court. The statement further says that Ms. Ali is being unfairly punished by – and I quote – a 'group of people who will do anything to please the regal family.'"

Tamara swiveled around in her chair to face HNC's political analyst, Dana Romero. "Dana, what are the implications for Ms. Ali and the government of Andover?"

"Tamara, if Patricia Ali is found guilty, this will end her political career. I wouldn't be surprised if she was forced to resign as Minister of Government," stated Dana.

"Is that a drastic step?"

"No. A poll conducted by the Rice Center shows that Ms. Ali has lost popular support. Furthermore, only 16% of those polled have said that they will vote of her in the next election."

A satisfied smile crossed Michael's face as he turned off the television. The King turned his attention to the many folders which required his attention when Princess Sophia was escorted into his office by Glenn.

"Michael," she seethed, "when is this bad publicity going to end?"

"What are you talking about? I've ensured that the regal family has stayed above this scandal. Why do you think I didn't comment on any of those rumors about Katherine?"

"I don't know. I just feel that this may be a bit too much for us right now."

The King could understand his sister's apprehension, but he knew all too well that her concerns were for naught. "Sophia, this is the first time in a very long time that change has come to the kingdom. Maybe it's time that Patricia Ali steps aside."

Princess Sophia thought about her brother's words with great care. It was an open secret within the regal family that Michael did not like Patricia Ali. Even though the monarch had to work with the Ministers of Government and sign their bills into law, Michael's relationship with Patricia was always contentious. From what Sophia heard, Patricia viewed the regal family as wholly disposable, while Michael thought Patricia was an ineffective leader. Yet, as Sophia thought of everything she'd heard in the past, she began to suspect that her brother may not be as innocent as everyone thought. "Michael, did you orchestrate this investigation by the Court of Magistrates to ensure Patricia lost her job?"

"Why on earth would I do that, Sophia?"

"I find it quite strange that this case went right to the Court of Magistrates, when it could have been handled by an independent body." The princess took a moment before saying, "The magistrates are appointed by the monarch. They will do whatever you wish."

The King rolled his eyes at his sister's insinuation. "Sophia, I have had nothing to do with any of this. We are the victims. Whoever is behind The Martyrs of Andover needs to be dealt with by the letter of the law. I have no say in how the law operates with regard to this issue."

"Do you know who is behind this group?"

Michael knew that it would come out eventually and he didn't want Sophia's endless conjecture to seep to the regal household. He leaned into his sister with a grave look on his face. "I need your word that you'll keep this strictly confidential." The princess nodded in agreement. "The Andover Secret Police have been investigating this group for months. I've been aware of their presence ever since."

"You knew… Michael, for goodness sake! You could have stopped those rumors about Katherine!"

"I didn't know they were planning on using my dead wife to get to me!"

Michael reclined in his chair in order to regain control of the situation. "Their claims were a shock to me, Sophia. I didn't know what they had planned. But now, they are being dealt with by the Court. That's all I have to say about the matter." The King rang a bell on his desk. A butler appeared and the King ordered him to bring coffee, tea, and snacks for the pair. Upon the butler's return from the kitchen, Michael asked, "How are you coping with Lady Margaret's dramatic exit to St. Martin?"

Princess Sophia couldn't contain her elation. "I'm relieved. I hope she never comes back to Andover."

"Sophia…" Michael sighed. He carefully sipped his tea. "I know things have been difficult with Lady Margaret…"

"Difficult? She tried to ruin my marriage and she tried to murder my best friend." Sophia clenched her fist. "I hate her, Michael. I'm just thankful that you've been able to keep it out of the press."

Michael nodded in agreement. The last thing the regal family needed was a scandal which emanated from Lady Margaret's inability to remain sane. Although Michael rarely agreed with his cousin's choices in life, he didn't know why she was unable to be happy. Maybe this time away from the kingdom would be good for her, thought the King.

"Do you think Edward will really divorce her," asked Sophia. "I know how much he loves her…"

"Between us, it would be best for everyone involved if they did get a divorce. It's obvious that their marriage was over a very long time ago."

"A divorce under your reign," cracked Princess Sophia. "How scandalous, Michael."

"If it's the best thing, then I'll urge them to pursue it in a hurry. I've always been fond of Edward. I do enjoy having him as a member of the regal family."

"Indeed," smiled Sophia. When Edward and Margaret's engagement was first announced, Princess Sophia had her doubts. Actually, she still thought Edward was all wrong for her self-absorbed cousin. However, Michael was right. It was a pleasure to have Edward in their family, despite the way Margaret treated him.

"What about you?" Michael asked softly.

"Excuse me?"

"If Margaret and Edward do get divorced, are you afraid she'll go after Prince Robert?"

"I wouldn't worry about that," Sophia told Michael. "Margaret knows better than to mess with me."

West Andover lay on the west coast of the kingdom, north of the County of Port Agnes, west of the County of Blake Hill, and to the northwest of the County of Kemp Forest. Many viewed this county of Andover as the most up to date, trendy, and exciting. While Old Andover was the home to the kingdom's government, Andover Palace, the Andover Securities and Exchange Market, and the old world charm of the kingdom, West Andover was the vibrant financial, media, diplomatic, and new moneyed enclave.

West Andover Palace, which was once the home of Princes Christian and Erich, was the current home of the Andover Diplomatic Council. However, the council's fifty year lease on the building expired this year and the property would revert to the regal family. Due to this reason, the Andover Diplomatic Council has just finished building a gleaming new headquarters for their renowned organization.

In the shadow of West Andover Palace, His Regal Highness The Prince of Kemp waited anxiously. The news of the Court of Magistrates' decision to investigate Patricia Ali stunned the prince. This was the first time in the kingdom's history that the highest elected official in the land had been investigated by the Court. Alexander was rightfully nervous. If the Court could reveal Patricia's part in their plan, he knew it was only a matter of time until his role was uncovered. The Prince of Kemp couldn't help but fret that his own father would turn him in, but what did the King know? "You came," he sighed.

From the shadows a haggard looking Patricia Ali walked towards the prince. She performed a slight curtsy out of duty. "How could you let this happen," she shrieked in a low, frightened voice. "You were supposed to protect us!"

"This not my fault! I had no idea this would happen!"

"My office and my home are being searched right now! My children are beside themselves!"

"You have to remain calm, Patricia."

"Calm? Don't give me that crap. This isn't your life on the line…"

"Look, we knew this could happen. Just stay calm. Please. We must consider the greater good."

"The greater good," she shot back. Months ago, this sounded like a noble task, but now, it felt like a terrific set up. "If they expose me, I'll expose you!"

The Prince of Kemp maintained his cool air. Thankfully, Alexander knew that Patricia had already been discredited by the press, the public, and members of her own party. She's grasping at straws, he thought. "My hands are clean. How will anyone trace these events back to me?"

"I can…"

"You have no power anymore. No one trusts you. They'll see it as your continued effort to discredit the regal family."

"You are evil," she gasped.

"Listen to me," he said calmly. "Our plan will go off without a hitch. This is just a minor glitch for the greater good. Trust me."

"Michael. What are you doing here?" Walter gave his cousin a tight embrace as they walked down the hunter green halls of Blake Manor. "Did Margaret do something?"

The King felt sorry for Lord Walter because he was the person everyone tended to go to with complaints about Lady Margaret. "I can't stay very long, Walter. I wanted to inform you that I've reviewed the dossier on Danisi Samantha Masoli."

Lord Walter felt his heart lurch into his throat. This single piece of paper could either spell the beginning of a fairy tale or the end of everything he'd managed to build with Samantha. If there were one aspect of regal life he could do without, this would be it. "And…"

"Everything's fine. Thankfully."

A wave of relief rushed through Walter's body. Suddenly, everything seemed possible. "Good. I couldn't be happier! I guess I'll tell Margaret about the engagement whenever she decides to grace us with her presence."

"You still haven't heard from her?" Michael motioned for the maid to fetch his overcoat as he and Walter stood in the vast foyer.

"No… To be honest, I don't understand why Lady Margaret does what she does anymore. I do feel bad for her."

"There's nothing we can do…"

"I know," noted Walter. "She just seems so angry with the entire world. I just hope for the sake of her son that she gets her act together before it's too late."

"Helena!" The Princess of Kemp ran down the corridors of Andover Palace as she spotted the young princess. "May I have a word?"

Annoyed, Princess Helena turned to her sister-in-law. "What?"

"I wanted to apologize for that night at Kemp Castle. I'm sorry."

"No you're not," interjected the princess, coldly.

"Princess..."

"I don't have time for this, Olivia. I need to prepare for a meeting and a dinner."

"Why are you so cold? I'm trying like hell to make amends and you blow me off. Why?"

Princess Helena crossed her arms defiantly. "My feelings about you haven't changed. I still find you terribly annoying."

"You have to reconsider...we're family."

"You're my brother's wife," corrected the princess. "You're only a princess by courtesy of His Majesty The King." Helena laughed to herself. "My father could have made you a princess in your own right before the wedding, but he didn't. My mother was a princess in her own right by order of my grandmother and my great-grandfather, Henrik, made my grandfather Duke James a prince in his own right. I think that clearly sums up how we view you."

Stung, Olivia didn't know what to say. When she and Alexander were married no one told her that she could be created a princess in her own right as a perk of being married to the heir to the throne. At the time, she gladly accepted the courtesy title as the Princess of Kemp, but now she realized that Helena's word held a lot of truth. "Can't we just put this behind us?"

Without a word, Princess Helena marched into her private suite, leaving the Princess of Kemp alone in the corridor on the verge of tears.

"Your Majesty, Mr. Ellison is on the line."

Michael rarely ate lunch at his desk, but the upcoming investigation of Patricia Ali proved to be more dramatic than anyone could have predicted. For Michael, it meant that he may have to swear in a new Minister of Government, but that wasn't the worse thing in the world. "Yes," Michael said brightly.

"Your Majesty, I want to inform you that Ms. Ali and the Prince of Kemp were spotted together near West Andover Palace two hours ago."

"Thank you, Mr. Ellison."

"What would you like us to do," inquired Kerr.

The King considered his options for a moment. "I know what must be done…"

28

Spring arrived days earlier than expected; however, the presence of new hope within the Kingdom of Andover was desperately needed. The last trace of the winter snow was replaced by the budding cherry blossoms, singing robin, and slightly longer days. The regal wedding was the talk of the kingdom, as well as Patricia Ali's legal issues. Andover was abuzz as to whether or not the Court of Magistrates would actually demand that Patricia Ali step down from her post as Minister of Government. Whatever happened, popular opinion erred on the side of the Court. Rather uncharacteristically, Patricia Ali adopted a low profile that no one could quite understand, yet the regal family found her diminished presence a welcomed twist in this ongoing tale.

While the Court announced that they would announce their findings in Patricia's case today, the King was in the State Dining Room of Andover Palace solidifying the final arrangements for his wedding. As the staff served the three course lunch, the Dowager Queen eyed her booklet of information carefully. By Cassandra's estimation, everything was going according to plan, which pleased her more than anything. The Dowager Queen raised her wine glass to her lips as Countess Sally Hall whispered something to Count Patrick Hall. Whispering is so rude, Cassandra thought hotly. "Is something afoot," she asked.

Countess Sally Hall smiled politely. Yes, the Dowager Queen did rank above her in every way that mattered, but she was beginning to find her impossible. No matter what Sally wanted to do for the wedding, Cassandra had the power to veto her plan. Or, even worse, Cassandra would say she would present it to the King and never speak of her idea again. It's not that Sally felt any malice towards the Dowager Queen, but she certainly knew who was running this wedding. "I just told my husband that we needed to refill his heart medication on the way home."

"Oh," muttered the Dowager Queen.

Nancy Hall shared a knowing look with her brother, Count Matthew Hall. They knew about the power struggle consuming the Dowager Queen and their mother. To Matthew, it was a marker for the years to come, while Nancy thought it was good fun. While Nancy laughed to herself, she caught sight of Prince Joseph's glistening eyes. He was the most handsome man she'd seen in a very long time. Their friendship had grown stronger since that fateful night at Hart & Sons. However, Nancy was very aware of the fact that no one in her family wanted her to become romantically involved with the prince. She could understand why, but for some reason, the temptation to pursue her future step-nephew was too delicious to pass up. Over the past few days, Nancy had spent more time in the palace than she would have ever dreamed of before because Sally refused to be alone with Cassandra. Nancy and Joseph had become the unspoken referees in their continuing power struggle.

"The last issue at hand is that of sleeping arrangements the night before the wedding and transportation to Andover Chapel." The King lowered his glasses to the bridge of his nose. "We have four carriages at our disposal… I will travel in the lead carriage with the Dowager Queen followed by Count Matthew and his parents. The Prince and Princess of Kemp and Prince Joseph and Princess Helena will follow in the remaining two."

"And everyone else," asked Matthew.

"The regal fleet will transport the remaining family members to and from the chapel. I think that's enough for now," sighed Michael. "Matthew, will you join me for a moment?"

Count Matthew Hall followed the King out of the dining room and into his office. Michael walked to his desk, unlocked the bottom drawer, and handed Matthew a six page legal document. For a moment, Matthew couldn't believe what he was holding in his hands. It was a pre-nuptial agreement.

"If you sign it, I'll give it to my legal team and that's that." Michael felt terribly uneasy. Glenn suggested that the lawyers deal with this matter, but Michael knew it would seem cold and official. Which is why the King insisted on handling this matter in his own way.

Matthew placed the document on a nearby table. "I knew this was coming… It's so…formal…"

"Matt, let's not make this any more uncomfortable than it already is," Michael exhaled.

Not wanting to start a fight, Count Matthew briefly skimmed the document. Everything seemed in order, but he still thought the gesture was wholly unromantic. This is what kills modern romance, Matthew thought ruefully.

"You're not happy about this, are you? Be honest, Matt."

"Michael, I'm not a fan of these things. It's as if we're planning our divorce."

"That's not the case. It's regal protocol. My father had to sign one before he married my mother. He wasn't thrilled about it either, but it's how we do things." Michael took Matthew's hand. Despite the nature of this exchange, the love they shared radiated through the toxic stratosphere. "This wedding will be our greatest day," Michael assured his fiancé.

Matthew nodded in agreement. Although the wedding was closer than he could imagine, he was still haunted by the endless news coverage of Princess Katherine. She was everywhere. Even though she died ten years ago, Matthew still felt as if she were a silent partner in his upcoming marriage. While he loathed that fact, he fondly remembered the days when he, Katherine, and Michael were best friends…before life got in the way. Those days were long gone, Matthew reminded himself. "To be honest, I have had…doubts…"

"What?" The King couldn't believe his ears. If Matthew was unhappy, he wanted to know. "Why?"

"It's silly, Mike. But with Katherine in the news for the past few weeks, it's been very trying. I know it's been very hard for you and your family, but the press has been outright cruel to me. One blogger even suggested that I killed

Katherine."

"That's insane," the monarch exclaimed hotly.

"I know. We were best friends once upon a time… I know I'm being silly. It's just that I've had time to rethink everything to death since that vicious story came to light. Just ignore me." Matthew ran his hand along Michael's arm with great affection. "Are you angry?"

Michael shook his head. "I understand where you're coming from, Matt. However, you'll have to remember that Katherine will always be a part of my life."

"I know."

"We're starting a brand new life together and I can't wait."

"Your Majesty," Glenn said, as he made his presence known.

"What is it," barked Michael.

"Sire, I have Mr. Conrad on the line. Shall I patch him through?"

Michael asked Matthew to excuse him as he took the call. Alone, Matthew wandered around the vast palace. The sheer size of this monument to power took Matthew's breath away. He saw corners of Andover Palace he never knew existed. What lurked behind the closed doors only teased Matthew's curiosity. One day, he vowed, he would spend time in every room within the walls of this palace. "Are you lost," a voice called from around a deep corner. Count Matthew took a step forward to see the Prince of Kemp watching him with a stern glower on his youthful face. The Count performed a low bow as Alexander said, "You should have an escort."

"I just left His Majesty's Office," explained Matthew. "Are you on your way to see him?"

"I don't see why that's any of your business," bristled the Prince of Kemp.

Matthew forced a kind smile. He knew Alexander loathed him, but he would not let the prince get the better of him. "Well, it was very nice to see you…" Matthew began to pass Alexander, when he called after him.

"You should consider backing out of this marriage."

Matthew froze in his steps. "Excuse me?"

"I never repeat myself." The Prince of Kemp shoved his hands into his pocket as he made his way towards his future stepfather. A feeling of intense superiority passed through Alexander. The young man turned his nose down at Matthew with great delight. "This little game you have roped my father into has been fine for publicity, but it's time you went back to the Netherlands or wherever you came from…"

"If Your Regal Highness will pardon me, I don't agree with you."

"I didn't ask you to agree with me," snapped Alexander. "Call off this sham of a wedding. Maybe then we can all get on with our lives."

"I don't take kindly to threats," countered Matthew.

Alexander's lips curled. "It's merely a suggestion."

Before Matthew could reply, Alexander's handlers appeared and whisked away the prince. He was fully aware that Alexander despised him, but this threat was extreme. Matthew decided not to tell Michael about his run-in with Alexander because he didn't want to start a war within the regal family. However, as Matthew left the palace and drove to Lord's Pass, he couldn't help but feel that everything was about to go to hell.

"You wanted to see me, Your Majesty?"

Michael motioned for Glenn to close the door to his office as the Prince of Kemp performed a dutiful bow. "The Court of Magistrates has reached a verdict regarding the Patricia Ali case."

The Prince of Kemp stiffened. He'd almost forgotten that the verdict would be delivered today. Thankfully, Patricia hadn't mentioned his name during the trial, which only strengthened their bond. No matter what the outcome of the case, Alexander was determined that their plot would still take shape. So what if a few minor details had to be made for the sake of the Kingdom of Andover? This was bigger than everyone, the prince reminded himself. "Why would I care about the verdict?"

The King fixed his steely gaze on his eldest child. Although he never understood the way his son's mind worked, he was able to see right through Alexander. Michael knew all too well that Alexander was behind The Martyrs of Andover. However, he had yet to devise a way to deal with his son. Whatever Michael came up with, he was certain that Alexander would be punished for his crimes against the regal family. "Son, this case stems from rumors about your mother. I thought we should watch it together."

"Where are Joseph and Helena?"

"Joseph is hosting the Halls and Helena is at an engagement with Princess Sophia and Prince Robert. Have a seat." Michael walked to the liquor cabinet in his office. He poured himself a double amaretto and a single scotch for Alexander. The King turned on the television, sat behind his desk, and watched with detached interest.

The Independent Broadcasting Channel aired live from the Court of Magistrates. The longest serving member of the Court, Magistrate Henry Cole, 1st Peer sat somberly in the center chair as the other four members flanked him on either side. While their expressions were hard to read, a sense of melancholy hung over the courtroom. After a protracted silence, Henry Cole said:

"We, the Court of Magistrates, have considered the body of evidence brought before use in the case of The Kingdom of Andover versus Patricia Ali, Minister of Government. She is charged with being a member of the subversive group, The Martyrs of Andover, which has accused the regal family of Princess Katherine's death. The charges have been taken into account and reviewed by all five magistrates.

"We have found that the physical evidence shows that Ms. Ali is a member of this group. Furthermore, it is the express view of the Court that she is responsible for the accusations against the regal family. The Court of Magistrates considers this a high offense. One person does not have the right to use their power and influence to manipulate the media – and the people of Andover – by using an emotionally charged event to further their agenda.

"It is our finding that the regal family was not involved with the natural death of Princess Katherine. Moreover, we have unanimously agreed that Ms. Ali shall step down from her position as Minister of Government effective at noon tomorrow. The Vice Minister of Government, Mr. Brian Josten, 2nd Peer, shall become the Kingdom of Andover's new Minister of Government upon the resignation of Ms. Ali…"

The King turned off the television. He took in the news with a sigh of relief. The nightmare that had infiltrated his life for the past few weeks was finally over. At least one part of it was, he thought. The King turned his attention to his son who didn't even break a sweat. "I could have turned you in, Alexander."

The Prince of Kemp couldn't believe what his father had just muttered. Alexander's blood ran cold. If his father knew, why didn't he turn me in, wondered Alexander. Would he ever turn him in? Was this some sick game? If the King knew of Alexander's involvement, he knew his role within the regal family was on feeble ground. Now that Patricia Ali had lost everything with the ruling of the Court of Magistrates, what was to stop her from turning on Alexander and ruining his life? There was only one step left to their plan… "I don't know what you're talking about," lied Alexander.

"Don't play the fool with me, young man. I know all about your alliance with Patricia Ali. How could you betray me and the family in this cold, hostile manner?" Michael couldn't suppress his rage any longer. He'd kept this bottled inside of his heart for too long and now he couldn't suppress it. "You've put this family through hell! Your brother and sister have been torn to pieces because of you! How could you even conceive something so malicious? You tried to have the entire kingdom believe that me and your grandmother murdered Katherine!"

"You probably did," screamed Alexander.

"Are you insane?"

"Don't play innocent, Dad. I know that you wanted to marry Matthew before you married Mom. The only reason you married her was to ensure the regal bloodline!"

"I loved her!"

"No you didn't. You never loved her," spit the Prince of Kemp. "You probably killed her so you could marry your little fairy boyfriend!"

"I cannot believe what I'm hearing, Alexander."

"You never loved me. Never. Everyone knows that Joey is your favorite son. I've done everything I could to make you proud of me, but you've always dismissed me. My mother was the only person who ever loved me…"

"That's not true…"

"Don't bullshit me, Dad! I've done everything I could to make you proud of me, but I've always failed. You probably don't even want me to be the heir to the throne. If you had it your way, Joseph would be the Prince of Kemp and I would be cast into oblivion."

Michael's head began to spin as he took in the full strength of his son's diatribe. He never knew that Alexander hated him this much. "Son, you need to calm down…"

"I do not. You deserved this!"

"That's enough!" Michael slammed his fist onto his desk. "I've heard enough. I've always been proud of you, Alexander. Always… Yet for some reason, you have always acted as if you don't want to be a member of this family. Even before your mother died, you tried to systematically push us away. What more can

I do? You won't let me love you. You won't let yourself be loved. I can understand if you're angry with me. I get that. There were plenty of times in my life when I was furious with my parents. It's natural. But this? Alexander, you've gone too far..."

Alexander bit his lip to keep from bursting into tears. This was the first time in his entire life that his father had ever spoken to him this way. Yes, his father had yelled at him before, but within this moment, Alexander felt for the first time that his father was willing to fight for his son's affection. "Dad…"

"Alexander, you've turned your back on everyone that cares about you. How could you do this to us?"

"I did what I had to do! I should be the King of Andover! Not you." The Prince of Kemp eyed on the portrait of his father in his regal adornments above the fireplace. "You don't deserve it…you should abdicate. Let me rule the kingdom in a traditional manner."

The King refused to believe what his son was suggesting. Michael knew his son was power hungry, but to use his mother's death as a means to obtain the throne was desperate, even for Alexander. "You've lost your mind," Michael whispered icily. "You don't even understand the brevity of this situation that you have created! And for what? To usurp me for the throne? You leave me no choice… I must do something with you."

"What does that mean," spat the heir to the throne.

"Get out."

"Dad, you can't kick me out…"

"Go now, Alexander or I'll have the Secret Police escort you to Kemp Castle."

"Dad… Don't do this… I'm sorry."

"You've always been a terrible liar, Alex."

Crestfallen, the Prince of Kemp grabbed his jacket and stormed out of his father's office. While the Prince of Kemp waited for his driver to bring around the car, Alexander began to wonder what his father would do to him. This wasn't a part of the plan, but now that everything had changed, Alexander knew his life would never be the same again.

Alone, Michael stared out of his office window as his mind played over his confrontation with Alexander. While he would have preferred for it to have been less dramatic, Michael knew something had to be done about his eldest child in order to protect the regal family and the people of Andover.

Heads turned. Photographers snapped with great delight. Gossip trilled. Needless to say, the day after the Court of Magistrates' decision to have Patricia Ali stand down, the kingdom was abuzz about a different woman…or lady.

Breakfast at Cabo was a very popular activity of Andover's moneyed classes. The five course breakfast menu normally took two hours to get through, which meant that only the well-heeled patrons of Andover society could take advantage of this decadent activity. However, as the mimosas were sipped and the eggs Florentine were served, the patrons shared one collective thought: She's back.

The rumors surrounding Lady Margaret's return to Andover earlier that morning were brushed aside. Yes, everyone cared, but her return had been rumored to death, which made her eventual return a welcome surprise. When she entered Cabo tanned and refreshed with a dashing young man of twenty on her arm, eyebrows were raised, while the tech savvy ladies who brunch sent text messages to everyone in their iPhone directory.

Lady Margaret surveyed the scene with a delicious smile. This was her moment, she told herself. Despite the fact that it was not warm enough for a summer dress, Margaret was a sight in her Pucci wrap dress. She grasped the hand of the dashing young man, Gil la Croix, a student from the University of Andover whom she'd met on the beaches of St. Martin. As the head waiter showed the couple to their table in the middle of the dining room, Lady Margaret planted a hot kiss on Gil's cheek in front of the entire restaurant. Yes, she thought wickedly, I'm back.

"I still can't believe this is happening," whispered the Dowager Queen. She fiddled with the string of cultured pearls that dangled around her neck. "A Minister of Government has never been forced to step down. I still can't believe that she had the gall to do those things to us!"

The King sat in reflective silence. Patricia Ali's press conference to announce her resignation as Minister of Government was set for noon. Michael did not want to be here today, but he had to swear in the new minister immediately after Ms. Ali stepped down to ensure a smooth transition for the kingdom. While this may not have been an ideal way to eradicate this woman from his life, Michael was secretly thankful that she was no longer a thorn in his side.

Princess Helena's iPhone startled her as it chirped to life. She dug into her Hermes bag as her father gave her an annoyed look. "I'm turning it off..." But before Helena managed to turn off her phone, she checked the message one of her girlfriends had sent to her. There, on the screen of her phone, was Lady Margaret kissing Gil. "Joey, look." Helena passed the phone to her brother, who shook his head in disgust.

"She has no shame," observed the young prince.

"Who's this," asked Princess Sophia. She took the phone from Joseph and saw her cousin's public indiscretion. "She's back," Sophia whispered to Lord Walter.

Lord Walter glanced at the image with a heavy heart. In the two weeks since Margaret had left the kingdom, life had managed to go back to normal. Now it seemed that she was intent on ruining her own life and casting a shadow over the entire family. "Aren't we lucky," sniffed Lord Walter.

Moments later, Patricia Ali walked into the Banquet Room of the Government Complex. Ms. Ali approached the podium as the regal family averted her gaze. In their eyes, this woman was the ultimate traitor. After a moment, Patricia spoke:

"It saddens me that the Court of Magistrates could wrongly accuse me of this heinous crime. I am innocent. This crime that has cost me my career is bigger than any one person. I hope that the Kingdom of Andover will survive into the future. Thank you."

With that, Patricia stepped aside as Brian Josten made his way to the stage, followed by the King. The King was handed the Shield of Andover, on which Brian placed his right hand. "Do you swear to adhere to the laws of Andover's constitution, act in the best interest of the people, and serve as the head of my government?"

"I do," responded Mr. Josten.

"I hereby proclaim Mr. Brian Josten as Andover's new Minister of Government," announced the monarch.

"That was painless," noted Princess Sophia as she reapplied her lipstick in the powder room.

The Dowager Queen sat on a settee behind her daughter. Although she did agree with Sophia's estimation concerning today's event, she did not approve of that woman's speech.

"Your Regal Highnesses." Patricia Ali froze by the door of the powder room.

Sophia and Cassandra turned their gazes to the lone woman. Before Sophia could say a word, Cassandra exclaimed, "You have betrayed the regal family! You deserved to lose your job!"

"Mother!"

"She did," insisted Cassandra.

Princess Sophia stood between her mother and Ms. Ali. "I think it would be best if we all kept our opinions to ourselves. This will not help anyone."

As the Dowager Queen and Princess Sophia prepared to leave the powder room, Patricia Ali said, "Be careful. It's like I said in my speech: This…thing…is bigger than any one person."

His Regal Highness Lord Walter was pleased that today's event at the Government Complex was short and to the point. He had a stomach full of nerves that he couldn't control. As he paced through the Sun Room at Blake Manor, he couldn't stop thinking about the future. If everything went according to his plan, his life would never be the same again. And, for the first time in a long time, that was a very good thing.

"I'm sorry I'm late," Samantha stammered as she walked into the room. "There was an accident a mile from here."

"It's all right." Walter smiled as he led her to the soft sofa in the center of the room. "I'm glad you're here." He gave her a loving kiss. "I just have to do this," he muttered to himself.

"What?"

Before Walter knew what was going on, he found himself on one knee before Samantha. His palms were sweating as he took her soft hand in his. "Samantha… will you marry me?"

Samantha released a gasp of shock. "Walter… I can't…"

Lord Walter quickly rose to his feet. He felt like someone had ripped out his heart and his soul in one swift move. This was the first time in his life he'd ever felt this way about anyone. Now, he was worse off. He felt like a fool. Maybe she was too good for him. Or maybe he'd misjudged the whole situation. Whatever it was, he knew he had to get out of the stifling Sun Room. "Oh… Well, I… Jasper will see you out."

"Walter!" Samantha darted across the room and grabbed him by the arm. "I… I wasn't expecting this. You caught me by surprise."

"Does it matter? You said no."

"I didn't. I can't accept now. I need to think about it for a few days. Is that all right?"

"Sure," he responded dejectedly.

"I should go." With that, Samantha gave him a kind kiss on the lips before leaving Blake Manor.

Walter sank to the floor of the Sun Room as he tried to come to terms with the spate of recent events. The only woman he'd ever loved had turned down his proposal. Worse, she wanted to think it over for a few days. Walter began to feel like a fool who'd fallen for a woman who was out of his grasp. Not only that, but he was an idiot for putting himself on the line and being so raw with his feelings. He should have been absolutely sure as to how Samantha felt about him before he asked her to marry him. In that moment, Walter knew that if Samantha refused his proposal, he would go back to the single life once and for all.

His Highness Edward often pondered his place within the rigid structure of the regal family. By all accounts, he was the lowest form of regal life and being married to Lady Margaret didn't help his cause. Edward always thought that the regal family felt sorry for him. Whether or not they viewed him as essential often crossed his mind, but during times like this, he didn't know where he stood in their eyes.

Edward threw his iPhone onto the sofa of the Drawing Room in his state apartment. He'd just finished a phone call with Olivia, who'd informed him of Margaret's much discussed return to Andover. It turns out that Olivia's sister, Wendy Alan, was having breakfast at Cabo the moment Margaret walked in with her newest boy toy. Apparently, it was the scandal of the week. Olivia then informed her cousin that the pictures were online. Despite his better judgment, Edward surveyed the pictures of his wife giving some randy rogue a kiss in front of the entire kingdom. To be humiliated by Margaret's indiscretions in private was one thing, but to be the laughing stock of the kingdom was quite another. Edward's internal rage began to boil over when he heard Lady Margaret's high heels click-clacking on the Italian marble floors.

"Edward," she cooed. Lady Margaret gave her husband a passionate kiss. "It's so good to see you. I've missed you. St. Martin was absolutely divine. You should have been there. But with all the drama, I thought it would be best to get away. I'm terribly tried." She walked into the Drawing Room and fell onto the sofa. “Where’s Sam?”

“He’s at the polo club with Joseph.” Edward tried to temper his anger as he stared at his wife. He couldn’t believe the ease with which she slipped into the kingdom without a second thought. If the past were any barometer for the future, he knew she would never tell him about this new sex toy she'd picked up in St. Martin. “You’re the talk of the kingdom,” Edward said calmly.

Lady Margaret tossed back her head with a devilish laugh. “They love me.”

“Who’s the guy?”

“Oh? Gil? I met him in St. Martin. He’s attending the University of Andover. Edward, he’s a genius. He’ll be the next great lawyer or politician!”

“I saw the pictures, Margaret.”

Lady Margaret smirked. She knew that her husband would crack eventually because he didn’t have what it took to take her on. “Oh. That? Everyone’s making a big deal out of a simple peck on the cheek… It meant nothing. You know how people talk.”

“This isn’t appropriate behavior.”

“Don’t tell me what is and isn’t appropriate,” she bristled. “You’re the one who wants to divorce me!”

“You tried to kill me…”

“That was a simple misunderstanding. I’m a passionate person. You knew that when you married me.”

“No matter what happens between us, this has to stop. You should have the common respect to keep your man-whore locked away until our own marriage is sorted out.”

“Gil isn’t a whore! He’s falling in love with me.”

“You or your title?”

Lady Margaret jumped to her feet. "Take that back, Edward."

Edward ignored her demand. "You have to stop your endless need to self-destruct. Do it for me…"

"No. You don't love me anymore."

"I do too…" Edward threw his hands into the air out of sheer annoyance. When was enough truly enough, he wondered. "Have it your way. I'm done. If this is how you want our marriage to play out, then so be it."

"What do you want me to do, Edward? Sit around and wait for you to love me again?" She let out a defiant laugh. "I will not be seen as a miserable, washed up woman who cannot get a man. I am more than capable of obtaining any man…"

"And what does that prove? Nothing. You're turning your back on me and our son!"

"Leave Samuel out of this," she snapped. "You want the divorce. You told everyone else in my family that you wanted out of this marriage! How do you think it made me feel to be the last to know that you didn't love me anymore?" Tears began to stream down her face. Margaret knew she couldn't lose her ground – not now. She maintained her steady stance as she said, "You betrayed me, Edward. I'm going to live my life and no one will stop me. I'll be seen with the youngest man possible and make a fool of myself! I don't care, but at least I'll be allowed to live!"

"Do whatever you want, Margaret. I'm through."

"You should have been there," simmered Alexander. He paced throughout the sitting room in the private quarters of Kemp Castle. Although his altercation with the King had happened hours ago, he still found it difficult to come to terms with the rift with his father. "He was so smug."

The Princess of Kemp nervously devoured a glass of wine. Even though she didn't attend this morning's ceremony, she did watch it on television. With Patricia gone, Olivia thought that this could be the new beginning she craved. If she could have her husband's child and they could become the reigning regal couple, all would be well, she deduced. However, in this moment, she realized how naïve she had been during the past few days. "He can't just take away your birthright," insisted the young woman. "You have rights! There are laws that even the King of Andover must abide by."

"He has regal prerogative. My father can make a regal proclamation and make Samuel his heir if he wanted to do so. He won't because he respects tradition." The nervous prince sat on a chintz footstool across from his wife. "But he could."

"How much does he know?"

"I'm not sure," muttered the Prince of Kemp. "He knows that Patricia and I were behind the story about my mother. That much I know. Yet, he let Patricia take the fall. Now the whole world thinks that she's behind The Martyrs of Andover."

Olivia shrugged with great indifference. She couldn't understand why her husband was so worried about the former Minister of Government when he had been spared. By her estimation, he should have been celebrating, not worrying about that woman. "Maybe this is for the best. We can concentrate on our future, Alex." Olivia stood with a small smile as she picked up the lunch menu prepared by the castle's chef. "What do you want for lunch?"

"How can you think about eating? Olivia, we have to stop him."

"Just let this go, Alex," she replied sternly.

The Prince of Kemp shook his head with great defiance. He knew his father better than most people. They may not have been close, but he knew his father didn't suffer fools, nor did he let anyone or anything slip past him. The King knew everything, recalled Alexander, and it was only a matter of time until his world came crashing down.

"Alex…"

"My father spared me from public ruin when he knew I was behind this whole debacle. I have to know what his next move will be…"

"Let it go," insisted his wife. She couldn't understand why her husband refused to take this as a gesture of goodwill between father and son, but she didn't have the time to care. She had more pressing matters on her mind. "Why can't you accept this as a blessing from the universe?"

"And give my father the benefit of the doubt? Olivia, his silence is deadly. Who knows what's churning in that mind of his? He could strip me of my regal entitlements tomorrow…"

"He won't…"

"He could," interjected the heir to the throne. "He could betray me years from now or he could simply banish me from the kingdom."

Olivia couldn't help but laugh at her husband's fanciful thoughts. "Banish you? This isn't the Middle Ages."

"I'm serious," he yelled.

"I believe you," she responded hotly. "I never thought that the King would act in that manner. But if he does…or if he could at some point in the future…we need to ensure our position in the kingdom."

"Go on."

"We need to ensure our place in the hearts and minds of the people of Andover. We need to make more regal appearances. We should double our official engagements. We need to do whatever it takes to make us more beloved than your father and Count Matthew or Princess Sophia and Prince Robert." Olivia's eyes began to narrow as she became lost in her own thoughts. No one would take away the one thing she wanted her entire life; not even His Majestic Regal Highness The King of Andover. "But most importantly, we need to stay in the line of succession for the throne."

The Prince of Kemp smiled at his wife, amazed by her sudden determination. This was the woman he'd fallen in love with all of those years ago. In this single moment, he knew that Olivia was on his side and she understood the brevity of the situation. He walked to her, kissed her passionately, and ran his fingers through her loose hair. "What now, Olivia?"

"No matter what happens, Alex, you have to trust me."

The King of Andover sat in his private quarters. Thoughts of Katherine raced through his mind. In the past two months, her laugh seemed to fill the recesses of his mind for the first time in years. Michael could remember the smell of her bespoke jasmine and lily scent, the way she held her head, the small scar on her left cheek, and the sound of her soft voice. Memories of their wedding became all too real as his wedding to Matthew drew closer.

Matthew. No matter how he felt about the reasons why he married Katherine, Michael had always loved Matthew. This was a chance for them to have the life they had always dreamt about when they were younger. Even though they hadn't spoken to each other until three years ago, the love they shared never died. In fact, Michael reasoned, it grew stronger. The strength with which he loved Matthew would never be equaled to how he felt about Katherine. However, Michael couldn't wait for his wedding day, which was closer than he could imagine.

Michael's eye spotted a copy of *The Pass Observer* on the coffee table. On the cover was Patricia Ali with a commentary about her term as Minister of Government. No monarch, by Michael's summation, had ever been betrayed so viciously by the head of his government. Her plot to unseat him through devious tactics unsettled the monarch. However, he was glad to be rid of her. Yet, he wondered, what would he do about Alexander?

The King let out a frustrated sigh. His eldest child was too unpredictable to be dealt with in an obvious manner. Ever since Alexander was a child, Michael felt that something wasn't right with their relationship. Alexander always seemed to resent him and for no reason at all. Michael never took it personally because he treated everyone the same way. But this was different. Alexander was so intent on destroying his father's life, that he used the death of his own mother as ammunition in his campaign for the throne. The King wondered where he went wrong with his oldest son. However, he couldn't recall the moment. Perhaps, reasoned the monarch, there wasn't a moment, but a time. By the time they realized how little they had in common, their lives were so far removed from the other that apathy was the only way to describe their father-son relationship.

What should I do about Alexander, wondered the King. He knew all too well that acting in haste would only worsen the situation. If he decided to bide his time, he may be able to strike when Alexander least expected his father to retaliate. The King walked into his bedroom as he tried to figure out a way to handle his son without causing any concern within the kingdom or the regal family. Michael began his reflective breathing while his mind emptied of all thought. A thousand options ran through his head about how to deal with Alexander. What could he do? What could be done? Michael's eyes sprang open. In that moment of quiet reflection, King Michael knew what he must do for country and crown.

30

A few days later, Her Regal Highness The Dowager Queen and His Regal Highness Lord Walter had afternoon tea in the serenity of the Blue Parlor at Andover Palace. In spite of their differences in the past, Cassandra and her nephew began to find common ground in their newfound friendship. Walter deduced that Samantha was the reason for this, but the fact that she hadn't accepted his proposal still bothered him.

Cassandra's dogs Maisie and Voltaire nipped at her heels, while she said, "Walter, have you heard from Samantha?"

"She called me this morning."

"Oh?"

Walter nodded as he sipped his black coffee. "She has an answer for me."

The former monarch clasped her hands together with delight. "I know she'll say yes!"

"Aunt Cassandra…"

"Walter," she interjected. "I know the human heart. That woman loves you. Why shouldn't she? You're a great man!"

"I don't want her to marry me because of…this," he said, gesturing around the Blue Parlor.

Cassandra blanched at the suggestion. "Nonsense! Think about it, Walter. Two regal weddings in one year would certainly detract from the scandals we've been forced to endure!"

Lord Walter nodded sagely. The last few months had been especially trying for his cousin, King Michael, as well as the rest of the family. Yet, somehow, they always managed to smile without ever letting the world know what went on behind the closed doors of the regal residences. "Why do you think

Michael hasn't said anything publicly or privately about the accusations?"

"I don't know. I suppose he doesn't want to give any more credence to those false statements purported by Patricia Ali." Cassandra spit as she said that woman's name. How she loathed her! "I'm glad she's gone."

"I never spent time with her, but I do recall how she wanted to make our family irrelevant."

"Indeed! She did!" Cassandra reached into her Hermes handbag and pulled out a glossy magazine called, *Swell Lives*. While this magazine did have interesting stories about Andover society as well as international society, it always carried hot gossip items. Cassandra knew she shouldn't have read it, but she did... religiously. "What do you think about Lady Margaret's behavior?"

Walter shrugged with great indifference. "Do I have to respond?"

Cassandra flipped to a page and handed the magazine to her nephew. "Have you seen this?"

There, in glorious color, Lady Margaret was photographed holding hands with Gil la Croix in West Andover. Walter's stomach turned as he read the salacious caption: "Lady Margaret steps out on His Highness Edward! Is this the end?"

"She's married for goodness sake," exclaimed Cassandra. "How can she let herself be photographed in this manner?"

"Aunt Cassandra, I don't know. To be honest, I'm close to giving up on my sister."

"You are," asked a shocked Cassandra. "Why?"

"She insists on being unhappy. She has everything she could ever want. Margaret literally has the world at her feet, but it's not enough for her. Edward's a wonderful man. But she's willing to throw her marriage away on that twenty-something guy who looks like he has an STD or two." Walter finished his coffee. "I don't get it."

Cassandra waved to the attending butler to clear away their brunch dishes. "Lady Margaret simply wants attention, my dear. I don't think she cares about the repercussions."

"You're right."

"However, one thing is certain: She's playing with fire."

The black executive Lancia Thesis came to a stop in front of a sleek modern apartment building, not far from the coast of West Andover. This area was populated with the high flying offspring of Andover's new money set. Needless to say, this wasn't a county of the kingdom His Highness Prince Robert liked to visit. Outside of his official engagements, he rarely came to West Andover because he loathed the perceived gaucheness of the area. Prince Robert sat in the backseat of the car for a few minutes before he summoned up the nerve to walk into the blindingly bright building. His assistant went in first to clear the prince's entrance with the doorman, and moments later, the prince found himself on the eighth floor of the twenty-two story building. He found apartment eighty-two and knocked twice. The prince could hear someone shuffling to the door.

"What do you want?" Gil la Croix stood before Prince Robert with a towel draped around his waist.

The prince took in this sight with mere disgust. It was one o'clock in the afternoon. Shouldn't this also-ran be dressed by now, thought the prince. "Hello. May I come in?"

Gil held the door open. "Members of the regal family never visit little old me," cracked the twenty-year-old kid.

Robert waited until the door was closed before he said, "Stay away from Lady Margaret."

"Why? We're having a great time."

"If you don't want to have your life turned upside down, you'll keep your distance."

Gil laughed haughtily. "I get it. You can't have her, so you don't want anyone else to have her."

Prince Robert did everything he could to stop himself from slugging this pompous jerk. "You don't know anything about her."

"Look, I don't need a washed up playboy telling me what to do." Gil padded down the hall to his bedroom. "Besides," he called, "she can't get enough of me."

Prince Robert's eyes took in the sight of the young man's apartment. It was rather big for a one bedroom apartment and no expense had been spared in its decoration or design. Maybe it stemmed from Robert's years in Andover Palace, but he found the modern furniture and harsh lighting too garish to be tasteful. A few minutes later, Gil returned dressed in torn jeans from a hip new designer and a rumpled shirt that simply said, "Loser's Always Win". "Gil, you don't know Lady Margaret like I know her. You are going to get yourself into more trouble than you can imagine. You'll have the press, the palace, and the entire kingdom in your life for years to come. You'll grow tired of the attention, but you'll always be the man who slept with Lady Margaret. Is that what you want?"

"Well," said Gil, "it's something we have in common." He shot Prince Robert a defiant look. "She tells me everything."

"Did she also tell you that she'll grow bored of you and cast you aside? She'll go back to her life and her family. She'll forget you exist. You'll never hear from her again."

Gil let out a pompous laugh. "If you say so. She and I have so much in common. I have to get to my class at the university. You can stay…"

"How much?"

"Excuse me?"

"What about five hundred thousand dollars?"

"For what?"

"To leave Lady Margaret and Andover…forever…" Prince Robert eyed the young man. He could tell that he was considering the offer. It was a lot of money just to go away, and Robert knew that Gil was nothing more than a decently bred opportunist. With a friendly smile, Robert made his way back to Andover Palace.

"Hello?"

"Margaret, it's Gil."

"Hi, honey…"

"You won't believe who just came to see me…"

"How dare you!"

Princess Sophia, Princess Helena, and the Princess of Kemp looked up with a start to see Lady Margaret standing in the doorway of Princess Sophia's sitting room. Sophia put her pen and notepad onto the table as she carefully studied her cousin. Although Sophia's staff knew that Margaret was not welcomed in her state apartment, she guessed that Margaret had elbowed her way into her home. Yes, Sophia surmised, despite Margaret's breeding, she had no manners. "What may I do for you?"

"Why wasn't I invited to this meeting," fumed Lady Margaret. "What is this all about?"

Sophia shifted in her seat. "We're finalizing the charitable posts we'll assume for the next year. You know we do this every year before the beginning of April."

Lady Margaret folded her arms. "Why didn't anyone tell *me*," she snapped.

Olivia let out a defeated sigh. She and Margaret had been close once, but she barely recognized her anymore. To Olivia, Margaret had become the kind of woman that other women always tried to avoid. However, like a bad song, she was everywhere. "We left numerous messages with your office," explained Olivia. "They never returned our calls."

"Well, you have my cell phone number! Why didn't you call me directly?"

"We didn't know where you were," interjected Princess Helena. "Margaret, don't make a scene. Just join us…"

"Why? You don't want me here," shouted Margaret. "You three princesses think you can treat me any old way because I'm *only* a lady. You can't do this!"

"Oh, shut up!" Sophia threw her hands into the air with sheer annoyance. She had finally grown tired of Margaret's self-pitying song and dance. "You know that's not true!"

"Aunt Sophia's right," stated Helena, hotly. "Anyway, Olivia's only a princess by courtesy of Alexander, not in her own right."

Olivia tossed Princess Helena a look of sheer embarrassment. This issue was such a sore spot with her, which was why Olivia suspected that Helena brought it up at every possible moment.

"Well," snapped Margaret. "You can all pretend that it's not the case, but we all know the truth. I'll never be good enough for your little club. If I weren't living in the palace before my mother died, you all would have petitioned the King to have me shipped off to Port Agnes House for the entire year!"

"If you're going to be a nuisance, could you please remove yourself?" Princess Sophia picked up her pen. "Helena, I think you should assume the duties for everything dealing with teenage women. You're the right age and…"

"Sophia," Margaret interjected casually. "Did you know that your husband was at Gil's apartment in West Andover a little while ago?"

Princess Sophia averted Margaret's smug gaze. The thought of her husband speaking with that person made Sophia's skin crawl. One of the many things that Sophia loved about her husband was his ability to mix well with her sort of people, not Margaret's. "So?"

"He tried to bribe Gil to leave Andover. He offered him half a million dollars." Lady Margaret moved towards Sophia until they were inches apart. "Your husband still loves me."

"Olivia, do you want the Kemp Council for Academic Achievement," asked Sophia, calmly.

"Margaret, stop this," insisted Helena.

Lady Margaret smirked. "It's true, Princess Porky. Ask Robert. Face it, Sophia. Your marriage is over and he still wants me."

Before she knew it, Princess Sophia sprang to her feet and grabbed Margaret by the shoulders. Her grip was so tight she could feel her nails digging into Margaret's flesh. Sophia's eyes were alight with fury. "My husband does not love you. You were nothing but an easy woman with no morals. You are an embarrassment to the entire regal family. The only reason Robert went to see that person was to stop the onslaught of negative publicity that has been swirling around you since the summer!"

Lady Margaret pulled herself free, as she pushed Sophia across the room. Sophia staggered to her feet as the other princesses watched in shock. "At least I live," she yelled. "You three sit around here like aging spinsters! I have excitement in my life and none of you can say that! None of you…"

"We're all ashamed of you," stated Princess Sophia, "including your own son."

"At least I'm able to have children. You'll never experience that, princess," spit Margaret.

Princess Sophia slapped Lady Margaret with all of fury in her soul.

Margaret stumbled backwards into an end table, which fell to the floor with a glorious crash. Horrified, Lady Margaret ran out of the room, holding her throbbing cheek.

Stunned, Olivia whispered to Helena, "She deserved it."

"Samantha…what are you doing here?"

Samantha smiled at Lord Walter with great warmth. She was dressed in a sleek black cocktail dress from her favorite boutique, Fort Mason, in Blake Hill. "I was on my way to a cocktail party at my parents' house, but I had to see you. I know it's rude to stop by unannounced, but I couldn't wait." Samantha took a deep breath. "Your proposal…it took me by surprise. I had a feeling that you may have felt…that way…but I didn't know you wanted to marry me. Walter," she sighed, "I love you so very much. If you'll still have me for your wife, I'd be more than happy to accept your proposal."

Walter rushed to Samantha and swept her off her feet with a passionate kiss. The moment seemed to go on forever. The sheer electricity that raced through their souls was only heightened by the fact that this was the first night that they made love.

"And then Aunt Sophia slapped her. I've never seen her so furious." Princess Helena sipped her iced tea as she finished recounting the events of this afternoon. She cut into her steak in the Europa Room of Andover Palace. It was so named due to the ceiling fresco and wall hangings of the Rape of Europa that Duchess Victoria commissioned for the palace more than eighty years ago.

Prince Joseph shook his head as the Dowager Queen said, "I can't believe Sophia would do such a thing."

"After everything that's happened between them," noted Joseph, "Margaret had it coming."

"But violence," croaked the former monarch.

Prince Joseph continued to eat his medium rare steak. It wasn't like his aunt to strike anyone, but he was all too aware of how vicious Margaret could be when it suited her. "She's the only member of the family to embarrass us week after week. I feel bad for Samuel. I want to take him away for the summer. He had such a good time with me last summer… He doesn't deserve this."

"And she tried to shoot Edward," squealed Helena. "Margaret's going crazy."

"Even Walter's calmed down," sighed Cassandra.

"I think Margaret's a sad person," opined Helena. "She seems to love the drama. Aunt Fiona wasn't like that, but it's Margaret's life. I mean, she's fifty-one! She needs to grow up."

The Dowager Queen remained silent for a long while. Cassandra knew all about Margaret and Walter's tumultuous childhood. While Princess Fiona and her husband, Lord Nicholas, were giving and loving, they were far from ideal. They spent the first twelve years of Margaret's life away from the kingdom. It usually fell to Queen Cassandra and Duke James to look after their niece and nephew at Kemp Castle. Sometimes, Duchess Victoria would keep the children at Andover Palace. The situation was never idyllic, but the problems that permeated Fiona and Nicholas' marriage didn't allow them to be the sort of parents that their children needed. It wasn't until the death of their youngest daughter, Lady Constance, when Nicholas and Fiona began spending time with their children, but by then, it was too late. By Cassandra's estimation, her sister and brother-in-law were never able to capture the love of their children because of their borderline neglect during Walter and Margaret's formative years. "Margaret's wounds run quite deep," Cassandra stated diplomatically. "We shouldn't pass judgment."

"You don't approve, do you," asked Prince Joseph.

"Of course not," she cried. "However, we must keep our personal lives out of the papers for the next few months. No more hundred thousand dollars nights out." She gave her grandchildren a terse look. "I'm serious."

Princess Helena shrugged defiantly. "It was only once. And Dad made us pay for it with our own money."

"Good," sniffed the Dowager Queen. "And Joseph, I would advise you to re-evaluate your relationship with Nancy Hall."

The young prince laughed to himself. He couldn't understand why everyone was making such a big deal about his relationship with Nancy. "Grandmother, we're friends. Why does everyone think otherwise?"

"We're concerned," noted Cassandra. "If you say that you're friends, then I'll have to believe you."

Princess Sophia sat in her bed as she tried to read *War and Peace*. After six minutes of re-reading the same sentence, she put the book on the end table near her bed. Her hand still throbbed from her encounter with Lady Margaret earlier today. How she hated that woman. Although Sophia would never strike anyone, Margaret had it coming. This hadn't been a year in the making, it had been years. Ever since they were children, Margaret seemed to be on a one woman mission to destroy her life. Not this time, Sophia thought resolutely. She didn't know when the change had occurred, but she was no longer the princess who was beautiful, yet perceived as spineless. She had her father's temper coupled with her mother's ingenuity, while Michael had inherited most of his traits from their grandparents, King Henrik and Duchess Victoria. Princess Sophia rang a bell and moments later the butler appeared with her nightcap. As she sipped the drink in peaceful silence, Prince Robert emerged from the dressing room clad only in his underwear. He climbed into bed and kissed his wife on the cheek.

"How's the book," he asked.

"Depressing." She handed her glass of brandy to Robert. "I heard you paid a visit to a certain gentleman in West Andover this afternoon."

Robert demurred. “I did. Before you hear it from someone else, I did offer to pay him to leave the kingdom.”

“Why?”

“I’m tired of the drama Margaret invites into our lives.”

“We wouldn’t have this problem if some people left well enough alone.” Sophia took another sip of the soothing liquid. “You need to let Margaret ruin her life. No one can save her.”

Prince Robert climbed under the goose down comforter. “I can’t stomach the thought of that upstart taking Edward’s place in the family.”

“You should have thought about that before you slept with his wife.”

“How long are you going to hold that affair over my head,” Robert snapped fiercely. “I’ve apologized for it more times than I can count, Sophia! I know I made a terrible mistake! Ever since it came to light, I’ve done my fair share of repenting!”

“Would you ever have admitted the truth if Margaret hadn’t been pregnant,” she asked in a soft, yet forceful tone.

Prince Robert cringed at the thought. “Sophia, I hope I would have…but there’s no use living in the past. Is there?”

“I suppose not,” she sighed. “You hurt me, Robert…”

“I know…”

“Just listen,” she interjected. “I’ve tried to give you everything. We’ve had our issues, but I’ve always loved you.”

“I know.” He took her hands in his. “I know.”

“I’ll do my best to let your indiscretion remain in the past.”

Prince Robert smiled softly. “Thank you.”

“It won’t be easy,” noted the princess. “You had an affair with the one person I loathe more than anyone else."

"But it's over."

Sophia knew she should have accepted that fact, but she couldn't do it. "Robert, you have to let Margaret live her life. Sooner or later she'll self destruct. And when she does, it will be the easiest way for us to get on with our lives. Can you do that for me?"

Unwillingly, Robert nodded because he knew that Sophia was right.

Her heart flew into her throat. This isn't happening, she cried helplessly. Yet the reality of the situation only proved one thing: Her son and husband were gone. Lady Margaret screamed for the butler, who promptly delivered a cream colored note on a silver service tray.

Margaret,

Samuel and I are spending the night at my father's house.

Call if you want.

-Edward

Rage filled her body. Within moments, Lady Margaret was waiting for her husband to answer his phone. "Edward," she bellowed. "You can't do this!"

"Do what? I took my son to see his grandfather for the night."

"This is kidnapping," she insisted.

"Samuel deserves a night of peace, don't you agree?"

"You can't do this..." Before Margaret could say anything else, the line went dead. This isn't happening, she told herself. Her husband couldn't take her son away from her whenever he wanted! Samuel was an heir to the throne. Edward's gone too far, she thought wildly as she stormed to Michael's private quarters in the palace. She ignored the attending valet as she burst into Michael's suite. There, in his night robe, the King of Andover sat reading a nineteenth century edition of *The Prince*.

"I tried to stop her, Your Majesty." The panicked valet bowed quickly. "I beg your forgiveness."

"Thank you." Once the valet returned to his post, Michael turned his attention to his cousin. "What is it, Margaret."

"I had to see you," she said breathlessly.

Michael snapped the book shut. "You could have called."

Desperate, Margaret exclaimed, "Edward's kidnapped Samuel!"

The King eyed Lady Margaret with great contempt. He knew she was capable of anything, but this was too ludicrous, even for her. "Excuse me?"

"I came home…and they were gone! Edward hung up on me when I demanded to know where they were…"

"They're at Edward's father's house in Kemp Forest," Michael said icily.

"You knew?"

"Edward told me hours ago. He and I thought it would be good for Samuel to be around Grayson for the night. With all of the antics swirling around your son, you should be relieved."

Lady Margaret could feel her self control slowly slipping away. Had she known Michael had given Edward his permission to remove Samuel for the night, she wouldn't have accused him of kidnapping his own son. Margaret realized that she had to salvage her own standing with Michael. "I didn't know…"

"Margaret, why must you paint Edward in such a heinous light? He's done nothing but love you ever since you two met. I highly suggest that you get your act together or face the consequences."

"What are you going to do?" Margaret chortled with great abandon. "I'm not your child. You can't order me about, Michael. Edward should have asked me if he could take my son…"

"He's Edward's son, too…"

"Do you think I'm so vapid that I can't see what's going on? This whole family is out to punish me for living my life! Well, I won't apologize for that! I have nothing left to lose. That's what everyone thinks. The whole kingdom talks about my downfall, so why not give them a show?"

"You don't mean that," said Michael.

She gave him a tight smirk. "I don't care what you think about me, Michael. I don't care what names your sister bestows upon me or what the Dowdy Dowager Queen thinks I should do. I'm me. And I'll be damned if I go down without living my life as I see fit."

Two weeks after Michael's late night incident with Margaret, he sat in the Freedom Lounge of Andover Palace with his wife's sister, Mary Walsh. As the staff served their meals, Michael and Mary made the necessary small talk to sustain them through this otherwise awkward encounter. Once they were left alone, Mary said, "It's a shame Helena, Alexander, and Joseph couldn't join us."

"Helena and Alexander are at an engagement in Kemp Forest. Joseph is at a reception in Lord's Pass." Michael took a sip of his afternoon cocktail. He knew he would have to reveal the real reason he'd requested Mary's presence this afternoon. "Mary, I…want to apologize."

She looked at the monarch with amazement in her eyes. "For what," she fumbled.

"I should have reached out to you once those terrible rumors about Katherine surfaced. Sophia told me that you came to the palace that day... I wanted to tell you in person."

Mary touched Michael's large hands. "Thank you. I was furious with you that day."

"I can imagine."

"I don't agree with the way in which you handled the matter, but I understand. I forgive you."

The King smiled weakly. After all, she was still a member of his family. "I do hope that you and Ted will attend my wedding."

"Michael…I don't know…"

"Do you have an objection, Mary?"

"No," she murmured. "I have…reservations… You have to understand that even though my sister has been gone for a very long time, it's a bit odd for me to see you with Count Matthew."

Michael nodded sagely. "He's the one, Mary. I wouldn't have proposed to him if I had doubts about him."

"Are you sure?"

"Very. If you come to the wedding, you will see that for yourself."

"All right," Mary replied. "We'll be there."

For Immediate Release by Order of Blake Manor

From the Office of His Regal Highness Lord Walter of Andover

Blake Manor, 1000 Country Road, Blake Hill, Andover 3500BH

> *Blake Manor is pleased to announce the engagement of His Regal Highness Lord Walter of Andover to Danisi Samantha Masoli, daughter of Earl and Countess Masoli. His Majesty The King and Brian Josten, Minister of Government, have approved the engagement, and with the rest of the regal family, wishes the couple a long and, happy life.*

With regards,

Blake Manor

***

That night, Blake Manor was lit up as never before. Life, it seemed, had swept through the dark halls of the regal residence. Outside, a stream of chauffeured vehicles belonging to the regal family and Samantha's family and friends lined the shale drive of the manor. Inside, the State Ballroom was a sumptuous feast for the eyes. No expense was spared for tonight's cocktail reception. Walter knew that he had to celebrate his engagement in style, which was why everything had to be perfect. So far, it was.

Lord Walter took in the State Ballroom with great delight. The staff milled around the exclusive crowd with deft precision. In one corner, King Michael and Count Matthew spoke with Samantha's parents, while the Prince and Princess of Kemp regaled a pair of Samantha's girlfriends with tales of their wonderful life. A wide smile crossed his face as Samantha and Edward stood by his side. "How's Samuel," asked Walter.

"He's asleep in his favorite bedroom." Edward's eyes darted across the room. "Has she come yet?"

Walter ground his teeth. "No. My own sister blew off my engagement party."

Samantha took Lord Walter's hand. "She'll come. Your office called her several times today. She'll be here."

"Where's Lady Margaret?" The Dowager Queen finished her third special drink of the evening. "This would never happen if Princess Fiona were still alive," she told Princess Sophia and Prince Joseph.

Princess Sophia rolled her eyes. "This night is about Walter and Samantha. Not Margaret."

"May I have everyone's attention?" Joseph gently tapped a bread knife against his cocktail glass. The room fell silent as Joseph said, "I would like to propose a toast to my cousin, Lord Walter and his beautiful fiancée, Samantha. Samantha, you've done the impossible by taming my wonderful cousin." Knowing laughter filled the room. "However, I can't think of any two people better suited for each other. I would like us all to raise our glasses…"

"Damn it! We're late!"

Everyone turned to see Lady Margaret standing in the doorway of the State Ballroom dressed in a tight Celine dress, with Gil on her arm. She stumbled into the ballroom in a drunken state as a hushed whispered infused the air. The King held his head in his hands, while the Dowager Queen had to be seated right away. Needless to say, the entire regal family was absolutely mortified, while their bewildered guests looked on with their mouths gaping open.

Walter stormed over to his sister, grabbed her by the arm, and led her into Drawing Room. "How dare you," he spat furiously. "If you were going to come here in this state, you shouldn't have come."

"What did I do," drawled Margaret. "I'm *here*, aren't I?"

Lord Walter released his grip on her arm. He couldn't believe the ease with which she seemed to excuse herself from her actions. "I am ashamed of you, Margaret. How dare you try and ruin this night. *My* night!"

"This isn't my fault," she chaffed. "Everyone's plotting against me!"

"Get over yourself. You're a member of the regal family. It's high time you started acting like one."

Lady Margaret let out a defiant laugh. How rich, she thought. "Me? You're the one who couldn't even commit until five minutes ago! You were the one who dated every unsuitable woman Andover, New York City, and Luxembourg had to offer. I played the game, little brother. *I* married the right person and had a child. *I* made our parents proud. What did *you* do?" Lady Margaret sized up her brother with contempt. "You lived abroad, dated everyone you weren't supposed to, and all but ignored your obligations as a member of the regal family until after our mother's death! Twenty seconds of 'doing the right thing' doesn't absolve you from your sins, Walter!"

"I…never claimed to be a saint..."

"No, you're trying to conform. How does it feel?" Lady Margaret made herself comfortable on the yellow sofa that dominated the center of the Drawing Room. She studied her brother with great care. "It's stifling, isn't it? To wave and be the person the whole world wants you to be, but you can't even pursue the things that make your blood race."

Despite the anger he felt towards his sister, he couldn't help but feel the sting of her words.

"We use to be the rebels. The rule breakers… We use to laugh because Sophia and Michael had to do the hard work, while we had the fun. What happened? When did you become one of them?"

"When I realized that I was making myself unhappy." Lord Walter shoved his hands into his pockets. His head still swirled with anger, although he had cooled down considerably in the last few minutes. "You have to know that this is uncalled for, Margaret."

"This isn't my fault," she belted. "Everyone – including my husband and son – has turned against me. What have I done to deserve this? Nothing!"

"You're no innocent and you know it. After everything you've done to Sophia, it's no wonder Michael hasn't kicked you out of the palace."

"Are you on their side?"

"I didn't…"

Lady Margaret threw her hands into the air. "Gil is the only one who loves me! My own brother has turned against me. And everybody wonders why I act out. You people make me do it!"

"That's enough." Walter walked over to his sister with fury in his step. He grabbed her by the shoulders and shook her violently. "Our parents would be ashamed of you."

"You can't say that…"

"You and I know it's true. You either straighten up or I'll have nothing more to do with you."

The words hit Margaret hard. He was her the one link to the life she knew as a child. Throughout their entire lives, they had relied on each other in times of pain and joy. Lady Margaret was so stunned, words failed her.

"I will keep my life and Blake Manor open to Samuel; he's always welcome. As far as I'm concerned, you're *persona non grata*, Margaret."

Hurt beyond repair, Lady Margaret ran out of Blake Manor, with Gil by her side.

The cocktail party announcing His Regal Highness Lord Walter's engagement to Samantha Masoli ended just before eight o'clock in the evening. Many of the guests had dinner at the best restaurants in Blake Hill, while the regal family decamped to their respective residences. Normally, the regal family would have stayed at Blake Manor; however, the murmurings about Lady Margaret's explosive visit were the last thing they wanted to discuss. However, Princess Sophia and Prince Robert stayed behind to chat with the engaged couple in the Drawing Room as the staff served a light dinner. Afterwards, Sophia found herself wandering the halls of the vast manor. Although she didn't grow up there, she did spend time there as an adult with Princess Fiona and Lord Nicholas on the weekends.

Minutes later, Princess Sophia found herself outside of Samuel's bedroom. She peeked inside to see Edward watching over his sleeping son. He was a devoted father, she told herself. She motioned for Edward to join her in the room across the hall from Samuel's. "How are you," she whispered.

"Absolutely livid."

"Edward…"

"It's not the mere fact that she's been so blasé with her own life, but she had to make a fool of herself tonight." Edward walked across the moonlit room, which overlooked the manor's tennis court. "She had no right to do that to Walter and Samantha."

Princess Sophia joined her best friend by the oversized window. "Walter's banished her from his life. Maybe we should do the same thing."

"Sophia…"

"We should. I don't even want to contemplate what the papers will say tomorrow morning. This scandal is the last thing we need." Sophia sat on the windowsill with great care. In a soft voice she said, "It's just another one of Margaret's scandals. If you ask me, I think Michael's done with her."

The soft moonlight bathed Edward's well-defined face. The thought of Margaret being banished from the King's life made him slightly joyful. Yet, he did feel sorry for her. Edward realized that he would always love Margaret and, for that reason alone, he loathed himself. "Sophia, let's not project about things that have yet to happen."

She touched his hand with great care. "I know my brother…"

"I only care about my son. I need to protect him."

"Of course you do. No matter what happens, I'll always be here for you, Edward." Her eyes met his in a moment of intense understanding. She touched his face gently before giving him a small hug and rejoining her husband downstairs.

As Edward stood alone in the vast bedroom, he wondered what the future held for his son, his wife, and the kingdom.

The next morning, the newspapers ran the story about Lady Margaret's drunken appearance at her brother's engagement party. Although the source of the leak was deemed confidential, the King had no doubt in his mind that someone from within Samantha's circle of friends had told everything to the press. "Mother, I don't know what to do."

Cassandra peered over her coffee cup. "Go on."

"Margaret. She's behaving in the most abhorrent fashion."

"That's because you were sequestered at Kemp Castle during her last public display of attention." The Dowager Queen shook her head with great annoyance. "Fiona was always at her wits end with Margaret. I don't think there's any hope left for her."

Prince Robert made his way into the Blue Parlor. Although he would have preferred not to dine with the Dowager Queen and the King without his wife as a buffer, he had to face them. In the months since his affair with Margaret was exposed, the tension between the King and his brother-in-law began to thaw. However, thought Robert, he was still considered a traitor by the former and current monarch. "Good morning," he smiled. The butler began to pour Robert's coffee when he spotted the newspaper on the table. "Why are they reporting this nonsense?"

"Don't ask us," bristled the Dowager Queen. "We don't seek this sort of press."

"Maybe Margaret's going through a rough time," suggested Robert.

The King rolled his eyes. "Does your wife know you're defending your mistress?"

Robert was taken aback by Michael's biting tone. "That's not what I meant…"

"Well," huffed Cassandra. "We've given Margaret the benefit of the doubt one too many times! Enough is enough."

"Aren't you being harsh?" Robert wondered aloud.

"No," snapped Cassandra. "The King's wedding is literally days away and that's what we need to focus on, not Margaret's antics. Can you imagine? She brought that boy to Lord Walter's engagement party… I was mortified!"

The King eyed Robert suspiciously. "It would be best for everyone if we all focused on the future. Let's let the past go. Whatever Lady Margaret decides will be her decision; not ours."

"Are you giving up on her, Michael?" asked Robert.

"I never said that," corrected the King.

Prince Robert was beginning to feel the pressure of this situation. He hated the way Margaret's own family turned on her whenever she stepped out of line. Although he was glad to be a member of the regal family, he never understood their ever shifting allegiances. No matter what happened to Margaret, he would always care about her. That fact alone made the current situation even more unbearable. Prince Robert excused himself from the breakfast table and went for a very long walk around the grounds of Andover Palace.

"I must say, I'm surprised." Lady Margaret sat in the Morning Room of Kemp Castle with a cup of Darjeeling tea in her hands.

The Prince of Kemp gave her a tight smile. After last night's event, he knew he had to speak to Margaret. It wasn't because he cared, but because he had a plan. "Why's that?"

"In the eight years you've lived in Kemp Castle, I've only been to visit you four times. The other visits have been with the rest of the family."

"What can I say? I'm apt to forget my manners."

Lady Margaret pursed her lips. "I'm no one's fool, Alexander. Why did you want to speak with me? You could have called me."

"Phone calls are impersonal. Besides, I had to tell you in person that I'm on your side."

Lady Margaret eyed Alexander suspiciously. In all of her life, her cousin's son had never expressed a modicum of interest in her. What did he want with her? In spite of her initial reservations, Lady Margaret kept her cool. "You are? Haven't you sworn an oath to devote your life to country and crown?"

"I have."

"Well, the King isn't exactly my biggest fan."

"So?"

"Do you think going against him is wise?"

The Prince of Kemp leaned across the table. "Margaret, we have a very judgmental family. They think that whenever someone steps out of line, they need to be dealt with in their own special way. I understand why you feel the need to have a young lover and all of that. Believe me, my father is the last person who should judge anyone. For goodness sake, he's marrying a man."

Lady Margaret couldn't hide her surprise at Alexander's candor. "What does this have to do with me?"

"Margaret," he said in a low, soothing tone, "things are going to change in the kingdom. If you want to be a part of that change, I have a wonderful opportunity for you."

31

It was the fourth of April.

In four short days, the regal wedding of the decade would occur at Andover Chapel. The hours seemed the fly by as the livery stables prepared the regal coaches, purebred horses, and the regal fleet of executive cars. Meanwhile, the regal women were in the midst of the final fittings for their gowns, while the regal men stood dutifully as tailors from Hutton & Company hemmed their bespoke tuxedos. Earlier that day, the extended members of the regal family made their way to Andover Palace to take part in the many rituals inherent to the family before a wedding.

In his official office, Michael listened as his head lawyer, Kurt Brenner, presented him with the final documents regarding the marriage. Moments later, Count Matthew joined the King and his lawyer with his pre-nuptial agreement in hand. "Count Matthew, it's very nice to meet you," said Kurt.

"You too, Mr. Brenner." Matthew sat on a sofa next to Michael. "Should I sign this now?" With a nod of Michael's head, Matthew signed the pre-nuptial agreement. "Wow. That felt cathartic."

Michael added his signature before returning the document to Kurt. "Matthew, there's more business we need to sort out."

Count Matthew eyed the King and Kurt carefully. His stomach began to twist into knots. "What?"

"Once you wed the King," began Kurt, "a regal proclamation will be issued stating that your style and title are: His Regal Highness The Duke of Andover, Consort of the King."

That title, Matthew thought again. It was so lofty that it made him doubt himself. How could he ever live up to the expectations of being the King's husband and the Duke of Andover? All of that on top of being a regal highness.

What have I done, Matthew wondered hastily. "Very good." Matthew responded with a smile.

"Now," explained Michael. "The style and title won't come into effect until the wedding day. I'll perform that ritual before the wedding. Mr. Brenner," Michael said, "thank you for your time."

With that, Kurt bowed and left the office.

"I wanted to ask you something," Michael said softly.

"Yes?"

"How would you feel if I created you a prince?"

Matthew's heart nearly fell out of his chest. This was all too much. He'd spent years dreaming of this day, but suddenly, the reality of the situation began to overwhelm him. Being styled as a regal highness and being called a duke was one thing, but being a prince in his own right? That certainly was the stuff of fairy tales. "I… Can you do that?"

"When I married Katherine, my mother made her a princess in her own right. She was the Princess of Kemp, Princess Katherine of Andover."

The sound of Katherine's name felt like a knife to his groin. "Oh. Is that why you brought it up?"

Michael gave Matthew a bewildered glance. How could he think such a thing? Michael loved Matthew more than words could tell and he wanted to give him everything. He'd only recently thought about making Matthew a prince in his own right, without even considering Katherine. "No. It's not," Michael said with measured anger.

"Michael, I appreciate the offer, but being your husband is more than enough." Matthew kissed the King with great care. "Have you decided what you're going to do about Lady Margaret? Michael, I don't think you should ban her from the wedding."

"I thought about it…and I'm not. I think it would be too drastic. Besides, she would turn the whole situation to her advantage."

Matthew felt out a sigh of relief. "I'm glad. I want our big day to go off without a hitch."

"Excuse me, Your Majesty." Glenn appeared in the doorway of the monarch's office with a low bow. "Mr. Ellison is here for his appointment."

"Matthew, could you excuse us? I'll only be a moment."

"Of course," nodded the Matthew.

Glenn led Matthew out of the office as Kerr Ellison walked in. He bowed before the King with great respect. "Your Majesty, we have news."

The King raised an eyebrow. These days, thought the King, news was rarely a good thing. "What is it?"

"Our intelligence suggests that something may happen during the ceremony. I would suggest that we raise the security level to 'high' until after the wedding day."

Michael closed his eyes. He loathed the fact that this was happening in his kingdom. The last thing the monarch wanted was for his wedding to be overrun by the Andover Secret Police. However, if the lives of his family and guests were at stake, he had to protect them. As the King, he'd taken an oath to protect crown and country. It was his duty. "That's very unsettling to hear, Mr. Ellison."

"I know, Sire."

"Make the necessary arrangements." As Kerr prepared to leave the office, Michael said, "Can we ensure that we have plain clothes security officials? The less attention they draw to themselves, the better." Kerr bowed once more before leaving the office.

Matthew returned to the King's side. He quickly took stock of his heavy mood. "What's wrong?"

The King shook his head. "Nothing."

"Michael..."

"I can't divulge state secrets, Matt."

"Oh," stammered Matthew. "I…"

The King placed his arm around Matthew's shoulders. "You have to understand that there are issues that concern the kingdom… Issues of great importance… I will never be able to share these items with you. Do you understand?"

"I guess…"

"There are also things which go on within the regal family that I will not be able to discuss. I need you to understand that I'm not keeping secrets; I'm doing what needs to be done for my kingdom. Will you be able to handle that?"

Matthew smiled. "I will."

"No, no, no. Anything made of silver goes on *that* table," instructed the Dowager Queen. She stood in the center of the Garden Room off the South Terrace of Andover Palace. A bevy of assistants swirled around her with wedding gifts from people from around the world. And, true to form, Cassandra made it her personal mission to oversee the delivery of each gift to the soon-to-be couple. Some of the gifts would be kept by the couple, while others would be auctioned off to raise money for charity. "One moment," she called to a passing assistant. "Who sent this?"

The assistant opened the large card. "It's from Her Serene Highness Princess Elena of Mecklen-Coburg, Ma'am."

Cassandra instructed the assistant to place the large gift on the table in front of her. The wrapping paper was all too familiar to the Dowager Queen. She had seen it throughout her childhood, but now, it rarely made appearances in the kingdom. The paper was decorated in the coat of arms of her grandfather, King Christoph's family, the Grand Duchy of Mecklen-Coburg. After Christoph left

Mecklen-Coburg to become the King of Andover, he had sporadic contact with his family. King Henrik continued to keep the lines of communication open, but life proceeded without a care which made the two lines grow further and further apart. Princess Elena was her second cousin and the daughter of King Christoph's third oldest brother, Prince Ludwig of Mecklen-Coburg. A tear rolled down Cassandra's cheek as she read the short card in Elena's elegant hand:

Your Majesty,

May you and the Count have a lifetime of happiness...

Send my love to your mother and your family...

Always,

HSH Princess Elena of Mecklen-Coburg

"Grandmother, are you all right?"

"Yes, dear." The Dowager Queen placed the card in its envelope. She gave Princess Helena a small smile. "Memories…that's all, dear. What brings you into this state of entropy?"

"I'm dateless! I'll have to go stag to my own father's wedding," moaned the princess. "Can you help me?"

The Dowager Queen led her granddaughter to a sofa at the back of the Garden Room. "Dear, why don't you call a young man you should have spent last summer with instead of that detestable Derek Sharpe?"

"I don't want to seem desperate! Grandmother you know everyone."

The Dowager Queen instructed her assistant to fetch her worn copy of *The Andover Peer Review*. "Joseph! Vincent," cried Cassandra as the two young men made their way into the Garden Room. "How lovely!"

Helena gave Vincent a warm hug. "You look well."

"Thanks," he smiled. "So do you."

"How was the flight?" Cassandra asked. She then ordered the staff to bring more chairs and iced tea.

Vincent shrugged coolly. “The regal jet is too nice. I swear.”

“It’s one of your entitlements,” acknowledged Cassandra. “Where’s your father?”

“He’s flying in the day before the wedding with my girlfriend, Vaughn. I wanted to arrive early and catch up with the family.”

“Wonderful,” exclaimed the Dowager Queen.

“Helena, do you want to come to Cabo,” asked Joseph. “You can have the Brie and egg salad without guilt…”

“I’ll meet you in an hour. Grandmother and I have something to do.” Princess Helena watched her brother and cousin leave. She then turned her attention to Cassandra, who was busy leafing through the hefty book. “Is there anyone? I can’t go to my dad’s wedding by myself. I’ll die. I’ll just die.”

“Nonsense,” huffed the Dowager Queen. “The trick is to find someone your age who’s suitable… Ah! Let’s see… Heath Lincoln!”

“Heath?” Princess Helena briefly recalled meeting him at various social events seasons ago. He was quite attractive without being too handsome.

“Now, he’s the maternal great-grandson of the first Minister of Government, Earl John Richmond. His father is an earl, as was his grandfather and great-grandfather.” Cassandra snapped the book shut. “I’ll have my secretary make the necessary arrangements on your behalf.”

“Thank you, Grandmother.”

“It’s what I’m here for, dear.”

“You’re the lucky one,” joked Nancy. “You get to rid in a carriage, while we’re stuck in cars.”

Prince Joseph gave her a playful punch. He sipped his beer as he took in the sight. Cabo was always busy at lunchtime, and today was no exception. What made today different from the rest was the fact that everyone was buzzing about the King's wedding. Apparently, it was the most sought after ticket in town.

"How long are you in town," Suzanne Hall asked Vincent. Suzanne had just returned to the kingdom for her brother's wedding, and she couldn't wait for the big day.

"We'll see. I have a few finals to take at Yale, but who knows?" Vincent bit into his caviar salad. "I do love Andover. I don't know why my parents insisted on keeping me away for so long."

"I do hope that the taxpayer isn't shelling out their hard earned cash for this decadent lunch." Derek Sharpe appeared at the regal table with a sneer on his face. With Patricia's recent banishment from the kingdom's political world, Derek was one of the first causalities. Now, he was appearing on talk shows and political radio broadcasts to speak out against the regal family. "A caviar salad," sniffed Derek. "How unnecessary."

Joseph clenched his jaw. He still couldn't process his former friend's betrayal. The prince didn't know why but, Derek had turned into a traitorous jerk who used Princess Helena to further his own agenda. "What do you want, Derek?"

Derek's eyes met Joseph's. "Your Regal Highness…you may want to watch your tone. You never know who's listening."

"Go away," muttered Prince Joseph.

"Why? The regal family should be brought down! You people serve no purpose in a democratic world! Kings and queens are so sixteenth century. Well, in the case of this family, the King is a queen."

Joseph stood to his feet so quickly that his chair fell to the floor with a mighty crash. He nearly placed his hand around Derek's throat, until Vincent stepped in between them and Nancy restrained the furious prince.

"You need to get lost," advised Vincent.

"Who are you?" Derek sniffed pompously.

Vincent stared down Derek. "I am His Regal Highness Vincent. No one speaks about my family in that manner." Vincent stabbed Derek in the chest with his index finger. "Get lost, you loser."

Livid, Derek pushed Vincent. "Fuck you."

Before Vincent could respond to Derek's assault, Joseph ordered his cousin to cool down. "He's not worth it, Vince. He's a bottom feeder who uses people to advance his own sad life."

"Me," countered Derek. "Your sister is the frigid one. She never gave it up once while we were together," he laughed.

Joseph turned to the passing waiter and ordered him to fetch the owner. "What seems to be the problem," asked the owner.

"I want this man removed. Now," bellowed the prince as he recounted the events leading up to this moment in time.

The owner, Gary Weitz, promptly ushered Mr. Sharpe out of the building and banned him from returning. As the restaurant returned to its quiet din, the regal party sat in silence as they tried to process Derek's intrusion. "I'm impressed," Suzanne said. "I would have slapped that ass."

"He wasn't worth it," muttered Joseph.

Nancy took a long sip of her cocktail. "Why did he even find it necessary to bother us?"

"He's a douche. I'm sorry I ever allowed him onto my polo team and into my sister's life," sighed Prince Joseph.

"You wanted to see me, Michael?" Lady Margaret sat in front of the King's desk. She wore a teal dress with black heels and an oversized hat to match. "I'm on my way to…a meeting."

"With whom?" The King consulted all of the regal schedules, which he always kept on his desk. "Your office doesn't have anything booked for you until tomorrow morning."

Lady Margaret cast her eyes to the frescoed ceiling. "Must we do this?"

"Margaret… I'm concerned."

"Why? You don't care about me," she snapped. "I want to bring Gil to the wedding."

The King could feel the blood drain from his face. His cousin had dreamt up a lot of inane ideas, but this was by far the most ridiculous. "You will not! I won't allow it."

"Why not?"

"This is my wedding day, not a tacky awards show. For one day, this family's drama will be put on hold."

Lady Margaret laughed. "You are such a hypocrite, Michael. I don't know why you're so incensed with perpetuating the myth that people actually live happily ever after."

"Some people do," retorted the King.

"We're not all so fortunate."

"Margaret, I wanted to talk to you about your marriage. I've put it off long enough, but after the wedding, we will evaluate the situation, and decide the best way to go forward."

"What is there to discuss," she asked incredulously. "Edward wants to divorce me! Gil is the only person who cares about me!"

"How much do you know about this person?"

Lady Margaret remained silent. "That isn't the point. We're mentally connected…we share a passion I've never known…"

"Enough," interjected the monarch. "This discussion is over."

"If you don't let me bring Gil, I won't come to the wedding!"

King Michael eyed his cousin carefully. No matter how hard she protested, he knew she would never do something so stupid. After all, she loved regal life more than anyone he knew. "Do it," Michael whispered in a warning tone. "I dare you."

Her Regal Highness Princess Sophia stood in the dressing room of her state apartment on a raised platform, while her personal designer, Clifford Pennington, fussed with the bodice of her dress. The princess caught a glimpse of herself in the three way mirror. A wave of sadness washed over her. With her older brother's wedding only four days away, thoughts of her own marriage infiltrated her psyche. Sophia's wedding day was the happiest day of her life. How she loved walking into Andover Chapel with her parents by her side, the kingdom at her feet, and Robert waiting at the end of the aisle, waiting to become her husband. It was a perfect day, she remembered. She also recalled walking down the aisle and spotting Edward in the sixth row, smiling at her as he'd done countless times before. For some reason, she found it comforting to have him there because she knew he'd always be there for her.

Sophia and Edward had been best friends for so long that the thought of marriage seemed like a foreign proposition. She often wondered what may have happened had she married Edward. But a thousand what ifs meant nothing. She loved Robert; she always would. He was her ideal. Robert was the man any woman would be grateful to marry. He was by her side during her two miscarriages; he always supported her. He loved her. But where had their love gone wrong?

She still couldn't fathom why Robert would sleep with Margaret. Sophia knew that no matter what she said or how she acted, she would never forgive Margaret for her indiscretion. Edward was the ideal husband and father, but Margaret treated him with nothing but mounting contempt. It was then that the single thought that had bothered Sophia for months crept back into her head:

Margaret only married Edward to spite her. That was it. Nothing more, nothing less. Deep inside of her soul, Sophia knew that Margaret wanted Robert long before the affair. She probably wanted Sophia's husband from the day Sophia met him. But that was a very long time ago…

"Your Regal Highness?"

Sophia came out of her reverie. "Yes, Mr. Pennington?"

"Is the bodice to your liking?"

She looked into the mirror with a faint smile. "Yes… It is… Excuse me..."

"Robert, you look dashing." Sophia stood in the doorway of their bedroom as Robert fiddled with his tie. "Do you need help?"

"Sure."

As Sophia began to tie her husband's tie, she said, "I love you, Robert. I love you very much."

Overcome with emotion, he swept her into his arms, and kissed her passionately. His slender hands ran along the small of her back, as her fingers slid through his hair. "Let's go."

"What," she asked breathlessly.

"This summer… Let's forget Port Agnes House and go somewhere… Anywhere… We can renew our vows."

Her heart began to flutter just as it did on the day they were married. "That sounds lovely," whispered Princess Sophia.

"Thank you for lunch, Olivia. It was lovely." Her Regal Highness Elmira placed her fork onto her plate. Although Elmira wasn't versed in the internal politics that were subtly at play in Kemp Castle, she knew that something was off. It was very odd for Elmira since everyone sitting at the table was related to her by blood and marriage. "Edward, how's Samuel?"

"Well," sighed Edward.

The Prince of Kemp let out a disapproving laugh. "Well? Ed, what do you intend to do about your marriage?"

Edward picked at his duck. "It's a private matter, Alexander."

"Have you discussed it with the King," pried Alexander.

"I have," Edward responded flatly. "However, with all due respect, I don't think that conversation is any of your business."

Alexander bristled at Edward's tone. He loathed being thought of as less than by the members of his family. "I'm the first person in line for the throne! I wish you people would stop dismissing me as if I'm a junior member of this family."

"No one said that," corrected Elmira. "Calm down…"

"I will not! Elmira, life in the kingdom is very political," snapped Alexander.

Olivia tried to calm her husband. "Why don't we have dessert outside?"

"You won't get custody of Samuel," Alexander proclaimed.

"Alex!" Olivia exclaimed.

Furious, Edward stormed out of the Great Room with Olivia trailing after him. "Edward," she called. "Please. Don't go. I don't know what Alexander was thinking. You have my support, but you have to remember that the regal family has more sway than we do."

"Thanks for the vote of confidence, Olivia…"

"I'm sorry… You know what I mean…"

"Look," he said, as his eyes darted around the castle's corridors. "My marriage has fallen apart. I've accepted that. But don't think for a minute that I won't do whatever it takes to protect my son."

Olivia bit her lip. "I hope it isn't for naught."

"When did you become so…much like your husband?"

The Princess of Kemp gasped. "That's not true."

"You can't see it, but I do…so do your brother and sister. Alexander has changed you, Olivia, and not for the better. Be careful."

She stood in shock as Edward thanked her for lunch and left the castle. Olivia tried to grasp what her cousin had told her, because, she reasoned, he was right.

His Regal Highness Prince Joseph and His Regal Highness Vincent stood in front of the King and they recounted the incident with Derek Sharpe earlier today at Cabo. "It's my fault, Dad," Joseph sighed. "I shouldn't have let that peon get to me."

"That's not true," insisted Vincent. "Derek was goading us. He said terrible things about the family. I had a role to play in what happened, too."

The King listened carefully. "What did Mr. Sharpe say?"

Vincent and Joseph exchanged a concerned look.

"He…said the King was a queen," muttered Vincent.

"Well," surmised Michael. "It seems understandable. Let's just ensure that the next time we dine at Cabo, we book a private dining room."

"You're not angry," asked Joseph.

The King shook his head because he was grateful that someone had finally put Derek Sharpe in his place.

Samantha lost her breath. She'd never seen a room as grand as the Drawing Room at Andover Palace. To be honest, this was the first time she'd ever been in the palace. Her parents were friends of the Dowager Queen, the late Duke James, and Princess Fiona, which meant they spent quite a bit of time in these wonderfully ornate rooms. With the news of her engagement to Lord Walter filling the quiet corners of the most fashionable boutiques, Samantha knew she was in a different world. She looked around the room once more before she began to eat the five course meal prepared by the palace staff.

The Dowager Queen continued to talk to Lord Walter about issues that were important only to them. Finally, she turned her attention to Samantha. "How is the quail, Samantha?"

"Lovely, Your Regal Highness."

Cassandra nodded. "Walter, I'm so happy you two have found each other. Now that the King and the Count will be wed in a few days, I can't help but think about your wedding. Yes, it will be a perfect affair. The right people from the right families..." Cassandra caught Walter looking slightly overwhelmed. "Is something the matter?"

"It's just...we haven't discussed the details of the wedding," said Walter. "But we want to keep it small."

"No more than one hundred people," stated Samantha.

"One hundred?" Cassandra shook her head. "That's a cocktail party! This is a wedding! When I married my dear late husband there were seven hundred guests! Walter, when your parents were married there were six hundred guests in attendance. Now, I think two hundred is a nice number. However, we can leave those details until later. Samantha, tell me, how are the people treating you now that you're engaged to Lord Walter?"

Samantha pondered this question for a while. It wasn't until that moment that she realized that people were treating her differently. Her friends and family still acted as they always had, but strangers showed much more interest in the details of her life. "It's different... All of this is so foreign to me."

"Are you happy," asked the former monarch.

“Yes.” Samantha smiled as she gazed at Walter’s masculine face. “I am.”

The Dowager Queen signaled for the butler to fetch her handbag. “I was going to present this to you on your wedding day, but I couldn’t wait.” She reached into the bag and handed Samantha a long black box.

Inside was a priceless, flawless sapphire necklace. “Ma’am… I don’t know what to say…”

“Aunt Cassandra, isn’t this Grandmother’s?” Walter distinctly remembered his grandmother, Duchess Victoria, wearing this piece of exquisite jewelry when she performed her regal duties.

“Yes. She instructed me to give it to the woman who would become your wife. My mother thought Margaret wouldn’t appreciate it and well, Sophia would never wear it. I hope that you will wear this gem on your wedding day, Samantha.”

Overwhelmed, Samantha burst into tears as Walter held her hand. “Thank you,” he said. “This means so very much to us.”

The Blake Manor estate was vast. Unlike Kemp Castle which served as a private estate and working farm that provided food to the regal residences, Blake Manor was an oasis of clam. The main house was what most people saw, but King Henrik had three lodges built for the use of the regal family which had its own private entrance to the estate.

It was in one of these lodges that Michael and Matthew lay on a rustic bed with a roaring fire in front of them. The stress of the last few months seemed to evaporate in that instant and nothing mattered. They were together and, after the next few days, they would never be apart. It seemed like a lifetime of yearning had led them to this moment. This was a moment of intense understanding, renewed faith, and optimistic planning for the years to come.

Michael fed Matthew strawberries covered with dark chocolate, and dipped in champagne. “Are you sure you don’t want to become a prince in your own right?"

"I'm sure," sighed Matthew. "I've only ever wanted us to be together… like this…forever."

"It's going to be a wild ride, Matt. After the wedding, there will be engagements, appointments, meetings, duty…"

"Sounds intense."

"Intense is good."

"Mike," Matthew sighed. "No matter what titles you posses or how you're viewed by the public, I'm thrilled to spend the rest of my life with you. You are the most wonderful man I have ever known."

The King's eyes filled the soft tears. He raised Matthew's face to his and kissed him with every bit of passion in his soul. They melted together while the rest of the world continued to drift away.

32

The King of Andover rose before dawn. Michael peered out of the arched window of his private bedroom suite with renewed hope. In a few short hours, Matthew would become his husband. Michael had thought of this day for years, but he never dreamed that it would happen. The fact that it was actually taking place in his lifetime made him truly grateful. Michael's mind drifted to the time before he married Katherine, their years together, the birth of their children, and her untimely death. The King still missed his wife, but he knew it was time to move on with his life. Would she be pleased with Matthew? They were friends a lifetime ago, which is why the monarch felt at peace with his decision.

By seven o'clock in the morning, Michael stepped out of the shower to find his barber setting-up shop in his dressing room, while members of the staff prepared his regal adornments for his ceremonial outfit. Usually, twelve people weren't necessary for Michael to perform his kingly duties, but this wasn't a normal day. He instructed his attending valet to hold his breakfast, because he had something to do. The King excused himself as he slipped on a pair of trousers and a cashmere sweater. Michael walked down the quiet corridors of the palace with a purposeful stride.

He stepped into the dimly lit chapel at Andover Palace. It was empty, except for a few candles towards the front. Michael walked solemnly to the front, lit a candle, and said a private prayer. The King had never been a religious man, but he often liked to pay thanks to his family members who had gone on to another world.

Ghosts from the past entered Michael's mind. The King could see his father, his grandparents, Princess Fiona and Lord Nicholas, and Princess Katherine in the recesses of his mind. Although Michael would have loved for them to have been with him today, he was at peace with their passing. As he rose to leave the small chapel, the King saw his son, Prince Joseph, walking towards him. "It will be fine," said Joseph.

"I know," Michael stated. "I wanted to pay homage to everyone who has moved on."

Prince Joseph stared ahead at the flickering candle. "I miss Mom. I always will."

"As will I, Joseph."

"I think…I know that you and Matt will be very happy together."

Michael gave his son a wry smile. After a few more minutes in reflective silence, father and son returned to the palace.

The morning maid drew the drapes just before seven-thirty in the morning. Count Matthew rubbed his eyes as the warm sunlight filled the vast suite at Andover Palace. He couldn't believe the day he'd dreamt of for years had actually arrived. Butterflies filled his stomach. Matthew didn't know if he could hold down any food, but he was due to join his parents and sisters in the Sun Room for breakfast before the wedding.

After a long, luxurious shower in the marble bathroom, Matthew dressed himself in a black James Perse tee shirt and a pair of black trousers. When he walked into the Sun Room, he couldn't help but notice his beaming family. For the first time in his life, Matthew didn't feel like himself. And, for some reason, it felt good.

"Your Regal Highness, please join us," smirked Count Patrick Hall.

Matthew sat at the circular table next to his mother and sister, Kate. "Not just yet," Matthew sighed. "But soon…"

"Well, I'd like to propose a toast." Patrick raised his glass. "Matthew, I think I speak for your mother and your sisters when I say that we want nothing but the best for you and the King. I hope that you two will have a lifetime of happiness and undying love. I can't think of two people better prepared for the journey."

Matthew's mother, Countess Sally Hall, began to cry, while Suzanne,

Nancy, and Kate toasted their brother. The Count took a deep breath, but it was impossible to hide his brimming apprehension.

The entire regal family and the Halls mingled amongst themselves in the Green Room of Andover Palace. Glenn informed the family that the carriages and cars were ready to transport everyone from the palace to Andover Chapel. Although they were not due to leave for another ten minutes, they continued to mill about until the last possible moment. Princess Helena examined her beautiful pale yellow couture dress by Mrs. John Langdon in the full length mirror, while Princess Sophia and Prince Robert chatted lovingly in a corner of the room. The Prince and Princess of Kemp welcomed Lord Walter and Danisi Samantha Masoli, while the Dowager Queen examined the scene. A flurry of tears came to her eyes. She was excited for her son, but she knew that Michael's generation was firmly in charge. Although she rarely mentioned it, Cassandra was very proud of her family. Despite their issues, they always did what was best for the family…in the end, anyway. She didn't know how much time she when her day of judgment would come, but she resolved to appreciate whatever time she had left on this great earth. Yes, Cassandra thought gingerly, the torch was firmly in their hands.

"I can't… I have to leave, Gil."

"Call me when you're done. We can do something," he cooed.

Lady Margaret smiled as she hung up her iPhone. She left the phone on the corridor table just as Edward emerged from the guest bedroom. Margaret admired the way he filled out his tuxedo. He looked too handsome, she thought wistfully.

Edward barely acknowledged his wife. He walked into their bedroom, removed a handkerchief from the bureau, and returned to the hall. "Where's Sam," he asked.

"Joseph took him to the Green Room a few minutes ago. If you don't believe me, call him."

He was quickly becoming tired of Margaret. It was time to cut the cord. "Let's make it through today – for Michael's sake."

"Edward… I'm sorry for the way things have turned out this past year." She played with the small diamond Cartier timepiece on her wrist. "I don't want to lose my son."

"I won't lose him, Margaret. I'll fight for him, no matter what."

"You won't win," she said, goading him.

"No judge in their right mind who give our son to someone as unstable as you."

"I'm a member of the regal family. We always win."

"Not this time," Edward stated emphatically. "Trust me."

"Then it's war."

In the privacy of the Throne Room, the King performed an ancient ceremony in front of the Henry Cole, 1st Peer from the Court of Magistrates and Brian Josten, the Minister of Government. Matthew knelt before the King as he listened to the regal proclamation that he was now invested and created as His Regal Highness The Duke of Andover. The necessary papers were signed by all present. Before the couple could revel in their joy, they made their way to the waiting carriages for their long anticipated wedding day.

The King climbed into the first carriage with the Dowager Queen. Their carriage was trailed by the Prince and Princess of Kemp, with Princess Helena and Prince Joseph in the following carriage. Count Matthew Hall and his parents followed Princess Helena and Prince Joseph in the final carriage. The three mile route from Andover Palace to Andover Chapel was lined with the people of the kingdom. Cheers filled the warm spring air as white and blue confetti fell from the windows of Old Andover. The regal fleet of executive cars carried the remainder of the two families.

By the time the party reached the chapel, the King let out a broad smile as he and the Dowager Queen stepped into the warm spring air. They waved to the crowd before stepping into the chapel through a private entrance. Dr. Cartwright, the spiritual adviser to the regal family, greeted Count Matthew Hall and his parents before leading them through a separate entrance into the chapel. The remainder of the party greeted the cheering crowds as photographers snapped their pictures. Reporters from around the world stood across the street as the wedding was beamed into millions of living rooms around the planet.

The invited guests began to file into the chapel. Member of the European and Asian royal families, Andover's political class, distinguished guests, diplomats, and the crème de la crème of Andover society filled the chapel. Princess Sophia greeted the representatives of the European royal houses, while the Prince and Princess of Kemp mingled with their Asian counterparts. Lady Margaret and His Highness Edward did their best to avoid the curious glares. His Regal Highness Samuel, who was all too aware of the tension between his parents, stayed by Joseph's side before finding his seat next to his uncle Walter. His Regal Highness Vincent introduced his girlfriend, Vaughn Phillips, to Princess Helena and Prince Robert, as Mary and Ted Walsh found their seats behind the regal family. Joseph and Robert greeted them warmly as the music from the string octet filled the chapel. Dr. Cartwright made his way down the aisle and to the front of the chapel.

A trumpet blared three times.

The guests rose and turned their attention to the back of the chapel. Count Matthew Hall, flanked by his parents, made his way down the aisle. Matthew's mind went blank as the familiar faces of his life stared back at him, some warmly, others harshly. It didn't matter, Matthew told himself. The official regal photographer snapped pictures of Matthew as he told himself not to vomit. Before he knew it, Count Matthew was at the front of the chapel; his parents kissed him on the cheek and stepped to the side.

The trumpet blared three more time.

All eyes locked on the King of Andover and his mother, the Dowager Queen. They proceeded to walk down the aisle with great importance and dignity. "I'm proud of you," whispered the former monarch. "I've always been proud of you." At the front of the chapel, she kissed Michael on the cheek and stepped aside.

The King and the Count stood side by side as Dr. Cartwright said, "Your Regal Highnesses… Honored guests; ladies and gentlemen… Please be seated. This is, a momentous day, not only for His Majestic Regal Highness The King and Count Matthew or the Kingdom of Andover, but for the world as a whole. In this moment, we are championing the rights of everyone and the eternal love that binds us all. I would like us to take a moment to absorb this thought.

"Now," continued the doctor, "I have known His Majesty since he was a teenager. I have had the joy of becoming acquainted with Count Matthew over the last few months. The love they share is one that will inspire poets, prompt people to dream, and make the world a better place. The journey they are about to embark on is one filled with many joys and sorrows, yet I cannot think of two people better prepared for the state of matrimony. Do you, their parents, give your undying love and support to your children as they enter this union?"

"We do," echoed their parents.

Dr. Cartwright continued: "Michael James Henrik, King of Andover, do you promise to give your undying love and support to Matthew Christian as you enter this union?"

"Yes," smiled the King.

"Matthew Christian, do you promise to give your undying love and support to Michael James Henrik, King of Andover, as you enter this union?"

"Yes," Matthew replied hastily.

"By the power vested in me by the Kingdom of Andover, I hereby confirm this marriage," announced Dr. Cartwright.

The couple shared a short kiss as the chapel filled with jubilant applause. As they parted, Dr. Cartwright declared, "I am proud to present His Majestic Regal Highness The King of Andover and His Regal Highness The Duke of Andover!"

The King and the Duke smiled broadly. They seemed to float down the aisle of the chapel, out of the large doors, and into the warm April sunshine. The crowd erupted in cheers as they tossed red, pink, and yellow rose petals onto the beaming couple. As the King and the Duke stood on the steps of the chapel and were joined by their families, everyone could see that after months of waiting and eager anticipation, the union was an unmitigated success.

The Official Ballroom at Andover Palace was filled with the most important people from around the world. Music filled every corner of the room, while waiters glided through the room with treats made especially for the wedding. Princess Helena stood near the front of the room talking intensely with Heath Lincoln who was, by Helena's estimation, the perfect man. She brushed his hair away from his face, prompting Heath to take her by the hand and kiss it, ever so lightly. Just feet away, Prince Joseph and Nancy Hall danced next to a dozen princes and princesses of Europe. Joseph whispered something in Nancy's ear that prompted her to laugh so heartily that the Dowager Queen and Countess Sally Hall took notice.

"Well," Cassandra said breathlessly. "It seems we may have to plan another wedding."

Sally caught a wicked gleam in Cassandra's eye. Without a word, Sally gave her new in-law a weary smile before excusing herself. Befuddled, Cassandra gasped when she saw a ghost starting towards her. She hadn't seen Princess Elena of Mecklen-Coburg in more than sixty years. Once she received the gift from

Elena, Cassandra called her cousin and invited her to the reception, but she never thought she would appear. "Your Regal Highness," Elena said with a creaky curtsy. "You look well."

"Elena," cried Cassandra. She grasped the woman for dear life. "I'm so glad you're here."

"As am I. My dear cousin, we have much to discuss."

"Vincent, why didn't you tell me?" Vaughn walked through the crowded ballroom with a glass of rare Merlot in her hand. "So, what are you a prince or something?"

"No," Vincent shook his head. "I'm a regal highness… I'll explain it to you later."

"I can't believe that we're at a king's wedding, at a real palace and the Prince of England is two feet away from me!"

"So…are you mad that I didn't tell you?"

Vaughn gave him playful smile. "No," she cooed. "I'm still in to you."

"Smile, Alexander. It won't kill you." The King sat beside his son and handed him a glass of champagne. "Where's Olivia?"

The Prince of Kemp glowered at his father. He wanted nothing more than to return to Kemp Castle and pretend this wretched day hadn't occurred. "She's talking to the American president's wife."

King Michael studied his son carefully. Michael realized that this day would be quite difficult for his children, but he didn't anticipate that Alexander would behave so appallingly in a public setting. "You should try to enjoy yourself, Alex. This ill will you're harboring towards me won't do anyone any good."

"I sat through that sham wedding," retorted Alexander. "That's all you'll get from me tonight, Dad."

Lady Margaret laughed as her husband finished telling her a bawdy joke.

These were the moments Lady Margaret missed the most. Edward was wonderful, she told herself, so why couldn't she just stay with him? "Edward," she whispered, "why don't you come into our bedroom tonight?"

Chirp! Chirp!

Margaret pulled her iPhone from her diamond clutch purse. Edward peered at the phone. It was Gil. Lady Margaret excused herself to take the call. Edward sat back in his chair as he took in the sight of hundreds of happy, content people. This life looked wonderful in pictorial spreads. However, to Edward, this wasn't life; this was a contradictory piece of hell. This was Margaret's world, not his. In that moment, Edward knew that his marriage was finally over.

"I must say that when I heard of your engagement to Lord Walter, I was quite surprised." Her Regal Highness Frances finished her cocktail with a curt smile.

"Why's that," Samantha asked politely.

Frances shrugged indifferently. "Marrying him could ruin your life forever."

Before Samantha could respond, Walter interrupted their conversation. Trepidation swept over Samantha as Walter demanded to know what was going on. "Your cousin just told me that if I married you, you would ruin my life forever."

"Frances, what right do you have to say that to her," Walter demanded to know.

"Because," spat Frances, "I know you." With that, Frances disappeared into the crowd.

Samantha eyed Walter carefully, but something in Walter's demeanor changed. She decided to brush off her concern. However, Walter wished more than anything else that Frances would never return to Andover.

"Do you want to dance?" Edward turned around to see Princess Sophia standing behind him. “My husband has been whisked away by the Italian prime minister’s wife.” Sophia led Edward to the dance floor. His forlorn mood melted her heart. She’d seen Lady Margaret leave the ballroom, but she didn’t want to mention it. Sophia reasoned that Edward needed to have a moment of bliss in this hyper-romantic setting.

As they danced, Edward looked down at Sophia. She seemed so small in his arms, but she was anything but small. He admired her endless strength, determination and zest for life. Unbeknownst to Edward, he held Sophia a bit too tight, but she never flinched. The princess merely smiled at her best friend as she placed her head on his shoulder. However, Edward and Sophia realized that their moment of glory had passed years ago.

The seven course reception dinner ended shortly before ten-thirty that night. Michael and Matthew spent more than two hours saying goodbye to their one thousand invited guests. They walked hand in hand down the vast corridors of Andover Palace to their private quarters, where the regal couple retired for the rest of the day and part of the next. Then, for the very first time, they made love in their own bedroom, and it was perfect.

Epilogue

The twenty-second of April was an important date for the regal family. First, it was Prince Joseph's twenty-fourth birthday. Second, it was the ninth anniversary of King Michael's accession to the throne. Lastly, the regal family had to attend a breakfast reception in Old Andover to officially welcome Brian Josten as the new Minister of Government. This morning would consist of breakfast at the Government Complex in Old Andover before attending a celebration in a nearby park to commemorate Michael's accession and finally, a birthday party for Prince Joseph at Andover Palace.

After breakfast, the regal family waited in the lobby of the Government Building with the the kingdom's highest ranking government officials. His Highness Edward, who had since moved into the guest room in Lady Margaret's state apartment, finished a call on his iPhone, and approached his wife. "I wanted to inform you that my lawyers have drafted my petition for divorce."

Lady Margaret didn't flinch. "You'll regret this, Edward. You've been warned." Edward walked away as Margaret called Gil.

Prince Robert witnessed this exchange. "I should talk to her," he told his wife.

"Excuse me," whispered Princess Sophia. "Leave her alone."

"Sophia…"

"No. Why do you care, Robert? Do you want to be with her?"

Robert threw his hands into the air with great annoyance. "I only love you! How many times do I have to say that? Unless…"

Her husband's silence unnerved her. "Just say it."

"Unless you want me to go to Margaret so you can be free. Is that what you want," he asked Princess Sophia, bluntly.

"Matt, is Nancy coming to the palace tonight," Joseph asked Matthew.

The Duke of Andover patted his stepson on the shoulder. "Yes, Joseph. You two are becoming very close. Is it serious?"

Joseph gave the Duke a coy grin. "I'm going into the armed services tomorrow. Nancy and I are just friends. We haven't slept together."

"You don't look well. I'll have the driver take you to the palace." The Prince of Kemp held his wife by the hand, but she brushed off his concern.

"I'm fine," she whispered. "I think I may be pregnant. And there's something else…"

The government officials embarked on the fifty yard walk to the celebrations in the park. They waved to the onlookers with great warmth as the regal family made their approach. Out of nowhere, the sound of gunshots rang out in all directions. Pandemonium broke out as screams permeated the air; bullets pierced the sky as people ran for cover. The Andover Secret Police wrestled the King to the ground. The Dowager Queen was pulled behind an armored vehicle, while everyone else was ordered to get to the ground. For what seemed to be an eternity, the sound of gunfire filled the spring air. The police rushed to the regal family as the emergency medical units sprang into action.

As the bedlam began to clear, Princess Helena stood up. Blood ran down her lily white dress and stained her hands. When she looked down, she let out a chilling, nightmarish scream. There, at her feet, lay her father. The King was bleeding out on the streets as the medical technicians rushed to his side to close the wound. Kerr quickly ordered the police to close off the area when someone yelled, "The King's been shot!" Instantly, the crowd and the regal family burst into a panic. The Duke, the Dowager Queen, and the King's children rushed to his side, but there was nothing they could do. As the regal family stared helplessly at the bleeding monarch, the Dowager Queen let out a bloodcurdling scream as one sobering thought ran through her mind: The King is dead. Long live the King.

www.ingramcontent.com/pod-product-compliance
Lightning Source LLC
Chambersburg PA
CBHW071339020726
47502CB00001B/167

* 9 7 8 0 6 1 5 3 5 0 9 3 6 *